The Hemingway Files

A NOVEL

H.K. Bush

Blank Slate Press | St. Louis, MO 63116

Blank Slate Press
Saint Louis, MO 63116

Blank Slate Press is an imprint of Amphorae Publishing Group, LLC
www.amphoraepublishing.com

Publisher's Note: This book is a work of the imagination. Names, characters, places and incidents either are products of the author's imagination or are used fictitiously. While some of the characters and incidents portrayed here can be found in historical or contemporary accounts, they have been altered and rearranged by the author to suit the strict purposes of storytelling. The book should be read solely as a work of fiction.

For information, contact:
Blank Slate Press
4168 Hartford Street, Saint Louis, MO 63116
www.amphoraepublishing.com

Manufactured in the United States of America
Cover Design by Kristina Blank Makansi
Cover art: IStock
Set in Adobe Caslon Pro and Avenir Next Ultra Light

Library of Congress Control Number: 2017939478
ISBN: 9781943075324

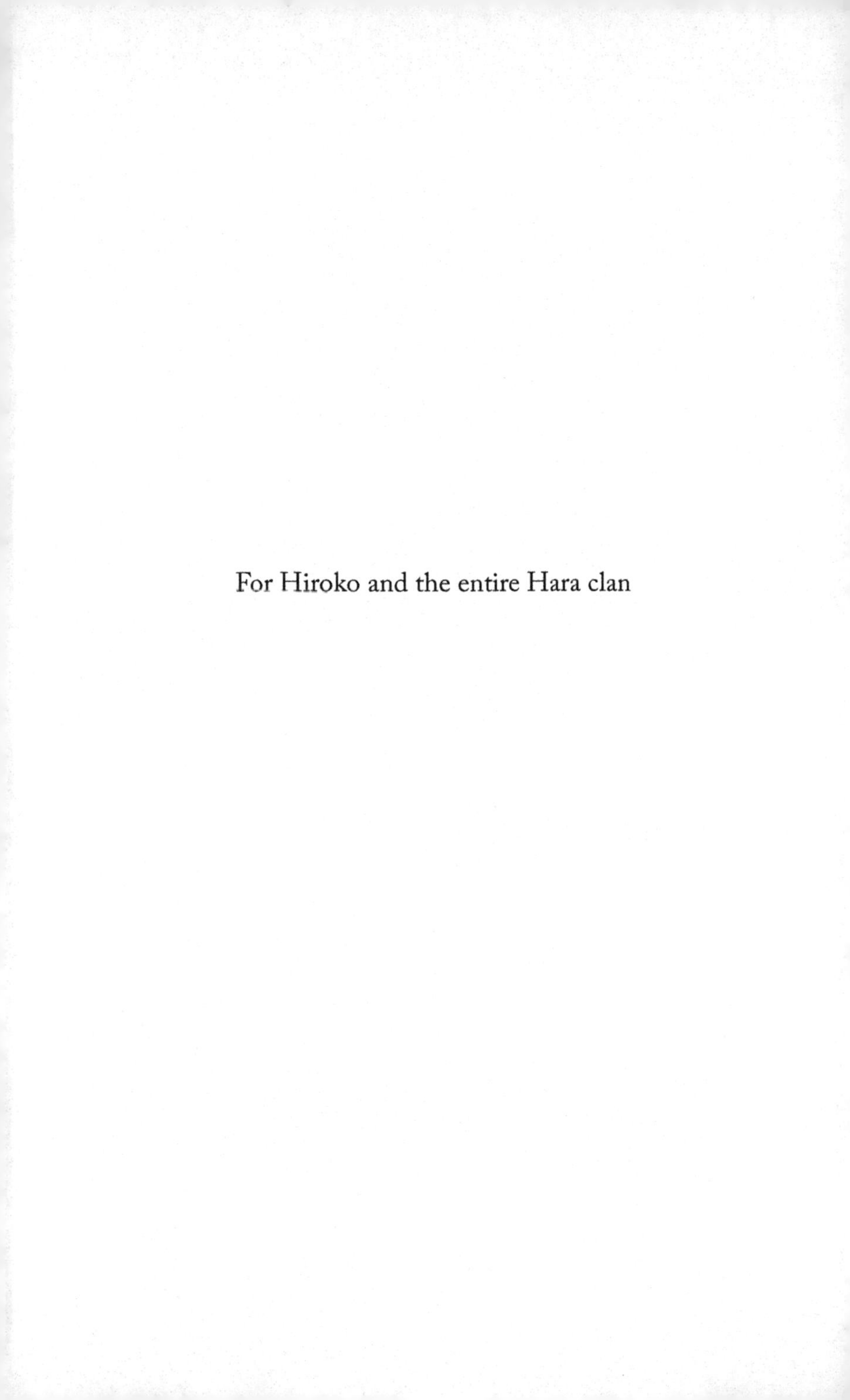

For Hiroko and the entire Hara clan

The Hemingway Files

Note to the reader:

The following story is based on actual events and real historical personalities. Some of the names and locations have been changed for the sake of privacy. Professor Martin Dean's untimely demise almost a year ago has meant that the final responsibility for publishing these documents has fallen to me, his second cousin and closest living relative.

I realize that as the information contained herein becomes widely available, academic specialists in a variety of fields will subject it to further scrutiny, and opinions will vary as to its accuracy. Indeed, I have already shared the contents with several colleagues who are well-known authorities on the authors discussed. While I am confident in the tale's accounts of key events and personalities, having done a thorough fact checking myself, I do recognize the need for scholarly interrogation of the book's central claims and overall historicity. And so I welcome all doubts and debate, and I look forward to the amiable conversations with my fellow researchers that will certainly ensue.

And yet, although factuality and narrative accuracy are crucial, I would advise readers to embrace the "story-truth" revealed here: that we remember the dead—return to their great written works—and reconnect with the invigorating power of the words, and the letters, that they have left behind for us, the living. Like my distant cousin Professor Dean, I have dedicated my own life to precisely these ideals.

—HKB, July 4, 2016

Part One

The package arrived in my departmental mailbox some time before Christmas break, but I didn't see it until several weeks later, well after New Year's Day of 2011—a rather unfortunate circumstance, since its arrival during Advent would have boosted my flagging affinities for the miraculous. Now I am revising this preface one last time, just over a year later, in spring of 2012, my mundane life having been permanently jolted by the parcel's marvelous contents.

The package contained, in short, and to paraphrase Prince Hamlet, "words, words, words"—the luminous sort of words upon which we have built our civilization. Or, as my former student Jack Springs described the gift in his last letter to me, it was "a box full of nothing but words." There may have been madness in the box—but as I eventually learned, method as well.

As that last reference might suggest, I am, and have been for the majority of my life, an English teacher, a mid-to-late career professor here at Indiana University in

Bloomington, Indiana, steady and politic, a woodworker and fisherman in my spare time, nearing the end of a long and (some would say) productive career. For reasons that evade me, and that in fact do give me some regret, I've never married, nor have I ever come close to approaching that foreign land of husband or father.

Some may argue that in fact I *have* fathered a certain kind of offspring, at least insofar as I have fostered a faith of sorts: the religion of great literature, the solemn belief in the ennobling power of words. On my best days, I've provoked in young minds a passion for the written word, the compositions of our great artists. But perhaps "midwife" would be more appropriate. Either way, it all sounds rather grand, I suppose. The reality of my days is much less romantic: I teach my classes, some brilliant, others desultory. I search for signs of life among pages and pages of student writing, from freshmen to doctoral candidates, pages often defaced by coffee stains, colas, tobacco, or the eccentricities of faulty, bargain-priced printers. It is often most exciting, and also most horrifying, during the humdrum act of grading freshman papers, performed ostensibly in the study of the most majestic expressions ever penned by human hands. Because it is among the youngest that we are occasionally rewarded with the briefest glimmers of promise and, every so often, even genius. And so in due course, I assign grades—and attend meetings about various departmental and administrative issues, hold office hours, advise English majors and listen to the unexceptional details of their everyday lives, and try to carry on some of my own research and writing. Almost all of these tasks involve the free market commerce of the mother tongue; I'm a purveyor of what are sometimes called the English language arts, including both the ridiculous and the sublime. My life is disciplined and predictable, some might even say boring, but I've grown comfortable with it.

And so it was on that frosty morning in January, a little over a year ago, that I found myself returning, after a long absence, to my campus office on the fourth floor of Ballantine Hall. There was quite literally not a single other person around. Classes were a week away, and most of my colleagues were either still out of town in warmer climes, at home enjoying a second cup of coffee, or safe between the blankets, sleeping an extra hour or two. At least eight inches of snow covered the ground, but I forged through it, intent on a day at the office, as is my habit, knowing that a huge amount of holiday mail would be waiting for me. I was drawn to campus by the promise of the mailbox.

It has long been my habit to work in the mornings. I am fond of the ambient drone of a computer or a mini-refrigerator, the stillness of letterhead, paper clips, and file folders, and I certainly relish the fact that almost no other professors (and absolutely no students) haunt the hallways before 9:00 or 10:00 a.m. I savor the monastic tone of an academic environment—the shelves of volumes, the piles of unread manuscripts and publishers' catalogues, the odor of slow deterioration, the decay of acidic paper and day-old coffee. And I relish the romance of a stack of unopened mail. I wonder—what secrets might be hidden between the worthless leaflets, the random advertisements from sellers of casebooks and curricula, the slick fliers for overpriced documentary films on authors of marginal accomplishment? Often nothing of value emerges, but until one works his way through it all, slowly and patiently, at least a sliver of possibility remains that some buried treasure will emerge.

Having been in upstate New York visiting my aging mother, I had not been to the office in over three weeks. And as it turned out, a major discovery was to be unearthed from among that early morning's rather large stack of mail, all of it stored neatly in my mailbox on that early Monday morning after Twelfth Night. As the first human visitor of the year, I was like one of the mysterious magi from the east, and the departmental office was shadowy, its doors locked and its confines silent as the stars on that far-off winter's night. I used my master key to unlock the windowless door and collect the ample plunder of mail hidden within, a booty that included dozens of letters and memos, several boxes of books, and various issues of periodicals and journals. From there, I carried it all to the frigid end of a long corridor, where stood my office.

Entering, I paused to savor the sunlight beginning to emerge through my south-facing window. The trees were bare that bitter morning, with the exception of a few stingy old oaks, which were about as forlorn as trees are ever likely to be. As I stood looking out into the glade below, the office seemed to yawn, as if waking from a long winter's nap.

I settled the mail on a side table, stuck my gloves in my coat pockets, and shrugged off my coat, hanging it, along with my hat and scarf, on the hook behind my door. Next I flipped on the small space heater hidden beneath my desk—which was, technically, against university rules—and grabbed my carafe, headed back down the hallway to fill it with tap water, then returned to plug in the coffee maker in preparation for a long morning of work.

My empty stomach, by and by, began to pronounce its primal warblings, so I pulled out my brown bag egg sandwich, settled into the easy chair in the corner, and began sorting through my mound of mail. Halfway through, I discovered my prize ("some have greatness thrust upon them"): a mid-sized cardboard box, easy to overlook, the kind commonly used by publishers to send out manuscripts or examination copies of textbooks. In the upper left hand corner was the only outward clue: "Jack Springs," the name of a favorite former student scrawled in black. It immediately struck me as odd that it had been sent from Kessler Boulevard in Indianapolis, instead of from Washington state, where Jack had been teaching for over a decade, and where, I would learn later, he composed its contents.

Inside I discovered several items: each with a large yellow Post-it note affixed to the front. On top was what appeared to be a book wrapped in brown paper and tied with a string; its note read, "Open me first." Beneath it was a business-sized envelope with "Professor Martin Dean" written on it along with a note reading, "Open me second"; and then came a medium-sized package wrapped in the same brown paper, also tied with string, and sporting a note instructing me to "Open me third." I also found another, smaller box, gift-wrapped in Christmas paper, its dimensions suggestive of a wallet or keychain. Taped to it was the final note, demanding "Open me last, after reading the story."

Now duty bound by the domineering tone of a Post-it note, I unwrapped the first package and was pleasantly surprised to discover what turned out to be a worn copy of *The Old Man and the Sea* by Ernest Hemingway. Opening the cover, I was stunned to discover that it was not only a first edition, but was inscribed with a personal message:

Dear Eloise,
I send my warmest greetings
(unlike the last time!).
Yours Always,
Ernest Hemingway, October 7, 1952

Signed and dated by the great author, Papa himself! This was a marvelous gift for anyone, but unlike some of the other things Jack had sent in recent years, this one was really worth a lot of money—possibly thousands of dollars at auction.

I settled the tattered novel, the package with Jack's manuscript, and the smaller, gift-wrapped box on my worktable beside me, then opened the letter envelope, and pulled out the note, which read:

December 13, 2010
Danforth Springs
1247 Kessler Boulevard
Indianapolis, Indiana

Dear Professor Dean:

It is with the utmost regret that I write to you today on behalf of my son Jack. As you are undoubtedly aware, Jack has been suffering this past year with an aggressive and largely untreatable form of cancer. It has only been in the past few months that the disease has made it impossible for him to carry on with his work at the university. He came home to Indianapolis in late September of this year to be with his family for what little time might remain for him. His mother Hannah and I, and his sister Susan, have had the privilege of spending these final weeks in the company of a young man who, as you know, had a rare gift for language and storytelling, a jovial gift of humor, and a kind of grace under pressure that we usually reserve for heroes in fairy tales. Only in Jack's case, the grace was real.

With great sadness, I must now tell you that Jack passed away, on the early morning of Dec. 7 to be precise. I am just now trying to deal with the kinds of things that no parent should ever face. Among those matters is the delivery of Jack's letter to you, along with the three other items enclosed here. Jack was extremely insistent about my sending these things to you as soon after his death as I might be able to do so. I recognize the value of the rare Hemingway volume, which Jack showed me with pride, but I have no idea as to the contents of the other two enclosures, nor of his letter to you, which is, of course, a matter of privacy. Jack wanted it that way, and whether you should ever choose to reveal any of the contents to me or his mother is completely up to you.

As for the items enclosed with this letter—he wanted you to have them on condition of his death only, and not a moment before. Even on the morning of the day he died, he repeated these instructions to me, though he was fitful, and in what seemed to be unendurable pain. Evidently these were materials of some great importance—at least in his fevered imagination. In the future, should you decide to share with us the nature of those contents, we will of course be your willing and eager listeners. But for now, I am honoring my son's dying request that they be delivered to you unopened and unexamined.

Professor Dean, I think you should know that he spoke of you with the utmost respect and admiration. You had a profound and lasting impact on his life, and he admired you greatly, though you may not have realized it at the time.

I apologize for my brevity here, but we are daily—and indeed even hourly—struggling to deal with this horrific set of events, especially my wife, who is simply overwhelmed. The funeral was just two days ago, and it is an unspeakable day in the life of any parent.

If I can ever be of further assistance, please do not hesitate to contact me.

Sincerely,
Danforth Springs

And so it was with this letter that I learned on that snowy morning back in January of 2011, that Jack Springs was prematurely dead at the age of 44. Like his father and mother, I felt the horror of parental grief sweep over me—the horror that there is something unnatural, even unjust, about losing a child as admirable and as brilliant as I knew Jack to be. The elders consider it to be their rightful honor to precede the young into death, that undiscovered country, to pioneer as it were, but sadly, this is not always our privilege. And perhaps, as many believe, it is life's greatest tragedy.

Two items remained: the neatly wrapped manuscript, dimpled and rustic-looking, and on top of it the mysterious box, wrapped in cheap holiday paper, red with white stripes, like candy canes. This prize bore a cheerful, royal blue ribbon on top—red, white, and blue—very American, I thought. Again I glanced at its imperial Post-it note, where Jack commanded me again from the land of the dead: "Open me last, after reading the story."

I seemed to intuit, and would learn soon enough, that for me, an aging academic getting too set in his old ways, stodgy and unsurprising in my lonely life among books, the joyfully wrapped box contained a key that could magically unlock a mysterious doorway in my life, an entrance into a new world, like the wardrobe leading into Narnia, the rabbit hole into Wonderland. But like Jack's distraught father, I complied with the simple instructions and left it unopened—for the moment.

Instead, Jack's holy parchment beckoned me, and it now gathered my fullest attention. Slowly, I worked the string that held the manuscript together. Finding it knotted in such a way that I was unable to untie it, I reached for the pocketknife that I keep handy on my desk, for just such tasks, and I severed the cord. The paper fell away, and I held in my hands a neat manuscript, printed out in the gentle, fourteen-point font that my old eyes prefer. On top, a single sheet was stapled to yet another business envelope, with a few pages inside. Its message was scribbled unevenly, all in upper case lettering, with a bold, black pen:

READ MY LETTER,

THEN THE MANUSCRIPT,

BEFORE OPENING THE SMALL BOX.

ejs

One must be struck by the sheer insistence of Jack's repetitive instructions; it was a carefully conceived scheme, and he had it all planned out, as the unfolding of the tale will elaborate. And so I did everything in the precise order he prescribed, and I'll ask my readers to do the same, as I present the materials exactly as I received them myself. First came his poignant letter to me, appended below. Ornery editor that I am, I have silently corrected stylistic blunders and several minor typographical errors within the letter, as I have done throughout the full manuscript. Otherwise, it read precisely as follows:

This is my letter to the world,
That never wrote to me,—
The simple news that Nature told,
With tender majesty.

Her message is committed
To hands I cannot see;
For love of her, sweet countrymen,
Judge tenderly of me!

Emily Dickinson

Dear Marty,

It's the day after Labor Day, 2010, up here in the Pacific Northwest, and like a labor of love, or maybe the labor pains of childbirth, this story is finally being delivered. A box full of nothing but words. But these words are not just for you; they are to be made public, eventually. This is my letter to the world, wrote Sister Emily. And, as Mabel

Loomis Todd did for sweet Emily, I'd like to ask you to do me a favor: in the near future, please prepare my manuscript for the world to read, as my editor, or literary executor, if you prefer. Don't worry, there's something in it for you. A labourer is worthy of his hire (KJV).

Parts of the story have been hibernating in a file on my hard drive for a very long time now. Some of it describes the quiet lives we lead as English professors—lives like yours and mine. But my mundane life suddenly got all mixed up with some adventures in the Far East, all recorded herein. My story includes fond reminiscences of Sensei and meandering visions of Mika, two characters you'll get to know in due course.

Sensei. Mika. Sometimes I just speak those names out loud, into thin air.

Even now, those two magical names ramify deeply, being as they are the hazy yin and yang of my first serious enchantments overseas. Their precious names hover and whir about me like bright, insistent hummingbirds, along with other recurring images:

- Starched robes cinched with deep purple sashes
- Steaming mugs of green tea, trays of rice crackers wrapped in seaweed
- Late night sounds of trains, swooshing in and out, *clack-clack, clack-clack*
- Antique wood-block prints: bawdy geisha, cone-shaped mountains, red *torii*
- "Great Wave off Kanagawa"

- Prussian blue and white fingers, dagger-like, plunging into tiny boats
- Old hillside temples, jutting into wind, anchored on thousand-year-old timbers
- Bald monks in wooden shoes, sweeping wide porches, incense painted on air
- Fresh crab brains, gooey as toothpaste
- Orange day lilies and white chrysanthemums, dozing in earthen jars

Remembering has never been hard, often in haiku-like form—mere images, as above. But not always pleasant images—sometimes I would awaken in the dead of night, sweaty, startled, remembering what I wanted to bury. No, it was getting it all down on paper, preparing to send it out to the world that's been the hardest part. But I always knew the story needed telling, and given the circumstances of recent months, I've finally found the guts to wrench it out, for you, my friend, and for all the world to see.

In fact, there are confessions to make. I've suffered my own fair share of guilt, maybe even trauma, admittedly an overused word these days. Michael Herr puts it this way: "The problem was that you didn't always know what you were seeing until later, maybe years later, that a lot of it never made it in at all; it just stayed stored there in your eyes." What a line: stored in your eyes!

The mixed feelings are hard to explain, and harder to justify. I was paralyzed by remorse for days and weeks at a time, followed by a month of remorseless ease and comfort, unmoved by the events recorded here. Maybe I'm just *kichigai*—crazy, out of my gourd, cowering at flashing red lights, sirens rotating around in my brain. Over and over I've heard the familiar screams: *Taskette! Taskette!* (Help! Help!) And I've had the repeated nightmares, and the clammy, sudden awakenings. Meanwhile, I've kept my silence, biding my time.

Only in the past half dozen years did I begin to take some action, searching for answers, doing what any good researcher would do. I devoured countless books about the effects of trauma on its survivors. Academic volumes, clinical data, mostly about the survivors of the deaths of loved ones. Earthquakes became a particular focus. I studied the grisly accounts of massive temblors all over the world: in Iran, for example (December 2003, over 26,000 dead), or Pakistan (October 2005, over 73,000 dead), or China (May 2008, over 87,000 dead). Haiti, earlier this year: over 315,000 dead! Strangely, I ordered books on Amazon filled with frightening photographs. The literary trope also captivated me: the biblical symbolism of earthquakes, the threshing floor of God's wrath, the shorthand of apocalypse. And I developed a fascination with the pragmatics of earthquakes, how mundane human lives are so easily and abruptly shaken to their core, how normal people respond to the daily tremors of their existence, and how unpredictable concussions reveal the hidden fault lines of our characters. I felt like my own world had been rocked, and underneath were all these deep, secret chasms and fissures.

As one expert put it, "Trauma seems to be much more than a pathology, or the simple illness of a wounded psyche: it is always the story of a wound that cries out, that addresses us in the attempt to tell us of a reality or truth that is not otherwise available." The story of a wound. I like that. Or, in some cases, hundreds, or thousands, of wounds.

Another expert listed the many characteristic symptoms of Post Traumatic Stress Disorder, and I was not at all surprised to learn that at least five of them described my own odd behaviors: 1) excessive vigilance; 2) feelings of numbness or cognitive deadness; 3) sleeplessness often featuring recurring, intrusive memories of the events; 4) compulsions to repeat certain events, including a weird fascination with similar forms of violence; and 5) a sense of isolation from others. One famous psychologist described in detail exactly how I felt a good deal of the time: "Normal life becomes permeated by the bizarre encounter with atrocity and violence from the past, so much so that this past can never be completely purged. The two worlds haunt each other; the phantoms of a violent past insist on making their eerie presence permanently felt, even as we wash the dishes, write letters, or walk the dog." And another psychologist described the three steps for full recovery from PTSD: according to clinical research you must tell your story, you must find a reliable witness for your story (usually a close and trusted friend), and you must work to create a new story altogether.

That's where you come in, Marty. Are you that close and trusted friend?

Until now, nobody alive knows what I'm about to tell you, though my old pal Jim Daymon probably has a strong inkling, along with a few concrete artifacts—clues that I entrusted to him many years ago. Jim used to live in a Zen monastery up in the Japan Alps, but I haven't spoken to him in well over a decade now. More about Jim later.

The story you hold in your hands is the result of much fear and trembling this past summer and culminates many years of restless drafting and false starts, the majority of it now consigned to a digital purgatory. Most of the words came spilling out over long weekends of camping and hiking with my black and silver German shepherd, Walt, and my trusty laptop in the amazing mountains and coastlines within a day's driving distance of eastern Washington. Unfortunately, these past few months, many Fridays and Saturdays I would wake up feeling terrible, barely able to walk to the kitchen for coffee. But I had to write out my letter to the world, and tell the story. It has, to some extent, lifted a burden and begun the process of redemption, if that's even possible at this late stage.

By now, of course, if it's all gone according to plan, you've already heard the news: the most important motivation of all this effort has been the solemn realization that I'm dying. During spring break this year, I was riding my bike out in Mt. Rainier National Park—one of my favorite places on the planet—and I experienced some sort of physical attack. It was in the Paradise section of the park, and I was marveling at the endless fields of purple and yellow wildflowers. Suddenly, I hit a very deep pothole in the road and immediately felt a sharp pain in my lower chest that took my breath away and sent me careening into a very large, and very old western hemlock tree. Besides breaking my collarbone, I lay there for quite a while, blinded by a throbbing pain beginning around my belly and through to the small of my back, until someone happened by and alerted the park rangers, who rushed me away to the nearest hospital. It wasn't that near.

It turned out that the bicycle accident was the least of my problems, and that the stabbing chest and back pain that had buckled me over and sent me headfirst into the tree was the real source of trouble. The ER folks attended to the collarbone and urged me to contact my regular MD for further testing. CT scans indicated a mass along my spine, and additional tests confirmed that I had prostate cancer that had gone metastatic (rare for a youngish forty-something like myself, but not unheard of). Stage IV, I was calmly informed, meaning not only that would I be dying soon, but I probably only had a few months of active living to enjoy—or endure.

All this was less than five months ago. My final weeks and days, almost certainly, will find me bedridden and, in the end, largely immobile. I am telling you all of this as abruptly and humorlessly as I was told by Dr. Koyama, my earnest physician back in Spokane. There was a mocking irony to his being of Japanese heritage, I remember thinking, though of course he was third generation. His father, though, had spent time at Manzanar as a little boy, so the tragic remnants of historical abuse still lingered in Dr. Koyama's sad smile. Or at least I imagined it lingered. As he put it that day, his palms pressed together, prayerlike, and his index fingers touching his lower lip: "Consider this summer to be your gift. What do you want to do with it?" He peered at me over the top of his reading glasses. "Or—what do you *need* to do?"

Physicians generally do not make good therapists, but in this case, he asked the right question. And so, learning that I probably only had a few months of serious energy left, I knew it was time to finish my story. I must now face those few dark secrets hidden away, and consider the best way to dispose of them. Honestly, I had no idea if I could do it. In fact, if my health had not changed, I'm sure I would have kept it all buried away, in some dark vault underneath the floorboards, like in a Poe story, just as I had for fifteen years. But now I had to figure out what to do about those secrets, and I didn't have a whole lot of time to do it, if modern science had anything to say about it.

I'm hoping that writing all this down will be redemptive. But I need to warn you up front: complete redemption, in my case, is partly up to you. Yes, today I'm feeling the old remorse rising up within me. So to put things right, at least in my own mind, I need the help of a trusted friend. It will require you to undertake "a few minor tasks," as Sensei liked to put it. You'll get to know him soon, in a way.

I realize you are an "old dog," but newness is good for the soul, though I'm sure the favor I'm going to ask will sound like climbing Mt. Fuji to you—and, in fact, climbing will be involved, as you will soon discover, so I suggest you order some comfortable walking shoes. There's no one else I can trust, Marty. My dad's too old, and his health's lousy anyway—and my death, I'm sure, will be a tough blow making things even worse for him. And Mika? Well—I could never reveal these things to her. Finally, I want it to be someone who truly cherishes and understands the treasures involved. That leaves only you. And so I have sent you this box full of nothing but words. And a key to unlocking them.

Basically I want to enter whatever awaits me in the Great Beyond through the doorway of tranquil sleep, made possible by the knowledge, or at least the belief, that I did my best for those remaining. So please be that close and trusted friend, and help me create a new ending to this story. As Emerson once wrote:

"A friend may well be reckoned the masterpiece of nature."

Best wishes, EJS

友

With this letter from my old protégé, I was catapulted into spring semester of 2011. Professors always hope to hear from former students; in fact some of the greatest satisfactions of any teacher are the achievements and adventures of star pupils like Jack. And here, being described as a trusted friend, was a poignant moment to be sure. But can you feel the horror with which I now read Jack's epistle?

He had left Bloomington in the summer of 1986, heading off for graduate work in the Ivy League. One often loses track of people, with or without the Internet, and this was certainly the case with professors and their former students back in those days—even the favorites. And so for roughly a decade, I heard nothing.

Our relationship recommenced in the waning months of the Clinton administration, just before Easter of 1997, when he wrote a lengthy letter to me, announcing with great joy, that after spending three years in Japan followed by a couple years teaching and writing in Seattle, he had finally been offered—and had accepted—a tenure-track position at Gonzaga University in Spokane. I had not even known at the time that he'd lived and worked in Japan, but of course, I was overjoyed to hear of his good successes.

Jack did not announce this news in an email, as today's students might, and in fact, I still have the letter, tucked away in one of my prized file folders containing them all. Those letters, it goes without saying, along with our unspoken commitment to snail mail, are now revered even more in my memory. For me, his letters had become Jack. In truth, we had not even been in the same room together since he left Bloomington twenty some odd years before.

Now, I will catapult you, my dear reader, into the larger tale followed by my own account of the adventure set in motion by Jack's elaborate plan. Yes, finally, onward to Jack's wonderful manuscript.

The majority of the lengthy chronicle you now hold in your hands was produced not by me, but by my former protégé, Dr. Eugene Jackson Springs, a splendid student whose potential and achievements were among the best it has been my privilege to witness and encourage. *I have only augmented Jack's story occasionally, at the end of chapters, with either useful observations and/or hard factual data, all of which I've italicized (like this) for the sake of my readers.* Jack's story, with my minor interruptions, is then followed by a briefer report of what came afterwards. My own participation in all this, as it turned out, required more than just editorial assistance.

I can divulge up front that I now understand why he kept certain details in the strictest secrecy for so long, and why evidently his own parents were not even allowed to hear the tale—until now, when all the world can listen.

Our great authors were an eccentric bunch: often bullies, sometimes even sociopaths. All were driven by mixed motives, by their love of truth and beauty, by their tempestuous and autocratic personalities, and by the impure motivations of lust, personal gain, and notoriety. And yet they penned those marvelous words, words, words.

The lyrical inventions of the great artists can indeed set us free, but if we're not deliberate in our careful use and stewardship of them, their narcotic effects can imprison us as well. Jack's confession is thus a cautionary tale. It illustrates a devotion that should certainly inspire us, even as it reminds us that some kinds of devotion also contain the seeds of our own corruption, and perhaps even destruction.

Part Two

Epistolary Friendships II

by

E. J. Springs

Completed Sept. 4, 2010

Dedicated to
Sensei and Mika

CHAPTER 1

You are our letter, written in our hearts, known and read by all men.

—St. Paul to the Corinthians, II Cor. 3:2

I find letters from God dropped in the street—
and every one is signed by God's name,
And I leave them where they are,
for I know that others will punctually
come forever and ever.

—Walt Whitman, *Leaves of Grass*

I have loved the letters of the dead, Yu-san. I have given my life to discovering them, the secret thoughts from one famous person written to another, the miscellany of genius writers whose forgotten words were to me the very breath of life. Their letters are, in most cases, part and parcel of the author. We hold in our hands the remnants of the dead.

—Sensei, circa autumn 1993

友

The real story begins in Japan, and it will likely end there, too, though that part remains to be written. How I ended up in Japan is a pretty good yarn, but I won't tell most of it here. Suffice it to say that I had never been there before 1992, and frankly had never even given Japan the briefest of thoughts. It was just some place far away. I had those old stale ideas about Japan, a mythic place with temples and *geisha* girls, *samurai* and *sushi*, all that, but beyond the stereotypes, I'd never thought much about it.

I left Bloomington in summer of 1986 and headed off to New Haven to begin work on my doctorate, thanks to my inflated letters of recommendation. Still, I felt like the insecure little corn pusher from the Midwest that I was. Before I knew it, I was defending my dissertation and searching for full-time positions in the field. But when the smoke cleared, I received zero offers. A PhD from Yale, but no jobs on the horizon. To say I was devastated is putting it mildly.

That was in the late winter of 1992, over eighteen years ago, but I can easily drum up the dread and alienation that took up residence in the pit of my stomach, the choking miasma that enveloped me every single day, rendering me limp, directionless. I felt trapped by the machine of higher education, chewed up and spit out on the pavement, like one of the homeless guys down on Chapel Street, on the wrong side of New Haven.

But suddenly an unseen hand beckoned me all the way to the Land of the Rising Sun. At the end of the very last week of February 1992, I found myself seated in the cluttered office of my mentor and dissertation director,

Sherri Fisher. I was literally hours away from giving up the ghost and accepting a temporary, one-year appointment at a no-name college on the outskirts of Wichita, Kansas. I could hardly even believe that Wichita had outskirts, but I had no other options, my money was running out fast, and I was making the rounds to my trio of advisors, asking them for their opinions about my renting a U-Haul and heading off for the Great Plains.

Long story short: Sherri knew a professor in Japan who had faxed her with inquiries about me. They had some prestigious three-year, post-doc available, called the Goto Fellowship, and my scholarly work fit the description perfectly. She produced the fax, written by the chair of the Department of American Studies at Kobe University, Professor Aoyama Daisuke. I was immediately ill at ease. I couldn't pronounce the name or even determine whether the professor was male or female. I read the fax twice, as Sherri continued shuffling papers. I had never once in my life thought seriously about living in East Asia, or even visiting there for that matter.

"So you know this—person?"

"Oh yes, very well, actually. I once spent two months at Kobe University, and have been back a couple times when visiting Japan. Aoyama-sensei is a gentle, friendly, and funny guy. I think you'll like him." She turned her chair to look me straight in the eye. "Actually, he's a Big Ten guy like you—he did his PhD at Northwestern, and lived in Chicago for about eight years, so his English is perfect. You'd like Kobe, and the school; it's built onto the side of a mountain that rises straight out of the Pacific, just a couple miles away. The fax mentions that the apartment they provide will be in the same building they put me—

very nice, very upscale, fully furnished, with a view of the bay. It would be a terrific set up, with an excellent condo to live in and lots of support from the university." She twirled a little in her chair, and surveyed me like a Cheshire cat. "To be honest, it would beat the hell out of eastern Kansas, Dorothy."

I didn't smile at her joke, as I was taking a moment to interpret this jaw-dropping news. It was hard to let it sink in. But within two days, we were on the phone to Professor Aoyama—which I learned was pronounced Ah-oh-yaamaa. And just like that, within three weeks I had held a moving sale, said my goodbyes in New Haven, boxed up the rest of my stuff and moved it back to my parent's house in Indianapolis, boarded a jet from Indy to Chicago to Osaka, and found myself settling into a wonderfully furnished condo, or "mansion," on the fifteenth floor of a tall building with a stunning view of the Port of Kobe and Osaka Bay. In Japan, the school year begins in April, and I barely had time to unpack my things and clear my head of jet lag before I was in the classroom, inspecting the Japanese students as they inspected me right back. I didn't have a dog, but otherwise I might as well have been Dorothy among the denizens of Oz.

友

The week after my arrival in Kobe, cherry blossoms sprouted, schoolchildren donned their freshly laundered uniforms, and the brand new school year began. April 1992. Somehow it made sense for the academic year to begin unsullied and new in springtime, as it does in Japan. The cadence is different than in America, where school begins at the end of summer, and progresses immediately to the cool weather and the fall of leaves. Japan's academic rhythm is more hopeful, beginning at the moment of fertility and renewal.

My schedule was pretty simple: six classes per week, ninety minutes per class, about thirty to thirty-five students in each class. That sounds like a lot of students by American standards, but the system in Japan is set up in such a way that the vast majority of students are disengaged, completely unprepared, asleep, or absent. But there are always in every class a handful of eager, bright-eyed, and passionate young people whose souls entirely revolve around both the learning of the English language and a love for all things American. Plus they all immediately called me "*sensei*"—Japanese for teacher—and treated me with far more respect than I'd ever encountered in America. It is obviously this group that makes teaching English in Japan (or anywhere) not just tolerable, but often both stimulating and powerfully rewarding.

The teaching was simple enough, but the office politics were a puzzle. Professor Aoyama, the head of the department, had assigned a "*sempai*"—an older, more experience faculty mentor, called Professor Miyamoto—to be my primary caregiver as I made the transition into the Japanese university system. "Miyamoto-sensei has some acquaintance with your area. He has written some interesting works on American writers, including Hawthorne and Melville. He is most experienced with foreigners, having spent two years at the University of Oregon. I am certain you will have much to discuss."

We didn't. Unfortunately, I immediately disliked Miyamoto. He looked oily to me, unkempt in appearance and attitude, very thin, with a pock-marked face. Every time I saw him, he seemed to be wearing the same old blue suit and silvery-blue necktie. His English was passable, but his gestures were unfriendly and his air sometimes snobbish.

"If you would need anything, Springs-sensei, please give your requests to Miyamoto-sensei," Professor Aoyama instructed. Miyamoto bowed in my general direction, and so I bowed slightly back, not really knowing what else to do. I fumbled with my hands, not exactly certain where they should go as I bowed. "Miyamoto-sensei is one of our most trusted colleagues here at Kobe University, and I know he will be a worthy guide for you in the coming days."

Again, a slight bow. Miyamoto, however, would not look me in the eye, which made me nervous, and would not even speak to me beyond the standard "*hajimemashite*" and "*yoroshiku onegaishimasu.*" At the time, I wondered why he had been appointed guide dog for the poor foreigner. In retrospect, I realize there were other forces at play, and that, it turned out, Miyamoto had connections in high places. Even though I had no knowledge of what was going on behind the scenes, I picked up the distinct odor of something gone bad. So from the start, I kept my distance and rarely spoke with him. Initially, he had little impact on my life—that came much later. But he always seemed to be a specter lurking just beyond my field of vision.

友

Life was foreign, but good. I taught my classes, went for long hikes along the steep mountain trails above campus, read books, graded miserable student papers, drank more lukewarm green tea than I had thought humanly possible, and generally kept busy with my own writing. I quickly became a regular at one of the campus hangouts, the Munchen Café, a sort of hipster coffee shop named after the owner's fascination with the southern German city, minus the *umlaut*. It was roomy for a Japanese bar, with a number of old sofas, and it had some prints of German Expressionist paintings all over the walls, especially Kandinsky. They also had special "Oktoberfest" pricing, on Monday and Friday afternoons, which was nice, so it was popular with students.

Since Kobe is a city set into a narrow plain wedged between Osaka Bay and the dramatically sloping foothills of the Rokko Mountains, the largest peak of which rises to 3,000 feet or more, the hiking was marvelous. Rokko National Park borders the campus and was only about half a mile up the hill from my apartment, so I could leave the somewhat depressing urban landscape behind by simply going for a walk.

The park itself was lush, with refreshingly cool, damp air the farther I ventured. I liked to hike uphill for a good distance, and then look out over the great, sprawling city: the tall buildings, the trains going east and west, the huge cargo ships being loaded and unloaded by massive red cranes, and beyond the port, the wide expanse of Osaka bay. It was so different from the flatlands of central Indiana or the urban grittiness of New Haven that I never tired of gazing down upon the hectic city scenes from a serene perch, 1,000 feet above the din.

Within the first few months of teaching, I discovered another hidden pleasure: the department had a fairly well-stocked, though rarely used, library on the top floor of one of the office buildings. I was given a key, and Hiromi, one of the departmental secretaries who spoke some English and laughed with her hand over her mouth whenever I spoke directly to her, showed me how to sign books in and out. The library's impressive contents covered the gamut of English and American literary studies, though its holdings petered out after about 1980 or so. But unlike many of my colleagues back in the states, I was never one for chronological snobbery. I still think that much of the best work ever written on American literature was from the '50s and '60s, and was thrilled to find scores of old volumes hidden away on those dusty shelves. Some had evidently never been opened. And in all the months of going there for long hours of quiet study, I never once encountered another professor. The departmental library became one of my little secrets—a place where I spent many hours of uninterrupted joy, alone and in silence, like a Benedictine monastic. Thanks to the contents of that library, the miracles of inter-library loan, and the judicious use of my book allowance for the newest works, I had available almost anything I might need for continuing my own research.

Eventually, I wondered about the riches of this musty old storeroom, and when the opportunity arose, I asked Professor Aoyama about it. It was June, and the air was sticky in his un-air conditioned office (Americans have become addicted to air conditioning). Professor Aoyama waved a fan back and forth as he talked to me. He was slow to respond directly, but after a few moments, took to his subject with gusto, bragging about the legacy of outstanding professors that the department boasted in the decades after World War II. Several of these professors—Saito, Urawa, and Goto—had gone abroad to the best universities in the world for the study of American literature: Harvard, Yale, and Princeton. It was through their tireless efforts that the library had been established and well stocked in the two or three decades after the war and occupation, he said. "These three men, and especially Goto-sensei, have been the guardian angels of the department—I believe that is the phrase you use sometimes back in America?"

"Goto? Is that the same as the Goto Fellowship?"

"Ah, yes, of course, sensei, that is correct. Thanks to him, we have hosted seven foreign professors over the years in our department. This year is the first time we have been fortunate enough to host two of you. And it was largely due to the generosity of Goto-sensei that these volumes were purchased over many years. As you know, Goto-sensei comes from a family of some affluence."

"Well, no, sensei, actually I don't know anything about that."

Aoyama recognized his error, paused, then shrugged his shoulders, and nodded. "Ah, yes, I suppose not. Well, you see, in the old days Goto-sensei himself would welcome the winners of the Fellowship with a wonderful dinner party at his old house up in the hills, but now, as he is getting quite old, he is rarely seen down here in the department. It is through the generosity of Goto-sensei that these fellowships exist in the first place. He is now nearly eighty years old, I believe, and retired from the department, though occasionally he is seen wandering around campus or spending a few hours in his private office, which he still maintains. He also remains chair of the fellowship committee, so he has some little influence in the choosing of the candidates."

Professor Aoyama paused and looked at me. Not

knowing what was expected, I nodded appreciatively, but said nothing.

"Goto-sensei took a great deal of interest in you," he continued. Surprised and a bit confused as to why the man would be interested in me, I simply smiled and waited. "He actually provided an additional fellowship this year for you, after the committee had already made the first offer to Professor Kilcoyne and he had accepted it, last fall. But once he saw your vita, which Sherri sent to us, Goto-sensei took a strong personal interest, allowing your recruitment to be—fast-tracked?—I believe that is how you say that?" He worked a paper clip between his fingers. "He is also, like you, a great fan of Hemingway. And so, as you can see, your appointment was largely due to the patronage of Professor Goto."

It was intriguing information. David Kilcoyne, a British teacher from Leeds whose work was focused on the Victorians, particularly Dickens and Kipling, was a decent enough fellow. On several occasion we had already enjoyed together a few bottles of Asahi Dry beer, usually over fried noodles and *gyoza*—fried dumplings. I knew he was also considered a Goto Fellow, but hadn't realized that traditionally there was only one fellowship award every three academic years. I remembered the fax Sherri showed me, which had said something about a "special provision" of some sort.

"What is it about my work that interests Goto-sensei?"

He hesitated, and I wondered if I had made a conversational faux pas. I sensed he was studying me, so again I waited for him to continue.

"*So, desu-ne*?" Perhaps the most common staple of Japanese conversation, the phrase can mean many things:

"Yes, isn't that a good question?" Or, a more general comment of agreement, such as saying "you know?" or "OK?" As time went on, "*So, desu-ne*?" or its shorter forms, including the simple syllable "*ne?*" (meaning, "isn't that right?" or simply "right?"), became a regular feature of my own conversational life in Japan.

I wondered if the conversation was over and shifted in my seat, but Aoyama set his paper clip down and said, "Yes, well I think I can say this much—Goto-sensei is … a collector of literary objects and artifacts. Yes. And like you, he favors the letters and personal papers of certain American writers, whose works he values above … all else, shall we say. Especially those of Hemingway, I should say, *ne*?"

I nodded in agreement, but was, in fact, very confused. I considered this revelation a moment. "And when will I get a chance to meet Goto, so I can thank him personally for his generosity?"

"Well, yes, of course, I think that will be arranged at some point in the future. Perhaps it would be better to say 'if' you get a chance," Professor Aoyama corrected me. "I am not suggesting that Goto-sensei is opposed to meeting with you, or anyone for that matter. However, I am sure you understand by now that the way of the Japanese can be rather difficult for foreigners. And never refer to him as simply 'Goto,' by the way. It is much too rude. It must always be respectful: Goto-sensei, or Professor Goto, *ne*?" He winked. "I must tell you that any meeting with Goto-sensei, assuming that there is to be one, will be entirely of his choosing. If you do see him on campus, I would urge you not to approach him and introduce yourself. Allow him, in his own timing, to be the one to initiate any contact.

This is the Japanese way of the old days, of the elder being the one to arrange for a meeting with an underling."

I was getting more, not less, confused, but kept nodding anyway. "Yes, sensei, I think I understand."

"And Jack-san. I hope you will understand, but do not be intrusive in asking questions about Goto-sensei, or about his family, especially with anyone here at the university. This sort of gossip would be extremely unfortunate for you, should he become aware of it. He is an intensely private person, and his family has a storied past from before, during, and obviously, after the war. The university is like a very small village in that respect." He leaned to look out his door to see if any staff happened to be nearby. "You may feel at times that you have great freedoms here at Kobe Univeristy, and in many ways you do, but do not be fooled by the outward appearances. The other teachers and administrators are always watching you very carefully, since as a Goto Fellow, you are such a … special foreigner. Again, it is all part of the Japanese way." Aoyama waited a moment, then proceeded. "I have known for some time now, for example, about your frequent visits to the library."

"Yes?"

"Of course, Jack-san. Your status here is very prestigious; it is quite an impressive fellowship, and it is in the name of a very powerful family, so of course we must be careful that … well, that nothing is done that will bring dishonor upon that name. You must have suspected that for some time now, yes?" Aoyama cocked his head, smiling a little. "That Japan is a land where everything … is observed?" He smiled coyly at this last comment.

I hadn't noticed, at least not yet. "Well—actually, not really. But I do thank you for your honesty about this."

"You are most welcome. And of course, as the chair of this faculty, I also must watch over you, and be responsible for any, shall we say, indiscretions? Of course, I had thought that you would have known all of this already. I sometimes forget that Japan is a country full of mysteries for *gaijin*."

Talk about mysterious. At that moment, I truly felt like a *gaijin*—a foreigner, an outsider—and was more confused with every word.

"Please respect all of this advice, Jack-san, and understand that there are very many ways to endear yourself to elderly Japanese men—but also many ways to alienate yourself from them. Older men who grew up in the pre-war era are especially difficult to please in this respect. There are certain rules of behavior when in the presence of the *sempai*—the master, I mean. Do you know that word? *Sempai*?"

The phone rang on Aoyama's desk, and after answering, he held his palm over the receiver and told me that he must take the call. It was my cue to leave, which I did, gladly.

友

It was the last I heard about Goto-sensei for many weeks. I never brought him up with any of my acquaintances on campus, except for one, David Kilcoyne, of course. Even he warned me about what Aoyama-sensei must have meant when he talked about the Goto family as having some amount of fame in Japan.

"These old-time Japanese blokes," he said, quaffing a cold Kirin beer, "they see the world quite differently, it seems to me. Look, I'm not saying it's *1984* or any of that rubbish. But there is a bit of the *samurai* spirit still around, yes? Surely you've felt what it means to be a foreigner, an outsider, a *gaijin*?" He took another long draught. "And you must have noticed that people are always watching you, hey? Out of the corner of their eyes, as it were. Personally—" he sat back and waved his hand as if taking in all of Japan—"I would venture to stay on the safe side, and keep my nose out of the closets. And gents like this Goto fellow are hidden in some closet somewhere." He took another long drink. "The social obligations get tiresome, anyway, as you must be noticing. The endless bowing, and the formal dinners and such. Who needs it?"

Kilcoyne had been here only four months longer than I had, and yet his thin seniority had an authoritative ring to it. He was also nearly fluent in conversational Japanese. So I took his advice, kept my mouth shut, and tried to find out about Goto through other means.

友

Admittedly, when I first read the name Goto, it did ring a faint bell. But I was initially unable to place it. A surge of mystery and caution filled me, however, though I could not say why exactly. Only later did the name and its myriad insinuations return to me, according to some sort of alienated majesty.

Common as it surely is, the tale of Jack failing to land a permanent position in the States is an embarrassment of riches in today's academic market, I'm afraid. This condition fills me with shame, to think he was unable to find a suitable position here in America, to lose a gifted young scholar like Jack to another nation, even if temporarily, seemed somehow unjust.

And yet, it stirred in me the memories of my own first experiences abroad as a participant in a generously funded

NEH symposium hosted by a university in Lisbon, Portugal. As with Jack, my selection to this prestigious award was magical. I'd never been farther from home than Florida, but in Lisbon, the sea breezes off the massive harbor, the windy and sweeping vistas, the nightly walks up the ramshackle hills of Alfama—home of the Portuguese folk style of music called Fado—the spicy seafood stews accompanied by the passionate and mournful songs of the singers ... it was heady stuff for a first adventure abroad, a powerful narcotic I like to call that "anywhere but here" addiction we all suffer, from time to time. It comes, as Ishmael put it, "Whenever I find myself growing grim about the mouth." Perhaps, as they say, everything happens for a reason.

CHAPTER 2

One steamy midsummer day, I was hunkered down on my sofa, half-reading a travelogue about old Japan, and half-watching a late afternoon match of the high school baseball national tournament, when the phone rang.

"Jack-san? This is Miyamoto."

"Yes, sensei? How are you today?" I straightened up and, in fact, made a slight bow to him, though he was on the telephone. I was acclimating to the Japanese way, all right. Still, Miyamoto had the habit of getting slightly under my skin, making me feel edgy, as if I were a lab specimen always under the microscope.

"Just fine. My days are rather full, with meetings and other matters. You *gaijin* teachers should be thankful that these matters are of no concern to you."

"I understand. You must be very tired from working so hard." That's a vague translation of the rejoinder statement common among Japanese in such situations, *otsukare sama deshita*. I remember David once advising me, "Begin and end with thanks, or else mention how hard someone has been working. And when in doubt, either bow, or say '*otsukare sama deshita,*' or better yet—do both! Profuse thankfulness—that's the ticket!" Followed by a long gulp of beer.

"Sensei, I have some interesting news for you. Actually it is an invitation. I have been in contact with Professor Goto. He has some little interest in your latest work, as it turns out, and would like to consult with you about it and ... certain other matters. He is wondering if it might be possible for you to join him for tea this coming Sunday at his home in Ashiya? About 4:00 p.m.?"

I listened carefully, trying to crack the code that is often implied in the way the Japanese extend invitations or make statements. The nuance and the heightened awareness required for communication in Japan is easily overlooked by foreigners, and having been in the country for less than six months, I was still a beginner (and to this day, I still feel like a beginner). I also had an engagement for that particular Sunday—I was planning to attend the annual high school baseball tournament, always held at the legendary *Koshien* Stadium in Nishinomiya, outside Kobe, thanks to some free tickets provided by a friend of Kilcoyne. The tournament is a kind of national obsession, every spring and culminating in August, since the summer tournament is the most prestigious, with losing players famously scooping up some of the "sacred" infield dirt of the mythical arena. My first thought, typically American, was to negotiate another date for meeting Professor Goto.

All of this may sound confusing, if you've never spent time in Japan. But sometimes an invitation is not exactly an invitation in Japan, and you are expected to turn it down. Other times, it can be a non-negotiable demand. In late summer of 1992, I was still in my honeymoon stage, my often bewildered yet always bedazzled lover stage, the codes of Japanese communication still perplexing. I couldn't quite pick up the signals. But as far as I could understand Miyamoto, I was actually being invited to meet, finally, with Professor Goto, in his home. Somehow, I wanted to confirm my instinct. So I asked him:

"Miyamoto-sensei, is this an invitation that I should accept? Actually I have other plans for this Sunday afternoon."

"Well, obviously you misunderstand the situation, Jack-san. Try to comprehend what is at stake here. You must cancel those other plans immediately! Do you somehow not recognize this?" His voice got louder, and tenser. I felt the stress he projected, stress he intended me to feel.

"But sensei, I have tickets to the baseball tournament at Koshien on Sunday."

He was astounded that I would consider this information relevant in any way. He barked into the phone, "Meeting your benefactor is such an honor that you must accept it, immediately. In fact, I think you must understand that Professor Goto has never met individually with any of the previous *gaijin* teachers, and so I cannot help but tell you that it is an extremely generous honor. It is a summons, and yes, you must go, Jack-san. And you must be early, and take with you something valuable from America as a gift."

I'd learned enough about Japanese manners to recognize that several aspects of Miyamoto's speech gave away his lack of respect for me. He frequently called me "Jack-san," which is over-friendly and somewhat condescending, and calling me a "*gaijin* teacher" was also slightly offensive. *Gaijin* emphasized my foreignness, my outsider status. I could tell by these little mannerisms, not to mention the strains of anger in his voice, that he considered me a bit of a fool. But even though I felt a strong aversion for Miyamoto, I sensed that in this case he was giving me good advice. So I accepted the invitation.

"OK. I get it. Thank you for … your help with this, sensei. And please convey to Professor Goto that it would be my extreme honor to visit him in his home this Sunday." I was catching on, I thought to myself.

"Fine, Jack-san. This is the proper and, in fact, the only response that is possible. I would have thought that you would know this immediately."

"Yes, sensei. I appreciate your humble advice." I held my tongue, on this occasion at least, and thanked him profusely. The "humble advice" part was my little American dig, however, and I could not hold it back. I doubt he got it anyway. Most Japanese have absolutely no ear for American-style irony. Again, I recalled Kilcoyne, who came up with the "profuse thankfulness" mantra: when in doubt, bow slightly and say *Domo arigato gozaimasu.* "Thank you, thank you, very much." So I did.

It was time to meet the man behind the curtain.

友

Five days later, armed with the directions prepared by Miyamoto, I was on my way up the hill toward Professor Goto's residence. It was raining hard, a warm, driving rain that could easily turn nasty, flooding the innumerable streams and rivulets that wrinkle the hills and race down to the sea. After leaving my apartment, I'd jumped on a train and reached Ashiya station by 3:30, waited in line for a taxi, and by 3:45 I got my first glimpse of Goto's property.

He lived in a massive, walled compound at the very top of a long winding road, almost three miles up the mountainside from the station. Squeezed into a thin area between Kobe and Nishinomiya, the estate was in the most affluent neighborhood in the entire region.

Upon arrival I stood before a medieval-looking wall and gate at least eight feet tall. The drive up had offered stunning scenery, and I wondered what the grounds within the compound were like. Outside the wall, large, exotic trees peered down upon me and lush plants, gleaming and swaying in the pounding rain, seemed to yearn for the inevitable arrival of cooler, gentler fall weather. Moss grew on shiny rocks and covered patches of earth in brilliant greens. The sound of gurgling water hung like music in the air. For a moment, I stood, mesmerized. Then, as Miyamoto had instructed, I buzzed the doorbell. Twice. Finally, a soft, feminine voice: "*Hai*!"

I fumbled momentarily. "*Hai*. Yes, hello. This is Jack Springs, to see Professor Goto."

"Ah yes, Springs-sensei, *dozo*, please come in."

The sound of another, long buzz accompanied the withdrawal of the gate, which slid slowly to the right. Nobody was in sight, so I walked into the well-groomed garden in front of the main building of the compound and approached the entryway. I stepped up onto the front porch and again rang a bell. Immediately the door opened and I was greeted by a slender, radiant Japanese woman, of medium height and with the standard long, straight, jet-black hair. She was wearing a traditional *kimono*, a fresh light pink one with tiny flowers of blue, green, and gold, and she bowed deeply to me, avoiding eye contact. But she was perfectly made-up, highlighting the utter smoothness of her skin, and high arching brows that suggested a playful heart. Hers was the sort of pristine beauty that one usually imagines to be possible only in the movies. Encountering it in real time was dazzling, but petrifying. I trembled ever so slightly, and began to sweat. I tried guessing her age but it was impossible: she might be twenty-five or forty-five. Beautiful women in Japan hold on to an intriguing youthfulness much more successfully than most of their American counterparts, who suffer from too much fried food and sunshine, and not enough walking and other forms of exercise.

"Springs-sensei, *hajimemashite*," she said. "I am honored to make your acquaintance. My name is Mika. Welcome to our humble home."

I bowed back, in the tentative way of the slightly taken-aback *gaijin*. "Nice to meet you, I'm Jack Springs." We stood in the *genkan*, the small foyer in almost all Japanese homes where you take off your shoes and step up into the house proper. The wood was a gleaming mahogany, and the walls were decorated with what appeared to be authentic Japanese wood block prints. I recognized several of them immediately, from seeing them reprinted in picture books or on postcards.

"Please come with me, Springs-sensei. My uncle will be with you shortly. He is being detained and it may be a few minutes, and so he sends his apologies." Her English was effortless and near fluent, with only the slightest trace of a Japanese inflection. I slid off my shoes and followed her. She led me down a long hallway that featured more beautiful Japanese prints and a few scrolls on both sides, until we reached a very large room with the *shoji*—sliding doors of wood and paper—already opened.

It was a traditional tea room, fastidiously clean, the staple image Americans have of what an old Japanese home might look like. It was almost completely empty and spoke of austerity and purity. There was an alcove along one wall, called a *tokonoma*, in which a single vase of flowers stood, artfully arranged in a burst of color. *Tatami* mats covered the floor, and in the exact center of the room was a low table with a pit beneath it for one's legs. A single, pale blue pillow, embroidered with what looked like a swaying dragon, was on the floor on each side of the square table. Stunning artwork adorned the walls: scrolls in the dramatic, yet subtle Japanese style of calligraphy known as *shodo*, the way of writing. And because the *shoji* screens had been pulled back to reveal a miniature garden, the patter of rain on glistening plants and smooth stones offered a soothing accompaniment to the art, like a living extension of the room. Just as Mika gestured with long, slender arms toward one of the pillows, a brief spray of sunshine broke through the clouds, illuminating the garden with an iridescent glow and filling the room with light.

"Please sit here, Springs-sensei. My uncle should be arriving shortly. Shall I bring you some tea? Do you like Japanese tea?" I gazed at her, trying not to stare but failing miserably. She moved slowly, every gesture elegant and precise, sleeves sweeping behind her arms like wings.

"Yes, please, I would like some tea. Thank you." I thumped down rather clumsily onto one of the floor pillows. Japanese sit as gracefully as large, limber birds, while heavy Americans tend to be clumsy as they attempt to lower themselves onto the floor instead of into a higher, western-style chair. It all took some getting used to. As I landed and arranged myself, Mika bowed several times, and inched away from me, facing me until she reached the doorway.

After disappearing, she slid the screen closed, and I sat alone in the splendid old room, listening to the rain, which had lightened up considerably, and the slight wind rustling the leaves just outside. I considered this new bit of information: "my uncle," she said. But that seemed wrong somehow: I had already calculated that he would be in his seventies or older, if he did graduate study in the years after WW II, while she appeared to be hardly older than a young woman in her mid- to upper-twenties. In fact, Mika had the unjaded look of a young woman, and her mannerisms were refined. Possibly "uncle" was just a term of endearment? Or possibly, she was some other relative? She definitely seemed too young to be his niece, or so I thought at the time.

I waited for the tea, which Mika soon brought in on a platter with some *sembei*, rice crackers. She served me without a word and vanished once again. The soft aroma of her presence remained, as did the memory of her movements in slow and graceful patterns, like a kind of performance imprinted in the air. I sipped the hot tea and gazed silently at the room's impressive contents. Another twenty minutes passed. Finally, there was a bustle in the hallway outside the door and a quick exchange in Japanese, then silence. A minute later the screen door slid open once again and Mika appeared. "Spring-sensei, my uncle will see you now. Please, won't you follow me?"

I lurched to my feet and followed her down the hall directly into a similar room on the other side of the house, though this one was much larger with an even bigger table and more expansive window that opened out onto another splendid garden. Framed against the greenery beyond was a small, graying Japanese man, clothed in the traditional cotton robes known as a *yukata*. His shoulders were slightly hunched, as if he'd spent many hours bending over a reading table, and he wore large, black glasses. A tiny black and white dog sat at attention at his feet. The elderly man placed his palms on his legs just above his knees and bent slightly.

"Professor Springs, *hajimemashite*. I welcome you to my home. Thank you for accepting my invitation. I am Goto Haruki. It is a pleasure to meet you finally." Again, more bows.

I did what any observant westerner might do: I mimicked him, bowing slightly again and again. I knew to wait until he had completed his bowing. Then he looked up at me, stood with a grace I found remarkable for one his age, and came forward, extending his hand in greetings.

"Professor Goto, it is a great honor to meet you finally. Thank you for your generosity and for your invitation today." We peered into each other's eyes. I had brought with me a few items as gifts: *omiyage*, as it is called in Japan, mementos of a visit. It is common to bring some sort of gift when visiting another person's home, and Miyamoto had made it clear I knew that. I presented the *omiyage* with both hands, bowing slightly. "Sensei, *tsumaranai mono desu ga … dozo.*" Please accept these small and insignificant gifts. I said it with all the humility traditionally expected, and then some.

A wisp of a smile flashed across his face. He seemed surprised I had brought him some *omiyage*, though of course he would have expected it from any sane Japanese.

"Thank you. This is quite unnecessary. I am honored by your generosity." He seemed genuinely moved by my respect for Japanese cultural traditions, and I was, reluctantly, thankful for Miyamoto's advice. He handed the unopened gifts to Mika, who was still attentively observing both of us. She received it with both hands. And there was more bowing.

"Thank you for the honor of an invitation to your home," I said with yet more bowing of my own.

Looking back, I recognize how paltry my gifts were to this person of such importance in my life, almost an insult. I had given him a very ordinary box of bean cakes that I had picked up in the main train station at Takayama, on my way back down the mountain from a day of hiking, along with another box of some local mountain herbs. In fact, the gifts were ridiculous; it would have been much better to have hand-carried some elaborate keepsake from my home in Indiana, or possibly from Yale. I learned all of this a week later, in a late night session with Kilcoyne. How he smirked at my little miscalculation! And he never forgot, either, often calling me "bean cake boy" as a pointed reminder.

But Professor Goto handled my silly gifts as if I had presented him with relics from the Lost Ark of the Covenant. He allowed my absurd presents to go unremarked, being too polite to laugh. Further proof that outwardly, the Japanese are among the most generous and refined people in the world.

"Please sit here, Springs-sensei." Again, I lowered myself to the floor with as much grace as an Indiana boy could muster. He sat opposite me, framed by the outside window, which produced a glare when I looked at him. "I understand you are a fan of baseball and that this was a great inconvenience to you to come up here today. For which I apologize."

Miyamoto! The man had obviously told Goto about my plans to go to the baseball tournament that day. "No apologies are necessary, Professor Goto. It is entirely my pleasure to come here today." I fumbled a moment in the silence. "Do you like baseball?"

"Of course. I love the old traditions, all of them. *Koshien* is one of the sacred temples of our national culture, and the high school tournament is a national icon, a wonderful comfort to us all. In fact, my own father took me many times to *Koshien*." His English was flawless and refined.

Silence. "My father was very fond of racing, and often took me to the Indianapolis Speedway. It was a very big deal in my hometown. Going to the racetrack every May was like Christmas to me growing up. Or like our fishing trips, every summer in Wisconsin or Minnesota. I think fathers and sons truly bond at such times."

He considered my analogy. "Yes. Those memories of *Koshien* are to me as precious as the ones you describe of the racetrack, with your own father. Baseball is one of the great imports from your country, along with Coca-Cola and Mickey Mouse." He smiled at this last phrase, so that I wondered if he were being slyly ironic or not. "But tell me more about the Speedway. I have heard of it, of course, but here in Japan, we do not have much interest in auto racing."

At first, I described in detail how much the Speedway had meant to me as a kid. I painted vivid pictures of the parades, the release of the colorful balloons, Jim Nabors singing the traditional "Back Home Again in Indiana," the awesome din of the race cars, the smell of hot dogs with relish and mustard, the harsh sunshine reddening dried out human flesh, the funny things that the inebriated folks did in the infield, the streakers running naked down the main stretch in the '70s, that sort of thing. I also mentioned the race's military components (it occurs over Memorial Day weekend): flyovers by fighters or bombers, the playing of "Taps."

He looked at me quizzically. "Taps? The military bugler for funerals?" I nodded. He thought a moment, then said, "I did not know the military element of this race. Being on Memorial Day, and including some of these elements—does any of this bother Americans?"

I didn't understand what he meant, and told him so. But it did seem odd, I acknowledged, now that he mentioned it. So I asked about memorials for the war dead here in Japan (another blunder, I later realized).

"Well ... of course, here in Japan, we have a specific location for venerating the war dead. It is Yasukuni Shrine, in Tokyo. But it is a ... a controversial location." He paused, then changed the subject back to the USA. "Tell me more about this aspect of the race—the American Memorial Day—do Americans consider the fact that some of your own war dead might include criminals?"

This sudden twist put me back on the defensive. But his pointed observations revealed immediately what a penetrating mind I was encountering. Americans are not prone to thinking of their military adventures in terms of war crimes. Frankly, in all the years of visiting the Speedway, these thoughts had never crossed my mind, and I told him so. My admission seemed to satisfy him, and he nodded.

"And how about here, sensei? Do you like any Japanese sports?"

His question caught me off guard, and my mind raced to think about a sport I could mention. The pause grew, and he filled the silence. "Do you like *sumo*?"

At the time, I wasn't the fan of *sumo* that I am now; it seemed nothing more than a trivial sport involving morbidly obese counterfeit "athletes." In my unschooled mind, I associated sumo with the absurd pro wrestlers that popped up on late night TV back home. How poorly I had initially discerned the delicate beauty of the struggle, the deeply meaningful ritual of muscle and sweat that for many Japanese is the quintessential sporting entertainment. So I lied to my host. "Yes, it's a fascinating sport."

Professor Goto seemed to recognize my tiny white lie. He sipped at his tea, rubbed his hands together. "When I was a youngster, my father and brother were huge fans of the old fighters, and, of course, I liked sumo myself. Azumafuji was a champion in my youth, and we all shared a great admiration for him. He hailed from Tokyo, which is unusual for the *sekitori*—the wrestlers. My father often took us to Osaka in the springtime to see the tournament. A few times we went on the train up to Tokyo, where the traditional sumo stadium was, to watch the matches for a few days. Those are some of the great memories of my youth. Azumafuji went on to become *yokozuna*—the fortieth grand champion. I even had a picture of him, signed, on my bookshelf. My father knew his management team, they are called "stables" in English. We often visited the practice sessions and ate *chanko-nabe*, the famous meat and vegetable stew-soup prepared by the sumo wrestlers themselves. A privilege of knowing the right people." He paused to reflect. "Since those days, regretfully, I have not watched *sumo* very much."

I waited for him to continue, but he was done speaking. At least on that topic. An awkward pause ensued. An insect buzzed along the window, and a gust of wind caught a banner and shook it. Goto-sensei continued his studied gaze, peering into me.

"You have a beautiful house here, Sensei," I said finally, unable to stand the silence any longer.

"Ah, yes, thank you. It is our ancestral home. It was built long before the war. Mostly wood, I'm afraid. I have tried to maintain it in a proper fashion."

"Did you grow up here?"

"Yes. My father built it not long after he began to have some success in his industrial concerns."

"What kind of business was he in?" This was a bit risky, but I wanted to hear some details from the old professor.

He grinned at this comment. "Do you truly not know about my father, Springs-sensei? He is rather well known here in Japan." He looked me in the eye once more, and I wasn't sure how to respond. In truth, I had not thought to research my benefactor's personal past, and had no knowledge of his family. Not yet.

Goto-sensei lowered his gaze to the table, gently brought his tea to his lips, blew on it, sipped, then returned it to the table. He looked off to one side for a moment. Then back. "I am rather shy about speaking of things from my past. All of that can wait, I should think. In Japan, we do not often wish to speak about our families to ... outsiders."

Here he looked at me in the eye briefly. I think he wanted to be certain I understood that I was very much an outsider. His glance insinuated I had much to learn, that I had somehow already violated some set of codes, even if just slightly. Now the word that he used for me, which was surely his translation of the term *gaijin* in Japanese, does not have quite the ring of negativity in English as it does in Japanese, but still it sounded a bit harsh to my ears. He'd said "outsider" in English, but I heard it from a Japanese perspective, a good example of the inscrutability of words, from one language to another. Several months in Japan had already made me rather wary about all of this—the problems of words. Even single words can hold so much cultural significance, a reality I was grasping inch by inch.

We sat there just like that for a moment, with that word "outsider" hanging in the air between us. I had no idea what to say next, and since he continued to sip his tea in silence, I ventured ahead, and changed the subject like any good American might.

"May I ask you about some of these lovely artworks? The prints in the hallway, for instance—they look like some by Utamaro and Hiroshige that I've seen in books."

He waited a moment, and a smile almost appeared. "You have a good eye, Springs-sensei. They are, in fact, original prints. I have found them to be some of the more legitimate Japanese artworks of the past few centuries. Utamaro's women are particularly stunning, I think. Do you like Japanese art?"

"Yes, especially wood block prints."

As I said this, Mika glided effortlessly into the room with another hot pot of tea. She kneeled before us gracefully, and brought the teapot to each of our cups, mine first, filling it with steaming, rich, deep green Japanese tea. As she filled it, a mysterious expression played on her lips. She did not look me in the eye, but she was fully there, fragrant as cut flowers in her splendid garment. She bowed, raised herself once again to her feet, and backed away. Kneeling at the door once more, she said in the slightest whisper, "*Shitsure-itashimasu*" (excuse me), backed out, and gently slid the door closed. Each moment of her presence was mesmerizing to me, though in pseudo-Japanese style, I was trying very hard to conceal my wonder.

Professor Goto picked up the newly freshened cup of tea, and brushed away a fly from his forehead. "Then I would like to show you some interesting items that I have in other rooms, if you have the time to come and visit me again in the future. Perhaps you have heard of the views of Mt. Fuji?"

That statement carried with it two dramatic pieces of information—one was that he possibly owned some prints by Hokusai, who was not only one of the most famous artists in all of Japanese history but who had already become my personal favorite. The other was even more intriguing: the suggestion that he might invite me back in the future. I had assumed that this was just a one-time deal, as so many social invitations are in Japan. Meet and greets, Kilcoyne called them, pure protocol. But he seemed to be saying that a return visit might be in order—if I played my cards right. I nodded and said simply, "Yes, of course, by Hokusai. *Fugaku Sanju Rokkei.* The "36 Views of Mt. Fuji." I'm a big fan of Hokusai. And I would be honored to see them. You sound like an art collector, yes?"

This last question he found somewhat amusing. He looked down and smiled, then allowed the slightest chuckle to play over his mouth, just for an instant. "Actually, yes, I have a few minor objects. Since my youth, I have enjoyed the wood block prints, what we call the *ukiyo-e*, the 'pictures of the floating world.' I also admire certain ceramic items from the past. I have a few minor scrolls, and other things—some *katana*, some other old weapons." He sat very erect, looking at me, with both hands resting on the table before him. "These are mere trifles, however." He grasped the tea again, gave a sip.

Who calls art treasures "mere trifles," I wondered?

"By the way," he continued, "I am impressed with your knowledge of my country. *Fugaku Sanju Rokkei.* Your pronunciation is good. It is a title that most Japanese no longer remember. Is it not sad that we lose so much of our histories, our past?"

Here he looked up again from the table, to peer at me. I was learning the give and take of eye contact among older Japanese gentlemen such as Goto-sensei. I also intuited that his was a rhetorical question needing no real answer, so I gave what I had learned to be the quintessential Japanese response to such inquiries: "*So desu-ne!*"

We talked further about matters of weather, Japanese food, even returning to the subject of baseball. I discovered he followed the perennial local losers, the Hanshin Tigers, one of Japan's older franchises, and we spent long minutes of silence together, studying the rather thin lines of dialogue we exchanged. It takes some getting used to, but I'd already come to understood these moments of silence to be a crucial aspect of interpersonal relations among Japanese men, very much foreign to most Americans, who can barely take ten seconds without someone trying to fill the empty space with inane chatter. While Americans need to be talking almost constantly, here with Professor Goto, silence was a mark of manliness and respect.

As we sat, a banner flapped in the wind and branches brushed against the outside shutters. In the distance, a dog barked and children's laughter rose and fell as they passed by on the road a hundred feet away. Professor Goto's tiny dog slept on a mat in the corner of the room, his rhythmic breathing soft as whispers. By and by, Mika no longer returned to refill my tea cup, and I knew it was time to leave.

I stood and bowed, and bowed again, even as my host tried to match me. Behind him was Mika, bowing as well. My heart fluttered as I said, "Professor Goto, if I can ever be of any assistance to you, I hope you will let me know."

This gesture seemed to capture his attention. "Yes, Springs-sensei, I appreciate that. Perhaps in the future there is some small assistance that you can provide."

"Of course, sensei. Anything." But even as I said it, I recognized that in Japan, it might actually mean something, unlike in America, where these kinds of empty promises are made all the time. The Japanese do not dare to make vain statements unless they truly mean them.

I had no idea what kind of assistance I could possibly provide to this wise, secretive, and evidently very wealthy old man. The wood block prints alone would be priceless, if authentic, not to mention the estate itself. I needed more information on the Goto clan, I thought, even as I was bowing my sayonaras.

Once outside, I lingered for a moment and watched as Mika bowed and smiled ever so slightly in my general direction. Traditionally, the host waits for the guest to leave their view, so I turned to head toward the train station. They had offered to call a taxi, but the rain had let up and the sun peeked through the clouds now and then, and I thought that after all the Japanese-style sitting, it would do me good to stretch my legs and hike down the mountain. And so I did, through a neighborhood of great wealth full of large, concrete-walled complexes protected by automated fences behind which expensive German automobiles sat in driveways shaded by fruit trees and well-groomed gardens, which gave way to panoramic views of the sea several miles below me.

As I snaked my way back down the hill, I realized that the blank, concrete walls surrounding each little empire were often topped with broken glass, further dangers designed to keep out peasants like me. Those walls seemed an apt metaphor of my first impressions of Professor Goto and his niece.

友

I sat quite a long time thinking through this account of Jack's first meeting with Professor Goto. There were so many clues hinting at what would come next—the description of a masterpiece painting as a "trifle"; the fascination of many Japanese scholars for American literary figures; Goto's surprise that Jack knew nothing of the Goto family; and, perhaps most tantalizing, Jack's obvious interest for the exotic Mika.

Jack states that even in this early meeting he found Mika's presence "mesmerizing," but I always wonder about such autobiographical claims. He is remembering it that way, certainly. But in the many years since the actual event, we should recognize that his evocation of the scene is as much a fiction as is Walden. *In this instance, phrases such as, "She moved slowly, every gesture elegant and precise, sleeves sweeping behind her arms like wings" demonstrate that the powerful impression Mika made on that first day is purely a reflection of the author's craft and powers as an artist. I must say, however, that it was here that I recognized how very important these two characters would become, or had become for Jack, through the passage of time and retrospect.*

Such are the immediate impressions of a lifelong literature professor, I'm afraid, a man whose passions include a desire to deconstruct, to question, and to divine the motivations of human creatures. With someone famous such as Thoreau, it can become addictive. But this was my former student and now deceased friend, Jack Springs. It was as if he had entered some sort of mythical realm, and who could say where that might lead him? Or where it might lead me as well?

CHAPTER 3

Besides teaching English conversation, I had been taking Japanese conversation lessons since my arrival. It was pretty difficult at first, but the immersion experience of simply being in Japan helped, and my basic abilities in the language were improving. I sat in a class with tiny tables and chairs evidently designed for students roughly half my size, six hours a week, paid for by the university (another perk). The class was peopled with other foreigners who, like myself, had come to Japan as professional workers. My little class, held each Tuesday and Thursday evening in a cluttered classroom in an office tower near Sannomiya station in downtown Kobe, was made up of two other American men working for Eli Lilly, the pharmaceutical giant from Indianapolis, my old hometown; two giggly Australian women who taught in local high schools; and a British banker with a dry and subtle humor.

The Americans, Frank Banner and Tom Scholes, were decent enough guys, former chemical engineers who now worked together in managing a brand new Lilly office a few blocks away. Like me, they were basketball fanatics from Indiana, hayseeds who understood the true Hoosier nature of the game. Geneva Schrick and Belle Latimore were the girls from Perth, teaching in the JET Program, a government initiative for conversational English instruction in the Japanese public schools, where all students take a mandatory six years of English. Richard Yeats (no relation to the Irish poet extraordinaire, he assured us) was a vice president of the Royal Bank of Scotland, with its Kobe headquarters nearby. He had a long waxed moustache, and strolled about with a cane (though he had no discernible need for it), and he knew all the pubs with Guinness within walking distance of his office, his apartment, and our classroom. He seemed much older than the thirty or so that he probably was, yet he still had quite an adventurous streak, and for that reason we became fast friends. I soon discovered that despite being a staid banker during the day, he was quite the free spender after a shot or two of good whiskey.

Richard's generosity ended up having an impact in my life long after he went back to the UK. Though we were around the same age, Richard was very well off, and he owned a nice car, large by Japanese standards, a maroon Nissan Skyline with leather seats and a fine stereo. Occasionally he would invite me to go for long weekend drives in the mountains where we would roll down the windows, turn up the volume, and whisk along twisting roads listening to his mix tapes of old albums by Pink Floyd, Zeppelin, The Kinks, Fairport Convention, The Hollies, and The Who (Richard's favorites). We liked to stop at designated trailheads and wander off into Mother Nature for long hikes, with only water and snacks in tow. A few times it got dark, and, having no desire to drive back, we would find a *ryokan*—a family-owned, traditional inn—to stay the night, soaking our tired bodies in mountain hot springs, sipping *sake* till all hours of the night. Richard would rub his eyes and say, "What do you say we find some shelter and stay out here tonight, hey?"

Richard had a funny habit of ending sentences with the syllabic "hey." It was an endearing routine, not unlike its Japanese counterpart, the sentence-ending "*ne*?,"and I usually agreed to his spontaneous whims. The "hey" was Richard's code for, "It's OK, do it!" He was a funny and decent guy, who quickly became my closest *gaijin* friend. After tedious months of study, we both quit the classes, confident we could carry on basic conversations anywhere we went—although I always traveled with my small, trusty, red-covered Japanese-English dictionary.

Once we quit, we did not see each other as regularly. But we did keep venturing out together on back roads, over mountains, and along coastlines. He'd call, often late on a Thursday or Friday, and say, "Let's drive out to Kanazawa, hey?" Great memories of those trips and my connection with his Skyline, and his whimsies, would eventually pay off in more ways than one.

友

Soon it was *O-bon*, the festival celebrating the returning of the spirits of the dead, and a time of entertaining the ghosts of the past, remembering their lives and demonstrating respect and appreciation for them. The school year in Japan has a generous break in August for the festival, and the government and all businesses shut down as well. All good Japanese make a pilgrimage home to pay respect to their parents and other ancestors.

With time off, I was determined to find out more about the Goto family, so I turned to the most convenient place for such learning: the vast array of books and other news sources available at *Kinokuniya*, the huge local bookstore in downtown Kobe, featuring works in English. This much I already knew: the 1980s had been the heyday of reporting on the "Japanese miracle," and dozens of books told the story in detail. The height of Japan's economic emergence had coincided with the two terms of Ronald Reagan, the boom years. But by the early 1990s, Japan's economy had gone into a sustained recession, mainly due to enormous overpricing in the real estate markets, a bubble that had finally burst. What were, by American standards, modest homes in Tokyo that had been valued at well over two- to four-million dollars at the height of the boom, had seen their values drop by over half or more almost overnight.

Despite these recent economic speed bumps, Japan still appeared "miraculous" to most westerners arriving in the early nineties, including me. So I took the train down to Sannomiya, the central shopping district in Kobe, and hoofed it over to the bookstore. Browsing, I picked up a book titled *Japan's Master Builders: Architects of the Post-War Boom*, and thumbing through one chapter almost by accident, it suddenly dawned on me that it was describing Professor Goto's family!

His father, Goto Kenichi, was born in 1890 in Yamaguchi, and rose to prominence very early after World War I as an entrepreneur. He made his fortune in steel, chemicals, and machine tools, and established Goto Heavy Industries in 1924. This massive conglomerate went on from these original industries to diversify into all sorts of other businesses: banking, railways, and the Goto Department Stores.

I had been seeing the Goto name all over Kobe, but for some reason it just never occurred to me that this was the family of old Professor Goto, staid member of my own faculty. He was the youngest of Goto Kenichi's two sons. The first was Goto Tsukasa, born in 1917 and now the chief operating officer of the Goto Industries, was one of the three or four wealthiest men in Japan. Tsukasa was reared as his father's successor, as is the custom in Japanese society for the firstborn, a sort of prince among the princes of the nouveau riche in the 1920s era. He was tall, handsome, cunning, and an outstanding athlete (baseball and *kendo*, Japanese sword fighting). Tsukasa graduated from Kyoto Imperial University, the most important school in western Japan, and after college, he served as a fighter pilot during the war, flying Zeroes over the Pacific. He shot down at least ten Allied planes, and luckily was never drafted into any *kamikaze* groups, due to his own serious injuries in a fire near the end of 1944. Coincidentally, Goto senior's company made millions producing spare parts for Mitsubishi, the builders of the Zeroes that would ultimately be flown by his son.

When his father died in 1969, Goto Tsukasa was his designated successor. The will specified that he take over the family business (his mother had been dead for over ten years). Not long after his father's death, Tsukasa moved the company headquarters from Osaka to a much more fashionable area of Tokyo, and had been living in a large walled estate near Seijo in Setagaya-ku for over twenty years, enjoying his status as one of the world's twenty most wealthy businessmen.

The book's chapter on the Goto dynasty (which I read standing up in the bookstore, a common tactic in Japan for which they even have a term: "*tachiyomi*," roughly meaning "standing & reading") shed much light on the family, but only made a few passing references to the second brother, Goto Haruki. He had chosen a quite different path from his older, more charismatic brother. Haruki had also been a pampered prince, but he was bookish, physically feeble, and quiet, and his interests led him ultimately to the far more solemn hallways of the world's great universities. Born in 1920, he was too infirm healthwise to fight in World War II: his asthma and bad feet precluded his service. Instead he began his course of study at Kyoto Imperial University near the commencement of the war's great expansion. It was the year before Pearl Harbor. From there, he went on to Harvard in 1948, having developed a passion for literature, particularly the American romanticism of the nineteenth century and the Transcendentalists of Concord, Massachusetts: Emerson, Thoreau, and their friend, Hawthorne (a closet Transcendentalist). Goto studied at the feet of the legendary Perry Miller, and was one of the first Japanese ever to receive a doctorate in American literature from an Ivy League university. He completed the PhD in American literary studies in 1955, focusing on the Emerson-Whitman connection. Next, he did a post-doc for three years at the Sorbonne in Paris, after which he returned to join the faculty at Kobe University in 1957, where he has been ever since.

The book mentioned Goto Haruki's own inheritance as "paltry," hinting at the scandalous injustice of the father giving his oldest son the vast majority of the family fortune. Of course, a paltry percentage of $2.8 billion is nothing to sneeze at. I doubted if he had been forced to miss any meals, or cancel any subscriptions over the years. The author also suggested there had been a fair amount of tension within the family itself. A minor statement in the book puzzled me: "[The Goto family's] war efforts were undertaken in support of the imperial court, for which the patriarch donated much of his treasure, and the services of his two sons. The older son became a decorated fighter pilot, while the younger son aided the imperial court by donating his highly polished skills as a creative writer." This mysterious comment managed to sink its claws into my head, and I often wondered how Professor Goto's "skills" might have been used.

Japan's Master Builders made me wonder why he had chosen to leave the family business, to pursue the path of a college professor. Of course, I knew that in Japan, professors enjoyed a much higher esteem in the public imagination than they do back home in America. It also seemed likely that there was some family rift, symbolized by the older brother's move away from the older Kansai region to the more glamorous contemporary center of power, Tokyo. Meanwhile, his younger brother retained the old family property (the one I had already visited). Were the brothers still close? Did they still share good memories, or any sense of brotherhood?

The book also made me wonder about the implications of my position in Japan, and the sources of my good fortune. I slowly realized, standing in that crowded bookstore, that my entire subsistence in Kobe was due to the financial magic of two of *Japan's Master Builders*: the late, great Goto Kenichi and his cagy son, Tsukasa, engineers of the family billions. The Goto Fellowship, of which I was the latest beneficiary, was established due to the generosity of a family who made its billions by manufacturing cold rolled steel, nails and screws, muriatic acid, horizontal lathes, industrial furnaces, and copper tubing. Goto's oldest son produced the structural components of industrial Japan; his younger son and I, meanwhile, made our careers by uncovering the structural components of literature, the works of the "master builders" of the west.

友

Besides wandering the bookstores, *O-bon* allowed my first solo venture into the heartland of Japan before classes resumed. Armed with my trusty Japanese-English dictionary, I had already planned to head north to escape Kobe's deadening humidity and heat. I'd contacted my old buddy Jim Daymon, and he'd given me clear and detailed directions to the temple where he had been living for some three years. After a very long train trip, it was more long hours on several buses to reach the remote section of the northern Japan Alps where the temple is located.

I stayed the first night in the city of Matsumoto, which gave me a chance to visit the famous Matsumoto Castle. From its top, I enjoyed breathtaking views of the dark mountains of central Japan, into which I would venture the next day. I imagined that somewhere hidden among those peaks, my friend Jim was probably sitting, *zazen*-style, thinking deep thoughts, possibly even looking toward me and that imposing, feudal castle, as I looked toward him.

The next morning I boarded a bus and headed up into those wild and jagged peaks toward the resort town called Kamikochi, which is one of the most scenic alpine valleys in Japan. That leg of the trip took an hour, and then I spent another hour walking some of the well-groomed trails around Kamikochi, mostly with old, retired Japanese men and women. At ten o'clock, it was time to complete the journey to the temple. As instructed, I found a taxi and gave Jim's detailed directions—he had provided them in English and Japanese—to the driver. It took another half hour, winding up and up into the humid morning air. Finally the taxi-driver pointed toward a massive, red *torii*: a gateway into a sacred ground, comprised of two massive posts supporting a large connecting top. Think of a *torii* as an entranceway resembling a huge Greek letter Pi.

To get to the temple itself, I had to walk a path that snaked its way upwards for yet another hour. It was probably only about two miles, but the vertical ascent must have been several hundred feet, if not a thousand, and it made for rough going, a true religious pilgrimage. I stopped to rest a couple of times, taking long swigs from my water bottle, wiping my brow. Insects buzzed around my head and ears. Every so often I encountered another, smaller *torii* gate to pass under, so that by the time I reached the top, I must have walked through a hundred of them. Clearly, Jim's hideout was not for the faint of heart.

Like its namesake temple located in Kyoto, the *Ryoan-ji*, which means "the temple of the peaceful dragon," is blessed with an amazing zen-style rock garden on its grounds. As I entered the area directly surrounding the temple, a bit sweaty from my climb, I noticed this garden, off to my left. Sitting on one of its large boulders was an old Japanese man in the humble robe of a Buddhist monk. His head was completely shaved, and he sat balanced and erect, in an almost perfect posture, looking out toward the south.

I paused to watch him for a moment, during which time he did not move, and seemed not even to breathe. I hesitated to say anything since I didn't want to disturb him, but finally I let out a very slim "*sumi massen*," excuse me. When he turned to look at me, it was without surprise. Rather, he seemed to know I was there, and as if he expected me all along.

He stood, saying *ohayo-gozaimasu*: "Good morning," and bowing for a long moment. I did likewise. Then he said, "*Springs-sensei desu-ka*?" Are you Professor Springs? This surprised me even more, but it turned out that Jim had told his fellow monastics that a friend of his would be visiting, and that this was the approximate date of my arrival (actually, I was a day later than I had told Jim, having underestimated the long bus rides and my own stamina).

"*Hai, Springs desu. Hajimemashite.*" Yes, I'm Springs. How do you do?

Then he rushed toward me, grasped my hand with both of his, bowed again and again, smiling with great pleasure, and said, "*Ubukata desu—Hajimemashite.*" More bowing, now bordering on uncomfortable. "*Chotto-matte, kudasai.* English very poor." And with that, he hurried away, in search of help, evidently.

I was left standing in the gravel path, my old duffel bag beside me, wiping the sweat off my forehead, when, a few minutes later, Jim appeared. He was smiling as always, thinner than I remembered, and was also wearing the robes of the temple. And he was completely bald, the sun glinting off his shiny dome. No bows for him. He approached and took me off my feet with a long bear hug. "Jack, old pal! You made it, man. Yes! Welcome to Dharma heaven, buddy."

He picked up the bag and led me to the temple. On the porch just beyond were several of the other monks, whom he introduced. One of them was Watanabe, the guy in charge. "Just call him Watanabe-*roshi*, sort of like calling him reverend in English." They all welcomed me with friendly smiles and an air of contemplation mixed with an earthy enjoyment of all things surrounding us.

My first visit of three days on the top of that mountain, nearly 9,000 feet up, where the air gets a bit thin, was one of the highlights of my entire stay in Japan. Situated near, if not on the border of Nagano and Gifu Prefectures, *Ryoan-ji* temple enjoys a nearly panoramic view of the surrounding mountains. The view is oriented both eastward, back toward the Kanto plain, the "new" capitol Tokyo, the Pacific Ocean, and America beyond; and southwestward, toward the Kansai plain, the ancient capitol Kyoto, and beyond that my home in Kobe. From this perch high above the central mountains of Japan, one can thus look either way and meditate accordingly. In the distance loomed two of the most famous peaks of the Japan Alps: *Hotaka-dake* and *Kita-dake*. *Ryoan-ji* literally soars into the heights, and is the perfect location for thinking about both old and new.

With the pair of binoculars my host provided the first evening, I could look down over 1,000 meters into the surrounding valleys and watch tiny automobiles slowly work their ways up and down the switchbacks. Birds of prey glided noiselessly through the gorges. Hot and humid in the valleys below, the air was pleasant at the temple, and there was always some sort of breeze, so the windows and the *shoji* door panels were left open during the days. At night, the air was a bit chilly, and I nestled down under the fresh futons, dreaming of sutras and *satori*.

Jim was still the fun kibitzer, excellent story-telling

poker player and all-around wise thinker that I remembered from our old days at Yale, where he studied the philosophy of religion and where we'd met playing pick-up basketball, another religious activity we shared. He described in amusing detail his adventures in the *Rinzai* school of *zen*, and introduced me to certain disciplines of the temple, such as measured breathing and meditation on zen *koan*, the riddles with no answers. His eyes would shine precociously as he told funny stories about Watanabe's use of the *keisaku*, or "discipline stick," a long, flat and flexible piece of wood used to hammer the shoulders of meditators who are losing focus or falling asleep.

He also introduced me to the concept of *kensho*: seeing one's true nature, or enlightenment; and he explained that, in the end, this was what zen was really all about. He said that the *Rinzai* master Hakuin had claimed to have eighteen major kensho and countless minor enlightenments. Jim said all this with a knowing glance, enough to make me wonder if he had seen his own, true nature. I guess I'm still seeking some level of *kensho*, and sometimes I've wondered if I should call this book *Kensho*.

While there, I tried to mimic the routine of the group: we ate together, often in silence. One time during meditation, which I tried to embrace like the others, I actually did get whacked a few times by Watanabe's *keisaku*. When bored, I could always take off on some of the paths leading even higher into the Japan Alps. And when we were alone together, Jim and I could talk about books or Japanese art (he was a self-taught expert), or just fool around and play gin or *go*, a Japanese board game he had learned to enjoy, which he taught me. I was terrible, but he was a patient teacher.

On my final day, Jim showed me some of the treasures of the temple, which were kept hidden in a dark and cobwebby vault underneath the floors of one remote side room. I was sure he was breaking protocol by showing me the vault, and so I was all the more eager to see it. The most important of the treasures were several *katana* swords once used by samurai, an old mirror that needed a good cleaning, and a number of ancient scrolls, some of which were said to be of the sutras. Nobody really knew, in fact, since these relics had not been opened in many years, perhaps centuries, as far as anyone seemed to recall. The scrolls were venerated for the mysterious words they contained, words that nobody knew. "It is better that we not know," Jim explained. "That way, I can imagine that they memorialize words of great power and healing. As such, the words grow in stature, and none of us can be disappointed." He said all of this with no discernible irony, as innocently as a spring lamb. I loved watching him handle the scrolls gently and yet with great purpose, as if they might get up and walk away.

Besides the scrolls and Jim's *koan*-like elaboration, I was particularly struck by the intricacy of the carvings and other embellishments on two of the swords Jim allowed me to hold. "It's so Japanese," he'd said, "though many of the old people feel the attention to detail, the wonder, has been lost. The men from before the war think Japan has become crass and unfeeling—many older Japanese will tell you this—it's a common view. The *katana* embodies the beauty of old Japan." He looked me in the eye. "When people lose this sense of beauty, it's very hard work to get it back, yes?"

Together we admired the swords, which we held in both hands as if they were newborn babes. Then he put them both back in their cloth garments, stored them in their dusty cases, and together we lowered the cases back down into their hiding place.

Later, on the bumpy bus ride back down the mountain toward the train station, I realized that Jim was now like one of those swords. Like them, it seemed to me, he was also hidden away, emblematic of another sort of life, one far away from the machinery and the commerce of the decadent modern world, searching for something above and beyond it. I could never really see myself in such a monastic setting, and could never see myself giving months or years to such an exercise the way Jim had. But in a way, the academic life of a scholar has its own disciplines and its own hiddenness. And so I was drawn back to *Ryoan-ji*, according to Jim's earnest invitations. I told him, and Watanabe-*roshi*, that I would return, and I did—twice. Once a year later, again in the steamy weather of August, when I went directly and devoted fifteen days to the life of a Buddhist novice. And another brief, final visit just before I would get on the airplane and leave Japan once and for all.

友

Obviously, when Jim elucidated his reverence for the katana swords and explained the contents of the old scrolls, it resonated with Jack, as it did with me when I read the description of the contents of the temple's treasure room. Scrolls containing hidden messages, unseen for centuries. Swords of rare beauty and craftsmanship, yet engineered for precise violence. They were metaphors of the rich detail of old Japan, signifying something precious and yet nearly lost, conveying a romance and a vigor that loses nothing in its exoticisms.

As a literary critic, I am naturally drawn to metaphors such as these, hinting at the contrast of these precious commodities with the heavy industries described by the historian of the Goto clan. The silent winds high in the Japan Alps of a summer zen retreat, followed by the audacious return to contemporary urban life in Japan.

I also now believe these sacred temple items also became symbolic of Jack's subsequent quest. And of his "idea" of Japan—its meaning, its purpose in his life, its kensho, perhaps. Even here, he was foreshadowing the direction of his journey, I now realize. The clues are all there.

CHAPTER 4

The new term began promptly in mid-September. Teaching American literature in a Japanese university, I was discovering, was a task requiring great patience. My teaching was much less about the literature and much more about simple communication in the English language. In a class of thirty mostly female students, for example, maybe four or five would have decent conversational skills. So it turned out to be a lot of basic English conversation, even at an elite university like Kobe U. I would assign easy English reading: stories by Hemingway or Cather or O'Connor. Soon enough I figured out that only a few would even attempt the reading. Many sat in the back all semester, lifeless and silent, and worked on other things, or slept. Already, the romance was wearing thin, and I often found myself becoming drowsy, too. The teaching hours were not long, and I quickly decided it was OK to engage these students in conversation on almost any topic that we wished to pursue. We did sometimes discuss the readings, but we also talked about music, movies, sports, or whatever—in bored, convoluted English.

I also spent more and more time perusing the contents of the departmental library. I kept finding valuable old volumes, hidden away on darkened shelves. Most interesting were the many first editions, often by the most famous writers of the twentieth century—Steinbeck's *Grapes of Wrath*, *East of Eden*, and *Travels with Charley*; Cather's *Song of the Lark*, *The Professor's House*, and *Death Comes for the Archbishop*; and Mailer's *The Naked and the Dead* and *The American Dream*—all in nearly pristine condition. And there were many more. Some of them had evidently never been opened. They were untouched and forgotten. I found a personal favorite, *On the Road*, signed by Kerouac with the inscription: "Keep it rolling, dharma boy!" And I found a handwritten note inside the cover of a first edition of *Howl*: "For Bobby: Satori times are at your beck and call. Remember the night we saw God? Most gregariously, Allen Ginsberg."

Now I'll make a small confession. Actually, it brings a smile to my face in remembering those two volumes in particular, because, you see—I swiped them. I just couldn't resist. They were signed by the authors, for crying out loud, and they were two of my all-time favorites. Anyway, I reasoned, they were just wasting away in that dusty, old library where nobody could ever see them. For weeks, the thought that it would be so easy to steal some of these valuable books kept crossing my mind. So finally, I just slipped Kerouac's memoir/novel, and the slim volume of Ginsberg's poems, into my backpack, and left. Nobody would ever know, I thought. Except me, of course. I had been instructed, and required, to sign out anything that I took from the rooms. But I didn't, on purpose. I had every intention of keeping them both, forever.

That was the problem. I did keep *Howl* and *On the Road* on my bookshelf back at my condo, for about a week. I would look through them sometimes and relish their wild and eccentric contents. "I saw the best minds of my generation destroyed by madness, starving hysterical naked, dragging themselves through the negro streets at dawn looking for an angry fix." What odd and exciting words they contained! And Ginsberg's handwritten note! But even though the howl of the poems spoke to me, the howl of my moral conscience assured me that it had been wrong to purloin the books. I came to see that such a vice, were I to allow it to grow, might easily destroy my own relatively stable mind with madness (there were lots of other attractive first editions calling out to me, waiting up there in the library's decrepit shelves). The words on the pages had enticed me, but they also chastened me, and forced me to admit the error of my ways. So at the end of a week, I smuggled *On the Road* and *Howl* back into the library and replaced them on the shelves from which I had taken them.

友

Soon enough, it seemed, near the end of September, the baleful Miyamoto again appeared at my desk with some news. "Sensei, I should tell you that your meeting with Goto-sensei was quite an honor, you must realize. He would rarely take such a measure as to meet with a *gaijin*."

"Thank you, Miyamoto-sensei. And by the way, nice suit." Miyamoto smirked just a bit, but I was pretty sure he did not understand my subtle joke. I'd already discovered that most Japanese are tone deaf to irony. I touched his greasy lapel and inspected it briefly—tiny chunks of dandruff were clinging to it, if you took the time to notice.

Even by then, I had grown weary of Miyamoto. He sometimes lurked behind me as I worked at my desk in the main office, and he often gave me glib and stupid advice about this or that. He was like the Orwellian big brother that we all get sick of worrying about, though in general he seemed bland and harmless. It would be a couple more years before I fully understood his more sinister aspect, and the reasons that made him particularly envious of my soon-to-be-discovered opportunities. For now, I had taken to gently mocking him to his face, in ways that only a native speaker of English might be likely to discern.

"What did Goto-sensei say to you at your first visit, if you don't mind me asking?" In the several weeks since then, Miyamoto had never asked me a single thing about our first meeting; had, in fact, never even mentioned it.

"What did he say to me? I don't quite understand you—about what? We talked for over an hour."

"I mean about your position here. Did he say anything about that?"

I shook my head and shrugged. "Sensei, I really don't understand your question. What are you getting at?"

He hesitated and looked down a moment. Then he glanced around the office, to see who might be in earshot. He lowered his voice, but he spoke with real emotion. "Jack-san, I think you should know that I have been an able assistant to Goto-sensei for many years. I have done justice to his requests, and I believe that I have earned some respect because of it. My hard work over many years has been hardly acknowledged by this department, however. And I do not take lightly your interference into these matters."

"Interference? What matters?" I was clueless about any of this.

He went on as if I were not even part of the conversation. "I'll have you know that he even arranged for me to have an apartment just down the hill from his own estate!" He stated this to impress me, evidently. "Obviously, Goto-sensei respects my assistance, if no one else does!" He paused and scratched his head. "Or at least he did, until you arrived!"

I could tell he was debating in his own mind what to say next. Miyamoto is one of those kinds of people who always act like they put other people first, but, in fact, are always thinking of their own interests. So I responded with more irony, just to see if it registered at all. "Sensei, no one appreciates you more than I do."

Peppering my comments with American-style irony, knowing that my Japanese listener would completely miss it, was becoming a secret vice. Predictably, he failed to get my little joke, delighting me even more.

"Well, Jack-san, for now I will just say that you should remember that I am your superior here in Japan, and that you are under my care and supervision. The matters I speak of should become clear to you in time. I have been asked by the chair of our faculty, Aoyama-sensei, as well as by other officers of this university, to make myself available to you for counsel and advice, and I am trying to do that for you right now." He fidgeted with his thin little tie, then wiped his brow with a smudged handkerchief. "I also suggest that you keep me informed about anything that Goto-sensei tells you about the affairs of this faculty or university. My advice is that you remember your place in all of this."

"My place in all of what, sensei?" I honestly had no idea at the moment what he was getting at (I do now, of course). "I truly honor your efforts on my behalf" (more irony), "but I would appreciate a little more information, if you don't mind."

He looked at me for his own clues. "I have said enough already, sensei. You simply need to be aware of certain aspects of the university's reputation that may be involved in all of this."

I tried to imagine what my visit with Professor Goto had to do with the university's reputation, but I could not come up with anything. "Miyamoto-sensei, I really am confused. Are you asking me to report to you what happens every time I meet with Goto-sensei?"

He glowered at me for a moment. "There is much at stake regarding your relations with Goto-sensei. Surely you must recognize this." He scratched his ear and looked away. Then suddenly he stared at me again. "Just try to hear the words that I am not saying as well." He turned abruptly, and left me in his wake. He was about as irritated, and irritating, as any Japanese person I ever encountered, virtually smoldering as he stalked off.

But now I was the one scratching my head. I gulped hard, truly perplexed. My initial interpretation of his mysterious behavior, and of this very unsettling (non-) conversation, was that he must be protecting himself from what he considered an invasion of his turf. But I had no idea, at that point, what was the nature of that turf. There was much more going on than met my foreign eye, I remember thinking. And I was right.

友

Miyamoto's rude interruption and dramatic departure actually kickstarted my curiosity once again about Goto and his past, so I put away my dull paperwork for an hour and tried to track down more information. The faculty kept some records, including off prints of the publications of professors, and yet I still knew almost nothing about Goto's research, except for the tiny bit about his interest in American writers like Emerson. I asked for help, and secretary rooted around in a cabinet for a minute and produced a listing for me to look at. But it was mostly in Japanese. Hardly any of his work had been published in English. I don't know why this surprised me. One essay did appear in the *Yale Journal of Criticism* back in 1966. It was called "Fathomless Elements: Some Late Letters from Mark Twain to his Pastor, the Rev. Joseph Twichell of Hartford." Almost everything else was written in Japanese, though for some reason the publications were sometimes listed in English: places like the *Japanese Journal of American Studies*, or the *American Review*. I asked for a copy of the list, and the office staff acted surprised, as if I were requesting classified state secrets, and as if doing so would have been a major breach of protocol. They clearly had no intention of providing such information without consulting the president of the university, or perhaps the prime minister himself. (The obtuseness of Japanese bureaucracies can be like something out of a Kafka novel.)

But they did refer me to Professor Aoyama, and I entered his office. After some pleasantries, I requested a list of Professor Goto's writings. He paused, thought this over, and ultimately produced it from one of the many large filing cabinets in his office. "Please ask the secretary to copy this, sensei. And please excuse me for now, as I must work on some other pressing matters." He sat back down and resumed what he had been doing, so I backed away. The secretary made the copy, and I was on my way.

Glancing at the list, the one title that leaped out at me was at the very bottom of the list: Goto's dissertation at Harvard, which he finished in 1956. It was titled, *Transcendental Friendship in Emerson's Essays, Letters, and Life*. Of course, it's hard to say much about a monograph based on the title, but it was clear we had research interests that overlapped. Along with the one essay on the Twain-Twichell letters, it appeared that Goto had a very serious interest in letter writing—as did I. And it also appeared that we venerated many of the same writers, like Emerson, Whitman, Twain, and so on. Even the main words of the title intrigued me: the idea that a friendship might become transcendental, somehow revelatory of the nature of God, or the Oversoul, and that such a friendship might be partly inspired by the writing of letters. I recalled that Emerson had written a lesser-known essay called "Friendship," which I could probably find a copy of quickly. All of this sudden information made me a little giddy. Perhaps we had much more in common than I ever suspected. And perhaps I could figure out a way to request Goto's original dissertation, through interlibrary loan.

But that would take some time, and I wanted more answers immediately. Of course, "immediately" is a relative term, and in Japan it often means some time within a week. So I managed to get in to see Professor Aoyama a few days later, and asked him about Professor Goto's scholarly work and his contributions to the university.

He was seated at his desk, both hands resting in front of him in repose. But he wore a serious expression.

Slowly, Aoyama began his response. "Ah, yes, Goto-sensei. Naturally you would have some interest in his work. He has been a stalwart in this department since the sixties. A very soft-spoken man, but a true lion in the classroom. An entire generation of students, including myself, sat at his feet as if he were the Buddha himself!" He laughed at his own funny saying and so did I.

"Possibly you did not know this, but I began my college education right here at Kobe University. It was in the early '70s, and all I knew at that time was that I loved books and wanted very much to become a teacher. But Goto-sensei—well, he had other ideas, it seems to me." Pausing, he looked upward and thought about how to say something. "He was simply a quiet inspiration for me—my *sempai*." He looked at me to see if I knew the term. "My senior, a mentor. He detected something in my character, I now believe. And his calm reading of those wonderful poems he assigned—well, yes, it had some sort of ... sublime effect on me. I wanted to become like him. That is his major contribution, at least in my own life." He nodded, smiling, as he recalled his own youth.

"And what about his research? Can you tell me about that?"

He scratched his left arm, thinking back. "Goto-sensei has been one of the leading scholars of American literature in Japan for many years. He helped to found the Japanese Society of Americanists, and has generously supported that endeavor with funding ever since. As for his writing, his two books are very famous among Japanese scholars of America. The first book was about the friendships of the many people surrounding Ralph Waldo Emerson. Of course it covered Henry Thoreau and Thomas Carlyle.

And a brilliant chapter on Hawthorne as a friend. But it was most important, I believe, in introducing Emerson's friendships with some of the women who were previously forgotten about, such as Elizabeth Peabody and Margaret Fuller. That was rather novel for Japanese scholarship, particularly where Goto-sensei indicated the positive ways that those women influenced the great Emerson and his vision of friendship and of the life of the mind. That Emerson had close friends who were women seemed an oddity at that time. Nowadays that seems rather obvious, but it was groundbreaking and rather influential back then.

"The second book was a collection of letters to and from Ernest Hemingway in the 1920s and '30s, mostly during the Paris years, along with very interesting commentary about the friendships revealed in those letters. Many of them were from Ezra Pound, another of Professor Goto's great interests. These letters were translated into Japanese by Goto-sensei himself, and they reveal his mastery of both languages, especially English, another of the hallmarks of his career. Beyond that, he has written many essays and articles, and published numerous documents that he discovered in archives and libraries around the world. Those would be his major achievements. We are all very proud to have had his company over these many years. Though he is rather ... well, quiet nowadays, his reputation is exceedingly rich in Japanese academic circles. He is a living legend, I suppose you might say."

"And what about his family, and his brother?"

Here Aoyama seemed to flinch a bit. He looked off to one side, then simply replied in a sly manner that Japanese sometimes utilize, when they do not wish to answer. "Sensei, it is an interesting matter, is it not?" (This was his vague translation of whatever evasive non-answer he would have used with a native Japanese underling who was getting too close to the flames. Possibly a long, drawn-out "*So, desu-ne*?") He now looked across his desk for his pen, and picked it up with some urgency, then pretended to resume some urgent work with the papers spread out before him. "Unfortunately, perhaps it is best to speak of those matters at some other time, as I have very much to deal with at present with the new term off to such a busy start. I do hope you can forgive me."

He noticed a form off to his right, and slid it toward the middle of the desk, peering down at it as if it were an original copy of the Magna Carta. Suddenly the meeting was over.

I stood up, bowed slightly. "Sensei, thank you for your time."

He looked up quickly, then down again. "Yes, Springs-sensei, it is my pleasure." And then began scribbling on the document.

友

The title of Professor Goto's dissertation at Harvard, "Transcendental Friendship in Emerson's Essays, Letters, and Life," struck a deep chord within me. As if one might be so lucky to enjoy such friendships. These are friends who come along—if we are fortunate—half a dozen times over our adult lives.

The discussion here of Professor Goto's research reminded me that Jack's last letter ended with a quote from Emerson. He asked me to be his friend, you will recall, and then he quoted the great author himself: "A friend may well be reckoned the masterpiece of nature."

Such romantic allure! But besides these meditations on the bonds of companionship, I must admit that my heart began to accelerate with the mention of archival, primary documents such as the letters that record such bonds—topics near and dear to my heart. Hearing of these materials, and of any scholar's longing for the solitude of the archives and for whatever secrets they might hold for the diligent detective, is perhaps one of my own key purposes in life—my own "kensho," as I might say now. There are of course the glorious repositories at which I have been fortunate enough to be invited to conduct my own research—the Beinecke Library at Yale, the Houghton Library at Harvard, the Huntington Library in Pasadena, and the Bancroft at Berkeley, being among the highlights.

But besides these crown jewels of western civilization, I've found sometimes even greater joy in the less well endowed dungeons off the beaten trail, those facilities of musty odor, poor lighting, and weak ventilation, with cheap bookshelves crammed into intolerably small spaces. And yes, especially in the old days, some not even air-conditioned in the stifling heat of mid-summer, when most college teachers have the luxury of time necessary for any serious archival research. What atrocious conditions in which to discover the hidden confidences of those great, enigmatic masters of the pen! In retrospect, I loved every minute of those experiences, although I understand that may be hard for the layman to grasp.

Chapter 5

About a week later, Miyamoto presented me with a second invitation from Professor Goto. He simply walked up to my desk as I was filling out some of the bureaucratic nonsense that is one of the *raison d'etre* of Japanese society. I turned to look up and immediately noted that my colleague was in another foul mood. The irksome Miyamoto spoke not to me, but at me, without emotion on the outside, but seething somewhat inside.

"Goto-sensei is desiring your presence at his house, this coming Sunday, again at 4:00 p.m. Is that convenient?"

"Why, yes, sensei. Thank you for bringing me that news." I was feeling chipper that day, and felt like rubbing it in. "Isn't it wonderful, to be invited again?" I noticed casually that Miyamoto's hands were clenched. "And his beautiful niece, Mika-san?"

From the look on his face, this last little *piece de resistance* almost gave him a stroke. Without a word he turned and lumbered off into the sunset, searching for a wall to bang his head against. In private, of course. For myself, merely speaking the magical name Mika produced a narcotic effect.

So on a balmy September weekend, I made my second visit to the home of Professor Goto. This time, I arrived a bit early, and Mika again responded first to the call from the front gate. When I knocked on the front door, she opened it to greet me, with Professor Goto standing just behind her, elevated a little on the raised floor just beyond the *genkan*. Together they resembled the moon and the sun, smiling down upon me, a partial eclipse.

"Welcome once again, Springs-sensei," he said to me.

I bowed as I presented to him more *omiyage*, this time, a fairly expensive bottle of very fine *sake* that I had gotten at a famous distillery outside of Nara on a day trip. I was a quick study, and Kilcoyne had mentioned this as a more appropriate gift. Again he handed it to Mika, unopened. He then mentioned his thanks for the box of red bean cakes that I had given him at our first visit, which I had purchased on my way back from one of my earliest day trips. "I noticed that you visited Takayama. Did you see the famous thatched-roof houses?"

I had no idea what he meant by that, and said so. "Actually, I was just switching trains there briefly. I had been up in the mountains, hiking around." As we stood there, I told him briefly of my other recent travels up north during the *O-Bon* holidays, and he began asking me many questions. He was especially interested in my stay at *Ryoan-ji*.

"And you did all of this traveling on your own? I am very impressed with your ingenuity, *sensei*."

We walked back to the same room in which we had had our first meeting. Again, the window was partly open, and again Mika came and went noiselessly, filling and refilling our large, ceramic tea cups. She also brought some bean cakes similar to the ones I had purchased in Takayama, along with other little snacks, on a dark red lacquered tray: *edamame* (steamed soybeans), served in their thick green husks, and some small local candies. He summoned two of his servants, an elderly cook/housekeeper named Natsuko, overweight and mildy curious in her odd mannerisms, one of which was a habit of staring blankly at various angles (Later, he told me, "She is quite slow in most ways, but makes the most delicious foods in Kansai!"); and a man he called Omori, whom he introduced as his gardener and chauffeur of some twenty-five years. He was old but stout, and looked to be physically powerful. Omori bowed without smiling, said nothing, then quietly backed away.

"He is as loyal as a police dog, and trained in the martial arts." Sensei assured me. "But like a dog, he rarely speaks. Though sometimes he does bark!" I laughed at this odd comment; later I learned that Omori was essentially a mute.

There were a few other pleasantries, but somehow this get-together immediately seemed quite different from the first one—it seemed like this was more of a business meeting of some sort. Professor Goto wasted little time with the rather bland conversations of our first attempt. For one thing, he asked me what I preferred to be called. I told him that my friends called me Jack. But back in my school days, some people called me Gene, which is also what my mother often called me.

"Gene?" He actually smiled and almost beamed directly at me. This seemed to intrigue him.

"Yes. Gene, as in Eugene. My given name: Eugene Jackson. Eugene was the name of my mother's dead older brother, whom she adored. I sign my professional writing 'E. J. Springs.'"

He nodded. "Ah yes, so you do!" He thought this over. "Eugene. It's funny to say, but that is also a homonym, for a phrase in Japanese—*Yu-jin*. It means friend, and sounds precisely the same as your name, Eugene. Although it is a rather strange word in Japanese. Not very common nowadays."

We both considered this coincidence, and he seemed pleased by it. "I spent many years in America, and I became familiar with your friendly customs. I would prefer to call you by some version of your given name, one that can be like a Japanese name for your stay here, as long as you feel comfortable with it." This idea seemed to give him some pleasure, as it did me. "Why not Yu-san? It sounds like a shortened version of Eugene!"

"Of course, Goto-sensei, that would be fine." I actually hesitated a bit when he said "Yu-san," because in my American mind there was something quaint if not a bit phony and melodramatic about it. But to tell the truth, Professor Goto's new name began to grow on me, almost immediately. I liked the sound of it—a Japanese equivalent. So I asked, "Perhaps you can show me how to write the *kanji*?"

This pleased him even more, so he found a card and pen, and before me inscribed my new Japanese moniker:

He presented the card to me, saying "Please learn to do this, Yu-san." And then he guided me, stroke by careful

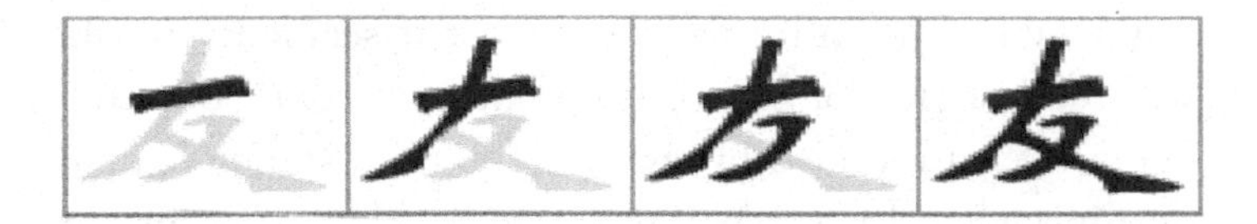

I accepted the card, then presumed to ask him what I should call him. Sensei, or Goto-sensei, would be just fine, he told me. But he seemed a trifle stiff in answering, as if it were a dumb question (which it was, and, once again, I recognized later that it was another of my ignorant breaches of protocol, strike three for the neophyte *gaijin*). I should have known, but somehow did not, that my position relative to him was not one that could allow anything in the vicinity of an endearment. In fact, however, it is from that encounter that I began thinking of him, and usually calling him, by a single name: *Sensei.*

We resumed our interview. After another cup of tea (there is much lengthy tea drinking in Japan, and it makes one wonder how their bladders never seem to fill), silence pervaded the room for several long moments. Finally, Sensei looked up at me directly. "Yu-san," he said, hesitating just slightly to be certain that it was a name that he might use to speak to me directly. "Last time you asked me about my family. Your story about the fishing trips with your father reminded me of when I would return with my own father to his homeland, in the far western extremity of Honshu Island, and how he taught me to fish with nets on the seacoast, just as he had done as a young man.

"They lived in Yamaguchi Prefecture, the remotest southwestern tip of the main island. It was a tiny village on the northern side of the prefecture, called Senzaki, facing the Sea of Japan. Very remote. I recall the journey on the trains taking an entire day, or at least it seemed. Senzaki was the last stop of one of the train lines, alone out on a peninsula, surrounded by the sea. The train station's grand opening when I was a boy was a great celebration for our people down there, a sign we were joining the modern world!" He paused to let the image soak in. "Those were magnificent times. The pine trees along the rocky coast, and the salty wind in my hair as I stood leaning into it ... " He paused again. "The wonderful poems of my youth."

Here I began to note the romantic yearning we both seemed to share about the past. I was noticing the initial crack in the blank walls surrounding the wealthy Japanese professor up on that trendy mountainside, and some light began to shine through.

"As you might know, my family has had its share of good fortune. But it was not always so. My grandfather was a mere fisherman. They lived near a rugged stretch of the sea that was quite forbidding, and yet quite breathtaking. And the sunsets—ah, they were iridescent. The sky was empty, yet full. Do you understand that, Yu-san?"

I nodded, though the statement seemed more like a zen *koan* than anything quite meaningful at the moment. He sipped again.

"My father, Goto Kennichi, the oldest child of my grandfather, was quite energetic and a very fast learner, as you might say. His life growing up was difficult. He learned to work hard all day long, every day. Cleaning nets, cleaning fish, hauling the fish to market, the harsh sun beating down, or the sleet in the cold winter days, the never-ending winds off of the sea. But there was always rice and fish on the table, with enough money left over for clothing and life's other essentials. It was a large family and they cared deeply for each other."

He paused to sip more tea. Chimes sounded from somewhere beyond the gardens. "My mother was from a hard-working family in the east, a village in the north of Shimane Prefecture, near the town of Oda. Her father was a farmer; Oda means "small rice field." They were somewhat more fortunate than my grandfather's family, growing much rice, which was a valuable commodity. So much so, that when my grandmother was … what shall I say? —being offered to my grandfather's family as a possible arrangement, it seemed to them to represent a coming up in the world. Ah, Yu-san, my English is so poor. Do you understand?"

"Yes, I think so. It was an arranged marriage, yes?"

"*So*! That's right. All marriages were in those days. My great-grandmother was a *nakodo*—an arranger of marriages, a matchmaker in the south, and she knew the brother of my great-grandfather, from way up north. In this way, my grandparents were brought together. This must sound strange to an American, but it was the way of life back then. This is how my family emerged, through this arrangement. And so in the year 1889, my grandmother met my grandfather, and they were married, after which they lived all their lives on that rocky seacoast in Yamaguchi. My father was born there, in 1890, even before the turning of the new century.

"At first, in the very early days that he barely remembered, there was just enough to get by. He would tell me stories about how long the winters were, and those times when the fish were not running, and there was very little food to go around. It is a triumph of the human spirit when people come together in a family and make things work. But as he grew into manhood, somehow they began to prosper. My father was a remarkable mechanic and a person of rare abilities with regard to machinery, things of that sort. He could fix things, and he would build contraptions for various purposes. He rigged machines that helped clean the fish, for instance. He did all of this while still a teenager. These stories are all among the lore of my family—part of the Goto legend, as they say."

He looked up at me with a bit of a sly grin. "Americans do like to believe that they invented dreaming! 'The American Dream,' yes, Yu-san?" We laughed together. "But it was a great moment in the history of my family when my father, having succeeded rather brilliantly in his schoolwork, was allowed to enter a technical school in Hiroshima, to study engineering and manufacturing methods. At that time, Hiroshima was emerging as one of the industrial centers in the south of our country. It was just before World War I, and Japan was becoming a modern nation. The times were ripe for industrialists and entrepreneurs, men with vision and stamina, dreamers who saw what Japan might become in the world.

"My father was one of those men, Yu-san. He understood that Japan would make its mark in the world through the production of the basic materials of the modern nation. Machinery, steel, chemicals, wire, electrical parts, hardware, and so on. The building blocks of industry. He liked to call these things "*kome*," which means rice grain. His first businesses, he would say, provided *kome* to the world industries: the basic ingredients. No meal is complete without rice, he would say. In many ways, the story of my family is the story of my homeland—providing uncooked rice grains to the world. But soon enough, we progressed from simply providing *kome* to making the entire, fancy meal. And we started getting our own rice grain from other nations. By the time of World War II, we Japanese were building airplanes, ships, locomotives, machine tools, armaments, electronics, appliances, and heavy machinery. And so was my father. In only twenty years, he had risen to become one of the chief engineers of our remarkable industrial emergence as a nation. There were many others involved, of course. But men like my father who helped inspire and guide the miraculous transformation, were rewarded with great affluence."

Professor Goto continued telling me about the rise of his family. That rise had many good implications, but of course, it also had many very bad ones. He hinted at some of these—the ways that his father contributed to the emergence of Japan's military dictatorship, and its alliance with Nazi Germany in World War II. His father's insistent participation in the cult of the emperor, even after the war. These historical realities received only the slightest acknowledgements in his story, but they hung in the air like a dark cloud. Evidently, Goto Kennichi had been an admirer of the regime and a devotee of the imperial family, including Hirohito, until the end of his life.

After an awkward moment, I asked, "And what did you do during the war years? Where were you living?" I remembered the small comment in the book chapter covering his family empire, the comment about his supposed "efforts."

He thought about my query. "I was in Kyoto, studying. And thankfully, the city was never bombed, nor seriously damaged. They were terrible times, and we all learned to ... make some contribution to the war efforts, in whatever ways we might be useful. My worst memories were about the attacks. We still had family living in Hiroshima, and when the city was vaporized, two of my favorite cousins, along with their entire families, were killed there in August of 1945, at the war's end."

A strong breeze raised the curtains slightly, a truck rumbled over the road somewhere outside the wall of the compound, and we paused to let the heartbreaking memory of Hiroshima sink in. He had not said it with any anger, it seemed, but with a heavy sadness. I wanted to interrogate him further about what he called his own wartime "contribution," but that was not the right opportunity. Then Sensei continued. "My brother Tsukasa was a much more prominent part of the war effort. He was cut very much in the same mold as my father. If anything, he is even more gifted than my father. He learned to fly, and eventually flew the Zeros during the war. He always claims to be ashamed of Japan's evil doings during those years, and yet there is still a hint of pride in his voice when he reminds me that he shot down Allied planes over the Pacific, many of them American fighters and bombers."

He paused, straightened the sleeve of his robe. "I recall when some older men killed themselves when Emperor Hirohito passed away, in a pathetic attempt to inspire young men to return to the old samurai ways of dying for the emperor. Such a grand waste! It was one of the most traumatic moments in post-war Japan: old, conservative men, killing themselves to honor the past! We call this specific act *junshi*: an expression of loyalty, repugnant as it may seem to Americans. And there was the gruesome act by Mishima, our great writer that many of us compared to your Hemingway. Yet my brother sympathized deeply with such visions of pride, as he would consider them.

He assured me that these lonely deaths were gallant and honorable efforts. It is possible that he might have even considered it for himself, though my brother has grown rather … comfortable in his wealthy ways. But still, Tsukasa might not mind dying in such a manner. He would think it to be for … a noble cause."

More silence ensued. Then, "I am afraid my elder brother is quite old-fashioned." He reconsidered his choice of words. "In fact, he is quite mistaken. I think we Japanese owe the Americans many more apologies for the things we did in those days. Most of us older Japanese are, in fact, deeply ashamed of our nation, and of what happened during those times. And yet, there is still that strong pull of national destiny, and honor, and the memory of the dead. It is why Japanese leaders still often visit Yasukuni Shrine, in Tokyo, our official memorial for all the war dead, much like your Arlington National Cemetery in Virginia, which I once visited. I recall standing before the Tomb of the Unknown Soldier at Arlington, and feeling a great calm, and yet also a great sadness there." I noted silently that this was the second time in our two meetings that he had mentioned Yasukuni Shrine. I resolved to find out more about it.

He stopped to consider the curious fact of history that had mysteriously brought us face to face across that table. Here he was, sitting and drinking tea with an American, talking about his brother's pride in killing Americans. "It is ironic, is it not, Yu-san? We are sitting here now, at this time and on this day, citizens of two nations that wanted very much to destroy each other less than fifty years ago. And yet we can be here now as friends, sipping tea, yes?"

I looked up at him again. "Yes, sensei." And I don't know why, but I felt the urge to bow forward slightly toward him. He recognized my gesture, and his eyes opened a bit wider, his eyebrows arching slightly. And then he bowed toward me, gently.

Another burst of breeze suddenly stirred some papers nearby. The thin curtains blew inward. A fragrance from outside, a blend of moisture and nectar, filled the room. We both looked up, and whatever that elusive magic was that had briefly warmed me just as suddenly disappeared. But the moment we bowed toward one another signified something, I was certain.

There was further talk about my family and my days at Yale, but the brief magic was gone. Soon it was time to leave that afternoon, so I gathered my bag and stepped out of the room toward the front entrance. Sensei followed closely behind, and Mika appeared again from an adjoining room. I turned to face them both, having put on my shoes, ready to depart. "Again, Sensei, this has been a most splendid time together. I thank you with all my heart." (This sort of language sounds a bit stilted to American ears, but that is how I had learned to speak to elders in Japan.)

"Goodbye, Yu-san. It has been most enjoyable." He paused. "Yu-san, I'd like to pursue some of our—common interests. I would love some good conversation about … well, for example, the secrets of young Hemingway and 1920s Paris, among other things. I also have some … items to show you. Does that sound at all interesting to you? That is, if you are not too busy? Perhaps we can arrange a regular time for our meetings?"

Sensei bowed, and as I bowed back. "Of course, Sensei. Whatever I can do, please call on me." And with that, I began to turn away and start down the path to the front gate. Again, the last image of the house was of the slender and beautiful Mika, bowing ever so slightly, as the electric gate slowly closed behind me. The sun was behind some clouds, nearing sunset; it had been a long meeting. I hiked down the mountain, and soon enough, I was back on the train, headed for my apartment.

Oddly enough, though, it was not the prospect of further literary discussion of the young Hemingway with an elderly Japanese professor that preoccupied me that evening, or throughout the following week of classes. Rather, it was the hope of seeing again his luminous niece, arrayed in another of her lovely silk *kimonos*. The moon, more than the sun, began to haunt me.

友

Suddenly as I read this chapter, the name began to emerge from the fog of my memory. Once, in London many years ago at a conference on Henry James, I had dinner with a colleague who brought along a friend from Kobe. Oddly, the man, whose name I now forget, mentioned a faculty member at his school who owned numerous wonderful collectibles, which he often would bring out to show his guests. This professor lived in one of the most fashionable sections outside of Kobe and often hosted extravagant, Parisian-style literary salons for any visiting writers or artists in whom he had even the slightest interest. My colleague told me that this particular figure was famous for his whim, his hospitable good will, and his eccentric passions for such things as Tiffany glass, earthenware ceramics, or the first editions and autograph letters of famous Americans.

But I also recalled there was some minor mention of this professor's shady family connections, including some aspect of the Imperial family and the war. Now, when I read this section, I suddenly realized he'd been speaking of Professor Goto!

It is one of the mysteries of the human memory, how all these things get stored away, possibly never to be revisited, and then, all at once, a song comes on the radio, or a scent wafts abroad, and the memory is reborn.

Chapter 6

The politics of my emerging friendship were often on my mind. I began wondering what Miyamoto and the other office spies/rats would think of me, having regular meetings with Sensei. By this time, even a glimpse of the slimy Miyamoto, with his ill-groomed suits and his pock-marked face, gave me the creeps. And I wondered why exactly, this rather negligible person should exert so much anxiety over me, so I started trying to fill in a few of the details.

A few days after that second visit, David told me that Miyamoto was formerly an "assistant" to Professor Goto, and had evidently helped him with certain "important" tasks. David had overheard a fairly loud (by Japanese standards) conversation, in which Miyamoto had been complaining rather vigorously to a colleague. David was a quick study in the language, and despite the colorful ornamentation and other assorted colloquialisms, he felt he could make a decent translation of some of Miyamoto's complaints: "I have been demoted to a mere go-between, an errand-boy. I must now consider Springs-sensei to be my rival—my enemy," he'd said.

Or at least that's what David thought he'd said. Whatever Miyamoto was ranting about that day (and David admitted he could only catch parts of the conversation), it was clear that Miyamoto saw me as some kind of threat—and not just to Sensei, but also to himself. So I began to return the paranoia, and started watching my back.

友

It had seemed at the conclusion of that second meeting that Sensei and I might be together again very soon, perhaps even the following week, but in reality things like relationships often do not gel as quickly in Japan as they might in the United States. So again, I went about my teaching, kept fairly busy, and promptly forgot about Goto for a while. But, I must confess I did keep picturing his lovely niece in her silk kimono.

Several weeks into October, I received another Sunday invitation, and then again two weeks later. Each time it was Miyamoto who would ask me politely (though stubbornly and rather glumly) to visit the home of Goto-sensei. These invitations became formal and sterile, but evidently everyone concerned somehow understood them intuitively to be the proper way of proceeding.

As my respect and fondness for Professor Goto grew, my disrespect and even loathing for his messenger Miyamoto grew in direct proportion. Once, as I came into the main, common office where all the teachers had a desk, I noticed Miyamoto surreptitiously peeking into one of my drawers, looking for who knows what.

"Can I help you, sensei?" I said, holding back the anger.

He was obviously surprised to see me. "Ah Jack-san. My apologies. I was looking ... for a copy of your syllabus." He looked both ways, then back at me. "For Professor Aoyama."

It was an obvious lie, but protocol forbade me from calling him on it. So I refrained from any response except to glare at him, hopefully making my feelings abundantly clear. My blood pressure shot through the roof, and I leaned toward him ever so slightly. After a moment, he spoke again.

"Sensei, I have also been instructed to inform you that Professor Goto is again willing to host you this Sunday. Will that same time be convenient?" I believe he felt threatened by my surprise encounter, and of course since I was much taller and far stronger than he was, he actually managed to act a bit humble.

"That would be fine, sensei." He remained standing precisely where I would sit in my chair, and I began gently to edge him away from my desk, the drawer still slightly open. I slammed it shut—at least, as much of a slam that would not seem improper in a Japanese office. "Now please, do you mind if I get to work?" And with that he bowed slightly, turned away, and left without saying another word.

It took me a long while to settle down. Six months into my contract, and already I sensed there was something desperately wrong with my situation. Well, something definitely wrong, I should clarify, with Miyamoto. Looking back, I recognize that even when I found him going through my desk, some tingling sensation arose from my inside—not exactly nausea, but some otherworldly sensation, ultimately unnamable. I associated Miyamoto with a malevolence of some sort, something I couldn't quite pinpoint. I still remember his uneven face, his overuse of cheap aftershave, and his smarmy indifference to me as a person. Even as I am writing this sentence it all comes rushing back. The deadness of his creepy eyes. And the shame and horror I now know was yet to come.

友

Soon enough, the Sunday meetings with Sensei all began blending together. Sometimes I would take him a book I wanted him to read, one that I had mentioned and that he did not know about. Oddly, given his adoration of Hemingway, he had never read the book most directly reminiscent of his best work, *A River Runs Through It*, so I bought him a copy. More often, he would offer in return a few Japanese novels to read, in translation, of course.

He urged me to read Kawabata, for instance, and to think of his stark language in terms of American Modernism. He insisted I study Mishima and Oe. "Two Japanese writers with, shall we say, very different views of our nation," he said. And he gave me a couple of books by the American Lafcadio Hearn, deeply romantic tales of the Old Japan.

"Yu-san, I should have mentioned that the word 'Yu' is a common sound in Japanese, and that with a different Kanji, it can also mean ghost," he told me. "Hearn felt that ghosts were a prominent feature of Japanese culture. I think I can agree with that."

During one of the visits, Sensei got to his feet, disappeared into the other rooms, and returned with an old volume with a dull black cover. He sat down and slid the volume across the table toward me with both hands. It was called *Japanese Homes*. "Do you know about Edward Morse, Yu-san?"

The name rang a bell, but not much more, and I shook my head. "Not really. Some American from New England, I seem to recall, who spent time here in Japan, yes?"

"Mr. Morse was a true hero of the American spirit, and a true interpreter of the spirit of Old Japan. This book of his describes the homes of the Japanese in the old style, about one hundred years ago. This room in which we are sitting is of that style, called *wabi*. It is a room of emptiness and of purity, I think. Somehow Morse understood the Japanese better than most Japanese.

"Did you know that even a hundred years ago, many Japanese were already ashamed of the old Japan, and wanted to leap ahead into the modern era? But Morse understood the very great price of doing that, Yu-san. Even by the 1880s, Morse was worried about the loss of Old Japan. That's why he convinced so many wealthy Bostonians to come to Japan and buy up large quantities of Japanese art—ceramics, pottery, paintings, *katana*, everything. Morse was himself a great collector. He began with sea shells, collecting for the pure joy of collecting. His accomplishments are still to be seen in the great collections now held in museums in the Boston area. Morse understood the beauty of these older things, even when almost no Japanese people could understand them."

He sipped his tea and thought for a moment, then proceeded. "He immersed himself in Old Japan. And then he shared his learning with other important Americans, like Fenollosa, who became an admirer of Japanese art and culture, and then the teacher of Ezra Pound. I have great respect for Morse. Please take this book and read it. I think it will help you to see how foreign eyes are often the most perceptive about the things of beauty in a culture."

Then the discussion went in a direction it rarely did. Sensei complained of his own family, and its rush into commerce and big business, and how his own sensibilities dictated that he must somehow resist it. "My brother was the perfect successor to my father. He was trained as the perfect business *samurai*: cagy, feisty, even ruthless, and willing to do whatever his master would ask of him. Even die, if he must. Meanwhile, I was more like Morse. I wished simply to observe, to study beauty. And while my brother was learning the ways of business, I was studying Basho and the *haiku*, flower arrangement, and the way of tea. I believe they resented my bookish ways. But they forgot that in the Old Japan, all *samurai* immersed themselves in such artistic pursuits. The way of the true *samurai* involved the whole person, including the artistic.

"During the war, I became a great enthusiast of *ukiyo-e* (wood block prints) and that is when I began my own collection of prints, scrolls, and old pottery. In college I became fascinated with the heroic and youthful literature of America, and so I also tried to immerse myself in it. These things became a refuge for me, at a time of great upheaval." He stopped and sighed just slightly. "General MacArthur understood the Old Japanese way—that when a nation is conquered, they must worship the gods of their conquerors." Then he put his right hand up along the side of his face, resting in thought. "For me, the great artists were the true gods of American culture—Emerson, Whitman, Hemingway, and many others … Their words were like holy scripture to me."

He waited, thinking. "You are here in Japan, now,

largely because of my love for these things, Yu-san. Our mutual love." He sipped slowly, letting this sink in. "I was drawn to your research primarily due to your impressive knowledge of Hemingway and his friend Ezra Pound. We share a common fascination with what you have so aptly called 'epistolary friendships'—the literary remains of the great authors.

"In fact, I will tell you many things of Hemingway in the future. Much of what you have written is of course correct, but I believe, shall we say, I may possess some ... items, that will prove invaluable in your future work."

"Items?"

He sat motionless, gazing out toward the hallway beyond me. "Books. Manuscripts, letters, that sort of thing. Items of rather rare notice." He even managed the tiniest of smiles as he said this. "Indeed, I own numerous things that might reopen certain debates regarding the ... well, central facts of Hemingway's and Pound's early years." More waiting and sipping. "The detritus of friendships, the fossils of the dead, like Morse's seashells, cast up onto the shore."

"Tell me more about these items, Sensei." I was ready to turn our talk in that direction, but again revealing myself as the eager, impatient American, who must learn to wait.

He lingered a moment over my request. He seemed to savor my desire, just slightly. Then said, "Yu-san, there will be much time for that, for extensive talk about Hemingway and Pound, and all the others. We are in no hurry for those ... secrets." More waiting. "For now, I wish to talk about Japan." He fanned himself, looking away, adjusting his pillow. Soon enough, he continued onto the earlier topic. But he had given me some intriguing clues.

"It may sound odd to you, Yu-san, but I chose to worship at the altar of these other, stranger American gods. I longed for the Old Japan of Professor Morse and Lafcadio Hearn. Hearn was obsessed with an incurable yearning for the inscrutable, for the deep layers of Japan. So was Fenollosa and Ezra Pound. My father recognized that I was, at an early age, a hopeless romantic, but he and my brother indulged my passions. To them, I was the spoiled, effeminate younger brother, an impractical man, of no earthly good in the New Japan. And possibly a traitor, in my study of the Americans."

A lengthy pause ensued, and I finally tried to fill it. "Do you have much contact with your brother?"

A gentle sigh. "He is in his world up in Tokyo, and I am still down here in my own, separate world, Yu-san. The remnant of the old world, Kansai, with its ancient capitals, Kyoto and Nara, both of which are now nearly spoiled. Just decadent old vestiges of a lost Japan, I'm afraid. Much of it defaced by tourist traps for foreigners." I thought about the contrast. "In any case, it is my brother's responsibility to return here to visit the relatives, and honor the dead and the place of his youth. Our family tomb is located in a famous temple in Kyoto. And of course the old family hometown in Yamaguchi. But Tsukasa has not been here in many years, and he would never consent to return to Yamaguchi. He wanted only to escape that world, and he succeeded. I, myself, have not traveled to Tokyo in an even longer time. So the answer is, no, we do not have regular visits.

"Fortunately, there is the one connection. Mika is my brother's only living child. His son died many years ago of an illness, without leaving him any grandchildren. Tsukasa was rather old when Mika was born, almost fifty I believe. She was a great surprise to him and his wonderful wife, now also dead. It was in the sixties, just prior to the Olympics in Tokyo, and of course the Games signified the emergence of a new and vibrant Japan. Hosting the Olympics was our entrance onto the world stage, a new beginning after the tragic war years. We were all extremely proud as a nation.

"And Tsukasa was such a proud father. His hope was that Mika could give him a grandson, or better yet two grandsons, for carrying on the family line." A wistful tone emerged in recalling those days. "She is the gem of my family, I think. But she is more like me than like my brother. She loves the Old Japan, and has worked very hard to master the arts of the tea ceremony and of flower arrangement. Of course she is also a beautiful young lady, as you can see for yourself." At which point he actually paused to gaze at me and grin. "And so she frequently takes the bullet train up to her father's home in Tokyo. She has access to much good fortune, and so she loves to visit the shops in Omotesando or Ginza and spend some of her good fortune on Italian shoes, handbags, jewelry, and other things that are of interest to young Japanese ladies. She is like me—a collector, but of the trinkets of Japan's modern culture, imports, I am sorry to say!" He laughed at this. "But I think it is a wonderful thing for an old man to have such a beautiful flower as her, who prefers to spend most of her time here in this tiny replica of Old Japan, rather than being colonized completely by the bourgeois culture of the New Japan in Tokyo, don't you think, Yu-san?"

As if on cue, Mika appeared with another tray of snacks and tea. She swept in, kneeled before us, and with the gentlest touch refilled the cups. "She is like a bridge between us, two aging, alienated brothers. A kind of interpreter between the old and the new, I suppose. Isn't that so, Mika?"

She bowed and then smiled, and actually laughed just a bit, an unprecedented development. "Yes, *Onii-san.* I adore both sides of Japan! When I visit the old temples of Higashiyama in Kyoto, my feet always feel much better at the end of the day when I wear my latest pair of Ferragamo sandals, rather than the traditional Japanese wooden *geta.*" Evidently she had overheard his catty remark about her expensive Italian shoes. And then she disappeared once again, smiling. Turning back to Sensei, I noticed him peering at me with a rather sly grin. And so I made a tiny nod in his direction. It surprised me that Mika could be a little sassy, which made her even more attractive to my American sensibilities.

In my mind's eye, Mika's lovely smile at that moment, followed by Sensei's wry grin, now seems pregnant with significance. Her slight gesture warmed me, and made me shake the tiniest bit. Even now, as I write this line, it produces a quiver of something primal. I think Sensei already understood the bewitching effect that his beautiful niece had on a young man like me, still in the prime of his sexual life, so to speak. And he was right. As the weeks went on and I returned again and again for tea and crackers, I was increasingly drawn to Mika. It was hard to resist, given her natural endowments and her stylized Japanese way of speaking and serving.

Yes, perhaps the feminist critics I befriended back at Yale will cringe at my depictions of Mika, and they are surely correct in ridiculing my lusty "gaze." In truth, women seem to underestimate the sheer power of the visual for healthy young men, as I was in those days. Just catching glimpses of feminine beauty and grace can produce intense, pleasurable feelings—the lust of the flesh, it's called. Yes, I felt them—increasingly with Mika, and by the end of those first few visits, I had developed a crush on her. I recall lying awake, unable to sleep, picturing Mika. I would imagine the smoothness of her hair, or conjure the Parisian perfume she dabbed on her unblemished skin. Simply stated, she was adorable—in a visceral way.

But it was impossible for me to say whether there was any affection from her. And behind it all was Sensei's looming presence, not to mention Miyamoto's slimy threats, if that's what they were. Was a relationship with Mika even plausible, I wondered? What would Sensei think if I were to pursue his niece? I had no idea at that time, but soon enough I would find out.

友

Professor Goto's reference to Jack's interest in "epistolary friendships" certainly resonated deeply for me. In fact, it was precisely in this important chapter that I realized how my own work and influence, as provocateur of Jack's literary scholarship, was a key reason he had been called to Japan in the first place. Indeed, while he was still an undergraduate, I had hired him as a research assistant, putting him to work in the Lilly Library transcribing the unpublished letters of T. S. Eliot. I also recognized that Jack's preoccupation with letters was not merely academic. Our friendship over many years modeled precisely the sort of relations he studied.

It all commenced years after his adventures in Japan. Perhaps rather strangely, for much of his last decade we had carried on what I can only call an extraordinary and even intimate friendship via the United States Postal Service—we maintained an unspoken agreement that there would be none of this Internet nonsense, but instead we would send real letters in envelopes bearing American stamps, moistened by real human tongues. And so, over the years, we kept to our silent covenant.

Beyond our occasional letters, what we mostly shared was a passion for our work as literary historians and critics. My own work involves nineteenth- and early twentieth-century American literature. Early in my career, I wrote a book entitled The Gilded Neighborhood, *about Nook Farm, the genteel village in Hartford where Mark Twain lived next door to Harriet Beecher Stowe. It was published by a top university press, managed to become an oft-cited text, and forever after made my name recognizable in the field. But I was unable to follow it up with the all-important "second book," instead pouring my energies into textual editing. Nowadays, I co-edit the journal* American Realism, *and I direct the ongoing efforts of the William Dean Howells Project here in Bloomington, a scholarly edition of the complete written works of an important American writer.*

Despite its more mundane associations, the Howells Project is probably closest to my heart, and indeed is the main source of whatever trifling fame I've achieved in my admittedly quiet and rather routine career. We at the Project are the curators of one writer's millions of words, the executors of a lifetime of careful scribbling. Often I feel a lot like a scribbler myself—slightly out of place in this age of wireless communications. I'm no Luddite, nor am I violently opposed to technology, but for old-timers like me, birthed into a different era prior to the Telstar satellite and its offshoots, wireless often translates, ironically, into disconnection. Lincoln spoke of the "mystic chords of memory" holding America together through the horror of a long Civil War, and one might be well justified to ponder what precisely connects us, in these latter days of miraculous "connectivity"? Despite all these innovations, here's what I still consider to be a perfectly fine answer: it's the words, words, words.

I recall that spring of 1997 when Jack reached out to me, announcing his new job at Gonzaga. Given the excruciating job market, it was great fortune he was able to locate such an attractive, permanent position at Gonzaga, a solid Jesuit university located in the desert places of eastern Washington, and where eventually he was rewarded with well deserved tenure.

It had been over a decade since we'd communicated, and after that initial silence, he slowly began cultivating a long-distance relationship with me, his former teacher and advisor. Since then we'd steadily traded postcards, sent each other books to read, even exchanged videos and CDs. With every gift, we included chatty, single-spaced letters, letters that grew longer as the years passed. They were highly nuanced, dense and jocular, the special kind of letter one receives from only a few friends over the course of a lifetime.

One package included a signed copy of his first book, Epistolary Friendships: The Power of Letters in American Authorship, 1870-1930, *which was based on his dissertation work at Yale, and published by the University of California Press. I had helped him edit in its final stages, and was flattered to see a few of my own ideas more fully fleshed out and well expressed. I recall working on his book during a steamy Indiana summer, when I sat for many long, undistracted hours on my screened back porch, overhead fan slowly rotating, listening to the distant sweet corn growing, the patient emergence of gleaming tomatoes that would soon be slathered with Miracle*

Whip and sprinkled with salt. I was glad to do this service for an old student, one who was emerging as a serious voice in the field of American literary studies, just like those ripening tomatoes. And after a long day of intense and focused editing, I enjoyed a few ears of sweet corn and sliced tomatoes, always kept in the fridge, chilling next to a few longneck bottles of beer.

Epistolary Friendships *was a book that told stories in pairs, mapping the way famous authors—Mark Twain and William Dean Howells, Edith Wharton and Henry James, T. S. Eliot and Wyndham Lewis, Ernest Hemingway and Ezra Pound—carried on their friendships through the writing of letters. It can be rather astonishing to study the letter-writing habits of such monumental authors. On many days, Mark Twain scribbled out twenty or more letters, all by hand. So did Longfellow, Howells, James, and many other great writers—thousands of hand-written letters over several decades. Many of those letters are available in libraries and other archives today, but hundreds—even thousands—are still missing or in private hands. Many were burned by their owners, destroying the secrets they contained.*

But every once in a while, an unknown cache of letters or an unknown manuscript will turn up in a basement, attic, or estate sale. Or at a fancy auction at Sotheby's. Or even on the black market, with millionaires outbidding one another for the privilege of owning some unique item of literary lore: an unknown letter, a buried photograph, or a first edition with annotations by the famous author who owned it. There's gold in those old papers, it seems—maybe even more so in our day of texting and social media, at least for those who have eyes to see it.

Jack's book was published in the fall of 2001, almost precisely as airliners were crashing into skyscrapers in lower

Manhattan. His fresh new volume, wrapped in its glistening dust jacket, arrived in my office just days before the tragedy. It sat on a corner of my desk for weeks, gathering dust, as all of us crowded around televisions, mesmerized by the spectacle of the shattered icon of American capitalism, the thousands of shattered lives, and clamoring for whatever new information might become available. The book and its subject matter seemed vaguely irrelevant in the aftermath of 9/11, as did a lot of other tedious features of academia. One of the most prescient images attached to 9/11 was the great cloud of paper fluttering everywhere in the breezy morning, like downy snowflakes. So a book about letter writing, about how words can hold us together, seemed rather quaint in the glow of images being replayed over and over on CNN.

Despite the sinister implications of those jetliners, my extended correspondence with Jack led to a deep and genuine affection. I looked forward to each exchange of letters and ideas—even as they became less frequent—and none more so than when his final package arrived last winter—plump, mysterious.

At first I believed it was simply the logical, final step of our own epistolary friendship. But I now know it was much more. Jack's adventures in Japan originated, at least in part, in our relationship so many years before. It gives me some joy to say that what Professor Goto recognized in Jack's work was, to whatever extent, also a recognition of my own minor contributions to the field. I say that with as little bravado as I can conjure. Obviously, when I first read Jack's manuscript, I had no idea I would be drawn into the narrative as more than a minor character.

But now I know better: I've become just as implicated in this literary adventure as anyone. In effect, Jack's story was destined to become wedded to my own story and would change my life in ways I could never have foreseen. An uncanny result, one that Jack had perhaps planned all along.

CHAPTER 7

Soon enough, the meetings with Sensei took on a new urgency. One day, after I sat for a minute or two alone, Sensei swept into the room, holding a pile of books, a few folders, and two pairs of white gloves. It was the day he commenced revealing some of his previously mentioned "items."

"Yu-san, I am sure you of all people might find these of interest."

"Yes, Sensei?"

"Do you mind wearing these?" He handed me a pair of the thin, linen gloves, pure white, then called for Mika, and rattled off some incomprehensible Japanese instructions. Soon enough, she returned with one of those specially-made boxes used in many libraries for the storage of valuable documents, such as letters. Deftly, she placed it on the table in front of us and backed away again. We both put on the gloves, and Sensei hurriedly untied the strings holding it closed and pulled out the contents, stored neatly in file folders. The tops of the three folders read, "Twain-Twichell 1897-1900."

"Do these look familiar, Yu-san?"

I inspected several of the leaves from the first folder. Months spent studying the handwriting of both Mark Twain and Joe Twichell prepared me for the examination, and I deduced the letters were written on paper from the correct era, and, by all appearances, looked to be authentic. I began scanning the one on top:

> Hartford. Nov. 2, 1897
> Dear old Mark,
> We have been reading, and re-reading, and again reading your "In Memoriam" with the accompaniment of a gray autumn sky and the falling leaves to blend with its unspeakable heart-breaking sadness; its aching, choking pathos. It sets all chords of memory and of love a tremble. It plainly speaks of the pain of Life's inscrutable mystery, the riddles of human experience.

I looked up at Sensei. "This letter is about the poem Twain wrote a year after his daughter Susy died. It was called "In Memoriam," after Tennyson's famous elegy,"

He nodded at me. I leafed through and found the next letter—they appeared to be ordered chronologically.

> Vienna
> Dec. 21, 1897
> Dear Joe,
> I was touched by your last letter—touched, I say, to the very bones. I hand it to you, old reliable Joe—your words are as a balm to this tired old heart. That pathos, as you put it—it *is* like a dream,

> or rather nightmare, and I cannot ever awaken. I languish in the study, grinding away on a shipwreck of a story about a town called Hadleyburg; or I sit in the parlor and listen to Clara playing piano; or, I wander out of doors, and look up and down the tired old city streets, but never finding the one I wish to find. Meanwhile, Livy moans in the next room, enervated and inconsolable. How do men outlive such days, Joe?

I glanced again at the date, and asked, "Sensei, are these what they appear to be?"

Professor Goto sipped his tea, then nodded. "I thought you would be a person who not only could recognize them, but would also appreciate such things, Yu-san. What do they appear to be?"

"Well, they look to be actual, autograph letters. The time is about a year after Twain's daughter Susy died, and it is still obviously very much on his mind, and remains a topic affecting his writing. But I thought I had read all of the letters from this period, about Susy, and I don't remember these. I could write down the dates and check a few of the standard sources to see if they are listed, if you like."

I thought I detected a slight grin from Sensei, and once more he glanced to the side, then snapped a rice cracker in half, putting it in his mouth and chewing. He then leaned over, grabbed a tome off the stack he'd carried in, and handed it to me. It was the scholarly volume listing all of Twain's known letters of the period, and I immediately began looking through it to see if the one just read was mentioned. After a moment of searching, he said, "That will not be necessary, Yu-san. Those letters are not listed in any of the standard guides."

That was a shock, of course, since undiscovered and unlisted letters from such a major author are a rare commodity in literary circles these days. My eyes went from Sensei back down to the letters I held in my hand. I paged through a few more, and a deeper thrill ran through me as I realized that I might be one of the only people to know about them, besides their owner. Overall, there were about ten letters from Twain and ten more from Twichell, a total of about eighty pages of autograph, original, unknown letters. Possible values at auction might be as much as $25,000, or even much more (auctions often produce much larger sums than can be anticipated).

"Are all of these letters unknown, Sensei?"

"Unknown to the standard sources. But not unknown to me—and now, to you!" He smiled in my general direction, without meeting my eye.

"Then I would like your permission to study them." He nodded, and I began reading through them. A mere ten minutes later, my heart pounding, I had to stop myself from jumping up and running around the room! I could swear I heard the blood rushing through the veins at my temple. It was obvious these letters contained new and intriguing information not available anywhere else. These moments of gleeful discovery are what veteran scholars live for. "Perhaps we should make these letters known, Sensei. Have you considered publishing these?"

"Yu-san, these letters must remain our little secret—for now. Also, any other items that I choose to present to you, today or in the future. I am showing you only because you have already proven to me that you are one of the world's experts in these matters. One must have ... trained eyes to comprehend the beauty of such items."

He paused for effect; he had my full attention. "In fact, I brought you here for this very reason, as I mentioned. I have so few people in my world who understand such things. I am hoping you will not betray my trust."

The comment about how *he* had brought me here caught my attention. Again, it sounded almost as if he had personally selected me for the fellowship. By this point in our emerging relationship, I realized this was plausible, but I had let that notion pass before. And I did again at that moment, focusing instead on the letters before me. "Can you tell me about how you got these?"

He thought this over. "I can tell you many things, Yu-san. But for now, I will assume you recognize I have remained quite interested in collecting, even to this day. Passionate, and some might even say—obsessed? In any case, I saw myself as a collector of lovely things, whatever I found valuable. Worthy things. Something that Walter Benjamin once said has stayed with me over the years: 'to renew the old world is the collector's deepest desire.'"

He saw me chuckle just slightly, I believe. "Yes, Yu-san. I proposed to *renew* something from our past. Is that really so quaint? Best of all, I had assets with which to do it. With assets, one can do many wonderful things in life, and I wished to use mine for the preservation of certain items." He hesitated again. "Yu-san, do you remember the Utamaro print outside in the hallway? Do you know the history of the *ukiyo-e* prints in Japan?"

"I'm not sure what you mean, Sensei. You've spoken of them before. I know they fell out of fashion for some time."

He nodded. "Yes. But it's even more disturbing than that. There was a time in our history when Japanese people became ashamed of those lovely pictures. They wished to become more 'modern.' Or what their intellectuals assured them it meant to be modern. And so they began to rid themselves of their past, and those items were sold off to foreigners. Many of the most beautiful wood block prints of Japan are no longer here because the Japanese people forgot how beautiful they are. This is a national disgrace. At least there were the wealthy Americans who saw their beauty and saved them. The Japanese lost their eye for them, but the outsider understood the beauty of the native art, once the natives had long forgotten."

Mika entered, bringing us fresh tea and tiny chocolate biscuits. It seemed reckless, having these valuable Twain letters on a table with snacks and tea, but Sensei seemed unconcerned. He began collecting the letters, putting them back into the box, then asked Mika to return the box to whatever room was its permanent home. I wanted to keep reading them, and Professor Goto sensed that, but simply said, "There will be more time for reading those later, Yu-san. And I have other things that you might like to see as well. For now, let us speak openly."

I ate a wafer, sipped some tea. "Yes, Sensei?"

"Yu-san, may I ask you something? I am sure you might have noticed that the people at the university have some interest in your comings and goings, yes?"

His comment seemed a bit melodramatic, but later I better understood the microscope under which I had been living since my arrival. I believe he was concerned about my loyalty, and perhaps my discretion, which I felt capable of honoring, though I wasn't ready to cut off a finger for him, or whatever. Still, I said, "Of course, Sensei. And please don't worry; you have my loyalties."

"Yu-san," he said, "I would like to ask for your assistance in the future with a few small but very special items that have come into my possession over the years. I hope that you will allow me to learn from you about such things. I would like to think of you as … a collaborator, if you are willing."

Even though his intentions remained unclear, I nodded, expecting him to continue. Instead, he was silent for a long minute. Then suddenly he spoke again. "I am sure you must have suspected all along that I have some little interest in your scholarly work. You have produced an interesting project with your dissertation. There are a few minor errors, of course, but on the whole I think it is worthy. I hope we can talk about that—next time, perhaps."

The bit about the errors caught my attention. *What errors?* "You read my dissertation?"

"Yes, Yu-san, of course. Why should this surprise you? Obviously, with the help of our library staff, I can read almost anything I want, from anywhere in the world. It is a fine piece of work, and you should be very proud. Of course, any research is only partial, and must depend on what is available. In the future, I wish to talk about these matters. And perhaps I can even provide a little information about certain aspects of your research."

Of course, he had made it clear that we shared common academic interests—why else would he have been inviting me to tea? Or, more to the point, why else had I been selected for a Goto fellowship when one candidate had already been selected? Hadn't I been told that my selection had been unusual? It is obvious in hindsight. But at the time, the fact that he had studied my dissertation was a huge surprise and a great honor. And hearing this after having held real letters written by Mark Twain was also quite intriguing. I was eager to discover what other "minor items" might be hidden in his storeroom, waiting to see the light of day.

"But not today. We have done enough for one afternoon, I should think." That was the signal our meeting had come to an end. So I stood up, made my salutations, and departed. As usual, both of them accompanied me to the entrance door.

"Goodbye, Jack-san. Mika bowed. Her long gleaming black hair cascaded forward over her shoulders. I turned to walk away, and suddenly Professor Goto spoke again.

"Yu-san, would you be willing to come for longer periods of time, perhaps next Sunday? I think we might even have dinner together, if you are willing."

His questions took me by surprise. I turned to face him. "Of course, Sensei. As I have said, I am at your service."

He hesitated, looked to the side, and stroked his chin briefly. One of his hands was behind him. "Yes, well. I would be honored if you would agree to somewhat longer meetings, so that we can go into more detail on various … topics. Perhaps even weekly, at least during the terms. I think we have much to learn from one another. Would that be acceptable for you? You must be very busy, yes?"

I had not thought of regular weekly meetings, but those letters—and the mystery of what else was hidden away in his old house—were certainly a great incentive. Plus, there was the nagging comment about the "minor errors" in my research. "I'm sure I could make myself available, Sensei."

"Is Sunday a poor day? Perhaps you wish to attend church services somewhere. I remember many Americans did so when I studied there in the fifties. I have asked for your audience on Sundays so far because it is the Japanese way. Would you prefer another day?"

"Sundays are fine, Sensei. I can come next Sunday again at 3:00 p.m, if that time suits you."

"Yes, Yu-san, it does. Please do come at 3:00. I have other items to show you, and I need your input on many other matters." He now bowed to me, said "Sayonara," turned away, and disappeared inside the house. Mika still bowed respectfully before me, hands on thighs. In twenty minutes, I was on the train, heading for home, but mesmerized by possibilities.

友

Often our visits involved Sensei questioning me about various aspects of the literary life: with an old shriveled up Japanese partner my only listener—and possibly Mika, bowing forward on her knees and furtively listening to us through the sliding door. But there was one other episode that winter that accelerated things for me, and it sticks in my memory as a turning point.

It was one of those early December evenings, about a week before Christmas, when the weather is threatening to turn nasty and winter pounds loudly on the door, demanding entrance, like in an old Robert Frost poem. Winds howled down from the ridges above, and the trees bent nearly sideways as I trudged up the hill, almost late for our appointment, a dreaded no-no for a *kohai* like me. I shuddered off my coat, worried that I was tardy, and asked Mika, "Is he ready?"

She shook her head. "No, he is not yet ready for you. Please follow me." She led me again down the long corridor to our meeting room, and we sat briefly facing each other across the table. She had a lovely set of beads decorating her long, ivory neck, and sat there as if a tropical bird had flown into the room. After an awkward pause—it was our first time alone in a room together—I noticed an old volume sitting at the exact center of the table. I reached out and placed my right hand on it, turning it to see what it was.

Surprisingly, it was *Moby-Dick*, an odd volume to discover sitting out on a table in a spartan, Japanese home. There were four or five yellow Post-it notes sticking out of the pages as well. I looked up at Mika, guffawed briefly, and smiled. "So Sensei likes Melville's old sea stories, *ne*?"

I had taken on the habit of inflecting my English sentences with the Japanese-style sentence-ending '*ne*?', meaning yes? or right? It is, for many Japanese, an habitual tick of their spoken language, just as "you know?" is for many Americans. The longer version, "*so desu-ne*?" had by then become similarly quite addictive.

She noted the volume and responded, "Ah yes. The Whale. My uncle is quite taken with that story. He will no doubt lecture you on Melville today." She paused, then asked me, "You know, of course, where Ahab meets the whale, yes? He has lectured me on it more than once."

But I didn't remember, and as I was about to ask her for an explanation, her uncle entered the room. "Yu-san, welcome. I see you are discussing the Great American Novel, yes?"

Mika rose to her feet, bowing and backing out of the room. She seemed mildly surprised by his sudden entrance, not to say embarrassed, and immediately disappeared into the hallway without another word. Sensei was now clearly in charge. He thumped down onto his pillow, across the table from me, and immediately began interrogating me about Melville, as if I were being examined orally for another PhD.

"Does it surprise you that I find Melville's novel so valuable?"

"Well, no, of course not, Sensei. It's a masterpiece."

"Yes," he sighed. "And yet so little understood—by Americans, I mean."

I hesitated because I had no idea where he might be going with this train of thought. Then I said, "Of course, the whale is a symbol that is meant to be misunderstood—or, perhaps we might say, a symbol of the impenetrable nature of things."

He leaped on my phrasing, and looked me directly in the eye. "Yes, that's true. The impenetrable nature of things. That is well put, Yu-san." He was quiet, stroking his chin. "Let us consider this a moment. Can you tell me the other supreme symbol in *Moby-Dick*, for what you are calling "the impenetrable nature of things?"

I thought for a moment. "Well, there's the doubloon, for example. The one that Ahab nails to the mast."

"Ah yes. The mast." I wondered immediately why he perked up to the second part of my response, dismissing my suggestion of the doubloon as being too easy, I suppose. He was pushing me to think deeper about Melville's symbology. It was much later that I began to I realize that Sensei was revealing his mind in a new and deeper way, in this seemingly nonchalant discussion of Melville. He was ushering me into the energetic and rather quirky courtyards of his literary sensibilities that day, a side of himself that he had been holding in reserve, a layer I had not yet even imagined, including, it turned out, his obsessive side.

"Tell me about the mast, Yu-san. I recall a crucial moment in 'Song of Myself,' where Whitman says that the 'kelson of creation is love.' A kelson, as you know, is a structural support on a ship, meant to bolster it. The center mast of Ahab's ship must be such a unifying and sublime eros. Might Melville be saying something similar?"

His mind worked at a rapid and invigorating pace. I remember thinking that while he might be old and wrinkled, it was I who had to struggle to keep up. Plus he had the advantage as he had prepared for our meeting that day. Hence, the many yellow Post-it notes.

"And so, the doubloon on the mast is missing the point?"

"The doubloon is mere money, a paltry thing. We must go much deeper." Just then, Mika appeared, with tea and *sembei*. Her scent wafted casually into the room along with the *ocha*. It took her a moment to situate the tray, and pour some tea. Sensei was always very patient about such matters. Then he said, "Let's forget about the doubloon for the moment, Yu-san. Tell me about the masts. Where are the ship's masts from, in *Moby-Dick*?"

I had no idea, and told him so. Such a detail seemed fairly arcane, I remember thinking.

He bit into a cracker. "And where was Captain Ahab injured? Where did he lose his leg?"

I thought about this. "Sensei, it's been several years since I've read the novel. I don't remember."

He pounced. "And yet all of this is crucial to the novel. I might also ask you, where does Ahab finally encounter the monster, and where does the captain and his crew meet their demise? But I will assume that the answer once again escapes your memory. This is what I mean, when I say that Americans have largely failed regarding one of the most important aspects of the novel's symbolism—as have you, Yu-san." He calmly unwrapped another *sembei*, and slowly bit into it. "I might add, that for me, it is of equal importance to the Whale itself!"

Then he wiped his palms together, and took up the volume resting between us on the table. "Please allow me to read a few passages to you, which might be useful to our discussion today." Opening to the Post-it notes, one after the other, he read me these passages:

"Her masts—cut somewhere on the coast of Japan, where her original ones were lost overboard in a gale." He flipped to the next passage:

> "Now, sometimes, in that Japanese sea, the days are as freshets of effulgences. That unblinkingly vivid Japanese sun seems the blazing focus of the glassy ocean's immeasurable burning-glass. The sky looks lacquered, clouds there are none; the horizon floats, and this nakedness of unrelieved radiance is as the insufferable splendors of God's throne."

He looked up at me. "'Freshets of effulgences'; that is a masterstroke, is it not?" And again he turned to the novel, and continued reading:

> "[of] Asiatic lands, older than Abraham; while all between float milky-ways of coral isles, and low-lying, endless, unknown Archipelagoes, and impenetrable Japans ... the Oriental Isles to the east of the continent—those insulated, immemorial, unalterable countries, which even in these modern days still preserve much of the ghostly aboriginalness of earth's primal generations."

And with that, Sensei closed the book. "Yu-san, my idea is that ... well, I believe that the crew of the ship face a dual mystery. *Moby-Dick* and Japan, both impenetrable mysteries, both of which evade the penetrations of science and of the modern mind. It is absolutely crucial to recognize that the Whale can only be found in the waters of Japan, yes? Do you see?" He watched for my assent, but I was still confused as to his point. "Melville says at one point something like this: the waters of Japan are the 'almost final waters,' and all the action at the end of the novel, and the hunt for the Whale, occurs as they penetrate further and further into the 'heart of the Japanese cruising ground.' The crew of the Pequod, as it turns out, must confront not only the White Whale. They must confront also Japan."

"So are you telling me that Japan is an impenetrable mystery for the American visitor? Isn't that just another great myth that the Japanese have about themselves? 'Poor Japan, it is just so inscrutable to foreigners'?" I smiled at him as I said this.

He actually laughed at my sarcasm, then quickly became serious again. "But you are missing my point. Don't you see? The crew must confront the great Other. In this sense, of course the Japanese are inscrutable—but so are the Americans, for us!" We both smiled at this. "Besides, words are inscrutable, as well as symbols. Melville's term before—"effulgences"—it is a brightness from something that remains unidentifiable. What you Americans glibly refer to as God. Ahab's obsession is to penetrate the very mysteries of God, or Being—this Great Other. It begins with an imperial pride—one might say, as evidently Melville believed, a very American pride. But its end is in destruction."

I will say this: it's funny what the mind remembers with precision, and why. Because I remember that meeting, almost twenty years ago, like it was yesterday. Sensei's brilliant interpretation of Melville was dazzling—not unlike the inscrutable beauty of Mika, pouring the tea. Beyond the general mystery of Japan, and its impenetrable nature, there was the confusion I was increasingly feeling about Japanese women, one in particular, and this even greater and much more specific mystery keeping me up some nights. Mika was beginning to get under my skin, and what I considered to be my growing understanding of Japan (another funny idea, in retrospect) allowed me to believe that perhaps I might actually have a chance with her. But in the back of my mind, I had real doubts. I also recalled how Ahab's mission ended.

Long-time foreign residents often comment upon their curious ambivalence toward Japan. As *gaijin* begin to grow more knowledgeable and confident in their understandings of their adopted home, they simultaneously become more conscious of Japan's great shortcomings. In fact, they also begin to despair of ever comprehending the "true" Japan. As Melville's inscrutable white whale swam along, I wondered if I could ever anatomize the Japanese.

These ambivalent feelings also characterized my longing for Mika. It was impossible for me to say whether there was any affection from her. But another Sunday, I happened to arrive a few minutes early. Sensei was away on some other visit or errand of his own, so Mika greeted me in our customary way and escorted me into the main sitting room. I sat for some time alone, until finally she served tea, as was her wont, and upon telling me that Sensei would return soon, hesitated at the doorway. "Wait, Mika," I stammered. At first those were the only words that came out. She paused, without quite turning to face me. Finally, I blurted out, "Please sit with me until Sensei returns."

It seemed like a very long time until I got any sort of response from her. She must have also been wondering how to respond to this foreign professor from America. Then: "Jack-san, since my uncle is elsewhere, I am uncertain if it is ... proper for me to be alone with you?" It was both a statement and a kind of question. I realized that it was a gesture of opening from her, however, so I insisted. And she did, finally, sit down with me. It was a graceful act to see her fold her legs underneath herself and rest like some precious bird on the floor opposite me. She cupped her drink with both hands and sipped almost imperceptibly. The sleek long hair swayed before me like the device of a hypnotist. For the first time we were alone in the room as two individuals, a man and a woman seated across an antique table in a magical old Japanese home, drinking tea. In reality, we were not alone. I later came to understand that Omori and the cook were almost certainly elsewhere in the house, perhaps even lurking nearby.

Sitting with her, suddenly I understood that, despite all of the treasures of Sensei's collection, here before me was his prize possession. I had certainly noticed Mika's beauty and grace, on every visit so far, and I knew I was attracted to her—how could I not be?—but now I sensed the vague possibility of something else growing inside me. At the thought, a thin sweat broke out on my forehead. She had turned up the heater underneath the table to counteract the damp and frigid air as it was surprisingly cold that day, but that was not why I was suddenly sweating. Mika noticed and asked, "Are you uncomfortable?"

"No, I'm fine." But in reality, I felt like an eighth-grader trying to make small talk at recess. She looked down shyly at her hands while I tried to think of something to say.

We chatted briefly about the trivialities of the day. Finally I realized we had one rather obvious thing in common. "How long have you been staying here with Sensei?"

"Well, that is quite a long story. It has now been almost ten years. I came down shortly after finishing my college years in Tokyo."

"I know your father is important up in Tokyo, so I've always wondered why you left to come down here to Kansai?"

She again was coy and hesitant. She thought about my question for a period of time, then smiled secretly. "That is also quite a long story, and hard to—how to say—summarize?"

She looked up to me for approval of her choice of vocabulary, which was obviously just right, so I nodded and said, "Yes, summarize." This seemed to give her more than a little enthusiasm and joy, which in turn did the same for me. My heart ached to find her approval, and it was just in these trifling gestures that I was beginning to realize that small wonder. In fact, I think we both realized that sticky day that some sort of bewitchment had begun to overtake both of us—or at least, I began to believe it for myself, and began fantasizing that it could become a two-way street. Whatever her feelings were, I allowed myself to embrace the fullness of the spell that she could cast my way—a fullness that I can still dredge up these many years later.

Perhaps she sensed the spell as well. So she began to spin her own tale. "My father is, as you say, quite important. Yes, and in many other ways that you have never even dreamed of. For example, he has become friendly with the emperor, and has visited the Imperial Palace, on many occasions." She now smiled shyly at me for a momentary pause. "Here in Japan we are very reserved about what we say about family to ... outsiders." This word also seemed to stifle her a bit—the use of "outsiders" was undoubtedly her rough translation of *gaijin*, which can be deployed in a derogatory fashion. "I'm sorry, Jack-san, I am not saying you are such an outsider as all that. You do understand, I mean outside the family, yes?" I nodded at this. "But I think you must know a little about the Goto Industries; it is common knowledge. My father, as you must imagine, is rather"—again she searched for a proper term— "shall we say insistent? Or autocratic? One must be of such a character, to succeed as he has in the world of big business and industry. And yes, he has been extremely successful."

She paused some more, nodding slightly. I was used to this idiosyncratic feature of much Japanese storytelling—frequent and generous pauses for reflection and emphasis. "Father is a very good man in so many ways. But somehow all of his business concerns have made him forget the things that some of us Japanese value even more—things like art, tradition, the past. Our history together. I remember how much he tried to help me achieve my own success, but he had a very rigid sense of what such a success might include. Meanwhile, I tried to ... reconnect?"

I nodded, and she graced me with a smile.

"Yes, to reconnect with my uncle down here in Kansai, near the old capitol, Kyoto. He was rather shunned by my father, since he was the one who had left the family business in pursuit of these other things. Literature, prints, things of beauty, the finer things in our world, I think. My uncle understood when I wanted to spend several years studying flower arrangement—*ikebana*. But my father considered this to be a great waste of time, and saw no practical reasons for doing it. Except, of course, that it might make me an even more attractive 'catch.' He was always the … pragmatist—I believe that is the American phrase, yes?"

Another nod from me.

More pauses.

"My father wished for me most of all to marry into a wealthy and prestigious Tokyo family. He had even had one chosen for me. Father had arranged for a *nakodo*—a go-between, or matchmaker—to find a worthy son-in-law, and I was ultimately introduced to one who had been approved by him. He was a son of the wealthy Uchida family, most famous for their factories near Nagoya and outside of Tokyo in Saitama, producing car parts and other machine products. The Uchidas did much business with the automotive companies—Toyota, General Motors, Audi, Fiat, Mercedes. They had deep roots in industry, like my own family. Their younger son's name was Kentaro, but he liked being called Ken, and actually he was a handsome and funny boy. But we had very little in common. He had no use for the things of beauty in the world, or old things; only pleasures and the things of wealth. He loved loud music, dancing, sports cars, and surfing in Hawaii, Australia, South Africa—wherever the big waves were at the moment. Or skiing at the biggest and most elegant resorts: California, Utah, Austria, Italy—anywhere but Japan, which he considered too "*dasai*"—meaning, old-fashioned. He seemed to be a good man, and yet somehow he was still the product of his environment, and sometimes acted very much like a child, and I was not able to go through with it." She looked at me and saw the astonishment in my eyes. "Yes, Jack, sometimes a Japanese woman can even turn against her elders! Does that surprise even you, an American?"

I looked at her in silence. What surprised me was she called me by my given name!

She blinked, diverting her eyes. "And so I said no, to Ken Uchida. This kind of rebellion is almost unheard of in powerful Japanese families. It was just after that when I decided to come south to Kyoto, and my uncle graciously provided a place to live temporarily and many important connections for me. That was almost ten years ago.

"I believe my father still has some hope that one day I will relent and return to Tokyo, and begin a family for him, with a carefully selected millionaire husband. Of course, I want children—but in my own timing. My silly dream of a romantic spark, of true love—I suppose it comes from all those American novels."

As she looked up at me and grinned shyly, covering her mouth and snickering softly, the image of a dashing hero sweeping a delicate Japanese maiden into his arms flashed through my mind. As ridiculous as the image was, my pulse quickened.

"My father has often told me he would immediately begin a new search for a worthy successor, if I were to give him notice. And he wants most of all for me to give him grandchildren—in fact, I should say, a grandson. He would like to enlist my son, if I ever have one, into his army as a potential successor for the family business. It is his way of thinking about me, I would say. Until I do this, my life is not meaningful for him. But I am now into my thirties, Jack-san, and this sort of success is becoming more and more unlikely. Here in Japan, it is not common for a woman my age to marry. I believe the American term is 'old maid,' yes?"

Mika, an old maid? The term conjured up a vision of the Widow Douglas, or of Emily Dickinson hiding behind her bedroom door in Amherst. But before me sat an attractive, even luscious, bright, bilingual, and extremely gracious young woman, just entering her prime. I shook my head, perhaps a bit too vigorously, and said, "No. Mika, that's not the right saying; 'old maid' doesn't refer to young women like you. You are—" I hesitated before blurting out, "Well, you're beautiful!"

This pleased her and she smiled, then covered her mouth again and bowed, slightly shrugging her soft shoulders. "But here in Japan, I am—damaged goods? Yes, and so for most men of any prestige, they would assume there is something seriously wrong with me, not being married with children at my age. I am afraid sometimes that I have missed out on all that, but I am not sad. In college I read many British and American novels about young women finding men to love, rather than simply ones to follow and obey, like house pets. Books by Jane Austen, Louisa May Alcott. *Anne of Green Gables*. I loved them all, and still do. I am afraid I have been bewitched by these western stories of falling deeply in love. All of this is why I felt I must escape the world of my father in Tokyo, and return to the world of my past, my family traditions. And so I came back to Kansai, and entered the world of my uncle, who has been for me like a father ever since. He truly does understand the value of words and symbols and true love, as matters of the heart that are superior to the matters of the business world and what my father calls 'the real world.'"

These last words echoed through the room just as another set of echoes emanated from the front of the house, and then, the hallway. It was the sound of footfalls, and evidently signaled the return of Sensei. Just as Mika completed her sentence about the "real world," I heard

Sensei call her name from the hallway. "Mika, *Tadaima! chotto kochira ni*. I'm home. Come here, please."

She quickly got to her feet and slid open the door to receive several packages that Sensei had brought along from his outside visits. With them in her arms, she scurried off to the kitchen. Sensei spied me over her shoulder as he gave her the packages, and immediately his face betrayed a kind of irritation toward me that was subtle yet obvious, his body language questioning the propriety of a young man in a room alone with his "young" niece, though again, in this case, she was over thirty. He was indeed of the old school.

But the tone of his voice, in perfect Japanese form, did not betray any such irritation—at least, almost none, to my untrained ear. "Ah, Springs-sensei, you have come. My sincerest apologies for being late. I trust that Mika has taken good care of you, yes?" His use of the formal "Springs-sensei," rather than the affectionate "Yu-san," was another subtle signal of his displeasure.

"Hello Sensei, yes, we enjoyed a small conversation about art and literature. I only arrived a few moments before you did," I lied. I still don't know why I said that, about having just arrived. In fact, I had been there half an hour before he showed up.

He seemed to catch me in this minor canard, and hesitated just slightly in taking off his overcoat, as if to study my slip-up. Then he said, "Art and literature? It is just as if I were here, then. That is our typical subject, is it not?"

He remained standing, stretching his arms, looking each way, bending his knees. Then he sat. "Let us begin by looking at an old set of papers I have here." He reached for a green library box, handing it to me. I opened it to discover hand-written notes that looked like a draft of an essay or lecture. The title was simply, "Friendship."

"That's a title of one of Emerson's essays, yes?"

He nodded, still seeming a bit ruffled by the idea of his niece being unchaperoned with a *gaijin*, I suppose. Nevertheless, soon enough the enchantment of the words on the page took over, our conventional tutorial-style meeting began, and all complications due to his absence were left behind.

友

Not long after that day, I learned there was more gossip going around the department, though David pretended to hesitate in telling me. He was a bit overly dramatic at times, playing his news to the greatest advantage. We were down at the Munchen Café on a cool and cloudy afternoon, tipping a few ales. David had been seeing a lovely young Japanese singer who went by Ryeiko. He had noticed her in one of the local clubs, and soon became infatuated. She was flashy, pretty, and boisterous, and he loved speaking his improving Japanese to her and taking her to expensive restaurants in Umeda, on Osaka's trendy north side. She also knew all the insider joints, the ones that stayed open all night and served twelve-year-old Scotch at reasonable prices—well, reasonable for Japan. And he loved regaling me with their drunken adventures. "She's wearing me out, pal," he winked.

Then he looked at me, slightly more seriously, and said, "The water's fine, old boy, why not come on in?"

I froze. "Meaning what?"

"Word around campus is that you have a thing for a certain lovely young Japanese maiden yourself—is it true?"

"Excuse me?"

"Drink up, mate, this one's on me." He motioned toward the waitress for two more of the same, then hunched forward toward me and lowered his voice. "Listen. Everyone knows about Goto's niece, and about your many visits to his home. Word is, she's quite the sorceress. Why play games? I saw her once walking around the marketplace near the station with the old man, and she is quite the doll. Why not go for it yourself?"

The two beers arrived swiftly, and David emptied almost half of his in one long draught. He looked at me, but I had no response. So he took another long drink, sighed, and wiped his mouth with his sleeve. "Oh come on, Jack. You know by now that everyone's business is public news around here. The university is like one big, unhappy family. You just haven't quite learned yet whom to ask about such things. Believe me, your many visits to see Goto are common knowledge. He's quite the legend in these parts, Jack old boy. And his luscious niece—she's just about your age, yes? I bet if you asked your students, they would even know about the rumors."

If true, I had once again underestimated the sinister aspects of this claustrophobic culture I had entered. And I was stunned enough to lie about my feelings toward Mika, even to one of my closest confidantes in all of Japan.

"David, the thought never crossed my mind about her. Anyway, she'd never have anything to do with a *gaijin*, right?"

That question was a dead giveaway, of course. He laughed, took another drink, and shook his head at me. "Jack, you never know with these girls. Some of them are fascinated with westerners. Look at me, I'm no Brad Pitt, but my girl is as lovely as a cherry blossom, yes?" Gulp. "She shows me off like I'm Prince Charles."

David peered at me with a knowing smile. "One more small detail, sensei." He leaned forward, voice low. "It seems our boy Miyamoto also has a bit of a crush on your Mika-san." Another gulp. "Word on the street is, he once made a play for her. Can you imagine? That toad with a rich beauty like her?" Pause, drink. "I may be off, but it sounds like he has been threatening to break your neck, or some such nonsense, if you ever touch her. Ha!" Gulp. "And you know, they say he's quite skilled at the martial arts—*karate*, *kendo*, that sort of thing—he's quite the *bushi*, a warrior, they say, despite all appearances." Gulp, gulp. "That's what my sources tell me, anyway."

Was Kilcoyne razzing me here? He had that sly humor one often finds in highly intelligent Brits, all deadpan and seemingly in earnest. Miyamoto a *samurai*? Whatever those "sources" might be, and assuming David wasn't pulling my leg, it seemed plausible that Miyamoto saw me as some kind of threat—and not just to Sensei, or to his access to whatever treasures Sensei might have hidden away in his house, but also to Mika. But most serious of all, evidently, my own private and emerging crush had already been noticed—by David Kilcoyne, his "sources," and possibly others as well. Like Miyamoto.

友

A few days later, I happened to run into Miyamoto—or rather, perhaps it was his strategy to make me believe it was just a coincidence. Again, I was sitting in my home away from home, the Munchen Café, having a cup of coffee and reading a newspaper, when suddenly Miyamoto appeared. I was virtually alone in the café one moment, and the next he was looming over me, holding a cup and saucer. "May I sit, Springs-sensei?"

"Yes, of course, sensei." I had to pretend to welcome his presence, despite our edgy relationship. "Please sit down." I even pushed out a chair for him, though my paper remained on the table, giving him little room for his own coffee.

He took his time, and presently it became clear that he had a specific agenda. "And how is Profesor Goto? Is he well?"

"Yes, he is fine." I decided then and there to pursue my own agenda, since he had barged into my afternoon. One of my tactics was to show Miyamoto that I knew some things about him. "I have heard that you formerly worked closely with Professor Goto—is that true?" Sip. Sip.

He absolutely glared at me for a moment, signaling his intention to control the conversation. "Yes, sensei. I did some … research for him, previously." He waited, and so did I. "And I should say, yes, I also traveled on his behalf. Many times, in fact. To Hong Kong, China, and even San Francisco, on one occasion." Sip. Sip. "I have heard that you recently have been asked to assist Professor Goto, in this way—is that correct?"

We were quite the social pair, at that moment. It was becoming clear to me, and certainly to him, that in a perfect world, we would simply move the tables out of the center of the room, and have at it. "Why yes, sensei, I may be asked to 'assist' him. In the very near future." I was lying about all this, of course—at least, I thought so, at the time.

"And what will you be … undertaking, on his behalf, if you do not mind me asking?"

Now I could twist the knife a bit. "It may be … unwise for me to say very much about the personal business of Professor Goto. I believe that you should ask Sensei for those kinds of details. Your previous intimacies with him should allow for that kind of information, *ne*?"

This approach clearly pissed him off. But like any good Japanese male of his age, he was calm and seemed almost unaffected. It was the stormy eye that he laid on me, just for the briefest moment, that gave away his ill mood. Then, "Springs-sensei, I wonder … How is Mika-san?" At this point, he took a moment to meet my gaze and smile in that almost imperceptibly Japanese way, in which a smile is the specter of a smile, almost not even there. I was proud of myself that day, I distinctly remember thinking, because I was starting to catch on to some of these minimal signals.

"She's fine, sensei. And thank you for asking." But his slight mention of her, now, made me uneasy and wary of his intentions. He was, in other words, twisting his own knife just a bit, tweaking me somehow with the reference to Mika. Since I began visiting Sensei regularly, Miyamoto had maintained a constant, though distant presence on the margins of my life, a malevolent one at that. And here he was again, irritating me, and now putting me on edge about Mika, just as I was beginning to think of her in more serious terms.

Miyamoto drained his cup. "Springs-sensei, I have had … a rather long friendship with Mika, as you may already know. I would be … very disappointed if you were to do anything that might … upset her. I hope you can understand my … concerns." Evidently he knew something about my feelings for her, as David had intimated, and he was there to make some sort of vague warning. Perhaps it was even true that he himself had fallen under Mika's spell, in his former life as Sensei's assistant. That's what I thought at the time, not understanding until much later, in fact, the month before my departure from Japan, the more sinister aspects of this "coincidental" meeting.

Before I could respond, he stood to take his leave. "Enjoy your afternoon, sensei," he said with a slight bow. I mumbled something back to him, and he left. Just like that, the strange interview was over. But after he left, the ghost of Miyamoto burrowed deep into my consciousness. Though he had said almost nothing of consequence, there was a distinct message in his tones and gestures. And it was deeply unsettling.

友

I noted with some poignancy the brief quote from Walter Benjamin, which may have come to Jack through one of my lectures years ago: "to renew the old world is the collector's deepest desire." We collect, that is—at least, we tell ourselves so—for the purposes of renewal, first to know the Other in more precise detail, but ultimately, to make a better world for us all. To "bring or gather together," which is the Latin root of the verb "collect."

While there remains so much handwringing among academics due to the so-called "crisis in the humanities," here we see reminders of why we do the things we do as teachers and as scholars. Our hope is to gather all things together, so to speak. And we hope that these dreams of unity are not to be deferred forever.

And yet, one wonders as we journey through this nether world full of outward tomfoolery and inward deceits. "The impenetrable nature of things," as Professor Goto puts it in his ingenious reading of Melville's white whale. His remarks bespeak a powerful yearning to penetrate both that whale, and more generally, the great Other. But alas, one can only penetrate so far. For the world is veiled, resisting collection, resisting a gathering together. A wise man once put it this way: "How often I have longed to gather your children together, as a hen gathers her chicks under her wings, and you were not willing?"

Chapter 8

My weeks took on a new life, leading up as they now did to those Sunday visits with Sensei. I got my teaching out of the way with ease—just show up and talk—and time passed very quickly. More and more, Sensei enticed me with multiple items that were indeed of interest to me. Almost all of them, he explained, had been purchased through agents, or at auctions where his agents made bids. He took great pleasure in detailing for me the date and price of the assorted transactions, most of them at auctions in New York, London, or Paris during the 1960s or '70s (evidently his heyday as a collector), and then he would carefully hand the item to me. Some of them I held in stunned silence, and he took obvious delight in watching me inspect his treasures: "Here's a signed first edition of Hemingway's *In Our Time* that I bought in 1961 for $800 at an auction in New York," he would say. Or "Ooh! Here's a set of typewritten letters (with a few autograph letters thrown in) from Hemingway to Adrian Ivancich, all circa 1950-55, around 120 pages total, which one of my agents discovered in 1968 for $12,000." Or "Ahhhh! Look at this one, Yu-san, it's the typed and penciled-over, original manuscript to Hemingway's volume *Death in the Afternoon*, purchased at auction in 1963 for $15,575." Ooohh. Ahhh! On and on it went. With Hemingway clearly at the center of his collection, he drew me deeper into his own obsessions.

Eventually, he returned to my own scholarly mistakes. Sensei had mentioned them weeks before, and I'd been mulling them ever since. He began by pulling from one of the nearby shelves a copy of my dissertation, evidently prepared and kept handy for my appearance that day. "See, Yu-san? Another example of what good fortune can conjure." He smiled broadly and handed me the tome. It was bound in those cheap-looking cloth bindings used by most American universities, in this case of a bright blue (my originals were bound in a dusty greenish color, so this was one produced from the original copy that he must have gotten through interlibrary loan). The volume had dozens of bright yellow Post-it notes stuck into various pages, and I assumed he had marked the pages where he either wished to discuss something, or possibly where he discerned some error.

"Please tell me about those errors you mentioned, Sensei."

"As you can see, I have marked most of them." *Most of them?* I felt the air whoosh out of me. *How many errors were there*? Patiently, he showed me a few little problems, some of them proofreading mistakes, but mainly a number of historical or biographical inaccuracies. Soon he got up and left me to go through the other marks in the book and figure them out for myself. As I reviewed his notations, his craftsmanship came through in the dogged manner in which he went through my work, mechanically marking each and every error, as if it were a tremendous lapse in rationality, a decided gesture of rebellion against something sacred. I remember my hands shaking, the heat rising to my face as I turned the pages. I was embarrassed, ashamed even, to have been directed by this small Japanese man to these tiny mistakes in my own native language or national history. It struck me as a further show of force, a metaphorical suckerpunch that dropped me to my knees in the face of his superior intellectual strength. As if any more evidence was needed. Yet, I knew he had not pointed out my errors in a spirit of ridicule. His attention to every detail was, rather, more the gentle prodding of a master artisan guiding his student in a particular direction, toward a particular problem and solution. What direction, though? What problem? And, more importantly, what solution?

"Sensei, these are egregious mistakes, and I appreciate your attention to my very poor work. But there must be something else, yes? What do you think are the most significant errors in my dissertation?"

He was at that moment standing to one side of the room, leafing through a picture book. He turned a page, and, without looking my way, said, "Yu-san, some of your mistakes are no fault of your own. One can only speak of historical facts, for instance, based on the available data. As you know, I am an aficionado of a number of American authors. I have shown you some of the things I have collected regarding Hawthorne, Melville, Hemingway, Mark Twain, Emily Dickinson, and many other writers, yes?" I nodded, and he paused, shut the book he was scanning, placed it carefully on a shelf, and came and sat down across the table from me again.

"Well, Yu-san, I wish to concentrate now on the one author whose life and works have been my greatest fascination. In fact, it is one of the reasons I went to America in the first place, and why I decided to study literature. I am referring to the most Japanese of American writers, I think. And like you, he was born and raised in the Great American Midwest. Can you guess his name?"

I remember being struck by the comment about someone being the most Japanese of American writers. I wondered about all the things he might mean, but I immediately thought again of the book that always seemed to me to be quintessentially "Japanese": *Snow Country* by Kawabata, one that Sensei had insisted I read early on in our relationship. Kawabata's spare, romantic prose, his preoccupations with lost love, and his celebration of endless skiing in the pristine snow, followed by steaming green tea, warmed *sake*, a hot bath, and a nice, fluffy *futon* brought to mind another Midwesterner.

"It must be Hemingway, yes?"

He smiled. "Very good, Yu-san. Good! I am impressed that you would notice this about Hemingway. You impress me more every time we meet. His prose is quite stunning to us Japanese. Indeed, I often have said he writes his sentences almost like little haiku. Every word, every sound, is precious. And he was such a romantic, in those modern times in Paris, just after World War I. There is a concept in Japanese—*natsukashiisa*—which is hard to translate, but that captures this sentiment, something like nostalgia in English, or fondness for the old things."

"The romantic yearnings of our youth, Sensei. And I agree about his writing. But nowadays, many critics dislike Hemingway for his arrogance and macho posturing."

"Oh yes, I know that's true. All so tangential to the true artist. Theoretical parlor tricks, trifles, I can assure you!" He said this with some little irony, a touch of glee in his voice. "But actually there is something charming and powerful about his masculine side, don't you think?" His eyes were bright as he warmed to his subject. "Yes, you can admit it! I love it when he goes to the bullfights, or skis in Austria. We Japanese, yes, we are still a macho society, I suppose. And of course, he ended up killing himself. In Japan, some consider death at one's own hand to be brave, the ultimate act of true manhood. I cannot quite agree with that view, but the heroic idea of suicide—this must sound very strange to you as an American, yes?"

"It's very strange, yes—and disturbing."

He stopped to think this over, nodding slightly, then proceeded. "All writers have their faults. One Japanese author said that it is the faults that produce great writing, like the fault lines that cause great earthquakes, something like that. Earthquakes reveal the fault lines and the true man underneath. It is hard to translate.

"In any event, yes, at times Hemingway was quite odd in his behavior, true enough. He was known to be conceited, even hateful at times. But always remember this: strange behavior does not change the prose, Yu-san. Hemingway is the greatest prose stylist I know, of all the Americans." I shrugged my agreement. "For me, Yu-san, it has always been about the words themselves. The rest is mere conversation."

Sensei got up again, walked out, and, moments later, returned with another book. He stood in the doorway, opened the book, searched for a passage, flipping through a few pages, then nodded and began to read aloud. As I listened, I noted again how well he spoke English and how slight was his accent.

"Then I went back to writing and I entered far into the story and was lost in it. I was writing it now and it was not writing itself and I did not look up nor know anything about the time nor think where I was nor order any more rum St. James. I was tired of rum St. James without thinking about it. Then the story was finished and I was very tired."

He paused and smiled at me, and said, "I recognize this as myself, Yu-san. And for me, I also write from a hunger, and enter into the writing—when I'm lucky. At least I used to. I can tell you this much, I certainly *collect* from a hunger."

He closed the book. "Now those are very fine sentences, Yu-san." He stopped, then looked at me. "Do you know these words?"

"Yes, Sensei. It's in a Parisian cafe, as recalled many years later, from *A Moveable Feast*."

He sat back down now, placing the volume on the table between us. After the slightest hesitation, he put both of his hands on the book, and slid it all the way across the table to me. "I want you to have this, Yu-san. It is a small token of our wonderful conversations, and our times together, which have been a great comfort to me."

I picked it up, inspected it, and by the date inside realized that it was another first edition. "I can't accept this, Sensei. It is too valuable." I slid it back across the table to him.

But he would not touch it. "You disrespect me unless you accept it, Yu-san." He looked around the room, his chin held high. "In any case, I have another, so it is just a small gift. Please take it." And so, still hesitating, I did. And then the meeting was over. It was not, apparently, the right day for Sensei to delve any deeper into my own woes as a writer, even though I could tell from his manner there was more he wanted to reveal. I now guessed that whatever revelation he was guiding me toward was directly related to Hemingway, and he said as much when he bade me goodbye at the front door.

"Yu-san, we will get to other matters about your coverage of Hemingway by and by." And so we did.

友

But before we got back to Hemingway, the relationship between Sensei and I changed again. The next Sunday, he recruited me into his cohort of foot soldiers, those who might carry out his specific tasks. Of course, by now I was a willing recruit.

As I seated myself, Sensei spoke up. "As I have mentioned, Yu-san, I have been quite intrigued with your coverage of Hemingway's letter writing and his friends in Paris. I have never told you about my own wanderings in that great city. I suppose of all the cities in the world, it is Paris that most captured my heart. Have you been there?"

"No, Sensei."

"Well, that will not do, Yu-san. I have many loyal connections, shall I see about housing for you? With the travel allowances from the university, perhaps it is the right time in your life to see the fabled City of Lights?"

"Perhaps it is, Sensei. Paris is one of the many places I would like to see in Europe."

"Paris is the most important of all the cities in Europe. It is the cultural center of the continent, I think. Hemingway understood as much, as did Picasso, Gertrude Stein, Pound,

Eliot, all of them. Of course, there is Italy—in particular, Rome, Florence, and Venice—all very dear to my heart, but relics of a much older and distant world. Paris is of the modern world. The epicenter, I believe."

A large fly buzzed around our little table, and he shooed it away. "I must gently insist, Yu-san, that you make a visit to Paris one of your priorities." He paused, looked away from me, and then went on. "In fact, I have been meaning to ask you to consider going to Paris as my assistant, my agent, so to speak, for there are perhaps some things that you might do for me once you arrive there. It would be a business trip, in fact—let us put it that way, yes? And I am just getting too old for that sort of travel, I'm afraid."

"You want me to go to Paris on your behalf?" I was intrigued and yet perplexed.

"There are a few items I am interested in that require a certain expertise. You could do me the favor of appraising them, in ways rather different from the amateurs who usually do that sort of thing for me. Perhaps during an upcoming break? Say, in spring? A wonderful season for Paris, not the regular tourist season, and not so hot and humid, as the summer. Fewer tourists, getting in each other's way, trampling upon one another, scrambling to take photos in the Louvre, without even seeing the art itself! In spring, you can walk the avenues without obstruction. It is a bit chilly, but I always regarded cold weather as the best time for extended walking. And Paris is certainly one of the world's great cities for walking. You will see for yourself, Yu-san. It is dazzling!" He was a good salesman. "And I can certainly arrange for a comfortable place for you to stay, near the center of the city, on either bank, as I know many people."

It was a great opportunity, a free trip to France, all expenses covered, and the idea more than intrigued me. I thanked him for his confidence and said I would give it some thought.

"Fine, Yu-san. Please do that. And since we are discussing travel—" He hesitated and seemed to have another proposal. "I have one other possibility that has come to my attention, just yesterday. In some ways, I am rather shy to ask." He looked up at me, somewhat forlornly, somewhat hopeful. He was quite a cagy guy, looking back. He was greasing the wheels by enticing me first with the idea of a trip to France.

"Yes, Sensei?"

"*So desu-ne?* I should explain that there is a particular … object, one that I have long coveted, and which may become available in the coming weeks. Perhaps, I thought, you might be willing to help me with this."

I chewed my rice cracker and heard the cold wind whistling through the pine trees. First France, and now, what? I swallowed and looked across at him. "Thank you for thinking me trustworthy enough to even ask, Sensei."

"You are quite welcome, Yu-san. I do trust you. In fact, I should like to ask for your help in advancing my analysis of … *Moby-Dick*. Together, perhaps we can venture even further into the rabbit hole of Melville's story."

I recalled Sensei's earlier mention of how I might "be of assistance" to him in the future, to which I had agreed, but his frequent hesitations of speech indicated he had some trepidations in asking for that assistance. So I assured him I was glad to help. But Sensei was never in a rush. As my assurances echoed off of the *shoji*, he swept some crumbs off of his *yukata*, scratched his head, and then sipped slowly from his teacup. Almost as if he wanted to be sure of my own proposition to assist him.

"Yu-san, it is rather sad to admit this … " Pause, sip. "But the days of my own lengthy travels are, well, shall we say, virtually over. Yes, in my youth I could be quite the … jetsetter? Is that the term?" I nodded. "*So desu-ne* … Yes, I did love to travel back in the early days. But now, I get headaches on airplanes, and can never sleep properly. And the jet lag."

I remember thinking he seemed to be stalling. He straightened a few papers on the table and wiped his brow with a handkerchief. "*So desu-ne*," he mumbled once more. "What I mean to say is … there is a certain item that I have been after for some time now, and it is presently being made available, if you understand. However, it is of such value that I would wish to have a … trusted friend collect the item and bring it to me. Formerly, I have had various assistants for such matters, but lately I have had some … disagreements? In any case, my former assistant is no longer someone whom I can trust in such matters. And … well, you see. I need to … train another helper. A *kohai*, if you will." He looked up at me. As he spoke, I thought of words rolling around in his mouth like rough stones in a rock tumbler. He looked everywhere but at me—the ground, the window, the ceiling. This articulate and eminently cool customer was suddenly jumpy about his impetuous proposal, so I let him off the hook.

I wondered about the former subordinate and under what circumstances he had been dismissed—or had left of his own accord. And I believe I even wondered if he was referring to Miyamoto. "Are you asking if I might be willing to act as your assistant in this case?"

He smiled and understood my generosity in relieving him with this comment. “That is precisely what I am asking.”

We spoke at some length about his plans for me. The “item,” which he preferred to keep unidentified for the moment, was in the hands of the widow of a wealthy real estate mogul in the Philippines, who lived in a suburb outside of Manila. Sensei explained that this Filipino collector had been a bit of a rival over the years. They had tried to outbid one another for various objects of common interest, as he put it, and in the case of this particular item, the rival had won out. That had been back in the early ’70s, over twenty years ago. Now that his rival, one Jun Escobar, was dead, the widow was making available certain unique items through the regular channels for such transactions in East Asia. In this case, the channel was a prestigious auction house located in the “Wall Street” of Manila—Ayala Avenue—just down from the Makati Stock Exchange and Makati Avenue.

I decided to see how he would detail his proposition, so for the moment I behaved as Japanese as I could and allowed my elder to speak. I sipped some tea, rubbed my temples, and tried to be as cool a customer as he was.

“Yu-san, I would like for you to do me this favor. In these cases, as my official agent in such a transaction, I can assure you, all travels and accommodations are … quite comfortable. Everything would be provided for you, first class, of course, including the air travel. Champagne upon take off, if you like!” He smiled obliquely.

To an Indiana boy, his talk of first-class accommodations was working its intended magic. I thought of wide, soft leather seats, a tray of cheese, and a cold carafe of dry white wine, served by beautiful stewardesses with silky black hair and inviting dark eyes. Then a limo whisking me off to a luxury high-rise hotel, and me overlooking the twinkling lights of Manila from the balcony of some presidential suite. "I think I could agree to help you with that, Sensei," I said. "But when would I need to go? I would need to make accommodations for my classes, of course."

"Now, first of all, at present, no immediate ... deal has been struck. However, I am extremely eager to gain possession of this item. And should I manage to do so, I would like to have the object hand-carried back into Japan, as soon as possible." He hesitated again. "And so, if I manage to do this, Yu-san—would you be willing to fly to Manila on my behalf? As soon as next week, or the week after, perhaps?" And he smiled and cocked his head to the side like a curious bird.

I mimicked his shy humor. "I think I could make that sacrifice, Sensei." But, in fact, the sudden challenge of making the trip unnerved me. The thought of visiting the Philippines had only crossed my mind once or twice. It seemed an exotic place with swaying palm trees and rumbling volcanoes. I had also heard about the Marxist guerrillas from the southern islands, the endless streets of abject poverty and filth, and the political instabilities of a nation on the brink of civil war. Still, I was sick of cold weather, and the idea of feeling the balmy sun on my face was enticing. And so I agreed to act, as Sensei had put it, as his "agent" in this matter of the mysterious item.

Within days, I received a phone call from Miyamoto. He was tense, and his voice, too hard-edged for a polite Japanese colleague, betrayed his unhappiness. "The trip to Manila is scheduled, sensei." His message was clipped, his tone altogether unpleasant. So what else is new? "Your tickets and other necessary instructions will be delivered later today," he said before hanging up.

So in the middle of February 1993, I made my first trip out of Japan since my arrival almost a year earlier. I flew first class and was picked up by a limousine service at the airport and delivered to one of the top hotels in the center of Makati. The streets surrounding my hotel were impressive, redolent with wealth both old and new. With a little extra time, I toured the palace where the Marcos regime reigned before they got the boot in 1986. The legends of Imelda's thousands of shoes were true; her dictatorial excess still on full display. I remember thinking those shoes—shoes of every kind and color, all displayed on shelf after shelf, room after room—were evidence of a different kind of collector, one of an obsessive and even creepy nature. Shaking off thoughts of Imelda Marcos, I continued exploring and eventually stumbled on a club near the hotel where a New Orleans native played the piano like Jelly Roll Morton on Valium—frenzied, incisive, yet somehow just passive enough for the "cool" crowd. Drinks were twelve bucks a piece.

The business side of the trip was straightforward and required only two hours out of the seven days I spent down there. An arrangement had been made for me to meet the middleman, by the name of Aguinaldo, at his tiny, disheveled antique shop not far from the hotel. He had been able to acquire the rights to peddle the object, whatever it was, for a healthy commission. I walked into the shop early one morning, and found him in the back room, with his feet up on a cluttered desk, smoking a foul-smelling cigar. He begrudgingly came out, leaving his cigar smoldering in a half-full ashtray. I introduced myself, clasped his sweaty hand, and immediately disliked him. After a few pleasantries, we got down to business.

"The item is in my safe. Has the professor explained the procedures?"

"Yes. I think it is all in order, yes?"

Then he snapped at me. "Well, to tell the truth, not really. The payment is not yet received. I phoned the bank at the end of business yesterday, and it was nowhere to be seen!" His face was almost comically contorted in mock alarm.

"Well … I know that Professor Goto wants the item very much. And I believe he is … able to raise the amount rather easily."

"Yes, Mr. Springs. You do not need to tell me this. Nevertheless, until we can confirm the transaction with the bank, I cannot turn over the property."

We returned to his back office and he seated himself, smoking away at the still-lit cigar, ill-mannered and grouchy. Eventually, he pointed me to a straight-back chair, then lifted his feet back onto his desk, leaned back, and glowered at me. The wallpaper was a sickly yellow from his persistent smoking, and I wondered about the tarry effects on whatever valuable objects he stored nearby.

"Can you phone the bank again, please, Mr. Aguinaldo?"

His face took on a reddish tint, and for a long moment he scowled at me as I sat in silence, waiting for him to blow like Melville's mighty whale. The humidity was climbing, and I found his company tiresome and unpleasant and his office even more so. So I tried a new tactic.

"Can you show me the item?"

This question made him even more ridiculously outraged by my presence. "The professor has told me that under no circumstances should I do so! Once the money has been transferred, and I have confirmation, I can release the book—it is already wrapped in several layers of protective brown paper. The transfer *must* be confirmed, at which time I can allow you to take possession of the volume."

He was very insistent about these matters, and repetitive. But a tiny detail had slipped out in this last remark: it was a book of some sort. Meanwhile, a plump vein popped out on the side of his forehead. I imagined counting his pulse by its tiny palpitations. We continued fuming in silence, sweating and staring at each other in his sleazy office.

Finally, inexplicably, and without warning, he picked up the aging rotary phone, dialed it, spoke rapidly in a native Tagalog dialect. He was quiet a moment, presumably waiting for confirmation, then slammed the receiver down with gusto. A moment passed. He rubbed his ear. Then, abruptly he stood, his back to me, opened his safe, pulled out the package, then shut the heavy door quickly as if I might reach in and scoop up all his valuables. He turned, handed me the package, and waved me away like I was a noisome fly. I said a hurried goodbye and got the hell out of there.

Two days later, I left Manila, never to return. At the Osaka Airport, I had to fill out a customs form. Technically, I knew I should report bringing into Japan something of great value, but, I had no idea what was in the package or how much it was worth. This lack of knowledge was strategically a very good thing, at least from Sensei's point of view. As I looked down at the customs form, pen in hand, I thought of the instructions he had given me before I left Kobe. "Yu-san, when you hand carry the item back through customs, it should remain wrapped, and I advise you to report that it has negligible value. The customs people will not question you on this." That was the first real hint that something was out of whack in all of this. The thing was, I just did not know the rules at that time. To be blunt, Sensei was simply asking me to obey orders and keep my big mouth shut—which is exactly what I did.

At the airport, I had only an expensive-looking Cross briefcase—provided by Sensei, and containing the mysterious volume—and my carry-on bag, a very cheap looking canvas roll-around that I had scored at a discount store in Umeda. It was a contrast that suddenly seemed to me to be obvious and suspicious. The good news was that I was indeed an American citizen, still highly favored in the eyes of the Japanese bureaucracy, so I was basically waved through, no questions asked—except for one. "Do you have anything to declare?" I hesitated just momentarily, then shook my head. He seemed to find my response dubious, but waved me forward.

There is a grainy and subdued image in my mind, as if I am looking down on myself from a security camera. I see a man who looks nervous, ill at ease, *guilty*. I remember being slightly relieved that the Japanese immigration agent was a scrawny kid who looked young enough to be one of my students and that he didn't have the foggiest notion that my briefcase contained a book valued at tens of thousands of dollars, or more. Breathing more easily because of the agent's youth or not, I was smuggling a valuable item into his country and was the sly and willing agent of an unseen powerful engine of deception. I was flush with both excitement and shame, and the image in my memory features a tiny drop of perspiration sliding down my forehead, ready to plop onto my passport as it is being stamped for reentry. At the time, the episode took on the shading of a sinister act involving illegal motivations and mysterious acquisitions, like a scene gone stale in an old spy novel.

In retrospect, however, it was no big deal at all. Veteran travelers do it all the time; they neglect to report their acquisitions abroad to the glum agents that greet them accusingly at international airports. Still, this first instance of tacit deception made me very uncomfortable. I felt presumed upon by my *sempai*, my teacher, and, to be honest, slightly betrayed.

友

The unwrapping of the mysterious volume, and the storm of confusion it unleashed in my own mind about things I had simply never thought much about, occurred on the first Sunday after my return to Kobe.

I presented the book to Sensei, still safe in its brown paper wrappings. He hesitated a moment, handed me another pair of those fine white linen gloves that he preferred for the inspection of old relics, and began pulling on a pair himself. Properly gloved, he then slowly unwrapped his prize. Sensei removed the paper as tenderly as a nervous bridegroom would disrobe his virgin bride, eliminating each layer of clothing, quietly and deliberately, lingering in anticipation.

It was a very old volume, and it took a moment before I realized it was another copy of *Moby-Dick*, evidently a first edition, meaning it would be worth somewhere in the neighborhood of $50,000—or more. Again Sensei picked up the moldering volume, hesitated, then carefully handed it across the table to me, with both hands. "Please look at the inscription."

I slowly opened the book and on the front page, I saw the following alien-looking inscription:

Beneath four blood moons,
A whale circles Nippon;
April snow camellia
—Ezra Pound, January 1916

I handed the volume back to him. "What do you make of the writing, Sensei?" A gloved thumb stroked the cover, and for a moment, he ignored my question. Finally, he spoke.

"This is something I have wished to own for many years, Yu-san. It is far more valuable than you might imagine, and, in fact, it holds the key to a mystery I have attempted to solve for many years. Of course, it is written in a first edition of the novel, which must seem amazing to the untrained eye. As with the other crucial details of *Moby-Dick*, however, Americans would overlook the true value of the book."

He still gazed at the inscription, then reached for a pad of paper and a pen, and scribbled down what he saw written there. Then he showed me the copy. "Here is the real prize; not simply because it is a first edition, of which I have another. No, this one is much more marvelous. The inscription is the handwriting of the previous owner, twice removed. I attempted to purchase this volume in 1972, over twenty years ago. It was placed up for sale by the widow of another previous owner, a couple years after his death. My rival collector, Jun Escobar from Manila, a true

Melville fanatic, swept in and cut me off. Now, finally, I have managed to take back this great prize!" He genuinely beamed at this sudden realization.

I listened, captivated, as he continued his explanation. "You may be surprised to learn this, perhaps, but this edition of *Moby-Dick* was once owned by Ezra Pound. He was in fact nearly as obsessed with Melville's sea monster as Captain Ahab was. Pound was a devotee of Melville's symbolic fantasy, I believe, because it is the quintessential story of inscrutability. Such is the modern, existential dilemma. In any case, like Melville and Ahab, Pound wished to penetrate the veil and stand face to face before the sublime. And like Ahab, Pound had … imperial ambitions of his own!"

And then Sensei did something that had not happened prior to this visit, and rarely happened afterwards. He slid around the table and sat beside me, his right thigh pressed against my left one. He reached for the book and held it open to the inscription, so that we could inspect it together.

"It is a unique masterpiece in my collection," he said, with an air of reverence. And again he closed the book, delicately.

"The haiku unites the whale and the island; even before the American critics noted this duality, Pound understood Melville's device. It is a splendid revelation, I must say.

"Not long after he etched this inscription, Pound published some of his oddest and most memorable verse, some would say his masterpieces. He attempted to compress into the most succinct form in literature, the image, an account of sublime mystery. Japan, the whale, these were also, for Pound, metaphors of this mystery, symbols of whatever the modern sensibility has let die. Pound sought an emotional intensity in a highly compressed form, a sort of fusing force. And he came to believe that it was the same burden of *Moby-Dick*, that this 'fusing force,' was really the ultimate purpose of all art and literature!" He paused, reflecting. "It is the only volume of Pound's library that is known to contain a haiku that he wrote himself."

Sensei now seemed satisfied with his oration, and leaned back on his left elbow, a boyish posture of relaxation that he had also never taken with me. He spied me coyly out of the corner of his eye. "And so what can you add to my analysis?"

"It is an ... unorthodox account of modern poetry, Sensei—as you know." I rubbed my temple. "And what's with the blood moons? From Joel?"

"Joel?" he asked. I think, for one of the only times in our relationship, I may have known something Sensei did not already know.

"Sure. The blood moons—from the Book of Joel in the Old Testament." And I could have said more, about the last days and so on—but refrained, worried about sounding like a whack job.

"Ahh! Joel, indeed!" But he actually seemed unacquainted with that section of the Bible, so I dropped it. Yet I could tell it piqued his interest. There was something behind Sensei's obsession, for the thing for which the symbols stood, the something that remained unnamed and evasive, that was both uncanny and exhilarating. Still, I let his unfamiliarity with Joel hang fire, and never did answer it. And yet I lacked whatever self-control was needed to resist becoming possessed of its enchantments, potentially deadly or violent though they might be. In short, from that day on, I was hooked.

After our study of Pound's volume, Sensei placed it into one of his green library boxes and carried it safely into the adjoining room, where he evidently kept his valuables. I knew it was nearby, if not right next door, because he was able to leave and return so quickly with his treasures. I sometimes heard him shuffling around just beyond the wall to my right. In fact, it was rather pleasant, to sit there and know that untold treasures were carefully indexed and stored in the room thirty or so feet away from me. Perhaps this old house contained more valuables than any storeroom at the Beinecke Library at Yale, or even the Lilly Library back in Bloomington.

When he returned, the seminar began again in earnest. "Yu-san, my gracious thanks for your help with the old book." Suddenly, after our initial rush, the precious antique was now just another "old book." "You have shown yourself to be a most worthy assistant, for which I am very grateful. And now, let us talk about your contribution to the study of the great authors, shall we?"

友

For this visit, Sensei had prepared by bringing out a number of library holding boxes and several reference volumes. These were already marked with Post-it notes. And there was my dissertation, squarely on the side table with the other materials. It looked like we were in for some serious work.

He pulled out the copy of my dissertation, marked generously with the accusatory yellow notes. "You have been a loyal helper. In fact, your loyalties inspire me to take you even deeper into the … shall we say, hidden treasures of my collection?" He even laughed at this, even if just slightly. "I think it is time to discuss some matters of history regarding young Hemingway. You see, the biographers have been quite mistaken about certain historical accounts of several matters.

"I'm afraid that you have also been tricked by these many false reports, Yu-san. This is a common occurrence in matters of biographical accounts. Surely you noticed this in your own work on Mark Twain, a well-known liar about his past adventures. Or should we say a teller of tall tales? In any case, a major difficulty with someone like Twain is learning to listen carefully enough to know when he is telling the truth, and when he is pulling your leg." He paused for a long sip. "Yes, the great authors are often notorious liars in real life!"

Another sip. "Hemingway, of course, has much in common with Mark Twain. He once famously had one of his characters say that all American literature began with Mark Twain's little book on Huckleberry Finn, something like that. Both of them were great tricksters, and so, it is quite easy to be led astray by the likes of Twain or Hemingway. One unfortunate result is that many errors of historical fact have been repeated by biographers of these two writers, and so most accounts are at least partially unreliable. Both authors often made up stories about themselves, or else they remembered things quite differently thirty or forty years after the fact. This is true for all of us." When he looked at me now, I think he discerned my disagreement, or my skepticism about the misleading content of the standard literary biographies.

"Perhaps I need to illustrate this, yes?" He opened my dissertation to one of the marked passages, and read to me from my own writing:

"The great disappointment of the Paris years involved the tragic loss of many manuscripts in winter of 1922. Hemingway's wife, Hadley, was preparing to join him in Austria, where he was on holiday for snow skiing. And so she gathered up all of his writing and put it together in an old, small valise that was useful for such a purpose. The valise contained everything—manuscripts of all of Hemingway's stories, various sketches of Paris in the 1920s, including the famous 'Six True Sentences,' several poems, and possibly the beginnings of a novel set in Chicago during World War I, along with their only carbon copies.

"On December 2, 1922, Hadley took a cab to the Gare de Lyon in Paris, and had her luggage taken to the platform and placed within the train. She went off in search of some Evian water for the long trip, and when she returned, the valise with the manuscripts was gone, although the other luggage had been left behind. Hadley was left in tears and desolation, and had to report the theft to Hemingway the next morning. His response was almost cataclysmic; he immediately boarded a night train back to Paris, arriving there the next day. Hemingway searched in vain for the manuscripts in the apartment, went to the Lost and Found at the train station, put an ad in the newspapers for a reward for the return of the manuscripts, and then in near suicidal despair did something that was too horrible for him to describe in his autobiographical accounts of these events. Perhaps, as some surmise, he got drunk and visited a prostitute. Perhaps he even held a gun to his head and nearly committed suicide. In any event, the loss of the manuscripts has attained a level of mythology in the study of the Paris years of the young Hemingway."

Sensei now closed the book, sliding it across the table towards me again. I picked it up, held it in my hands for the first time in a while. Hearing my somewhat plodding graduate school prose being read to me aloud made me cringe. "It sounds a lot like a graduate student, yes, Sensei?" I asked.

"Well, in fact, it does not. You write a crisp prose, Yu-san. I hope you will manage to keep from spoiling that. But the style is not the issue at all. Your account of those events is predictable enough. But allow me to ask a few minor questions about this story, *ne*?" I nodded my consent.

"Why would a thief take only a small valise, when there are other larger pieces of luggage?"

"I had wondered about that myself. I suppose due to the weight of the other pieces, and just wanting to get away less conspicuously?"

He smiled my way. "Yes, perhaps. What about the advertisement in the Paris newspapers? Have you seen this ad yourself?"

I shook my head no.

He nodded. "And what about the night train back to Paris? Can you tell me the specifics of that trip? Which train did he take? Or, why did his friends Jack Hickok and Lincoln Steffens visit the Lost and Found a few days later, if Hemingway did so himself?"

I now had a look of confusion, and said, "Sensei, I don't know about Hickok and Steffens. As for the train, well, no, I can't give any specifics, of course. But these are all facts from the biographies, generally speaking."

"Not facts, Yu-san. These are simply the commonplace details of the biographies. Actually, I will say that these literary legends commonly develop over time. And surely you know who was the greatest artist of the Hemingway myth, yes?"

"Hemingway?"

"Precisely."

Now another long break, for sipping tea and for me to turn these ideas over in my mind. After some time, Sensei continued.

"Some of the biographers have lately begun to realize what Carlos Baker had been saying for many years, namely that decades later, Hemingway himself would turn the story of the stolen manuscripts into a tragic moment in his young life in Paris, a tragedy whose pain was nearly unbearable. Poor Hemingway, the tragic hero-writer of Paris! It was a tempting opportunity for Hemingway to generate pity for himself. He could help generate the mythic elements by which the very greatest writers should be remembered by their followers."

"And so, according to your theory, these events never actually occurred? If so, how could one go about showing this theory to be true?"

"Oh, yes, some of those events did, in fact, occur, Yu-san. The valise containing certain manuscripts was taken to the trains by Hadley, and it was promptly carried off, perhaps even stolen by one of the many petty thieves who lurk about the Paris stations. Or perhaps," he smiled, "that valise was the object of some other person's attention."

I looked at him, puzzled. "Well, maybe it was. But how could we ever know if that were the case?"

"Yes, how could we know?" He was in his element, a

long-time professor teasing the truth out of his curious student. He was in no hurry to divulge his secrets.

But I was getting a little tired of the game, and wanted a direct answer. So I asked for one. "You expect me to believe that all the biographers are wrong, and that you alone have discerned the truth? Sounds a bit shady to me, Sensei." I smiled as I said this, but I meant it.

He was polite despite my cocky tone, but he managed to remain evasive. "Yu-san, you still misunderstand a little, and sound a bit naïve as well. Allow me to explain a few things, first. I must remind you again that a person with true devotion, time, and money can arrange almost any kind of acquisition, or find almost any information. Sometimes it means that one must be willing to … to make certain decisions, or request certain acts, that are not always … how can I put it? Not always acceptable under normal circumstances." He wiped his forehead with a napkin. "If you wish to say that the ends justify the means, then by all means, do say that."

I looked him in the eye at this. Was he making some sort of confession? I thought of my trip to Manila. Was it part of certain decisions or acts in which the ends justified the means?

"But if you must know. Yes, Yu-san. I, too, have stooped low, in order to find out things about authors that I have wished to discover. It became a kind of obsession for me at one period in my life to discover secret things that nobody knew—except me. And I have also done things, or more accurately arranged to have done on my behalf, acts that were—what shall we say?—somewhat outside the blurry lines of human ethics, not to mention the rule of law?"

He regarded me with a precocious grin and must have noticed the quizzical look in my eye. "Yes, I am admitting this to you now, because for a long time I have wished that you would know what kind of person I truly am, and have been. I have felt some guilt about many of these matters, in fact. Perhaps you feel that guilt somewhat yourself, Yu-san? There is a kind of voyeuristic thrill, isn't there, when you find something in an archive that nobody else has ever noticed? Isn't there a bit of a seductive pleasure, when reading the private thoughts of an author, concealed in a diary, or a notebook, thoughts never meant to be seen by another human's eyes? Surely you know this erotic feeling, yes?"

A long pause ensued as Sensei sipped more tea, and ate more *sembei*. Then he delicately unwrapped a fine piece of Swiss chocolate, popping it into his mouth, and closed his eyes. I was almost stunned by his frank intimation of acts that were immoral, if not illegal, in attaining these kinds of literary treasures. But it was hard for me to think about how to broach such a topic. So instead I said, "In your wide experience, Sensei, where *do* we draw the line in terms of the ethics of collecting and examination? Is all fair in love and war, or something like that? Because *that* sounds a little naïve to me!" As soon as the words were out of my mouth, I knew I was dangerously close to crossing some unseen line in our relationship.

He glowered at me a moment. Tensions were rising, if only slightly. He held the chocolate in one side of his mouth. "Yu-san," he began, emotionlessly, "I had thought that you would feel flattered to be the first one to hear of all these new discoveries, besides Mika, of course. I can handle some skepticism—we are both scholars, and trained to think this way. But I would have also thought that you might have some faith in me as well."

Now he waited, allowing some moments to settle us both down. "Please excuse me for challenging you," I said.

"I expect to be challenged, Yu-san. But I require your respect as well, and your patience. And I must tell the story in my own way. I assure you, all my evidence is at hand, and within these walls. All your questions will be addressed, I promise."

He brushed his hands together, and looked from side to side. Then he headed off into uncharted waters, one of his habits that often infuriated me. "Now. Do you know the story of the old Boston sea captain who retired to live out his last years in Florence? He was, of all things, a passionate devotee of Percy Shelley, whom he believed to be the greatest poet of all time, a romantic bard who delivered the dictations of the gods, as he saw it. This salty, old captain was rather obsessive in his great devotions, you see. It was in the 1870s, I believe." He talked slowly while still working the chocolate around in his mouth as it melted, covering his mouth with his right hand in the Japanese style. Finally, he swallowed the remnants of the candy.

"Well, the story goes that this sea captain discovered that an elderly lady, once intimate with Lord Byron, was living in a villa nearby, just on the other side of a door he passed almost daily. Through the grapevine he learned that this old lady held a large cache of papers from both Shelley and Byron: letters, old drafts of poems, perhaps even unknown diaries and journals. Well, the captain made it his mission in life to bring these papers to light, and to secure for himself a place in literary history. So he disguised his purposes and approached the woman about renting rooms in her large, mostly empty villa. Do you know of this old tale?"

I shook my head no. He wiped his hands on a napkin, and sipped still more tea. "History does not tell us whether this old captain ever succeeded or not. His name was Silsbee, by the way, and he had been a proper New England man for most of his life. The woman was called Claire, an old lover of Byron's, advanced in age, who lived in the Via Romana in the middle of Florence in a dilapidated building from the Renaissance. Captain Silsbee became excited to think that, everyday as he walked by her building, hidden behind its mossy walls was a woman whose lips had pressed the face of Lord Byron, and whose ears had listened with rapt attention to the voices of the other great British poets of Byron's time. It was indeed a heady brew of temptation. Can you forgive old Captain Silsbee for trying to communicate with this legendary figure, Yu-san?

"Sadly, we do not know to what extremes Silsbee was willing to go. What we do know is that he was hypnotized by the idea of holding in his hands the old letters of the dead poet. He was tempted by the very same things that tempt both you and me. And sometimes, in being tempted," he said, as he brushed some crumbs off of his robe, "we do things that other people consider improper, or not quite ethical. Yes, I would admit to that. But wouldn't you agree that the world deserves to see any letters and diaries of Shelley that remain to be discovered? In this case, don't the ends of literary knowledge and wisdom overcome any questionable means of producing them?"

With this Sensei got to his feet and slowly worked his way to the hallway and then toward the back of the house. Several minutes later he returned with an old book, which he handed to me. "This is for you. Perhaps it will help you to understand my own obsessions on these points." He smiled in saying "obsessions," in a kind of ironic joke to himself. I looked at the volume. *The Complete Tales of Henry James, Volume 6: 1884-1888* was on the binding. It was musty and weathered, and from the looks of it, came from the 1950s or '60s, or thereabouts.

I leafed through it. "James, huh? To tell you the truth, he was never one of my favorites."

This also amused Sensei. "I felt exactly the same—that is, when I was younger, like you. But James is one of those acquired tastes, I think. Like fine wine, he improves with age. When you get to be my age, perhaps your view of Henry James will change.

"In any event, I must insist that you take this and read it. I assume you have not read *The Aspern Papers*, then?" He took the book back, and began looking through it. There were faded pencil markings in the margins, and evidently he had a particular passage in mind. "Ah yes. Anyway, this is the story James wrote after he had heard the tale of our Captain Silsbee from Boston. He was so intrigued that it became the germ for what I think is one of James's most perfect fictions. He invented a dashing romantic poet, Jeffrey Aspern, to be the principal subject of admiration for the story's nameless narrator, who would do almost anything, or even perhaps die, for the joy of discovering new manuscripts by his idol. I know of no other story that captures both the joys and the horrors of this sort of literary fascination—perhaps a kind of mania—for collecting."

He looked at a marked passage, studying it for a moment. "James captured perfectly the feelings of grandeur about literary relics, and he knew the moral qualms that one might have about doing whatever it takes to find and secure those relics. James understood the, shall we say, narcotic effect of collecting. But perhaps you do not quite understand, Yu-san."

Sensei closed the book, offered it to me with both hands, and regarded me intently. "You see, these writers are for me like gods. And their papers are like relics of their greatness, even those they wished to burn. Yes, it is a kind of lifelong infatuation. But as James says so truthfully, I really have no need to try and defend this position. It is for me very much like a kind of religion, you see." He was now looking me dead in the eye, almost rapturous.

I smiled just a fraction, which Sensei must have caught. He smiled right back, in that funny, enigmatic Japanese way of his. Then after a moment his smile vanished, and he added, "Does it all sound so funny to you? If so, it only means that you have not fallen completely under the spell of the narcotic. However, one day you may very well find that you are like me and like Captain Silsbee, and even like Ahab." He paused and then added, "Yes, just three old sea captains, drifting about on the oceans of our lengthy days, searching for the words of life by which we might be saved." He stood, and bowed. "Please excuse me for now, Yu-san. The time has gotten away from me, and I must deal with other matters just now." He began backing himself ceremoniously from the room.

The idea of becoming like old Silsbee, run aground in Florence in the 1870s and looking for an anchorage, was sobering, but my mind was churning away at the enigmas surrounding Hemingway's early manuscripts. I nearly fainted when he said he had to leave. "Sensei, you must finish telling me about Hemingway."

"Yes, well, of course. Next time. And you will read the stories by James?"

"Yes, of course, but—"

"Then perhaps we can discuss them as well—next time." He turned his head slightly to check the large clock on one of the bookshelves behind him. "Yes, James does tend to grow in stature as time ticks away. But all that is for another day, I think."

I now stood up as well.

"Let's continue with that story next time. It hinges on Pound, and my rather odd conversations with him near the end of his life."

"What?! You met Ezra Pound?"

He smiled at my outburst. "Why yes, Yu-san. I have suggested to you repeatedly, the magic that money is capable of performing. I think you should have suspected that a man of my means and passions would have arranged meetings with many of the great writers of my lifetime. In fact, besides Pound, I have visited with the likes of Robert Frost, Pearl Buck, John Steinbeck. I spoke with T.S. Eliot in London after a lecture he gave, and bought him a drink afterwards as we discussed the Marx Brothers, of all things. In fact, I attended his memorial service in Westminster Abbey. That's where I first laid eyes on Pound, who also attended, though I did not meet him until a few years later, in Italy. Sadly, I never met Hemingway," he said, shaking his head in disappointment. "It was not for lack of trying, I can assure you. But by the time I became truly serious about such things, he was in great decline and hard to pin down." He paused and his gaze clouded. Then he looked up at me. "But I did manage to meet Hadley and had a very pleasant afternoon chatting with her, up in New Hampshire."

He was momentarily inspired to continue when he detected my wide-eyed amazement at these last revelations.

"Yes, Yu-san. Hemingway's first wife. And I also made up for my failure to shake hands with Hemingway by meeting many others. I had lunch with Dorothy Parker, whose booming voice actually scared me a little. She was a formidable figure indeed. I even met Alfred Hitchcock. He attended a reception I gave for an artist friend. I can still picture the room—one of those over-decorated ballrooms at the Bel Air Hotel, in Los Angeles. It was back when the Japanese were still not welcome in good society. I believe it was only my wealth that enabled many of the Americans I met to overlook my heritage."

My jaw must have been hanging open because he chuckled. "Do you find all of this so hard to believe, Yu-san? These are just people, like you and me. And I must admit I was always drawn, at least in my younger days, to glamour and celebrity. I was stargazing, yes, it's true! You see, money, to be crass, opens almost any door in life, and I was not above using it for just that purpose." He enjoyed the moment, though it was in the form of a confession.

He checked his wristwatch once again. "Now, I must be rushing off. But believe me, my knowledge comes directly from the lips—and documents—of Ezra Pound."

"You actually met him." I could hear the childish awe in my voice.

"Twice, in fact. Or at least some distant part of him. I can assure you that by that time in his life, he was a rather distraught and bewildering figure. He was old, dying, and largely in another world psychologically, I would say, and had gone many years barely speaking to anyone. But it was Pound all right."

He was finding his shoes, and putting on his coat, with me trailing behind him. Mika stood in another doorway, watching us both with great curiosity.

"It was in Venice, 1967. He'd been out of the St. Elizabeth mental asylum for about a decade by then. But forced incarceration takes its toll. He rarely spoke, as I said, and was living with an old friend, Olga Rudge, a violinist. She owned a decrepit old villa in the San Gregorio section of Venice, not far from the train station. Perhaps my remarks are unkind, for he was gracious enough in talking with me, and about certain things, his mind was clear and sharp as ever. He knew all about Paris in 1922, for example, even if he could not recall what he had for lunch that day!"

He was ready now and heading out the door. I couldn't believe he would leave me hanging like this. But in a flash, he had vanished into the back seat of his Mercedes, with the silent Omori at the wheel, and then they were gone. I moved as if in a dream, and soon realized I was halfway down the hill heading toward the train station, and wondering how I would manage until our next meeting.

友

These were shocking revelations, to be sure. Regarding the biographies of famous figures, I can verify that certain legends are repeated endlessly as facts—scholars obviously depend on the work of earlier scholars, creating a sort of echo chamber of received wisdom with much of it rarely, if ever, called into question.

I put down Jack's pages, stood to stretch my back, and looked out the window at the barren trees in the courtyard beyond my office. It was darkening, and I thought perhaps I should head home to finish the manuscript in front of a warm fireplace. The sun was disappearing and the moon rising, both suspended in the frosty air.

Like everything else, people are born and they die. Lives—even extraordinary ones—are fragile things fraught with everyday conceits and frailties. Regarding Twain and Hemingway, it is well known that they both worked diligently to establish and shape their own legends. These were obsessive personalities who cared deeply what others thought about them, and so they worried over and tended to their own legacies.

I know far less about Ezra Pound—though I do recall he is said to have rarely, if ever, spoken during and after his time at the asylum. What a sad depiction of the once great mind that in those final years of his life he was reduced to a mere shadow of his former self. And yet, I find it difficult to muster much sympathy for this forlorn character, a traitor, in fact. He is a hard person for me to like. His devotion to Mussolini, his subsequent condemnation for the United States, and his blasting of Jews, especially bankers, all well documented in his countless radio broadcasts during WW II, turned him into an enemy of the state—and a bit of a clown. After a brief stay in a military prison near Pisa, he was shipped home and then confined to a facility for the insane outside of Washington D.C. for over twelve years. Though publicly he recanted many of his hideous beliefs, privately he maintained a hateful prejudice and a gargantuan, imperial conceit.

Reading this account of Professor Goto's supposed meetings with Pound, I admit I was deeply skeptical. And yet, like Jack, I could hardly wait to hear the rest of the tale.

Chapter 9

Sensei sent word (through my nemesis) that he must be out of town for awhile, and that our meetings would need to be postponed, so the next few weeks crawled by—long, dreary conversation lessons littered with bad grammar and unread assignments. I did manage some time in the library, rooting around to discover what I could about Pound's final years in Italy.

I killed some of my free time by taking walks, reading, and doing a bit of writing of my own. And one Friday night, I went out for drinks and dinner with my old buddies from the introductory Japanese class. We met downtown, at our old stomping grounds near glittery Sannomiya station in Kobe, and haunted the back alleyways in search of the best *sake*, *gyoza*, or *yakisoba*. I had become a connoisseur of *gyoza*, small fried pork dumplings, a staple of late-night pub grub throughout Japan, and was eager to share my expertise.

Predictably, we ended up in one of the gaudy karaoke parlors, drinking pitchers of beer and taking turns belting out old tunes by the Beatles, Motown, Elton John, Rod

Stewart, or Frank Sinatra, howling slightly off-key into microphones that often screeched and popped with feedback. Of these old friends, my favorite was Richard, who announced that his three-year commitment was up, he would not be renewing, and that he was heading back to the UK. He missed his "Mummy's shepherd's pie," he explained.

He had been downing beers for a couple of hours, and spoke passionately into the microphone that he was officially tired of living in Japan, disliked being a mere "Japan-hand," and desperately required a return, as he put it, to the "real world" of British wheeling and dealing with the Royal Bank of Scotland. He was sloppy drunk, and was actually swinging a bottle of Irish whiskey around like a flashlight, pointing it at us one by one as he spoke, so it was hard to tell at the time whether there was any truth to his confession. I only vaguely recalled Richard's announcement the next morning, severely dehydrated and with a blinding headache, and needed to confirm that it wasn't something I'd dreamed. So as soon as my headache subsided, which took a few days, I called him to find out. Yes, it was true, he reported. He would be leaving by the end of the month, and was holding a "sayonara sale" to unload everything he wasn't taking with him. Such sales were frequent occurrences in the *gaijin*-world of Japan business life and offered a last chance for those leaving to sell their stuff and for those left behind (like me) to find major bargains. For one thing, Japanese generally dislike used products, unlike their thrifty *gaijin* counterparts. As a result, it was usually Americans or other foreigners who swooped in to buy various household goods for pennies on the dollar.

So I went up to Richard's place to check it out. I knew my position at the university would not be renewed after the end of my contract and doubted I would stay in Japan even though there were other opportunities for well-connected *gaijin* English teachers. As a result, I only scooped up a stack of books and an old reading lamp for my desk. I headed for the door as other scavengers appeared, but just as I was saying so long, Richard stopped me.

"How 'bout my car, Jack?"

"Your car?" His remark caught me off guard.

"Well, we had some nice times with it, hey? And anyway, it's over four years old now, so nearly worthless to the Japanese. Anyhow, I only got a week to sell the damned thing. What of it, hey?"

I eyed him with some residual envy. Yes, I remembered sailing up long mountain passes into the Japan Alps, with "Dark Side of the Moon" blasting from the speakers. But I didn't have that kind of money. "Richard, that would be great, but I couldn't possibly pay you a fair price."

He eyed me right back. "Well, old mate, how does this sound, hey? If I can't sell it by next weekend, it's yours for whatever price you can hand me as I bolt for the airport. Nobody's even looked at it so far, and I'm so busy with everything else, well ... Can you think about it?"

For a moment, I hung fire; then relented. "OK, Richard. *If* you can't sell it. I'm sure someone will want it, though."

But the following Saturday morning, the phone rang at 7:00 a.m. "Hey, mate, you up?" Richard. "Meet me down here at my place at eight. The car's yours, hey? My flight's at three."

I got ready in a huff, hustled down to the train, stopping quickly at the bank to withdraw as much cash as I could afford (300,000 yen), and arrived at Richard's just past eight. The money was in a fancy envelope, Japanese style, and he didn't even look at it. He handed me the keys for the cash. "Thanks, mate, I owe you one. Enjoy the car. Papers are in the glove compartment. Decent deal, hey? Sorry to be so rushed, but I'm meeting someone in ten minutes. Can you give me a ride down the hill?" Which I did, depositing him at the arranged location, outside Sannomiya Station. He got out, then leaned into the window, and grasped my hand in farewell. "Thanks, old pal, we had some fine times, hey? Gotta run now. I have too much to do. Best wishes." And with this, he palmed his hands together and performed a small Japanese bow to me, both honorifically and comically. Then he was gone.

And that's how I ended up with such a fine ride in the Land of the Rising Sun. It was perfect for the American in me, and my spirits soared—temporarily, at least. After considerable searching, I finally secured a tiny parking spot a few blocks up the hill from my condo. I paid a hefty fee and the car spent most of its time squeezed into the small space, but on weekends, I would get up early on a Friday or Saturday morning, just as the sun peaked into my windows, make some strong coffee, and head out into parts unknown in my blazing Nissan, often with no map and no destination in mind. I'd throw in a change of clothes or a book I was reading, but a few times I just hit the road with a fresh steaming cup of coffee.

It was an inviting way to begin my days off—not knowing where I would be as the sun went down, and in fact not really caring very much. Typically, it was somewhere in the towering mountains of central Japan, which were always calling to me. Gasoline was expensive, but I had little else on which to spend my generous salary, and with nothing going on until my meetings with Sensei resumed,

I had no particular reasons to be back till Sunday evenings, or even early Monday mornings.

Finally I received word (again through my nemesis, Miyamoto) that I had been invited to spend the following Sunday afternoon with Sensei. Eager to hear more about the intrigues of Hemingway's manuscripts, what Pound had to do with any of it, and the tale of Sensei's encounter with Pound in Venice, I showed up early. I admit I was also eager to see Mika once again. But it was Omori who answered the door, and Omori who directed me into the room to wait for Sensei. He bowed, pointed, and left. Not seeing Mika's graceful movements, not watching the swinging curtain of her jet-black hair, not inhaling the aroma of her powdered skin—well, it was a major disappointment.

As I waited patiently in the sitting room, Sensei lingered for twenty minutes elsewhere. I fidgeted with my notebook, looked at the various books on the nearby tables, and thought sullenly about the absence of tea (and its server).

Finally he emerged, smiling and ready to talk. "So you wish to hear about Venice, yes?" He rubbed his hands together, and sat cross-legged, as alert as I ever recall seeing him. "Those were my glorious days, Yu-san, and so it is a pleasure to tell you about them. I was so young, and in good health. My job here at the university allowed me to do as I wished, and in 1966, I had arranged to be stationed in Freiburg, Germany for a year, as a visiting professor. I learned from a colleague there that an older professor in the French department had known Pound from the pre-war days, and still corresponded with him on rare occasions.

"I made it a point to get to know her, and we became rather friendly. She was an Alsatian French woman called

Hélène LeComte, obviously of fine breeding and magnificent natural beauty, though she was by then quite aged."

He remembered this unexpected good fortune now with a kind of bliss. "We became a bit of a pair as the year unfolded. Hélène was large, amiable, and liked to drink good whiskey. She also knew all the finest wineries in the region, especially in Alsace, just across the border in France. And a region in Germany called the *Kaiserstuhl*, near Breisach and the Rhein. She taught me how to taste wine, actually. Wonderful, white Burgundies, and crisp Rieslings and Pinot Gris. It was nothing romantic; she was already rather old. But she still had great charm and retained some of her youthful beauty. She showed me around town, and we took walks into the *Schwarzwald*. Many boat rides on the river. Yes, we were quite friendly." He took a moment, relishing images of dinner with Hélène, perhaps enjoying schnitzel and wine together at some outdoor café in the Schwabian Alps. "Honestly, I never understood what she saw in me! Yes, Yu-san, she must have been quite a beauty in her youth, before the War!" I could see that Sensei was still intrigued by her, and that he may have entertained a small crush on her back in the day.

"Finally she told me one day about Pound. I never asked, rather she just instinctively brought it up. She described her correspondence with him, and I asked her for more details. Suddenly one day, she showed me a few of Pound's letters. They were quirky, often incomprehensible, but also at times hilarious in that odd style of his. She offered to introduce me to him, and I managed to arrange, through her aid, a couple of interviews with him in Venice."

"But Sensei, I did some reading this past week, and some biographers describe Pound in those last years as unwilling to speak or be interviewed. Some make it sound like he was even demented, near the end."

He found this amusing. "Nonsense! Pound played his little games. These are all well documented. And he was wracked by guilt and shame for all his political mistakes. But his grasp of history and art was still monumental. He simply wished to choose when to speak and when not to. He was certainly clear and articulate whenever I spoke to him, I can assure you. After my visits, I heard he even welcomed Allen Ginsberg, who sang Hare Krishnas to him, smoked marijuana, and insisted that Pound listen to records by Bob Dylan and The Beatles. What a scene that must have been—it was at Pound's 82nd birthday party! Yes, he was all there."

I tried to picture Pound listening to Ginsberg's loud cries of ecstasy. "So what was he like? What did he say?" I was nearly panting with anticipation. I wasn't interested in any more stories of Hélène LeComte.

Sensei took his time, now recalling that first meeting over twenty-five years ago. He must have been himself a relatively young man—about forty-five, certainly no older—a rising literary scholar going to meet one of the most influential minds of the century.

"He wore an old black robe of some sort. Silk, probably. He spoke very little, but when he did, it was deliberate, often brilliant, with a kind of vocabulary that can only be described as wayward, weird, yet compelling. He could be extremely funny, then angry. Occasionally he made odd references to people like Cicero, or he would quote some obscure historical figure like Martin Van Buren, as if everyone should know all about him—it was all very off-putting. He made reference to obscure historical points, or esoteric poems I had never heard of. I believe he expected everyone else to be as brilliant as he was, and if not, then to hell with them." He smiled. "Very American, I remember thinking. But I had gone for a purpose, and that was all I cared about. It was still rather early in my career and, like our old Captain Silsbee, I knew precisely what I wanted."

"And what was that?"

He looked at me with some surprise. "Why, Hemingway's valise, of course!"

Sensei got to his feet, walked over to the corner of the room, near the alcove, and there he lifted up for me to see a small briefcase, yellowish and slightly soiled. It was one of those old style cases, covered in dyed leather, metal at the corners, and it had evidently seen some duties over the years. He looked at the case as he held it in both hands, then brought it to me, and graciously handed it down toward me. "Look inside," he told me. "Carefully!" And he handed me yet another pair of white gloves.

I opened the valise by snapping the locks holding down the top, and an earthy aroma, the smell of old books and library stacks, slightly damp and mildewy, rose to my nostrils. The first things I saw were two old, dog-eared manila folders, each holding a sheaf of paper, typewritten, and battered. And each folder had a penciled title: "Bread and Wine" on one. "Big Shoulders" on the other, thicker file. I gently pulled both folders out and opened the thicker one first. The top page, faded and dirty, was bundled together with forty or fifty pages. On the top page was typed:

"Big Shoulders"

by Ernest Hemingway

Barely breathing, I set that file down and opened the other one to reveal what appeared to be the first page of a story titled "Bread and Wine." I set it down and looked back in the valise to pull out several more old manuscripts. My heart thudded against my breastbone as I sat there stunned, confusion muddling my thoughts. This valise supposedly did not exist. It was like the jarring moment in Poe's tale, "The Purloined Letter." I suddenly realized that the object I had been searching for had been there in front of me, right in the room with me, all along.

I looked up at Sensei. My mouth was agape, in awe I guess, and I just shook my head, almost as a complaint, not really knowing what to say. Then, finally, "But ... how can this be?"

Sensei had been working on some rice crackers as he watched me open the case and examine its contents. His fingers fumbled with the plastic wrappings while studying me with his eagle-eyes. He was like an old grandfather, watching a child open a longed-for Christmas present, looking for the sheer joyfulness to take over the child's face. He seemed to savor the silence as I sat there, absolutely dumbfounded, still looking through the contents of what appeared to be Hemingway's valise, circa 1922, Paris, France.

"Yes, it is true, Yu-san. The valise does survive, along with its contents. You see it with your own eyes, yes? You hold its contents in your own hands. And the irony of all of this is that the biographers had the evidence available all along, but were simply not able to put the clues together because of the Hemingway myth. The myth tells us that all of his great early work was lost forever. And Hemingway played that myth for all it was worth."

"So he knew all along that the valise survived?"

"Well, that is one possibility. But I do not suspect that to be the case. It is well established, however, that Hemingway knew that some of his acquaintances wanted very much for him to destroy those early manuscripts. They felt that his simple tales of America, Chicago, fishing in Michigan, and so forth, represented an old-fashioned art. One person in particular was insistent about this, and felt that Ernest's youthful works were holding him back from becoming the true artist of the new style. This critic felt that such stories were not worthy of Ernest's talents and efforts. I have personally received evidence from this person, and can prove it is true: two letters from this most famous friend, stating these things very clearly."

"Which friend?"

He looked surprised. "Are you not able to guess, Yu-san? I am a bit disappointed, actually. It was Ezra Pound, of course!"

"Pound? Why would he care even the slightest about Hemingway's stories? I don't get it."

He was ready for my questions, and patiently opened one of the thick biographies he had set on the table earlier. James Mellow's *Hemingway: A Life Without Consequences*, complete with Post-it notes sticking out. Sensei turned it toward me and showed me a quote from Pound calling Hemingway's loss an "act of GAWD."

"But what does that prove?"

"In hindsight, everything. You see, Ezra thought of himself as God!"

I grimaced at his point. "That's it? Your theory is based on that?"

He found this amusing. "It is no theory, Yu-san."

I was getting irritable and called his bluff. "Sensei! Please finish the story!"

He chuckled, shaking his head at me slowly. "You

Americans! So impatient, and impertinent." He was pulling me along, playing with my short fuse, and enjoying every minute of it even though it was clear I wasn't enjoying it at all.

"Very well," he said finally, after eating yet another cracker. "It is quite simple, really. Pound thought Hemingway was stuck, his writing stale, and that he needed a fresh start. Hemingway obsessed over those old manuscripts. Pound had read it all, including the parts of the novel set in Chicago. He told Hem it was terrible; that he should put it aside. Pound emphasized that the true, the beautiful parts of the work would remain with him, that he would retain the valuable material in his mind and heart, that the essence and greatness was a part of him and would stay with him, but that he needed to look at it anew. But Hemingway was very obstinate, a stubborn young man. He wouldn't listen. Finally, Pound decided there was only one thing to do: destroy all the stories and old manuscripts himself. Which is precisely what he did. Well, he didn't destroy them, exactly, but he got them away from Hemingway, which was the whole point. With the help of a co-conspirator, Pound arranged for all of those materials to be gathered and placed in a small valise, ready for his select agent to take it all away at a moment's notice. And that is how it happened. It was an inside job, Yu-san!"

"Inside job?" This was too much. The story was getting stranger with every detail. "How could there be another person involved? How could this happen without Hadley knowing something about it? Anyway she's stated repeatedly that it was she who put all the materials into the valise. So your story falls apart, Sensei—" I stopped. "Wait. "Are you telling me…?"

He nodded, a wide smile spreading across his face. "Very good, Yu-san. You have just completed the circuit."

"Hadley was the other person?"

"Of course. It all makes perfect sense. Ezra Pound was such an impressive and charismatic mind, along with being one of the Hemingway's closest friends, that he was capable of convincing Hadley to do almost anything, so long as she felt that it might benefit Ernest. I finally saw the connection myself in the mid-1960s and the solution seemed obvious. It was Hadley and Pound all along, although it took several more years of investigating to lead me finally to the valise you now see on the table before you."

"But how could they keep it a secret all those years?"

"It was in everyone's best interests to keep the secret. Hemingway's volatile temper was of legendary proportions. And anyway, there's not much in there, as you can see for yourself. Hemingway invented the rest, all on his own, and there was little interference from the critics and the biographers. Like children, they just believed the stories that the great author told them." He paused and looked off into the distance. "Yes, they all just played along. Until I put it all together and confronted the main actors in the drama. You know, Yu-san, there is a wonderful moment in an old movie by your great director, John Ford. The movie is called *The Man Who Shot Liberty Valance*. It's about a man who becomes famous for shooting a dreaded criminal, although, in fact, he did not shoot him at all. At one point, a reporter says, 'When the legend becomes fact, print the legend.'"

I nodded as I ran my fingers across the case's worn leather. I knew the movie well and had watched it many times.

"Well, that is what happened with the story of

Hemingway's valise," Sensei continued. "The legend became the fact, and forever after people quit searching for the lost valise. Except that when I began looking through these materials in the years just after the War, I was not completely satisfied with the legend. I felt that there was something wrong about it, something missing. And as I have told you, I had considerable financial backing for whatever curiosities I might be interested in uncovering—this was my major vice in life, or at least one of them. And so I went after the materials with the help of private detectives and some other snoops I have worked with over the years. I was determined to find out if the legends were true or not. And what I discovered, that no one else had ever taken the time to find out about, was that there were a couple of people still alive who had different versions of the story to tell. But nobody had ever asked them the right questions about it, or if they had, they had never asked with large amounts of cash in their hand."

My eyebrows must have shot up. "You mean that you had somehow deduced that Pound still had Hemingway's old manuscripts?"

"I assumed at that time that he must still have them, or that he knew who did, or else that the papers had been lost for good, or burned, or were a fabrication from the beginning. Those were the possibilities, as I saw it at the time. Though I did, in fact, have an opinion. And I turned out to be correct."

I frowned. "What *was* your opinion?"

He took some time for dramatic effect. He brushed the crumbs off his robe and resettled himself on his cushion. "You see, Yu-san, my hunch was that there never was much of value in the valise. Or, rather, I believed that *if* there had been a valise, it probably contained a few minor items, but was never the great loss Hemingway made it out to be. And perhaps even Hemingway himself knew all along that he was playacting. Possibly he himself destroyed most of those early works, some night in a drunken rage. All in the service of enlarging his growing myth."

This made no sense. "But Sensei, you have this valise, and the manuscripts," I said, gesturing to them.

He smiled at this. "Forgive me for that slight prevarication, Yu-san. It was just a parlor trick. A trick, I should say, that I have long desired to play on someone just like yourself. Someone, that is, who could appreciate it for what it is."

I sat there gazing at him in confused silence. He waited me out, but I couldn't think of anything to say. So he continued. "It is indeed a valise of the style and color of the period, yes. It may even resemble the one that Hadley lost in the train station. I had one of my agents in Paris purchase several valises of the correct age and style as described to me by several eyewitnesses, including Hadley Hemingway. But no, the actual valise, I am afraid to say, has been lost or destroyed over the years. As for the contents. Yes, two of the documents you have just seen are in fact originals, and so far as I know, both unique and completely unknown to the world outside of these walls, at least since Pound died. And from everything I have been able to put together, they were both originally inside of the valise that night in 1922, when it was supposedly stolen in the Gare de Lyon in Paris. That much is true and not a trick at all."

"Sensei, I don't understand what you are telling me."

He had my full attention; he smiled, shook his head, and began his explanation. "As I said, it was Pound all along. He was confident that he knew what was best for Hemingway. Don't forget that he convinced T.S. Eliot to throw out huge sections of *The Waste Land.* Eliot's epic poem was the monumental achievement of the era, and Eliot was no fool—Pound was simply brilliant, and in full control. So Eliot listened to him—and, in fact, Pound was right. He considered himself right about everything, and he truly believed that he knew what was best for other people, besides Tom Eliot and Ernest Hemingway. He persuaded Hilda Doolittle to write poetry a certain way, and to change her identity to the more mysterious "H.D." He even dared lecture the great James Joyce on the art of writing fiction!

"Honestly, I was a bit embarrassed that the idea had never occurred to me before. Or to anyone else, evidently. Old Ezra was one of the great monomaniacs in American literary history, sort of a Rasputin figure, charismatic, even mesmerizing. That is why I compared him to Satan. His later, unfortunate history with Mussolini and the Fascists is a true indication of this rather sinister streak in his personality, I'm afraid."

We sat motionless for a moment as I waited for him to continue. He pulled to him another green library box, laid out beforehand so that he could have it handy for just this moment in the story. "There is more evidence, but before I show you, I will tell you about Venice. Finally, yes, Yu-san?" He shot me a smile, and I nodded, helplessly caught in his web of stories, no longer sure what to believe, what truly had happened or what was simply an old man spinning a tall tale.

"I arrived in Venice in the summer of 1967. It was very warm, and I spent several days roaming the back alleyways and crossing the hundreds of tiny bridges that constitute the unique, odd, charm of the city. I had never been there before, and it had a hypnotic effect. This was the same city that had done its magic on Byron, and many of the great American writers—Hawthorne, Howells, James—and now, evidently, on old Ezra Pound. I had heard that he still went for his daily walks, even at his advanced age, and that often of an evening, he would dine with Olga at a nearby restaurant called Cici's.

"And so, secretly I would go at night and sit in a far corner of Cici's to wait for my target to arrive. On several occasions he did so, and I watched him struggle through the maze of tables, cane in one hand, and sit at the same place each night, inspecting the passersby, ordering the same meals, sipping at his wine. They rarely spoke, but I could see that there was a great affection there, and a kind of peacefulness. Pound was a formidable, almost a frightening presence. I was sizing him up, I told myself, preparing for our meeting, scheduled later in my second week in Venice.

"Finally the day arrived, and my audience was awaiting me. It was still quite light out—the sun stayed high in the skies until well past eight o'clock—and I made my way to Olga's house a few minutes from my hotel. I was quite nervous.

"We made our introductions, and I will be brief in describing our conversations. He pounced upon me with relish. 'So you are the friend of Hélène? And so how is old Horse-Blanket?' I'll never forget that first remark. The nickname, if it was one, was certainly new to me. The thought of calling the dignified Alsatian beauty 'Horse-Blanket' took a moment to digest. Possibly it was just an eccentricity, or an attempt to intimidate me, or throw me off. So I responded, 'Hélène is well, and sends her best regards.' And I must tell you I *was* intimidated, so I went immediately to the subject of interest. I asked him about the valise, and if he knew of any reasons that Hemingway might fake its loss.

"This shocked him, I now believe. He had gotten so used to the myth that he momentarily stuck with it. 'Why yes, of course, it was a great tragedy, a great loss,' he assured me.

"What if I were to tell you that there is some evidence of a conspiracy? That one of Hemingway's friends worked to rid the world of those early manuscripts?' I stopped for effect and looked into his fiery eyes. They blazed, like live coals. He looked right back at me, hard. I might have melted, then and there. I believe I was shaking and hid my hands so he wouldn't see. 'What sort of nonsense is this?' he demanded. 'What are you all about here?' He drilled right through me with those eyes, and started to his feet. 'How could a so-called friend do a thing like that? I'll have you know that Hem was like a brother. He helped me get out of the nuthouse, dammit, and sent me a huge check in support when I *did* get out. Which I still have, by the way. I never cashed it!'

"I did my best to calm his ruffled feathers. 'Yes, Mr. Pound, I know all about that," I told him. 'And I understand your affections.' I slowed down and looked at him directly, gathering my courage. 'But is it not true, that sometimes an older brother must step in, and do something that seems rather rash, so that the beloved younger brother can go forward in life?'

"He relaxed back into his chair, and sized me up a long moment. 'I've seen you watching me, you know, down at Cici's. Did you think I'm too senile to notice a skinny little

Jap, night after night studying me?' He paused for effect. 'What do you want from me?'

"I thought for a moment. 'Just a good story,' I answered. 'A story, shall we say, that can stay in this room.' I hesitated to make the final move. Then I told him, 'I can make it very much worth your while. I am a man of great means, Mr. Pound.'

"This information perked him up. I had been told in no uncertain terms from Hélène that Pound had always been obsessive in his fear about not having enough money. In reality, at this point in his life, he had more than enough money for anything he would ever need. Olga had taken care of all that. Nevertheless, Pound always insisted on being able to take care of himself financially, and to be assured that he would always have whatever he wished to have, was a great pearl to dangle in front of him. So my offer of money, put in this very casual way, called out to him.

"He said, 'So, we're negotiating now, for the story? Is that it?'

"If you wish to put it in those terms, yes."

"'But you have already done that, haven't you? You've put it in those terms, I would say. Well …' He stroked his old white beard. He had the wrinkled head of an ancient prophet, and his eyes were beaming, having just come down from the mountain of visitation. 'Shall we say, then, that if you make me the right offer, I might satisfy your strange desires? For I do, as they say, have a story to tell. Yes, and you are not so far from the Kingdom as you might imagine, Professor.'

"'But do you expect me to name an amount without hearing your story, or without seeing the goods being purchased?'

"He thought this over. 'Come back tomorrow night, then. Same time. I will show you … the goods, as you put it. Will that be convenient, Professor?'

"I agreed, and he rose to leave me without speaking further. Soon enough I was out on the street, strolling back to my hotel with a glorious smile on my face. I had the answers to questions I had been investigating for years, just within my grasp.

"The next evening, I arrived at the house prepared to pay whatever price might be necessary to secure the evidence I was seeking. I was quite curious about what form Pound's evidence might take. He received me immediately, and had a strange and almost unearthly look on his old and weathered face. He seemed slightly agitated, and wished to transact our business with great alacrity, I thought.

"'I believe this is what you are looking for, Professor.' He handed me an autograph document, signed by his own hand, as I immediately recognized."

And now, with a flourish, Sensei reached for one of his green library boxes, and pulled from it a single sheet of paper. "Here it is, Yu-san. The signed document that Pound handed me that evening, twenty-five years ago."

I took the leaf from Sensei, and began perusing it. It was abrupt and to the point, as I imagined Pound to have been. The paper reads, in full, as follows:

> *Yessir, it's true. I asked Hadley to bring all the stories to me—all of 'em. Commanded her, really. She was one that needed to be told what to do. Gotta see 'em, I bellowed. Bring 'em to me! Hadley was an easy tool, and she worshipped Hem. Anything to help the old man. And being*

Gawd, I easily convinced her. And in 1922 Paris, I was Gawd!

When I had Hem's stories, I immediately saw that my strategy was correct. I studied those silly tales—almost all of it cheap, vulgar trash, written by an ignorant youth. Just children's stories, fit for the flames. But my, did we invent a fine conspiracy. And nobody ever suspected! In some sense, my best poem ever. A myth for the ages!

Of course, I protected Hadley, and I swore to her that I would. We played our hand just right.

ps. Not everything was directed to the oblivion of flames. Two of those old stories survived. They were the best of the bunch: "Bread and Wine" and "Big Shoulders."

Would ya like to see 'em?

Signed, and sealed,
E. Pound, 1967, Venice, Italy

I looked up at Sensei, flabbergasted. "This is from Pound?!"

"His own hand. It is just as he wrote it and gave it to me, the second time we met. He insisted that I write a document to him, saying I should not reveal any of it until all the principals had been dead for at least twenty years. And he did produce the two stories, or rather one complete story, "Bread and Wine," and one large fragment of an aborted novel, "Big Shoulders." Those are the manuscripts I have already shown you. I knew immediately that I would not leave his house that night without closing a deal, so the negotiations began in earnest. He certainly had a weakness for cash.

"So I said, 'Name a figure, Mr. Pound, and we can begin our discussions of a proper payment.' He did name a figure, and I did not even make a counteroffer. Instead, I produced an envelope with a large stack of both Deutsche marks and Italian lira, and patiently peeled from it an equivalent amount. I even added some to it. And I handed it directly to him. 'Will that satisfy you?'

"He did not even take the cash. Instead, he looked me directly in the eye, in the haunting way that he had. The old evil eye, from a gothic tale. I actually shuddered. But I did not reveal any second thoughts, and held the money before him. He finally took the wad of cash, almost apologetically, saying as he did, 'Remember, it is to remain a secret, till twenty years after I can't be bothered by it anymore. Or the others, either.' And he turned and hobbled out of the room, his cane in one hand and the cash in the other.

"I never saw him again. That was over twenty-five years ago, and I have kept my end of the bargain—until tonight!"

Holding Pound's letter in my hands like a sacred text, I asked, "And when do you expect to make this discovery available to the scholars?"

He smiled, I assume at my American impatience. "It is not something we need to hurry, Yu-san. Every year that I withhold my secret, its value doubles, I should say!" He enjoyed his little treasure now, laughing as a child might with a new toy. "Of course, it is already unique, and thus almost impossible to appraise. What you hold in your hand may in fact be one of the most valuable single sheets of paper in American literary collecting. And you are only the fifth person to know of its existence—at least, to my knowledge. This should be a matter of some small enjoyment for you."

"Five people? Me, you, Pound… ?"

"And Mika, of course. She knows the contents of all my collections." He waited me out. Then, "Can't you guess the fifth?"

I thought it over. "Hadley?"

"Of course. I needed corroboration. Otherwise, how could I know that it was not some hoax by the aging poet, desperate for some easy money? So I managed to set up an interview with Hadley, two years after visiting with old Ezra. She was living in a farmhouse, up in New Hampshire, where she had settled with her husband, the writer Paul Mowrer, after he retired from journalism. It was near the end of the 1960s, and reporters and biographers were still contacting her with various questions and so forth, digging around for more information about the great Hemingway. She graciously invited me to her home, and provided directions. The day I arrived, I parked my rental car, and as I strolled up the front walk, I could hear piano music coming from the house. I stood on the porch a moment, listening to what sounded like a piece by Schubert. Then I pressed the doorbell, the music faded away, and a pretty, rather simple woman answered the door. It was Hadley, wearing a brightly laundered white frock, alone in that big old house, answering the door herself. I found this to be quite charming, an image I still can conjure in my mind. Immediately I liked her even more than I had imagined I would.

"She brought me into the sitting room, then went out for cold drinks—iced tea, a very American refreshment. We sat and chatted briefly, then I circled in for the necessary information. 'I've been to see Ezra Pound, and he told me a remarkable story about the Paris years.'

"She looked at me, her face blank. 'Yes?'

"'It has to do with the lost manuscripts.'

"'Oh, that damned, painful subject again!' She looked almost relieved, and spoke in a mocking, rather funny way. 'How many times must I tell it?'

"'It seemed a little rehearsed to me. And suddenly I went in for the *coup de grace*. 'I wonder if you might comment about this letter that Pound gave to me?' I handed her a copy of the document.

"She began reading, and very quickly her eyes became wider, and her head turned downward just slightly. Then she brightened and looked at me. 'And so just what exactly is all this supposed to mean? That we are to take seriously the words of an old, broken down genius, who spent twelve years in an insane asylum?'

"I took a moment before responding. 'I believe he is telling the truth, Mrs. Mowrer. There is other evidence to support his story, and so I cannot think that it is an invention. Unless you can tell me otherwise.' She began to protest, but I kept going. 'I should also assure you that I have promised Mr. Pound that I would never reveal any of these secrets until at least twenty years after the passing of any of the … major players in the drama, so to speak. I must tell you that I have long suspected some sort of conspiracy. It was only in recent years that I finally discovered what seemed to be a workable explanation. And so I visited Mr. Pound in order to test my explanation. He was altogether forthcoming in our conversations, and spoke as any sane, highly intelligent man of his stature should be expected to speak.' I waited a moment. 'And he also produced some very old manuscripts.'

"She sat motionless and rather fatigued-looking for several long moments. She consulted the copy of Pound's letter once more, shaking her head as if she couldn't trust her eyes to read the words on the page. I wanted to launch into another long statement, but felt it was correct to wait for her to respond.

"Finally she did. 'He told me he would never reveal to *ANYONE* what we had done.' She stamped her foot in a moment of petulance. I could see her mind working, trying to determine how to respond, what tack to take. I waited. Finally, she looked me in the eye. 'It was all for Ernest. I wanted so much for him to be recognized as the great writer we all knew him to be. And now we can all see that greatness so plainly. Ezra was our wonderful friend, and his wise advice had already changed so many people's lives. Tom Eliot called him the master craftsman.' She looked at me for some kind of sympathy.

"'Can you verify that Pound's account is accurate?'

"She put her face into her hands, then looked up once more. 'And is this to remain secret? Can you assure me of this? Because I simply cannot stand to be dragged once more, again and again, into the newspapers. When Ernest died, it was all just too much. Every reporter forced me to relive the tragedies over and over again. And this coming out …'

"She covered her face with her hands, and I said, 'Your story will be safe with me. Until at least another twenty years, or more. It is my solemn promise, Mrs. Mowrer.' Again she peered into my eyes, I think searching for an assurance that my promise could be trusted. And I had every intention of keeping it. I believe at that moment, she understood that to be the case. So she said, 'Yes, Professor. Ezra's account is correct. We put together the story about the valise. I thought that he could do the same for Ernest that he had done for Tom Eliot … I believed that Ezra knew what was best …'

And she quitted the tale. I had no need to prod her. She said little beyond what I have now told you."

"That's it, Sensei?" I wanted more.

"In terms of substance, yes. I already felt that I had the story, and was only there for corroboration. And I had received it, a confession of sorts. I felt pain for her at that moment, Yu-san. She was now just an amiable, slightly overweight older lady living in a farmhouse in New England, whose life had been fairly normal for a long time. And my brash inquiries served to resurrect those jarring memories of her youth, when she had found herself at the center of one of the most legendary bohemian cultures ever assembled. One day she was a pretty teenager growing up in Chicago, the next she was surrounded by the most brilliant and colorful set of intellectuals that we have perhaps ever seen in the western world. And now, in her dotage, she was alone in her farmhouse, playing an old, slightly out-of-tune piano, answering her own door, and serving iced tea to complete strangers.

"Presently our conversation ended, and I left her. But I now knew that Pound's tale was real, and that I had in my possession a relic of mythic proportions: a unique document, composed in longhand by Ezra Pound, proving to the world that my theories were substantially correct."

He paused, appearing triumphant. "You see, I had proven my thesis. It was the culminating achievement of my career. And yet," he wavered a second, "until this very day, I had never told any other person about it, outside of Mika. You are the first American scholar to know these things, Yu-san. Hadley died in the early '70s, and I have held the secret well beyond my promise. For all these years, I have been alone in my triumph, in the academic world—until now."

He called for Omori, made a request for sake, and when it was brought, he poured two tiny porcelain cups to the brim. So we lifted glasses and toasted Sensei's discoveries. He drained his cup of sake, then peered at me. "And what will you do with these secrets, Yu-san?"

Pause.

"I'll just have to think about that one for a while, Sensei." I looked down at my cup, at the exquisite craftsmanship, so delicate I could see my fingers through the fragile porcelain. "But don't worry—the secret is safe with me."

友

And I have been thinking about it—for over fifteen years. All that time, it has remained our little secret, like the details of a couple's romantic honeymoon, high up in the mountains, surrounded by wind and trees. The story about Hemingway and Pound would also become the culmination of my intimacies with Sensei, though, of course, I could not have known it at the time. Over a year and a half of slow cultivation had climaxed with these revelations of Pound in Venice. I was certain that it couldn't be topped, even by that great literary magician, Goto Haruki.

As it unfolded, ours was a short-lived honeymoon. Midwinter turned abruptly bone-chilling, and soon enough a moist chill began to dominate the early mornings. Cold, rainy winds came off the ocean, up the mountainside, and into my living room when I left the windows open—which I frequently did. One night, I awoke with the curtains blowing in almost horizontally, and although I had recently been let in on one of the greatest literary deceptions of modern times, my immediate concern was now a head cold from Hell. Meanwhile, Sensei left town for weeks on end, visiting the hot springs of Kyushu to escape the cold, and I stayed home on Sundays, sulking.

It should have been a momentous season for me. But the rain ushered in the dreariest and most discouraging times I had in Japan—at least, until the final days. Empty juice containers, piles of used Kleenexes, old copies of the *Japan Times*, and dirty dishes littered my now too tiny apartment. For almost a week I lay in my bed, reading when I felt like it, napping or just staring out at the city and ocean beyond. Occasionally, I turned on the television and dozed while listening to news on NHK, most of which I couldn't understand.

Classes were done for the year, and my head cold gave me plenty of motivation to skip going to the office. The lines at the stores, and the crowded sidewalks of urban Japan, were no longer amusing; they were now simply annoying, as were my classroom and office duties. Worst of all, I was getting restless, and I knew it.

友

When my visits to Sensei resumed in March, they seemed less intriguing, less energizing. For one thing, I was seeing less and less of Mika. Each week my heart would flutter as I awaited the person who would answer the door. The difference between Mika and Omori was like the difference between the vast blue of the Pacific Ocean spreading out before me and a half-full glass of tap water down at the local *bento* shop. And Sensei too seemed to be changing—he seemed more despondent, and often would send word to me canceling our next visit. Meanwhile, the talk I had had with Mika that one afternoon so many months back, unattended by Sensei, seemed to have become a distant dream. Looking back, it certainly injured my friendship with Sensei as well, though at that moment, things were destined to get much worse. For most of winter and spring of 1994, we only met a few times. But somehow the buzz was fading, and we both sensed it. Maybe the climax of our relationship had been achieved, and it would be all downhill from then on.

There was still the highly anticipated trip to France on his behalf. One week in late January, Sensei detailed the mechanics of my upcoming journey. It was certainly exciting, and would evidently require very little on my part, but there still was an air of mystery surrounding the precise nature of my "assistance." All I knew was that I was to assist in the evaluation of "certain documents."

So, on a balmy day in March 1994, I boarded a Japan Airlines flight bound for Paris. Sensei had it all arranged for me, months in advance. He had purchased a business class upgrade, which I learned was the only way to fly. Once I arrived at Charles De Gaulle Airport and exited customs, I was greeted by a wordless and nameless person in a black suit and cap who held a cardboard sign saying "Professor Springs," and who ushered me to a black metallic limo and whisked me into the center of old Paris. Sensei had also arranged for me to stay in a seventeenth-century building of cold limestone, with much glass and marble inside. It was situated a stone's throw away from the Closerie de Lilas, the old nightclub in Montparnasse where Hemingway and his friends reigned like princes in the glory days of 1920s Paris.

My silent driver carried my things up to the second floor—or, rather, the third floor; this aspect of European thought eluded my American instincts. The landlady spoke to me busily in a sort of French that did not sound much like the courses I had taken years before. Her hands moved franticly, like frightened birds. I understood about twenty percent of what she said, though I got the impression that she was very happy to have me, and that Sensei was someone of very great importance in her world.

Her name was Madame Clairaux, and she wore thick glasses, a crocheted shawl of bright red, and extremely strong perfume of some sort. She insisted I sit with her in her dusty nineteenth-century-style parlor and have tea. My head was shaky from the long flight and all I wanted to do was sleep, but I smiled broadly and ate a tiny Parisian pastry of some sort as she chattered on in her incomprehensible French. My nods only encouraged her further. Finally, teacups drained, she escorted me up the stairs to my rooms, and showed me how to use the door keys—one for the front entrance on the boulevard, and another for my apartment. She patiently took me around the flat to show me how various things worked, and in ten minutes was on her way.

It was late in the afternoon, and I was alone in a fairly extravagant apartment in the City of Lights. My flight back was eight days later, so I had plenty of time to explore. I only had one duty to attend to—to meet with one of Sensei's agents, as he called him, a Monsieur Gluckstein. Sensei had assured me that I could easily examine the documents in question in less than an hour, and then advise him about their authenticity. I did not know of their approximate value at that time, and on that first day in Paris I had not even known what they were or who had written them. What I did know was, that if it all worked out as he planned it, Sensei would green light the exchange, and would have funds wired into this agent's bank account. Then, I would receive the documents and hand carry them back to Japan. I was on a need to know basis, like a scene out of a Robert Ludlum novel, so it seemed very intriguing and romantic.

There were also a few other dealers whose offices Sensei asked me to visit, but the main purpose of the trip was evidently the rendezvous with Gluckstein, which was to be later in the week. So I had five days to deal with the jet lag and to get accustomed to my temporary residence.

I spent most of my time aimlessly wandering up and down the hypnotic streets of central Paris. It was cold but dry, and with a heavy coat and a wool cap, the days were perfect for serious walking. The streets themselves were the loveliest I had ever encountered—endless cafes with finely-dressed patrons sipping coffee and reading newspapers, stunning vistas of old churches, villas, and perfectly symmetrical bridges, and the raging root beer foam of the river Seine, stampeding its way to the sea. Octagenarians of both sexes, dressed up like models in glossy fashion magazines, walked slowly through the alleyways or along the river, with tiny dogs on leashes. I visited museums, sat for long silences in countless churches, and took lengthy breaks in those same cafes, substituting wine for coffee as the afternoons lengthened into evening. It was one of the great weeks of my lifetime, and I swore I would come back again and again. But I never did.

In due course, I met with Gluckstein in another of those omnipresent cafes. The meeting had been set up at a rather grand venue on the Rue de Rivoli, near the Saint Paul metro stop. Sensei insisted upon this location, claiming it had some of the best pastries and croissants in the world, of all things.

He delighted in such details, always insisting on "the best."

I arrived first, about ten o'clock on a promising Parisian morning, and took a seat, one of only three other people at the cafe. The pastry and coffee were, as promised, splendid. As I waited, I read a *Newsweek International* that someone had left on a nearby table. Twenty minutes later Gluckstein bustled into the café and came directly to my table, as if from some sort of intuition.

"Ah, professeur, I am late once again!" He smiled as he said this, and I was immediately at ease with him. Gluckstein was short, squat, wearing thick black spectacles on the bridge of his prodigious nose, a heavy wool suit and a cape, of all things. He was overfed, and thus overweight in the least offensive way, and he made the most of his God-given natural appearance by smiling and winking a lot, as if he were in constant touch with the frailty and ridiculousness of human culture and society. He carried with him a polished leather satchel and a blue and red checked umbrella, though the sky was fair and there was no sign of rain. He also had in his front lapel a bright red rose. Gluckstein was a charmer, from first impressions, but Sensei had told me to be on guard for this aspect of his character—as a businessman, he was a killer.

We sat for some minutes, and he asked me my impressions of his "adopted" city. He informed me that he was originally from southern Italy ("*Oui*, my name does not sound Italian, *n'est-ce pas*?"), and that he had come from a long line of collectors and dealers of curiosities and art, including paintings, prints, sculpture, stained glass, jewelry, antique books, and other curiosities. For over thirty years, he said, he had maintained a reputation as one of Paris's premiere dealers, out of a tiny shop he operated in the

Rue des Rosiers in the Marais. His family business back in Ravello, on a mountaintop high above the Amalfi Coast, was now run by his brother and nephew, and continued to be one of his chief suppliers of his curiosities. "They are worth far more up here in Paris," he winked.

He leaned in slightly. "Perhaps there is something I might be able to locate for you, Professor Springs?" He peered into my face, quizzically. "I have an extensive network, and also deal with civil authorities and private investigators, if your request might involve anything of a more confidential nature." His eye widened slightly as he moved just a bit closer toward me.

"Well, no, I can't think of anything for the moment. But thanks just the same."

This seemed to disappoint him just slightly. He looked away, fanning himself with his handkerchief. "Yes, well then, *alors* ..." Gluckstein rambled on a moment longer, then suddenly and decisively snatched the satchel up off of the chair next to him and unclasped it. He pulled from it a manila folder thick with what looked like old papers. And just like that, he handed the folder across the table to me.

"These are the documents that Professor Goto is interested in. I am sure he has explained it all to you already."

I didn't have the heart to correct him—I actually had no idea what was under consideration. All I really knew was that it must be something I had particular knowledge of, to be commissioned to come so far at such a great expense. Or at least that was my understanding on the morning of my meeting with Gluckstein. I eagerly opened the folder and began reading the document on top, an autograph letter:

Hartford. July 15. 1900

Dear old Mark,

Now you must know that I love you for I have let you alone a whole month—and more. And that for a man hunted from pillar to post by all creation as you are, is worthy to be credited as an act of grace and mercy. You are yourself to blame for waking me up now. Your midnight report of the dinner with the "Red Robin of London" was a sheer delight. Her mistaken conception of "what Americans all believe" deserved all the abuse you could muster, and I cannot criticize your befuddlement a bit (nor your irritation). I earnestly hope sometime to appear in person in a gathering of that illustrious clan somewhere, and to listen in rapt attention as you indicate to this robin the weaknesses of her views, and the misery with which you are forced to hear them. It would be a most memorable occasion.

So you are to summer in England. After then, what? Will you be coming home to America, at long last?

We are booked for the short-term at Judy's new cottage on Long Island, near Easthampton. Part of us are already there and the rest are going in a few days. . . .

I skipped ahead. The letter went on for several pages, and ended:

With love to Livy and the girls,
And yours affectionately, Joe

I turned the next page to see the following:

London
August 3, 1900

Dear Joe,
I am raging this afternoon, having just read more news about the nonsense being rained down upon the poor Filipinos, all in the name of God, progress, civilization, and so on. Why it is that the Americans consider it their right to pontificate to the world how clearly they perceive the will of an inscrutable God, I cannot say—but they do so as regularly as the sun sets, and generally do it without a shameful second thought, or even the tiniest trace of a grin on their faces. Airing their smug pieties is one thing, but to do so in the service of exploiting the poor Filipinos—well, Joe, it's an act of the Christian imagination that must make a solid man of the cloth like yourself blush in shame.

Forgive my smoke and heat, Joe; it's been a rather humdrum morning, with rain pouring down and the women off at a gallery showing. They left here with higher expectations than I was able to muster. And so here I sit, remembering the old days, when bloodshed and horror in the name of God were carried out, at least, against our own countrymen, and not upon these innocent and freedom-seeking outsiders whose very language and culture remain a mystery beyond our grasp. It can be a tiresome and even shameful thing, being an American abroad these days.

As for that "Red Robin" that I had mentioned, and her foolishness in such matters: Yes, it is a terrible thing to be lumped in with the rest of the crass Americans, who are all up in a lather about God and country and so forth. I did tell her a thing or two, and I suppose in the context of what the British think of as "high society," well, yes, it was rather unexpected. But mark my words—it's a dinner that none of them will very soon forget!

Affection all around, Mark

The letters appeared to be very much like the ones between Mark Twain and Joe Twichell that I had read in the past, both during my graduate years at Yale, where many of them are stored, and at Sensei's, the day he had shown me some unknown others. However, I did not recognize any of these, either.

I thumbed through this sheaf of pages. Overall, it was made up of approximately a hundred pages of autograph letters, all of which were written during the years 1898-1902, back and forth, from these two close friends, probably almost forty individual letters and postcards total. Obviously the ones by Twain were far more valuable individually; but as a complete lot, this was a terrific cache for scholars, since they looked to be a sequential "run," each letter responding to the previous one, roughly speaking.

Meanwhile, as I continued to examine the cache, Gluckstein calmly ordered an aperitif and croissant, watching the colorful Parisians tread by on the sidewalk. A few times he let his eyes rest happily upon me; he was the kind of dealer who took real joy in presenting to his eager clients a trinket that gave them pleasure.

Finally, he spoke. "Well, monsieur? What do you think of my merchandise?"

"Where did you find these?"

He grinned, wiping his mouth with a napkin. He sipped at his drink. "Monsieur, that is of course a matter of no concern to you. My clients, as you must know, wish to remain anonymous. And my business must rely on this aspect. Otherwise, my clients would go elsewhere, as you can imagine." There was some real delight in his eyes as he told me this. "I am a man of some secrecies, you see."

As I listened to Gluckstein from across the table, it was like a spotlight went on in my brain, and I suddenly realized that there might very well be something illegal going on in all of this. Now, looking back and retelling this adventure in hindsight, this sounds so naïve as to be almost laughable. But in all honesty, up to that very moment, it had not really occurred to me. Or else, perhaps I should say, whatever possibilities of impropriety might exist in all of this, I had suppressed somehow. But now, seated at a tiny table in a café in the Marais, it dawned on me. This might very well be hot merchandise, stolen from an archive, or perhaps a rival collector.

"Can you tell me how much Sensei is offering for these letters?"

He chewed on his croissant, slathered in jam. Then he wiped his mouth with his linen napkin, put it down, and winked audaciously. I almost laughed out loud. "Monsieur, this is of no real concern to you, as I told you. Professor Goto is a gentleman who insists upon all matters remaining confidential. I am of course also a businessman who works under such conditions." His very Parisian English, according to which a word like "conditions" came out "con-DEE-She-ONS," sounded rather like Inspector Clouseau. Any moment he might stand up and fall to the ground, his cape flying into the air, or else he might bowl over a waiter with a tray full of dishes.

"My understanding is that it is your task to inspect these documents, report back to your superior, and if he accepts your evaluation as definitive" [day-FEEN-it-TEEV], "for you to take possession of them and hand carry them back to Japan for delivery to Professeur Goto. That is all of the instructions I have been given, and to go beyond them is not in my interests. The Professeur has been one of my great and trusted clients for many years, even longer than you might imagine."

And so I did it. I counted up the number of leaves, the number of letters, and the dates, and found a telephone to call my "superior." I provided my report, barely able to hold back my enthusiasms, though I still suspected there was something fishy going on. Within minutes, Sensei made up his mind and spoke very briefly to me in the following manner:

"Yu-san, please tell Gluckstein to proceed with the arrangements as discussed before. Within twenty-four hours the transaction should be completed, through the agreed upon agents. Once he has received the payment, he is to deliver the goods to your apartment, at which time please verify that the entire package is the same. I would ask you to hand carry all of these documents back through customs. As old letters you can report that they have negligible value, and the customs people will not question you on this."

Here again was another hint that something was slightly out of whack, similar to my feelings of confusion at the end of my trip to Manila. Once again, my ignorance of the value of the papers, from Sensei's point of view, was strategically an advantage when reentering Japan. And, once more, Sensei was telling me to shut up and obey—which was, for the second time, exactly what I did. And once again, it ticked me off. Again I felt presumed upon. And again I felt betrayed.

友

It was another two weeks before Sensei and I met again. When I got back to Japan, he was away in the south again, and I was jet-lagging anyway. Since school was out, I had almost nothing to do regarding my teaching for another two weeks, so I spent much of my time worrying about the meeting. I didn't want to compromise our relationship, but I needed to somehow convey how I felt about being manipulated during the recent trip to France and on my prior trip to Manila. The problem was I had no idea how to even broach the subject.

On the day of our meeting, I trudged up the hill as a light snow mixed with occasional sleet swirled down from the cold, gray March clouds above. When I finally arrived at his house to deliver the goods, Mika met me at the door. It had been awhile since I'd seen her, but I was prepared, just in case. I presented her with a gift-wrapped box of candy purchased at a famous boutique near the Arc de Triomphe. Like Sensei, I had learned she cherished nothing but the best.

"Ah, Jack-san, *domo arigato*!" She seemed genuinely pleased.

We bowed at one another, still quite formal in our approach. Like with some of the overly eager young students in the first row of my classes, I regularly imagined a sexual spark with Mika, but I could never tell if I might be able to turn it into a raging bonfire. I remained confused about the possibilities of our having a relationship, though, in fact, it had been many long weeks since I had even glimpsed her. Since meeting her for the first time, I had suppressed those types of thoughts. Or at least I tried to suppress them. I could still feel the daggers of Sensei's glowering look, the day he discovered us sitting alone in the tearoom. I even pictured the limpid Miyamoto, slamming his forehead into a stack of bricks, and screeching at the top of his lungs. Thus did my fears curtail my lingering lust.

Anyway, I couldn't quite figure out how to play it, I guess—and thought of it as a stalemate. But in my daydreams, Mika's long swaying hair tumbling down onto her silk *kimono*, which was wrapped tightly around her lithe body as she leaned forward gracefully to refill my teacup—this had become my image of a sort of feminine beauty that was both exotic and down-to-earth. My Muse, so to speak. Ironically, it was on this cold afternoon of what would turn out to be my ugliest confrontation with Sensei that I was destined to comprehend the extremity of my desire to know Mika on some other level than mere waitress. But for now it would have to wait. So I asked, "Is Sensei ready for my visit?"

"My apologies, Jack-san, but he has been detained with other things and begs your forgiveness. Please come into the sitting room and he should return shortly. Can I offer you some tea?"

We went into the room that had grown so familiar to me. I thought of it as if it were a place frozen in time, like a reading room in one of the world's great museums, a place where the past brushed up against the present, and the passage of time was irrelevant, if only for an hour or two. The table at which I had sat and studied Sensei's wonderful collection awaited my leaning elbows, but today it was empty save for an old Japanese fan and a single, bright green and red volume.

As I sat and waited for Mika to return with a tiny porcelain teapot filled with steaming green tea, I thought about how much I had come to love these Sundays with Sensei. Leafing through his many portfolios, often filled with autograph letters or manuscripts by my favorite authors—a set of pages from a diary by Stephen Crane, some unpublished letters of Willa Cather, a few rejected early song lyrics by George and Ira Gershwin, the receipts from an Italian vacation of William Dean Howells—had become an addictive behavior pattern.

Mika entered the room, bringing her tray of tea and snacks. She poured and started to leave just as I opened my mouth to ask that she stay. The words died on my tongue when I heard the front door open and "*Tadaima!*" ring out. Then the sound of shoes brushing against a mat, then slipped off, the rustling of a coat, a cabinet banging shut, a sneeze, and finally someone walking down the creaky wooden hallway toward me.

Mika was still standing beside the table when Sensei entered the room. His eyes flickered between his niece and me before he spoke. "Yu-san, my apologies for being delayed. Have you been treated well by Mika?" There was a tiny inflection of jealousy and alarm in this question.

"Hello Sensei, yes, she has been most gracious, as always."

He gave her a slight nod and then turned to me again. "I met an old friend whose husband was long ago a colleague of mine. I had not seen her for many years—her name is Toyoda-san, her husband was a great scholar of Keats. He died about three years ago, and by chance I saw her today, and we talked for some time."

He seemed to be rambling and I remembered the awkwardness of the previous time, now months ago, when he had caught me sitting alone with Mika. I cleared my throat. "I've just been sitting here, reading this odd little book." I showed it to him. It was another of his treasures: a first edition of *The Wonderful Wizard of Oz*. It just happened to be out, lying on the table in plain sight.

Still standing over me, he shook the folds of his robe, brushing himself off. With what I thought was great deliberation, he lowered himself to the *tatami* across the table from me. "Mika! *Ocha*!" This command for tea was slightly more testy than usual, and I couldn't stop myself from glancing up at Mika as she hurried from the room to get more tea. Sensei and I sat in an awkward silence a moment. "It is a curious book," he agreed. "The poor wizard. A charlatan from the plains of Kansas. I often felt just as weak and empty as the wizard, in my work as a teacher. Worried that my own … ignorance, and imperfection might be revealed for all to see."

"Why did you put this particular story out today?"

He stopped to think. "It was not me. Perhaps Mika was looking at it?"

That was all we said about Frank Baum's children's book. I waited for another opening. Silence.

"So how was your friend?"

"Friend?" He had forgotten his own story.

"Toyoda-san? Your colleague's wife?"

He faintly recalled the episode, seemingly still worried that I had once again besmirched the honor of his precious niece, I supposed. Then he stroked his chin and paused. "Ah yes. She is not well. She looks rather haggard." He sniffled, rubbed his nose. "I assume that there are financial difficulties for her and her daughter. They live near Kobe Station, in a shabby old apartment that is rather poorly constructed, she told me, and I believe she is not able to find other arrangements."

I nodded. Time drifted for a moment, then I mentioned the papers. "Sensei, I wanted to ask about my assistance. In fact, I think we may have some problems."

"Problems?"

I struggled to find the way to explain my regrets. Although I had rehearsed my complaints many times, now my mouth went dry, and the words I wanted were nowhere to be found.

"Well, I wondered about the customs on the documents. I had the same questions when I brought back the copy of *Moby-Dick* from Manila, of course. I had not quite realized—"

Mika reentered the room, bringing another tray of tea and snacks.

"I mean, I wondered if ... well, doesn't sneaking documents or valuable books through customs amount to illegal activities?" In Japanese conversation, that last sentence was pretty American, meaning blunt, and as soon as it was out of my mouth I realized it was not how I wanted to say it.

Sensei appeared to take it in stride, but I could tell he

was upset. He tilted his head to one side, as if considering something of great import. He picked up a teacup and brought it to his lips, blowing on it. Then he put it back down without taking a sip.

"Are you referring to bringing the items through customs without notifying the authorities?" he said. "Or do you have other concerns?"

At that moment I wanted to ask about Gluckstein, and how he was able to find the documents, and whether working with such an "agent" was itself shady, but I hesitated. "Well, to tell the truth, yes. I wish you could explain to me why you failed to warn me about this whole smuggling operation. It put me in a rather uncomfortable position."

"Smuggling?" he said with a laugh. "You make it sound like some sort of drug business!"

I did not smile, and he quickly realized I was not in a humorous mood. He looked me straight in the eyes. "Yu-san, this is just a minor act of rebellion against rules that are simply outdated and unnecessary. As you Americans like to say, we do not need the government poking into all corners of our personal lives. Anyway, there is no customs charge on works of art or rare books. What the Japanese government does not know about my personal collections is really none of its business. I do not think that there is anything wrong with what you did to assist me."

This last statement sort of irked me. "You don't think so? Well, isn't that the sort of decision I should be involved in?"

"You seemed quite willing to go to France on my behalf, and through my arrangement, to undertake this work. I had assumed you would trust my judgment."

Tempers were on the verge of flaring, and we both felt something new and sinister brewing between us. I waited a moment, just looking at him with a grim resolve not to lose my temper, but that last line about "trusting his judgment" also began to irritate me. So I said, "I'm old enough to know the facts and to make my own decisions!" It came out like something a petulant teenager would tell his domineering parent, but I went on anyway. "And who is this Gluckstein fellow? He comes across a bit slimy for my tastes. Is he some sort of underworld figure? Where does he discover these priceless documents? Tell me there isn't something fishy about all that?"

Sensei was fluent in all sorts of idiomatic terms, like "fishy," but that word did catch his attention. "Fishy? Do you mean illegal, or even immoral? Yu-san, I have known Mr. Gluckstein longer than you have been alive. His business caters to many of the finest residents of Paris and throughout Europe. I believe his credentials are impeccable. As for where he gets his merchandise, I am not privy to such things. Perhaps you would like to interrogate him about all of that. For nearly forty years, I have instructed him to contact me whenever he learns of literary or historical materials that might fit my collections. You are insinuating that it is stolen merchandise, or some such thing as that, but this is where I believe you are overstepping your boundaries into my own business. Your charges are against Gluckstein's character as well as against my own. What you are saying implies a complete lack of trust in who I am."

I was just as tense as he was, but I reached for some words that might cool off the situation. We were fast approaching a point of no return. "Sensei, you've been a friend and a *sempai*, and I've valued our times together.

It's been a great honor, looking at all of these items you've collected over the years. But surely you must realize how this last experience raised certain questions for me. And how it compromised my own sense of personal conscience. I felt violated by doing things with no understanding or context. I feel like you used me."

Looking back, I now see that for Sensei, I had crossed a line. For him, it was my trust in his integrity that had been violated, and challenging him face-to-face was the final insult. Sensei evidently desired a Samurai-like loyalty of unquestioning obedience from one like me—a student much younger, much more naïve, and untested in the world in which he lived. He not only desired it; he required it. And so he turned on me.

"Are you really so high and mighty, Jack-san? Are you truly beyond such moral equivocations? I do not think so." He waited a moment for effect, then revealed his trump card. "Did you enjoy owning, if even for a short time, those first editions by Allen Ginsberg and Jack Kerouac? How did you live with yourself, after stealing those valuable books, and taking them back to your own apartment?"

This brought a smile to his face. No, it was a sneer. My jaw dropped open, literally. *How could he have known about that?* My mind whirled as I tried to work it out, and my only answer was that somehow there were devices within the library for surveillance. I fumbled for a response. "Sensei, I simply borrowed those to read. I did not feel any need to sign them out. And I returned them a week later." All three sentences were lies; my intention at first, when I put them in my backpack, was to keep them, which I did for over two weeks, till my conscience forced the return. So now I was lying about my own actions. "Anyway, what gives you the right to snoop into what goes on in the library? And if you thought my intent was to steal those books, why did you wait until now to confront me?"

He broke a piece of *sembei*, putting it into his mouth and slowly chewing it. Then he wiped his lips with a napkin. "Jack-san, I do not snoop. You misunderstand me. I pay lackeys such as Miyamoto to snoop on my behalf. In fact, the university has put you under Miyamoto's charge from the very beginning, as I recommended they do. I am certain you have noticed this.

"But what the university does not know is the extent of my abilities, and my very strong desire to safeguard the books in the departmental library, most of which were donated by me. These are not difficult things to arrange. As you know, the library owns many books of excellent historical value, though generally these are of rather minor monetary worth. Rather than hire a full-time librarian for a library that gets almost no use, I discovered how easily one can install a system that is activated by movement within the rooms of the collection. Miyamoto handles all of that. He was the one who reported to me that you had 'borrowed' those books without signing them out properly. Since you arrived, you have been almost alone in visiting this library anyway, as you must have noticed. So if anything went missing, it would be obvious who must have taken it."

He thought this over for a moment and again almost laughed. "I might add, I also resent your interest in another of my possessions. I have noticed your growing fondness for Mika, and I am afraid that it is not something I can endorse, Yu-san."

A pause, then a shy smile came to his lips. "Yes, I can read the signs quite well. But as you must know—now that you have been among us here for almost two years—such an arrangement is not possible. In fact, I can assure you that her father would never allow such a … liaison." He paused with sinister effect. "And I can assure you, his activities can be much more 'fishy' than mine."

I was dumbfounded, but he didn't stop there. "You also might be surprised to learn how much our growing relationship has disturbed Miyamoto's world," he said, biting into another *sembei*, again rubbing his hands together. "Yes, I do not think it is going too far to say that you are his archrival, at least in his own petty imaginings, and that he might be persuaded to do almost anything to return to his privileged status here in my household. As you must know, he formerly was much more active as my assistant, but we have had … well, many disagreements over the years, and I grew weary of his selfish ambitions. He also said and did things to Mika that were disturbing to her, and quite beyond his … well, his means. He had, shall we say, disrespectful … intentions. Clearly he is nowhere near her breed. So since then, and with your arrival, his work for me has been almost entirely curtailed. But I have occasionally asked him to help me, mainly, to keep an eye on you." He made this confession with obvious relish, and I could almost feel his knife twisting in my gut.

"I suppose he does not think very highly of you, Jack-san." He smiled as if sharing an inside joke, and then took another bite of rice cracker. He rubbed his hands together once more, brushing off any residual crumbs. "In any case, if you feel unprepared to help me in the future, I can easily arrange a suitable replacement."

All of these disclosures revealed an entirely different side of Sensei. I had hitherto misunderstood him, or else had turned a blind eye. He was menacing, angry that I had confronted him—*challenged* him—and obviously felt he needed to show how much more powerful he was than I had realized. I had indeed been naïve. Blind to the vast control—or the *illusion* of control—he exercised over our lives. Me, Mika, Miyamoto, and, presumably, everyone else in the English department: we were pawns on his chessboard. As far as my feelings toward Mika went, I now perceived the remnants of a deep-seated xenophobia, a prejudice I had assumed must be impossible for such a liberal, cosmopolitan scholar. And the idea that Miyamoto had been my predecessor as *kohai*, or maybe henchman, further diminished my image of Sensei as enlightened academic. Then, as with another twist of the knife, I realized the surveillance equipment in the library could also be installed elsewhere, such as in the condo building that Sensei owned. The idea that Miyamoto had scrutinized security tapes of my home life floored me—even though I had no evidence for it. I suppressed a shiver as anger washed over me.

In short, that afternoon was a turning point. Sensei suddenly struck me as ruthless, cold, and manipulative, and I must have looked like a mere underling challenging his motives. Worst of all, I'm sure we both felt powerless to repair the breach that was widening with every passing moment. Nearly two years of slow and patient relationship building had all washed away like a sandcastle in a typhoon.

That moment is seared in my mind, in fact. Without a hint of remorse, he had peered at me and stated, "I can easily arrange a suitable replacement." I was speechless. Without thinking of the consequences, I got to my feet. The air in the room was absolutely still. Sensei looked up at me, surprise etched in his expression. I'm sure my fists were clenched in rage. But he remained seated, arms and legs both folded in defiance. Tree limbs swayed in the wind just outside the window. An NHK news broadcast emanated from some other chamber in the house, describing further economic downturns. I bowed slightly. "Sensei, I see that I have displeased you, and I've let you down. You have always been a most gracious host, and I owe my life in Japan to you alone. But for now I think I should leave." Another pause, as I looked around at the familiar room. Sensei said nothing, made no gesture of reconciliation. "I regret our differences of opinion. And I am genuinely sorry you feel betrayed." I needed to get out of there before I said something I would truly regret. So bowing again, I backed out of the room.

Sensei sat there in stubborn silence. I think he was seething with anger, too, although I also detected some confusion and sadness. We both sensed at that moment that something unnameable had been ruptured in our relationship. Perhaps we both wished to offer an appeasement of sorts, but neither of us could muster a word. Sensei's rigid Japanese manner overcame whatever romantic sensibility was wrestling with it, and as I walked down the hallway, he remained silent. The old wood floors squeaked with each of my footfalls. I stepped onto the tiled entryway and found my shoes. Except for the faint radio broadcast, the house was still.

That silence, as I opened the front door and let myself out into the cold windy early evening, was the last thing I heard in Sensei's home until nearly one year later.

友

It was shocking, to say the least, to realize Jack had been caught up in doing the legwork for a man whose substantial literary collection had been accumulated by, perhaps, questionable means. And the recognition that an old academic, not unlike myself, can be revealed suddenly to contain twisted and even menacing traits of monomania and conceit was more than a little disturbing. I was shocked, that is, but also entranced by a sort of self-revelation. For Goto's journey was one on which, but for the grace of God, each of us might embark, if and when we become obsessed by the delights of this or that passing shadow. The delights of those sirens we pretend are of no temptation or consequence to those of us of superior character, may, in fact, lead toward ignoble acts. Perhaps it's a good thing I am lashed to the mast, so to speak, by my lack of Goto's deep pockets.

The chapter reveals not only the underhanded side of such businesses as collecting and secrecy, but how quickly a breach can occur among friends. And, in this case, perhaps, even more sinister, the shifty side of controlling others and bending them to one's imperial will. It was here, for both myself and for Jack I believe, that portentous rumblings from deep within the crust of the earth began to shake us to our cores.

Chapter 10

Suddenly it was April, and the busy time of starting new classes, and long, almost endless meetings in the department ensued. Springtime that year was stunning, with the cherry blossoms praising the sun and skies all over Kobe, and the hills singing almost as cheerfully as the Salzburgian variety depicted in movie lore. Unless you've lived in Japan through a long winter, it's hard to communicate the elegance of the cherry blossoms in their full glory. The beauty of striding down the hill to the university, and, on weekends, walking the well-marked paths of the nearby national park, or driving Richard's Nissan up into the craggy canyons and valleys of central Japan, all punctuated by rapturous cherry blossoms, was enough to send my benighted spirit soaring and assure me it was still good to be alive in Japan.

Work, more than the wonders of nature, was quite redemptive in that respect. I had terrific classes my final year in Japan. One in particular was a group of seniors I met with weekly, outside the classroom, for informal discussions on a variety of topics. These conversations took place at what I had dubbed our "Munchen coffee-train," a regular meeting I had managed to keep going for almost two years, except for breaks in August and January. Mondays and Fridays at 3:00 p.m., the coffee train kept chugging along. Some of the students who came regularly had been in classes with me over the entire time of my stay, and most were young women: charming, shy, with their long black hair and irregular yet beaming smiles. They were excellent in conversational English, and wanted to stay in practice. Yuko, tall, willowy, and with that mildly erotic innocence that so many college women have in Japan, had been around the longest. She had an amazing knowledge of old British and American rock and roll, which obviously gave us an immediate connection. Now that she was graduating, she spoke hopefully of going to live in London and working in some aspect of the music business. As a senior, she came to almost every meeting of the coffee-train, along with her silent and rather disturbing cohort, Minami, who still could not bear to look me in the eyes and almost never spoke, but who laughed even if the jokes were not funny to anyone else, covering her mouth obsessively. I had heard only about a dozen sentences issue from her in over eighteen months.

Yuko and Minami had been twinned in my mind since I began teaching in Kobe. In other cultures, one might think they were lovers, but that did not appear to be the case. Perhaps they were just friends spending time together. I sometimes got the feeling Yuko was waiting for me to make the move on her—an energy that eluded me, though in truth, the thought did cross my mind. But then, all at once, she made a move, something I thought I would never see from a Japanese-born woman. It was not long after my falling out with Sensei. Considering what she said to me one late Friday afternoon—"Jack-san, you look so lonely"—I must have been looking pretty forlorn indeed.

I glanced up at her, and caught a glimpse of something warm and sparkly in her dark eyes. "I'm OK. Just tired, I guess."

Minami was not there, probably away on one of those rare occasions when the two were not bound together. In fact, we were all alone at the Munchen. The sun was drooping below the trees, the barista in a back room. Yuko hesitated shyly, then pounced. "I've been wanting to ask you ... possibly, can I cook you dinner tonight? Do you like *yakisoba*?"

I admit the combination of fried noodles and several bottles of cold Asahi Dry, followed by a lusty encounter with a young, beautiful student was a powerful temptation. But somehow I begged off and got away with my scruples intact. That surely sounds Spartan to me now, in my dying days, when some hot noodles with Yuko sounds like a pleasant prospect. It remains memorable all these years later because it was the only time I was offered such an opening—at least so far as I was able to pick up. And who knows? Maybe Yuko just wanted to feed me and practice her English. But that night, lying in bed, again my fantasies drifted off toward a detailed bodily investigation of Japanese women. A "close reading" and analysis, as I might undertake on a poem by Ezra Pound. Eventually, of course, my imagination led me, lamely, to Mika. Her overpowering effects on me had a claw in my brain that I had no luck pulling out—and I admit, still haven't.

A few of the male students also came regularly to the coffee-train. Some of these were also students I had met the first year and who kept coming back for more. Tohru, Eddie, and Kenichi among them. Eddie was tall (6'3"), and he played forward on the school basketball club. Once he learned of my days as a gym-rat back in Indiana, he invited me to scrimmage with them, which I did every Wednesday afternoon for about a year. (He could actually dunk, a pretty unusual ability among Japanese players, who tend to have hands too small to palm a regulation basketball, and arms and legs slightly shorter than they would be on North Americans of the same height.) One evening we rented the classic film *Hoosiers*, and watched it together. I laughed at the dubbed Gene Hackman chewing out the players in a high-pitched, nasal Japanese voice.

The star of the senior class was Kenichi, still hanging around me, and still desperately dreaming of securing a job like mine. He loved American literature and spoke eloquently of the haunting tales of Poe and Hawthorne, considering them to be very much akin to the ghost stories so prevalent in old Japanese writings, including the *Noh* dramas, many of which were preserved by those lonely and eccentric American expatriates, Ernest Fenollosa and Lafcadio Hearn, Kenichi's favorite. Kenichi often wore an old blue sweatshirt with PENN STATE emblazoned on it, commemorating a long visit he had made to see a friend who lived in State College, PA. While there, he visited New York City, Boston, and Washington DC—all on his own, via buses and trains. He was understandably proud of this accomplishment. I thought so highly of his abilities that I encouraged him to think about graduate school in the States. I eventually wrote some letters of recommendation for Kenichi, and he managed to get a TA position at the University of Texas, and took a PhD there. That led him to a decent job at Hiroshima University, a position he still holds, along with some prestige and notoriety within the American studies community throughout Japan. He has translated numerous works into Japanese, and produced a fine volume describing the Hawthorne-Melville relationship, making brilliant use of their letters and journals.

Kenichi's success is a source of great satisfaction for me. It makes one feel like a midwife, I suppose, an academic birthing process that one both inspires and oversees. He occasionally still sends me letters, nowadays mostly e-mails, and it all started with those happy coffee-train meetings at the Munchen Café. It was a mild form of bohemianism, in their eyes, and I was the reigning presence, a pseudo-Walt Whitman at the head of the table. At the time I saw it as all about the students. But eventually I discovered how important this little group was, not just for the students, but also for the maintenance of my own sanity and enjoyment during those last alienated months in Kobe. I found myself looking forward to the coffee-train more than just about anything else; to tell the truth, I think it was the students like Eddie and Kenichi (and yes, Yuko) who kept me dragging myself out of bed each morning.

The Munchen Café and the coffee-trains helped to fill the hole in my life that had been produced by my falling out with Sensei. But the rift kept gnawing at me. I knew I must wait and not initiate anything, or at least I felt that way. But for several long months, I heard not a word from Sensei. I even wished to hear from Miyamoto, in the vain hope he might deliver another invitation or some request for my assistance. These messages never arrived, however. When I saw Miyamoto on the campus grounds, he forged ahead without acknowledging my presence. I had my own pride, and never once initiated a conversation with him. We were total strangers, functionally speaking.

Finally, I admitted that I missed seeing Mika as well. I fantasized about her more and more, often as I lay awake in my bed late at night. My room would be dark and quiet, with ambient noise drifting up from the late night taxis on the streets below. I could easily conjure images of her brilliantly fashioned silk garments, and the swaying black hair, and the way she moved so gracefully in and out of the room. I even recalled her particular odors: the faint sweetness of some Parisian scent, or the mild dustiness of some skin powder that she was fond of brushing on to her slender torso and unseen legs.

Yes, it finally dawned on me that I needed very much to see Mika again—and on more intimate terms, perhaps, than we would ever be able to achieve. I also wondered if she thought about me in similar ways, in the dark as the breezes fluttered through the open curtains on a sultry midsummer night. But I did not act on my desires.

Days and then weeks paraded forward, and soon enough we were deep into autumn. The mountain forests were changing their colors in anticipation of the final blaze of glory in late October. The weather was sunny, almost perfect, with brisk breezes offering the balancing counterpoint to the day's heat. The clear air of the mountain heights was rejuvenating to me in ways that almost nothing else in Japan was, at least since my time with Sensei had evidently run its course. And the many long months of silence led me to believe that it had.

One day, while driving toward Kyoto with no particular destination or agenda, it hit me that my time in Japan was nearing its end, unless I could come up with a compelling reason to stay. I thought about American football, of all things, wondering how the Colts were doing, and suddenly decided that three years was enough. There *was* no compelling reason, and it was time to go home. I could not put off finding a permanent position any longer. But then another, more vital realization hit me, again, suddenly out of the blue: the only truly compelling reason to stay would have to be Mika. She was still stuck in my brain, though I had not seen her in nearly ten months.

My car probably played a major part in my thinking that day. As cultural critics are fond of reminding us, cars are quintessential American symbols of power, movement, possibility, and even sexuality. I suppose, then, it makes perfect sense that my own cogitations about lost love came tumbling together one late October day as I drove through the hills. Almost without realizing it, I pulled off the road and sat there for a while. I remember it was just past 10:00 a.m. Then, I suddenly recognized what I had to do. I backed the car into a dirt pathway and turned around to head back to Kobe, spraying loose gravel into the ferns nearby. Other issues besides trees and mountains pressed into my mind with urgency and speed, and I had to attend to them, abruptly and certainly. Once and for all.

The thing is, I remembered that conversation one day with Mika, about the tiny farmer's market that congregated around one of the train stations near Sensei's house on Saturdays. She had said she often went there on Saturdays to buy flowers and fresh fruit for Sensei. Just like that, I had hatched my plan. I would go to the market, paperback tucked into my back pocket, and find a decent vantage point from where I could sit nonchalantly and await her arrival. It could all seem like a coincidence, but it would afford me the possibility of talking with her, and possibly meeting on a more regular basis.

And that's what I did. By the time I got back to town that day, it was already well past noon, and most of the merchants had begun closing up shop for the day. I sat there for an hour or two, but saw no sign of Mika. Undeterred, the next week I got up very early, took my place between the station and the market and waited. Hours later, as the monotony of the watch began to take its toll, I decided to pack it in. This same procedure was repeated the following Saturday, when there was a bit more chill in the air. After a couple hours, a slight drizzle began falling and a few of the sellers began packing away their wares. I was just on the verge of calling it a morning when I looked up the hill toward the station. There she was. Mika, carrying a canvas bag in each hand, and wearing of all things, blue jeans, a denim shirt, and a large straw hat. Her clothing suggested a new side of her personality, making her appear as American as John Wayne, or at least like someone who might be with the Duke in *The Searchers* or *The Quiet Man*.

I called out, like a loud American, "Mika-san! Hello!" And, as I did so, I jumped up and began walking briskly across the street toward her.

She hesitated, then smiled. "Jack! What a surprise!" Her smile seemed genuine. "*O-hisashi-buri desu*! It's been so long! We both miss seeing you, though Uncle is too proud to tell you this. He has mentioned you more than once."

Even after almost three years in Japan, I was still having trouble decoding the local stylings of sentences like these.

"Should I contact him, then? It would be a pleasure to visit him again, and it was a very bad day when we … parted ways."

She shook her head. "No, that would not work, I'm afraid. He is … very proud. He is just too set in his ways." She had a plaintive look in her eyes and she looked up directly into mine. "But we have both missed you, very much so."

If I had ever wanted to grab her and plant one on her luscious lips, it was at that moment, standing amidst the chaos of a noonday street scene as the rain began changing from drizzle into a more sustained shower. We were under the awning of a furniture store, and I did manage to find the resolve to take her hand. "Mika, can we see each other? I mean—can we meet, maybe have dinner sometime?"

The next minute was one of the longest and most painful stretches of time in my entire life. I awaited her verdict, heart in my throat. Then, she looked up again. "Well, Jack-san. We both know … well, that what you are suggesting is not exactly … so proper. However—" She looked around, as if she expected someone to be watching her. "I do know a very fine fish restaurant, down by the seashore. The owner is an old friend of my family, and if we were to go there, well … I think it would be acceptable. If you will allow me, I would even like to treat you to lunch. Do you like fish?"

I was in heaven. I had asked the unaskable question, it seemed, and somehow had received the unthinkable response. "I live for fish!" I blurted out. If she had invited me to a restaurant where they served steamed hardware, or bowls of doorknobs, I would have been just as delighted. So we arranged a date and time the following week.

And so on the designated day, we met at Sannomiya Station and walked up to where I had stashed my car nearby. From there we rode down the hill and turned east, passing through a rather seedy part of town. This actually surprised me a bit, because I would have guessed that her restaurant choice would be splendid and rich in every way. But the restaurant's location "down by the seashore" referred to the unpleasant, formerly industrialized areas close to the port, and the restaurant itself was a very small space hidden beneath a railroad trestle.

From the outside, it looked sleepy and dirty, but when she led me in, she said a very long hello to the owner, who let out a boisterous "*Irashai-mase*!" Welcoming customers is high art in Japan. We found ourselves seated at a long bar overlooking the cooking units. The chef's specialties included both sashimi and various kinds of grilled fish.

I was a Midwest boy, of course, so until my stay in Japan, my idea of a "fish restaurant" was catfish, trout, or the local Long John Silver's. I had, of course, learned to eat a variety of fish in Japan and I did like standard forms of *sushi*, but this place was for connoisseurs and it featured all kinds of mysteries. And, despite my years in Japan I had never quite become an aficionado of exotic *sashimi*—raw fish, without the rice. I squirmed slightly as I watched the waitress bring out a long, blackened fish to one of the tiny tables, where two large women immediately attacked it with their chopsticks.

"So, Jack-san? What kinds of dishes do you prefer? Do you like *fugu*?" She meant blowfish, which, if not prepared correctly, contains lethal toxins that can kill the unsuspecting customer. *Fugu* is, at least according to some, one of the gold standards for true connoisseurs.

What should I say? I did not want to appear a novice, so I said, "Maybe, if you want some."

Surprisingly, she shook her head derisively. "*Yada*!" (Japanese for Yuk!) "It is not one of my favorites. Please tell me, what dishes do you like, Jack?"

In a glass case before us were fresh slabs of all kinds of

fish, nestled in crushed ice, beside various other side dishes. Along the far wall was a massive aquarium, filled with lively fish that nonchalantly went about their fishy lives, awaiting their sudden execution in the interests of culinary teleology. Customers could simply point a finger at one of their fattened number and within minutes it would be served on a platter, still twitching if you were lucky. The walls were jammed with pictures of sumo wrestlers—the proprietor was a huge fan, Mika said, and the place was a favorite when the wrestlers were in town for the Osaka tournament each spring.

"Mika, it would please me very much if you chose some of your favorite dishes, to sample." And so she began quizzing the chef on what was fresh, what was best that day, and so on. The method of the place was to pour endless small glasses of cold beer or sake, and then to sample dish after dish after dish of tiny but beautifully rendered variations of fish, fish, fish. Mika basically gave free rein to the chef, whom she called Takata-san. She addressed him also with the term *taisho*, a designation of the excellence of his craft. He was a large, balding, prodigiously-bellied man who easily and quickly produced some of the most delectable food I had ever encountered.

One by one, she ordered up a variety of Japanese delicacies for me to sample. And she refused to tell me what they were until after I had sampled them. This put me in an unfamiliar and awkward position, but I am proud to say that I passed with flying colors. We began with some of the famous local octopus from Akashi: chewy, but delicious and cold, dipped in the soy sauce, spiced up with *wasabi*. Each small sample was followed with something new to me—succulent, sliced sea cucumbers (*namako*) in soy sauce, vinegar, and grated white radish; fish *foi gras*, another delectable treat with a cheesecake-like texture (*ankimo*); and jellyfish with cucumber salad (*kurage*). So far, so good. But one final dish that made me sweat and immediately go for the beer was the crab brains (*kanimiso*). It looked to my untrained eyes like a dab of dark greyish toothpaste. Mika smiled, and told me it was one of her favorites, and so she had saved it for last. But for me, it was the hardest to swallow, and it made me slightly light-headed once I discovered what it really was. But for the pleasure of dining with Mika, I gritted my teeth and took the medicine.

As we ate and sipped our beer, we talked about movies, books, museums in Tokyo, visits to China and Korea, my own travels in Japan, and so on. The topics came and went quickly, like the selections of old Japanese *enka* music that wafted through the tiny restaurant. I asked about one lovely song. Mika tilted her head, listening intently for a moment. "Ah yes! Hibari Misora. One of the legends." She explained that *enka* was a sort of Japanese rhythm and blues, featuring wistful country-style lyrics, heavily nostalgic and heavily stylized.

As the music played, the television was left on, soundless as an NHK announcer read the news. Customers came and went, some lounging around for another beer or sake, while others stood waiting for a table of which there were only six in total, lined along the wall directly behind us. It was a popular place.

Suddenly, about an hour into our lunch, Mika noticed the time. "Ah, sensei. I must be going. I almost forgot I have an appointment!" She immediately gathered her things, and nodded toward Takata that we were done. There would be no bill, since exchanging money would seem crass for a regular like her, and it would be settled later. So I have no idea about the total cost, but I can safely say that this little joint under the railroad tracks ended up being the place where I enjoyed the most expensive meal I ever had in three years in Japan. And it was good—but, even better, far, far better, was my time with Mika alone. Or so I thought.

The taxi she had requested arrived quickly, and she jumped in. She rolled down the window to say farewell. I blundered out, "Mika, can we do this again? I owe you a meal. I need to pay you back."

She waited a moment. Traffic bustled by. "Perhaps, Jack-san. But I am going to Tokyo next week to see my father. And I don't know when I can return—maybe not for another two or three weeks, at least."

Disappointing news, which I think she easily sensed. The taxi began inching away. "But maybe when I return? You obviously know that I come to the market almost every Saturday morning, yes?" Smiling, she threw these promising questions out the window at me. I tried desperately to think of the right word for parting. But before I could answer, she was gone.

友

A couple days later, I was snoozing on my sofa, television on but muted, and some Japanese *enka* droning on from my stereo—Hibari Misaro, in fact. Suddenly, a fist began pounding gently on my front door. I say "pounding gently" quite specifically, since Japanese people rarely seem to be over-emotional in anything, including attempts to appear forceful. The knocking startled me, one of those sudden awakenings when you feel you are either drowning or being threatened by some unseen force, when you don't even recognize you had dozed off in the first place. Silence, then more pounding, slightly less gently, then a muffled, "Jack-san."

Miyamoto? I checked my watch. It was late, nearly eleven o'clock. What was he doing pounding on my door at this hour?

"Hold on, I'm coming," I called. I slipped on my robe and stumbled over to the door, kept the chain secured, and cracked it open. I rubbed my eyes. "Yes? It is late and I was asleep. What do you want, sensei?"

"Jack-san, can I speak to you a moment?" That was when I noticed the other man—very large and not very intelligent-looking—looming about five feet behind Miyamoto. He stood as if he were at military attention, with his hands clasped behind his back. He did not look at me. He looked like an enforcer of some sort, like someone out of a B movie. His flashy clothing, deeply wrinkled face, generally greasy appearance, and what looked like a nasty scar from a knife fight on his right ear indicated that he had some sort of mob connection, what the Japanese call *yakuza*. He fit all the stereotypes of a Japanese wise guy. Or, perhaps my memory is again playing tricks on me. In any case, I was suddenly scared and certainly on the defensive as I unlatched the door.

"Yes, sensei? What can I do for you, at this very late hour?" I wanted to be sure he caught my irritation, even with Guido the Goon lurking behind him. So I yawned and stretched my arms, just to make sure he got it.

Miyamoto had a devilish attitude about him and took his time. He peered behind me into the condo, as if he were looking for someone else. Spying on me, I thought, looking to see if I had a girl up there. "Jack-san, we are here on behalf of the Goto family. I need to … explain some things to you. May we come in?" I noticed his use of the "we" plural and wondered if Guido understood English. He had not moved or seemingly even taken a breath since I opened the door.

"It is very late, sensei. Please just tell me what it is you want." I remained firmly in the doorway, blocking their entrance. A rather ballsy move, in retrospect.

My brazen attitude seemed to catch him off guard. Then he said, "This will not take long. I just thought that you might like some … privacy, in case your neighbors were listening."

"My neighbors are all asleep. Like I was. What is it?"

He looked down the hallway both directions. "Very well. I'm here to … advise you concerning your relations with Mika-san. It is in your best interests to leave her alone and to never see her again."

So it was about Mika.

"Relations? What are you saying?"

He cleared his throat, smiling, ready to go for broke. "Sensei … we know that you met with her last Saturday and that you dined with her at Takata's place. You insult me to suggest I am not fully aware of these actions."

"These actions? You make it sound sinister. It was just lunch."

"Nevertheless." He relished this word, maybe it was the word of the day on some English vocabulary schedule he had. "Nevertheless, such a rendezvous cannot be repeated. You are to stay away from her. Is that understood?"

"What are you telling me? Are you threatening me? What if I do see her again? Anyway—we do plan to meet again." I lied. "I promised her." Sort of true.

Miyamoto briefly rubbed his ear, then down the side of his face. Guido stood eerily by, statue-like. Finally, he spoke. "I think you would be much better off canceling those plans. I am here to say that it is in your best interests not to approach Mika-san again in … such a manner. She is … even now, being prepared for other plans."

Other plans? "Who sent you here?"

"As I said, I have come on behalf of the Goto family."

"Professor Goto?"

"That is not important." He paused, scratched himself. "But maybe you should understand—more fully. Most directly, I have come here on behalf of Mika-san's father, Mr. Goto."

So now Miyamoto was tied up with the other Goto. Or was he? What did he imply with that phrase, "most directly"? My head was still fuzzy from being awakened so suddenly, and something alien was swishing loudly through my bowels, alerting me to the necessity of relieving myself in the very near future. I had no more questions and no curt reply. So I simply said, "Is there anything else?" Suddenly Guido shifted his weight, and crossed his burly arms over his chest. He now looked like one of those demon warriors guarding the gates of a mountain temple. All he needed was a fiery sword.

"Yes, Jack-san. I need to know that you … understand this arrangement."

Arrangement? Another vague Japanese styling. "If you mean, will I keep away from Mika, you can tell your boss that he has no power to tell me how to live my life."

This seemed to amuse Miyamoto, and a sudden gleam came to his eyes. He even chuckled, then waited a moment before saying, "Yes, of course, I will be happy to convey your message. Nevertheless"—again, he used his fancy new word—"I must warn you that Mr. Goto does not like hearing … disappointing news. Are you certain that this is what I should tell him?"

Oddly, Miyamoto's line about conveying "disappointing news" to his stern boss reminded me of some dialogue from *The Godfather*, and I suddenly beheld in my mind the image of a bloody horse head turning up in my bed. Maybe he had recently seen the film, and wanted to act like the cagy Robert Duvall character. Maybe he was imagining himself as some kind of *consigliere* to the great Goto dynasty. Delusions of grandeur, I thought.

I was tired of Miyamoto's insinuations, but *nevertheless,* the thought of Guido banging my head on pavement, or throwing me down a flight of stairs, was not very pleasant either. "Tell him … that I only had a lunch with Mika, and that we are only friends." Then I really hit bottom. "And that I will leave her alone and have no … romantic plans for her. Is that better?"

He smiled his sinister smile. "Yes, sensei. Much better that I take that message to Mr. Goto. I know you would not wish to … have another late night visit from my colleague, Endo-san." He gestured behind him to his silent partner, who noticed his name and Miyamoto's gesture, and bowed slightly in my general direction. "Thank you for your time, Jack-san. I will let you return to your rest."

And without a word, I slammed the door, though gently, in the slightly rebellious manner the Japanese style allows.

友

By now, winter was nearly unchallenged. Cold winds were a daily routine, snow or freezing rain were regular visitors. Oily puddles turned the streets into obstacle courses. As my final Thanksgiving and Christmas in Japan approached, I was becoming haggard and ready to pack it in. The only thought keeping me engaged was the slim idea of rejuvenating my friendship with Mika. The fish restaurant had now become, at least in my feverish imagination, the mythologized highlight of my three years in Kobe. But Miyamoto's tacky threats, along with his intimidating, tattooed sidekick Endo, got its claw as firmly lodged inside my brain as Mika's luminous face—so much so, that I found it hard to reconcile the two competing urges: 1) go after Mika, or 2) save my own neck from being crushed by some *yakuza* thug.

Nevertheless (as Miyamoto might say), I could not let my nemesis's threats—or, for that matter, the Moloch of Japanese manners and ideology—determine my fate, Endo's surly demeanor notwithstanding. It took me almost a month to gather the nerve, but I succeeded. She had mentioned that she might return from Tokyo within a month. So I returned to the Saturday morning farmer's market. The first week, four hours of lurking proved futile, as did my efforts the next several weeks. Finally, just a few days before Christmas, the sun appeared, the temperature turned balmy, and right on cue, as if the fortuitous weather were an omen, Mika appeared in full radiance. This time, she was walking along with an elderly, conservatively-dressed Japanese woman. Both were laughing together about something. The older woman giggled in the typical understated style of refined Japanese women, with hand over mouth. Mika, whose hands were once again occupied with two filled shopping bags, was laughing out loud, her mouth open, in a boisterous and unapologetic fullness.

Her clothing, like her laugh, was again that of a typical Midwestern American girl—bandana, denims, sweatshirt, and boots. It was an image that surprised and delighted me, and I have never managed to shake it in all the years since. Right in mid-laugh, as it were, she looked up and spotted me observing her. This caused her to stop, then smile my way, then immediately glance sideways toward the older woman, who continued chortling away, hand over mouth.

Our eyes locked, some hundred feet separating us, across the open lot. I called out to her, waving with both arms now, again, acting like a true American. The gesture caught the attention of the older lady, and they both looked at me and bowed, almost as if it were in tandem. I got up, walked across the pavement, and bowed myself.

"Mika-san, what a pleasure to see you again. *O-hisashi-buri.*" I bowed again, knowing I needed to be formal, given her elderly companion.

There was some embarrassment, and finally she spoke. "Jack-san, *O-hisashi-buri.*" She gestured toward the now rather stern looking woman. "This is my friend from Tokyo, Toda Setsuko." More bowing. "*Hajimemashite,*" we both said. "*Oba-san, Springs-sensei desu.*" We chatted briefly, then I abruptly asked, "Mika, can I speak with you a moment?" I looked at her companion, my eyes imploring her for permission to speak alone with Mika. Getting no sympathy, I proceeded anyway and guided Mika gently away, with a hand on her arm. The tiniest frown worked its way over Setsuko's crusty demeanor as we strolled across the street together, out of earshot.

"I've been hoping to run into you, Mika. Actually, well, our lunch together meant very much to me."

She waited a moment. "Yes, Jack-san. I truly enjoyed our time together. And I hope you liked my choice of restaurant. I'll never forget the look on your face as you tried the crab brains. You were very sweet, pretending to enjoy it!" This memory made us both laugh.

Suddenly she grew more serious. "Perhaps you have heard, but I am back in town to look after my uncle."

I hadn't heard, of course. "Why? What's wrong?"

"Jack-san, he is not well. He is quite ill, in fact. Since you have left, he seems to be doing more poorly than for many years." She hesitated. It was awkward trying to talk to her, with the older companion hovering hawk-like a short distance away. "I'm sure he thinks of you often."

Three years in Japan, but the local nuance of sentences like these still danced around me like gypsies. "Perhaps now is the right time to contact him, then? It would be a pleasure to visit him again."

She shook her head. "No, that would not work, I'm afraid. He is ill, but still very … self-important. He is … too proud." She had a plaintive look in her eyes and she looked up directly into mine.

A sudden, almost incomprehensible sadness gripped me at that moment, standing amidst the chaos of a noonday street scene as the sun disappeared behind some dark clouds, and a light drizzle began falling gently. We moved under the awning of a pharmacy, and I did manage to find the resolve to take her hand.

"Mika, can we see each other, again? Can we meet, maybe have dinner sometime? Like I said, I owe you a meal."

Immediately her eyes broke free from my gaze and she looked down. For the briefest moment she allowed me to hold her hand, then gently removed it from my grasp, both of us absolutely aware of the continuing gaze of her friend, Setsuko. Over the din of the marketplace, she spoke the fateful words that, for all practical purposes, brought my tenure in Japan to a close.

"Jack." They were seemingly as hard for her to say as they would become for me to swallow. "I am engaged. I am to be married in the springtime." With this announcement she looked up again to my eyes, smiling in that feeble way suggesting that such a smile is not genuine. Then she looked back across the way toward her older companion, smiling all the more. "In fact, you have met me at a rather awkward moment. You see, Setsuko is my *nakodo*—the woman whom my father has enlisted to find my husband. And she has found me a wonderful man, one of the young executives in one of my father's businesses. His family is very prosperous, with an old *samurai* lineage." She waited and smiled again. "I believe you Americans would call someone like my Hiroshi a 'go-getter.' My father calls him one of his young tigers. He and his parents live near my father, in Setagaya, up in Tokyo."

I was stunned by all of this, of course. "But I thought you told me that you could never allow yourself to do such a thing for your father? What about all that talk about falling in love?"

"But I do love him, Jack-san." It did not ring true, however. A moment passed. "He is a good man. And my father assured me that this time, if I did not comply with his wishes ... well, I can only say that there was some damaging information that he was willing to release in case I continued to be rebellious." Now she looked me in the eye again, this time with some terror, it seemed to me. "He simply cannot come to terms with the idea of his daughter remaining unmarried and childless, well into her thirties. And he demands a grandson." She was staring straight down at the ground.

"What damaging information? You mean about you?"

"No, Jack-san. About my uncle. And his … services to the government, during the war. And some later, dubious business dealings. It would involve much disgrace for him, as well as a substantial part of his share of the family fortune. My father can be quite ruthless, as you must know by now. I have no choice, you see."

More hesitation.

"And of course, I'm sure you realize. He would never agree to any marriage to someone … who does not meet his specifications." She straightened up. "That would include an American," She told me. "Even an American of great wealth." Then she looked me directly in the eye. "Certainly not a professor."

That last sentence was like a sharpened dart. "But Mika, don't you have a choice? Our lives are all choices. Look at you," I said, gesturing toward her American outfit, though this time it was not quite as brash as the cowboy costume. "Is that something a traditional Japanese woman would wear to the market on a Saturday morning?" I actually laughed at my own little tease. But she only smiled wanly.

"This clothing? Well, I wish to wear it for now, because in just a few months, I may never be allowed to wear it again, at least not in public." She explained this to me with an utter sadness. She even laughed a little, though it was one of those laughs of despair that signal our resignations in life. "I am sure you can never truly understand all of this, Jack. But I also know what I must do. My uncle … " She caught herself, and for just a moment it seemed she might sob. "Well ... he needs me to do this for him, and so I must obey my father. I will be leaving Kobe at the end of December, to be back in Tokyo for the New Year and to begin preparations for the wedding."

I was deep in shock, of course. I noticed out of the corner of my eye that Setsuko continued keeping watch over our conversation. Lamely, I asked, "So that's it?"

She looked up, tears actually welling. She brushed them aside, and stood erect. "Yes, sensei. That's it."

The conversation was over, but I tried to keep it going. "Well, we can at least meet sometime for tea, or just to talk, right?"

"No, I don't think that would be a good idea. Anyway," and here she glanced back toward Setsuko, "my movements are now being ... observed. My father has many enemies, and the idea of a scandal would make some of them very happy indeed." The image of Endo rubbing his hands together, eager to cast me down a stairwell, flashed through my mind.

I understood, so I said after a moment, "Right. So I guess we should say our goodbyes." Another long, painful locking of eyes. "Well, thanks for all that great tea and *sembei*!" I even managed to guffaw at this, and she also allowed herself to giggle precociously into her hand. And then I took her hand, freshly giggled into, and held it one last time. "You meant a lot to me here in Japan. Much more than you'll ever know, I'm sure. But I want you to know that, and I give my best wishes to you, Mika. I hope you find happiness." With that, I turned, shooting a look of animosity in the direction of Setsuko, and walked away down the street.

A few seconds later, I heard her voice for the last time. "Goodbye Jack-san. I also wish for you to find happiness!"

I turned, myself on the verge of tears, but instead made a little joke, throwing up my hands, and shouting "*Banzai! Banzai! Banzai!*" Three times for good luck. It brought a smile to her face. But then, as I headed off back down the road, the laughter turned to loneliness, and turning the corner, I understood that my effulgent hope of romancing a beautiful Japanese woman had been dashed to pieces, and as I continued down the busy sidewalk, it vanished into a distant past. I never saw Mika again.

友

Days poured into weeks, like rainwater through a downspout. It was the end of 1994, and the soggy holidays came and went, but the lifeless holiday season in Japan, where most people work until New Year's, seemed secular and very bland to me. But the end of the school year was nearing, and I had officially told the powers that be that I would leave Japan as soon after the holidays as was allowable. Technically, the school year would not end until late February, and it would be best, they informed me, if I could remain until then. I was in a compromising mood, so I booked a flight for the final day of February and contemplated what my life would be like back in the States. But in my heart, I was ready to get on the plane already.

I had no job lined up for fall of 1995 and no real plan to get one. In fact, I hadn't sent a single job application letter. My flight would take me back to Indianapolis, through Detroit, and at least temporarily to the house of my youth.

I would begin my re-entry into America in the large, mildewed basement room I occupied during high school. Like Mika, I was another thirty-something returning to the ancestral home. It was vaguely troubling, if not quite shameful, when I pictured myself eating a Midwestern meat loaf dinner with my aging parents, watching college basketball's "March Madness" with Dad as he slowly rocked away in his chair, reading the *Indianapolis Star*. The family dog Caliban, now overweight and arthritic, would be lying on the rug beside us, asleep. Most irritating of all was the thought of calmly making my bed each morning, rather than facing the grim reproaches of an angered mother. Making the bed was a big deal for Mom.

Going back to Indy would relieve the immediate pressures of not having a clue where I would end up in life. But I also knew that I couldn't possibly handle my parents for very long. So in those waning days after the holidays, I finally began the task of searching for a position for the next fall. I had already missed the major feeding frenzy of job applications that commences in October and November. So that opportunity was long gone. Nevertheless, I hunted through the job listings and sent out a couple dozen half-hearted letters for positions not interviewing at the MLA Convention, already past. Many of those were either one- or two- year temporary jobs, or sometimes post-docs designed for brand new doctoral grads. Or they were heavy-teaching positions at what appeared to be substandard institutions, either at tiny liberal arts colleges in states I had never visited, or at regional state universities with directions in their names—often, multiple directions, like "Northwest" or "Southeast." I can't say any of them excited my interest particularly, especially after a decade at elite institutions like

Yale and Kobe U. But my savings would not last forever, and you have to pay the bills. So I sent out my letters and waited.

Meanwhile, I began auctioning off my own possessions through the notorious enterprise of the sayonara-sale, like all the other *gaijin* before me. By the beginning of January most everything of value had been spoken for. I packed up the many books I had acquired and shipped them home to Indianapolis. The only major item left was the neat and clean Nissan that I had bought from Richard. I assumed that I would be able to unload it for a couple grand just prior to my own departure, just as he did. But it didn't turn out that way.

Pretty much everything else was in place, and I began waiting out the final few weeks of my Japanese sojourn. I was ready to head home, parents' basement or not. My colleagues at the department held a year-end *enkai*, a dinner party to bring closure and drunkenness to the group as a whole. As a result, I was essentially liberated from any further duties, or social events, with the school. There remained only one unresolved issue in Japan, but I tended to try my hardest to sweep it under the rug: The failed relationship with Sensei. Try as I might, it nagged at me like an old mule. Despite Mika's advice that I should not try to contact him, and her implication that I should never visit him without an invitation, the thought certainly did cross my mind. In fact, by the first part of January, only about six weeks before my scheduled departure, I had essentially decided that I must attempt a final visit, Japanese protocols be damned.

And I did make a final visit. But it didn't happen the way I envisioned. The visit was the defining moment of my life, but I had no way of knowing it at the time. Even now, as I begin to recount that fateful day, I get antsy. A tingling sensation starts deep down in my gut and radiates out toward my extremities. It's not exactly queasiness. And oddly enough, it's not remorse—although I freely admit it should be. But it is otherworldly, creepy, maybe something akin to deadness, and it still lives as some sort of hideous presence lurking at the core of my being, a thing that is ultimately unnamable. And the more I dwell on it, a visceral and psychological horror comes rushing back, as it has now as I sit here and prepare to record it.

I look back over that last paragraph and see how lame my sentences sound. Show, don't tell, is the old writer's adage. So now, all that's left is to spin the tale and try to put words to this unnamable something. As a friend once told me, we almost never realize the decisive events of our lives at the moments we are living through them. Realizing comes later—if at all.

友

So much crucial data in this chapter gets lost upon first reading, I fear. The sadness of losing Mika is palpable, of course—but it coincides with the related, perhaps greater sadness of leaving Sensei behind in the Land of the Rising Sun, which became far more intense, I now surmise. But you are not yet fully acquainted with the reasons for that great sadness, dear reader.

Perhaps it is most appropriate to have our narrator admit that it has in fact required—lo, these many years—even for him to "realize" the meaning of all these interrelated events and personalities. Jack's use of the phrase "Realizing comes later—

if at all" is quite telling. It will remind scholars of the verb's usage in nineteenth-century America as a marker for what later, post-Freudian psychologists would term "latency": an inability among the grieving and the traumatized to latch onto the "reality" of a particular loss. Time is required to make death "real."

Now, rereading this chapter with its references to horror and the inability to "realize" what did, in fact, happen, reminds me of a quote that Jack hid in plain view, for all to see, in his preliminary letter to me, the letter that initiated this entire, lengthy process of recovery wherein he describes his own anguished memories as "the story of a wound that cries out, that addresses us in the attempt to tell us of a reality or truth that is not otherwise available."

A wounded lover, I might add—as are we all, to some extent—or will be, by and by …

Chapter 11

I was sound asleep early on a Tuesday morning when I had the strangest sensation, mid-dream, of being flipped a few inches into the air. I had been up very late the night before, during which I had had many beers and sakes and almost nothing to eat. So being flipped into the air might have been a fantasy attributable to a very bad hangover. That sounds uncanny to begin with, but I still have the non-negotiable memory of being both awake, asleep, and airborne, all at the same time, if even for the slightest moment. I hit the mattress and then was tossed up over and over, like a child bouncing on a trampoline.

Meanwhile, there was general havoc all around me. Furniture began moving all to one side of the bedroom, books came flying out of bookshelves, a clock fell off the wall and bounced along the floorboards. The sound was like a huge wave in a sea-cove, splashing onto ancient rocks, just before a storm hits. But the storm in this case was hitting me, and pretty hard, too. Above, a map of the world was torn from the wall and came floating down, gently covering one of my feet. It was all in slow motion, and seemed to go on and on and on.

The largest bookcase fell over with a heavy crash. A bottle of Chianti broke into shards of glass, spilling its blood-like contents onto the rug. And the building rumbled on. I fell out of bed—or was, rather, tossed—and found myself sprawled on the floor, face down. The wreckage and sheer insanity of it all continued, the building still rumbling on as if someone was trying to turn on a reluctant car engine. It seemed to last for many minutes, not mere seconds.

Finally the initial disaster began to settle down. Wearing only my pajama bottoms, I covered my head with both arms and lay prostrate and fearful, face to the floor. The initial shock waves gradually subsided into powerful vibrations punctured by occasional outbursts of Mother Earth's anger. But nothing else fell down, at least not onto me. I did hear something fall in the dining area. Then I heard one tremendous explosion from outside, followed by a number of smaller crashes.

I struggled to my feet once I figured it was safe to do so. Dust and a few pieces of paper were floating down upon me, and I tried some lights, but they weren't working. My first impulse was to get out of the building, but my rational side told me that it had been an earthquake, and that the worst was over. Of course, I was mistaken about that.

Trembling like a scared kid, I felt as alone on this earth as I ever had. I found some clothes to put on—socks, sneakers, a pair of blue jeans, a T-shirt and sweater. Then I pulled on a hat and coat for the cold winter weather outside. I moved steadily over to the window to look out, and though it was still dark, I could hear sirens and general commotion on the streets fifteen floors below me. I also saw a number of fairly large fires breaking out. But the most horrifying sight was of one of the buildings just a few blocks down from mine. It was buckled right in the middle, and its upper floors had toppled over like a kid's Lego castle. Gazing around the other nearby streets, I saw other buildings in nearly as ridiculous a state of emergency. In the distance, toward the bay, I noticed the gleaming Sannomiya Hotel, now cracked in half and leaning to one side. Broken windows and bent iron were everywhere. One of the hydrants right below me was gushing water heavenward. Dozens of people began to emerge out of the buildings and into the streets, in varying degrees of winter dress. One man appeared dazed and naked, except for a pair of boxer shorts. A couple of dogs ran by, loose and free, something you never see in urban Japan.

I located my essentials and prepared to get out of the building. The shock of possibly being trapped in another high-rise about to be broken in half was a focusing motivation. I found my wallet, passport, car and apartment keys, my journal, a few toiletries, pharmaceuticals, contact lenses, some underwear, socks, and a couple shirts. I threw it all into my knapsack and took one more look around at the doorway. That's when I spotted a flashlight, which I grabbed, and then headed instinctively to the elevator.

I actually pushed the down button frantically several times and waited a second or two before realizing it would never come. Duh. I didn't even know at that time where the stairs were, and the general darkness in the building made locating a stairwell even more challenging. Good thing I had the flashlight. Meanwhile, I could smell something burning. What it was, or where it came from, I could not quite tell, but again it was highly motivating. As I started down the stairwell, it was even darker, and smokier, than my floor was. There were also several other tenants weaving their lonely way down the ten or more flights to the sidewalks. One guy, braver than the rest of us, was checking floors, pounding on doors, though how anyone could have slept through that experience was beyond me. I respected his courage, but continued descending the stairs. Finally I reached the lobby, also choked with thick smoke, and sprinted out the front door.

General chaos greeted me on Minato-dori, the large avenue outside my condo. One ambulance flew by, siren blaring. Debris had fallen off of various buildings into the street, and the ambulance weaved back and forth to miss the larger pieces. One man held a towel to the side of his head and limped by. A younger couple ran by, the mother clutching a newborn while the father carried bags and a stroller. I saw an old lady seated on a bench, clumps of debris in her hair and clinging to her clothing, gently rocking forward and backward, talking to herself, with an eerie smile on her face. At least she had found some kind of peace. Another woman, in a green bathrobe and curlers, with cream on her face, was smoking a cigarette while holding both hands outward, shouting, "Eriko! Eriko!" I also vaguely noticed others, hurrying in all directions as best they could, given the debris, which was everywhere. More dogs wandered by. There were cats cowering in shadows. Sirens wailed near and far. And ever so slowly, the sun rose over Kobe, Japan.

Once I got out to the sidewalk and scanned the nearby surroundings, the scale of the event began to sink in. From the looks of it, the roads were damaged but passable. For a moment I could not think of what to do, where to go.

But suddenly, I looked down the street toward an older residential neighborhood and saw a house on fire. And I immediately understood there was only one place to go.

I ran around the corner, stumbling over a huge chunk of concrete, sprinted up the hill a couple blocks to my Nissan, and jumped in. Revving the motor, I headed up into the mountains, where the road looked fairly open, rather than down the hill into the city. I guessed correctly that the quickest way to Sensei's would also be the road less traveled, and also the one least likely to have debris and human traffic at this desperate hour.

友

In all, around 5,300 persons were reported to have been killed by the Great Hanshin Earthquake, a 7.2 magnitude temblor that jolted Kobe awake at 5:46:51 a.m., on January 17, 1995. The quake is still the only one measuring over 7-point magnitude on the Richter scale to strike directly in the center of a major urban population area. It was the largest casualty number recorded in Japan since the Great Kanto Earthquake, which occurred on September 1, 1923 in Tokyo, killing 142,807 persons. In 1995, most victims were crushed to death by the collapse of their houses, and/or burned to death by the fires that followed the earthquake. Half of the dead were over the age of sixty. Among the victims, 59 percent were women, and 41 percent were men. About 170,000 houses were destroyed or heavily damaged in Hyogo Prefecture and Osaka Prefecture. Hundreds of office and apartment buildings were also severely damaged, many beyond repair.

On the first day of the earthquake, there were about

a million houses without electricity. For over a week afterwards, almost a million had no gas or water service. A large number of reinforced concrete office and residential buildings, including my condominium, were damaged at the middle or top floors. The number of refugees without homes—which should have included me, though I violated the law by squatting in my severely damaged building for over a week after it was officially condemned—was at least 310,000. Many of these refugees were without homes a full two years after the temblor. I heard later that my own building was pulled down several months after the quake, having sustained serious damages beyond repair to the foundation and other important structural elements. It remained a vacant lot until finally rebuilt in 2004, again as a high-rise condominium tower of twenty-two stories. In all, at least 50,000 buildings were destroyed immediately by the quake, and many thousands were later identified as irreparable, and listed for demolition.

Kobe's city officials attributed the large number of deaths among the elderly to the growing number of younger people living in the suburbs and the fact that many elderly people lived alone in the quake-stricken areas, and the fact that a large number of homes in the area were built before and immediately after World War II. In the Kobe area, most of the old traditional Japanese wooden houses have heavy ceramic tile roofs and clay filling. Designed to resist typhoons, these older houses presented a poor resistance to the devilish forces of an earthquake of such magnitude. Thus did hundreds of elderly Japanese die, crushed to death in their sleep by heavy roofs as another chilly dawn approached.

友

I knew the back roads leading up into the Rokko Mountains well, having spent many of my countless weekends exploring them with my new car. I began my trek slowly, since the roadways were clotted here and there with debris, fallen poles, and other damaged materials. By the time I hit one of my favorite roads into the park area, most of the debris, and people, had disappeared from view. As so often occurred in my long walks in the mountains, I was pretty much alone—for the moment.

The path I chose led up abruptly into the mountains, switching back several times, then coming out on a long ledge overlooking the city and the bay. It would lead me northeast for several miles to another winding lane, which would lead me back down to Sensei's neighborhood. What I saw when I came out of the forest and onto the overlook was nothing short of apocalyptic. I rolled down my window and heard dozens of sirens and alarms going off. Occasionally there were shouts in Japanese, or shrieks, that drifted all the way up the slope. Smoke was rising from countless sites, and raging fires dotted the neighborhoods. Many buildings appeared to be leaning this way and that, and some were simply toppled over. I took a few long moments just to gaze at this surreal scene, and then hurried off for my destination.

Heading back down the mountainside, I entered the area near Sensei's compound. I had to work my way down, then back up again, where a fair amount of damage littered the streets leading up to his residence. Fires were already going strong all around me. I was edging my way along the final road up to Sensei's dead-end location, a road that dropped off immediately to my right, when I saw a massive boulder blocking my path. It had evidently been broken off one of the cliffs overhead, and was deposited there as some test of my commitment. I tried maneuvering around it for a minute or two, then realized that it was a lost cause. I was still a quarter mile away from his house, but I had no choice. So I turned the car around and parked it, right there in the middle of the road, its back bumper almost touching the granite slab. Oddly, I put on the caution blinkers. I remembered the flashlight, and had enough good sense to grab it again. Then I headed up the hill.

Before long, I heard a scream from one of the large homes. "*Taskette! Tasketteeeeee!*" Desperate, lonely calls of "Help!" I hesitated for only a second. I looked into the property, which was partly hidden behind the kind of six-foot stone walls that were popular in the neighborhoods of the wealthy Japanese. A side of the home was caved in, and burning. Heavy roof tiles were scattered across that side of the lawn like a deck of cards. "*Taskette!*" The call came with much agony. But my decision was nearly immediate—I needed to ignore the call for help. I needed to find Sensei.

Sometimes, even now, fifteen years later, I hear the cries of "*Taskette-Taskette!*" in my sleep. Yes, I do have regrets. Many regrets.

My first sight of Sensei's house was similar to the one I saw just moments before: roof tiles were on the ground, and the whole front entranceway of the house was demolished. A single, large crack had actually torn the stone wall in the front of the house like a piece of cardboard, many of the windows were broken out, and a light gray smoke was rising from a few places, but I saw no immediate signs of fire. The crack in the wall was helpful. I didn't know the code to the gate, so I just stepped through the wall and into the property. An uncanny silence pervaded the complex, though the distant sirens and general melee continued, providing an ambient mood of disaster. I ran up to the front and found it impassable; pieces of wood were literally stuck into the ground like tombstones. I circled around to the side and then to the back of the building where there was similar destruction. The backside had large windows that came down almost entirely to ground level, and both of them were broken out. I looked around for a piece of lumber, and used it to take out what little shards of glass remained, then stepped directly into the darkened room. An eerie silence greeted me, and for the first time, I was in Sensei's home with my shoes still on.

"Sensei! SENSEI!"

I could barely see what was in the room. I flipped on the flashlight; thankfully, the batteries were fresh and the beam still strong. Furniture, dishes, glassware, books, and unidentifiable debris were everywhere. Large sections of the ceiling had fallen in.

I inched my way through all the destruction, shouting again and again, "Sensei! Are you here?!" Only silence. I went from room to room. It was a large and impressive building, but now it looked like a bomb had gone off in it. I was not used to entering from the back, and I spent a few minutes inspecting the rooms I had never been in. I pointed the light into another room, one that appeared to be a sleeping chamber for a servant. Heaped into one corner were the gruesome remains of a body, covered with plaster and wood. I turned the body enough to see that it was Omori-san, Sensei's old gardener/chauffeur/companion, with a terrible gash across his face. My amateur examination found that he had no pulse. Then, from elsewhere, I faintly heard a voice: "Yu-san!"

It was weak, but it was Sensei. "Sensei! Where are you?" I released my hold on Omori-san.

Only silence. Then, "I am in our meeting room, Yu-san. Please come."

His politeness continued even then, I thought. I stepped out of Omori's room and followed the corridor around to the kitchen area from where I had entered, and then to the long hallway leading to the front door. Screens were tipped backwards and forwards along this hallway, some at forty-five degree angles across it, making it a kind of obstacle course to negotiate. I smelled smoke.

"Sensei, I'm coming!"

I fought through the screens and found the room. I was deeply moved when he called it "our room." But today, our room was a mess. Like the others, it was topsy-turvy. A priceless Utamaro print was lying on the floor just outside, the glass cracked and the picture penetrated by the side of a screen. The room itself was even worse than the others. Much of the ceiling had collapsed, and the floor was littered with debris. Tables and vases were knocked over, pictures fallen off the walls. I looked in and pointed the flashlight frantically around the room.

"Sensei? Where are you?"

"Here, Yu-san." I looked toward the voice and saw a futon for sleeping. I could make out the legs of the old man protruding from underneath one corner of a heavy oak bookcase, covered with part of the ceiling. I pointed my flashlight toward the mess and saw that on top of it all was a massive wood beam, the structural strength of the roof, along with even more clutter and debris. The end of the beam was near my feet. I stuck my flashlight in my coat pocket, placed both hands beneath the beam and tried to lift it. It didn't budge. I rubbed my eyes. It seemed to be getting smokier, and I realized it was surprisingly warm in the room.

I worked my way through the rubble as best I could. My first act was to look him in the eyes. I put the palm of my left hand on his forehead. He was damp and feverish. "Sensei, I'm here. How do you feel? Can you breathe?"

I already knew that there would be no way for a single person to do much good. He was trapped under a ton or two of dead weight, and the miracle was that it had not already killed him. It had to have been at least an hour or more since the quake hit. And yet I was struck by the fact that he looked at me with compassion and even joy. When I think of that moment now—it was odd, yet consoling—Sensei showing compassion for me, being happy to see me, at that moment and under those circumstances. He had his right arm free to move, and first he grasped my left arm, and sort of shook it. Then he mimicked my own movement, and placed it gently on my own forehead. "Ah, Yu-san. You have come back for one more visit, I see." He actually smiled, but then grimaced in great pain.

"Sensei, don't try to speak." I was lost for words. I looked him up and down, flashed the light up toward the ceiling. "I need to go for help. I can get you out of here."

But he grabbed my arm with his free hand. "No, Yu-san. That is not necessary. We both know."

Tears welled up in my eyes, but I tried to stay brave. "But Sensei, I need to get you out of here, get you to the hospital." Though I knew it was not to be. "Where is the pain worst?"

"My stomach, Yu-san." I tried feebly to feel around underneath the pile for his abdomen. Pulling out my hand, it was coated with rich, warm blood. It was not a massive issue of blood, but just enough, I suspected, to be fatal eventually.

I think, looking back, that we both knew, in that instant, that he would not last much longer. "Stay with me, Yu-san. Let's have—" he winced again, his face contorting in pain. He took a shallow breath. "Let's have one last meeting."

"Meeting?" I was incredulous, but I somehow understood. "About what?"

He seemed to think about my query. "About the words, Yu-san. About all those wonderful letters." He winced and tried weakly to push the debris off of his chest. "Pound's *haiku*. Hemingway's stories. The words I spent my lifetime collecting. The meetings have always been about the words and the letters, have they not?"

"Yes. Of course … the words, Sensei."

He tried again, feebly, to move the weight off of his body. I pulled on it with him. The bookcase shifted, but only slightly. He settled back into his position of fate, lying there on the soiled and bloody futon. "First, I need you to follow some directions. Can you do me this service? Afterwards, we can begin our meeting. By chance, do you have water? My throat is parched."

"Yes, sensei. Anything." I ran back out toward the kitchen, located a bottle of water from the now silenced refrigerator; still cold to the touch. Hurrying back, I held it to his lips, and he drank deeply, over half the bottle in one long draught. This revived him considerably.

"Good," he said, panting. "Thank you. Now I need you to rescue some of my collections. In fact, I want you to have some of them." More uncomfortable fidgeting beneath the weight. "Can you look into the next room, where I keep many of my things?"

"But Sensei, there's no time."

A renewed energy flashed in Sensei's eyes. "Yes, Yu-san. You will do this. For me."

I nodded, stood up, and walked out to the hallway, pointing the flashlight and peering into the designated room. The shades were pulled and it was completely dark, and the room was damaged, but navigable. "Yes, Sensei, I can get in OK." I quickly opened a couple of the shades, which helped.

"Good." He waited and thought it over. "I want you to open the closet screens." I did this. "Do you see the safe?"

Of course I did—it was huge, taking up half the closet space, and was almost as tall as I am. The rest of the closet was filled with file cabinets and stacks of those dark green library boxes that were often the focus of our meetings together. I told him that I had access to all of it.

"Good. I want you to open the safe." He gave me the numbers. On the second try, it clanked open. On top was a large, faded green volume. I took it out and read the gold words on the binding: *Leaves of Grass*. A first edition of Whitman's masterpiece, circa 1855, by itself probably worth several hundred thousand dollars or even more, since it contained an inscription by the author. Below it were a number of other books, several file folders, other valuable commodities such as coins and medallions, and several more library boxes. Then *Moby-Dick*, with Pound's inscription: "April snow camellia." There was also a large stash of cash, both yen and dollars, and some jewelry, as well as other documents. I picked up the Whitman and went back into Sensei's room with it.

"Here's the *Leaves of Grass*, Sensei. There are lots of other things in there. What would you like me to do with it all?"

With his free arm, he actually handled the leather-like covering of the volume, admiring it one final time. "This is for you." He breathed in sharply, and actually pushed the book at me. "There are other first editions in the safe, all for you. *Fanshawe*, some of the others I've shown you, the Stowe, Emerson, Dickens, the rest. *Old Man and the Sea*. Of course, Pound's copy of *Moby-Dick*, Yu-san. Don't leave that one. Take as many of them as you can save."

He winced, his breathing labored. "Since our previous meeting, there are some … new materials on Pound and …" He stammered, his voice still firm, but growing faint. "They are in one of the green boxes, in the safe. Do you remember those strange *haiku*?" He grimaced. "The blood moons? From Joel."

I was amazed that, pinned underneath debris from his fallen roof, on the very edge of death, he felt it necessary to speak in detail about these treasures, but he did. "Take those files, Yu-san. And don't forget about … Nook Farm. There's a large binder of … materials there. Very … crucial. Perhaps some day you can … solve the puzzle. It may be part of some … occultic formula. Save those, they are original and unique. Very valuable!" He actually chuckled at this last comment. "You must try to solve that mystery, on your own, I'm afraid!"

"Yes, Sensei, of course," I assured him. I had no clue why he referred to Nook Farm just then—the genteel neighborhood in West Hartford, home to Mark Twain, Harriet Beecher Stowe, Isabella Beecher, and others. Maybe just his mind wandering.

"And I want you to have the Hemingway files also, Yu-san. They are in there, marked, as I showed them to you last year. And be sure to take the Hemingway valise, as a memento of our times together. It must be here among the clutter somewhere." Another smile. "Perhaps you can play the joke on someone else, the one I played on you!" A weak chortle. "I wish I had those other books, *On the Road* and *Howl*, here for you; the ones you 'borrowed' from the library. I know how much you fancy them. But anything after the War is not so valuable to me." I also now laughed, with tears in my eyes. Still razzing me, right to the end.

He drew in a ragged breath. "Everything else in the safe should go to Mika-san. There are some files in Japanese, look for those. Find the materials on Mishima. And there is … much cash, and some jewels, and other documents of value." More strained, raspy breathing. "Yu-san. I must tell you, I regret … interfering in your … friendship with Mika. I know how … seldom one can approach … true romance. Yes, I do regret that." He was growing short of breath. "But my brother … he would never allow such a thing. And he is … quite ruthless, as you must know. I am sorry for that."

He was running out of time. "Don't bother talking, Sensei. You're losing strength."

He even smiled again. "We must have our meeting, Yu-san, remember." He breathed in and out, laboring now. "I must insist. As for the other documents in the cabinets—well, I had hoped to give them to the university. For now, I can only say that I leave it all to your discretion. They are for the Americans, I should say. The most important things are in the safe. Is there more water?"

I held the bottle to his lips again. He drank slowly, finishing the bottle. Again, it strengthened him for the moment. "You know of my obsessions with Hemingway, Yu-san. But he is not the author of my favorite book in

America. Do you know what that is?" As he quizzed me one last time. I tried to hold back the tears, but failed.

I wiped my face with the back of my hand. "No, Sensei. What is your favorite American book?"

Again he reached out and touched the green volume. "You are holding it in your hands." It seemed to give him considerable pleasure to inform me of this.

"*Leaves of Grass*? Why Sensei, you surprise me! It turns out that you're a hopeless romantic, after all!" By then tears were streaming down my face.

He noted my attempt at gently mocking him, and faked surprise, his eyes growing wide for just a moment. "Hopeless? Me? No, Yu-san. Once again, you have misunderstood. True romantics are of all people the most hopeful. That silly phrase—'hopeless romantic'—is a sign of a weak mind. Have you learned nothing from me?" he joked, instructing me to the very last, but it was nearly over. He grew silent for a long while. I took his hand, and he did not resist.

His voice was now a mere whisper, but he kept talking. "Whitman knew some things, and his words ennobled people. He forced us to think about what we might be in the world. Without words, the people remain powerless. Without beauty, life becomes ugly and unlivable." A brief moment passed. "It is why both of us 'romantics' became teachers of literature, I'm sure. Sowing in hope. Otherwise, the words are just ... scratches of ink on paper."

His face tightened, he gasped for breath, then exhaled. "Is it too late to say that I'm sorry we lost this last year together? You have been ... yes, I think, a good friend to me. And I am sorry to think you felt I lied to you, or mislead you." He stammered. "In fact, I did."

"No, Sensei. I understand it all now." And in that moment, I did understand.

He was losing steam, but still he kept on. "*Yu-jin.* A companion. I recall the day I named you. Do you remember?"

I choked back a sob. "Yes, Sensei. I remember everything."

A long silence ensued. "Perhaps you could read to me from that book, Yu-san."

I nodded. I could barely speak, but I took a deep breath and opened the volume to the first page and began to read:

I celebrate myself, and sing myself,
And what I assume you shall assume,
For every atom belonging to me
as good belongs to you. . . .

Sensei grabbed my arm with what little energy remained. "No, not that one. Read to me from 'The Sleepers.'"

It happened also to be one of my favorite poems. But since the first edition does not have the titles of poems included, or a table of contents, it took me a minute to find it. And so I began to read aloud again, the meticulous, loping lines casting a spell on us both, like a hypnotic trance.

I wander all night in my vision,
Stepping with light feet, swiftly and noiselessly
stepping and stopping,
Bending with open eyes over the shut eyes of sleepers,
Wandering and confused, lost to myself, ill-assorted,
contradictory,
Pausing, gazing, bending, and stopping.
How solemn they look there, stretch'd and still,
How quiet they breathe, the little children in their
cradles.

Sensei, his eyes now shut, was mumbling something to himself. He flinched fitfully, then seemed to settle down. A wan smile formed itself on his dry lips. I continued reading from the poem.

I stand in the dark with drooping eyes by the
worst-suffering and the most restless,
I pass my hands soothingly to and fro a few inches
from them,
The restless sink in their beds, they fitfully sleep.
Now I pierce the darkness, new beings appear,
The earth recedes from me into the night,
I saw that it was beautiful, and I see that what is not the
earth is beautiful.
I go from bedside to bedside, I sleep close with the
other sleepers each in turn,
I dream in my dream all the dreams of the other
dreamers,
And I become the other dreamers.

I stopped another moment, and looked down at Sensei now. And I could tell that he was gone. It was finished, and I knew it.

I closed the book and placed it gently beside him, and wiped the tears away from my eyes. Suddenly I realized that the fire was raging, out of control in a nearby room. I tried to figure out how to leave this gruesome scene, and the only thing I could think of was to cover him up somehow. I stumbled to my feet, swung the flashlight around and into the hall, and noticed a light green curtain on the floor. I pulled it into the room and covered the remains of my teacher, my friend.

The smoke was thickening, and I knew that my time at Sensei's house was quickly coming to an end. The first thing I grabbed was the copy of *Leaves of Grass*, just within the reach of his right hand. I looked for the old valise, which I figured should be across the room somewhere. Hemingway's valise, as Sensei liked to call it. Hunting through the debris, I noticed its faded leather gleaming from beneath a table. It had been badly scratched but was in working order, so I pulled it free, and threw the old volume of Whitman inside. Archivists would faint with horror to see how I treated Whitman's treasure that day.

Locating the valise had eaten into the window of opportunity I had remaining in the house. I looked down the hallway and saw the glare of fire from another room at the other end of the house. I understood that it was now a matter of rescuing as much of the materials as I could, in whatever time might remain. I took the valise into the room with the safe, drew out the Hemingway files, and threw them in with the Whitman, with a few of the other books—*Fanshawe*, *Moby-Dick*, *Representative Men*, *Uncle Tom's Cabin*. There was the heavy green library box, with the Pound materials he had mentioned: a thick file folder, which I took out and put into the valise. I rooted around and located one marked "Nook Farm"—Sensei had made special mention of that one as he faded away. On top I placed Hemingway's signed copy of *The Old Man and the Sea*. Being full, I now closed it, clasping the locks of the case. I set the valise outside the doorway, and went back to the closet.

I needed to rescue whatever I could from the safe, first of all, to present to Mika. It took several minutes. I located a few boxes, and filled them with the contents of the safe, then carried them out towards the back. First, I cleared the path of the fallen screens, to create a safer passage out to a back door, which I managed to twist open. It led into the garden, which was now surprisingly peaceful. All of this took even more precious seconds. Then I carried out the boxes for Mika, stacked them near the back of the garden at a safe distance from the building, and headed back inside. The hallway was passable, but I knew I had only another trip or two into the recesses of the house before I would need to abandon ship. My eyes stung, and I was coughing from the smoke. A fire was now raging in the kitchen and back apartment where I had spotted Omori's body.

I went back to the storage closet and started going through the cabinets and boxes frantically. I figured I owed it to Sensei to rescue whatever I could, and especially to find the most valuable and the most rare of his items. This was a considerable task, and ultimately impossible: the heat was gathering, and Sensei had many wonderful possessions. The things in the safe were simply his favorite items; many other treasures were in those neat green boxes. There were letters written by Edith Wharton, a diary of a Civil War general from Missouri, a volume of autographed poems by Yeats, the manuscript of an unpublished essay by Mark Twain. Thankfully, many of the boxes were labeled as to contents, so I scanned quickly through a couple stacks and pulled out the ones that seemed most promising.

Given a day of leisure to go through the stuff, perhaps I might have chosen other things than what ultimately was salvaged from the flames. But time was running out, and black smoke and heat began filling my lungs. I decided it was time to cut my losses, so I started dragging the boxes I had set aside into the hallway. On the polished wood floor, now cleared of the screens that had earlier been in the way, I could easily drag out most of the things I had set aside, and so now began doing it. But suddenly, as I looked up at the back door, a human figure appeared in silhouette. I froze.

"What are you doing?" a voice asked, in a broken, yet familiar English.

It took a few confused seconds for me to realize that it was Miyamoto. "Put those things back where you found them," he shouted, moving into the house.

I did drop them to the floor, and then stood my ground and faced him. "Sensei gave me these things. He's dead now, killed in the quake."

"Is he? And you expect me to believe that he has given you these valuables that you are now carrying out of his house? How convenient." He was now moving slowly toward me, with his arms held at both sides, menacingly I thought.

"Yes, he did. What are you going to do about it?" It was hard to think, hard to talk.

The blaze intensified. Miyamoto glanced into the kitchen, then the room with Omori-san. "You should have known your place, Jack-san. You should have stayed away. Now, I cannot allow you to leave."

I suddenly recalled that Miyamoto had once boasted to me that he studied the martial arts. He did not have the appearance of a very intimidating fighter, but I also knew that my own prowess was fairly limited. Anyway, the house was on the verge of total collapse, due to the growing fire, and I knew we were now in grave danger.

"Help me get these things out of here. Let me take what Sensei has given me, and you can have the rest, I don't care. Just move out of the way!"

"I will NOT move out of the way. If you will kindly move away from those boxes now, I will permit you to leave."

We were now less than ten feet apart. Flames were literally leaping out of the room just behind Miyamoto, and

I knew there was no other way out. I put myself instinctively into a defensive posture. "Get out of my way," I told him.

With that he leaped toward me, and to the best of my ability I thrust him to one side, into the wall. He scrambled up and punched me, sending my head snapping back. Stunned, I stood there letting him hit me again. But then my anger rose. He awoke within me the slumbering animosity that I held, not only for Miyamoto himself, but for all the rat fink nonsense he represented, all the repression of institutional Japan. And for his threats, and for getting between me and Mika. I remembered the creepy night he showed up at my place, with his henchman, Endo, looming behind him. I didn't give him a chance to hit me again. I reared back and struck him in the nose. I felt his blood spray as his nose cracked sideways. And then I smashed my first into his face again, this time for Guido, I guess. Then the third time, I caught him square on the jaw with a powerful left. I would have kept pounding him, but he fell to the ground and the back of his skull cracked against the doorframe leading into the hallway. His eyes opened wide momentarily, and he jerked upward. I saw his tongue jut wildly out of his mouth for a fraction of an instant. Then he fell backward again, eyes open and mouth closed, motionless now but for one strong exhalation.

I figured he was just dazed and resumed pulling the boxes out the back door and into the garden. Flames from the kitchen singed my hair and jacket, but I decided to make one last pass through the rooms. Several boxes remained that I desperately wanted to save, but I just couldn't do it. The walls would surely be coming down any second. Then I realized the safe was still standing open. Though it was by now nearly empty of its treasures, instinct told me, weirdly, that I must shut and lock it, to remove any suspicions that might linger in the minds of curious investigators whenever they would get around to Sensei's property. Maybe it would preserve the remaining valuables, I thought. So I quickly closed and locked the safe.

Finally, though I had second thoughts, I knew I had to pull Miyamoto to safety outside. I shook him, trying to revive him. He was out cold, barely breathing. I saw around the back of his head a pool of what looked like black blood, swelling almost imperceptibly. As much as I disliked the guy, I knew I had to get him out of the house so he wouldn't burn to death or suffocate in the smoke. Turning his body headfirst toward the back of the building, I towed him down the hallway. I had to pick him up to get him out the door, but I managed to do it. In the garden, I laid him out on his back. I pulled a few of the curtains off the back windows, and covered him up in the January chill—and yes, I left him right there in the cold. He was nearly lifeless, and blood was still seeping from his head wound.

Now outside for good, I could see that other homes in the area were facing similar emergencies. I had many opportunities to be a hero that day—to help Sensei's neighbors, most of them old folks like him. And as I left the yard with the first load, heading for my car, I thought I even heard Miyamoto say something. Maybe he yelled out in agony, or maybe it was a neighbor, or just my imagination. But I imagined later that I could hear him calling for help. "*Taskette! Jack-san, tanomu yo!*"

But I had to get the boxes and other items out to my car, which was a big job since I'd had to park on the other side of that boulder, a good way down the hill. So I started going back and forth, lugging stacks of boxes. It took four or five trips, but I finally managed to get everything into the car.

On the last trip, I checked Miyamoto. He was dead. Another large puddle of blood had formed around his skull; the clumsy fall into the door jamb must have fractured it. I shook my head, stood for a moment with palm on my forehead as if considering my options, then decided there was nothing I could do for him. I had made my choice about what was valuable and what was not. So I turned and left the property. Back at the car, I got in, started it up, and headed back down the road out of the neighborhood.

As Kobe burned, I decided to get as far away from it as I possibly could. With a car full of precious documents, I made another decision, and headed up into the Rokko Mountains that looked down upon the vast area of destruction below. I drove north, toward central Japan, and away from the coast.

友

It's funny, the things I remember about that day and the things I don't, or the many things that remain blurry. I remember every word of Sensei's last lesson, and the sad look in his eyes as he lamented the time we'd spent angry and apart. I remember the voices calling for help. I remember the rage that washed over me as Miyamoto launched himself at me. I remember the impact of my fist connecting with his face. I remember telling myself it was not really my fault that he was dead. (Maybe that's true, maybe not.) And I remember the cold, logical decision to close and lock the safe. The decision not to recover Miyamoto's dead body. And how I valued, instead, the boxes of letters and manuscripts above the men and women in the damaged, smoldering houses surrounding me. All "for the words," as Sensei might put it. Shouldn't I feel some remorse?

Yes, I should. But, in fact, I feel almost nothing—except now and then when that shadow of horror awakens and claws at my gut—and so I refrain from looking back directly at those moments.

I've never spoken of the events of that day, but have known for years that I must someday write something down. I've often wondered if I'd suffered some kind of post-traumatic stress syndrome, a common enough prognosis these days, something I usually associate with military vets and others who live in the line of fire. If I'm honest, I have to say I do not regret what happened. And I don't, or perhaps, can't, feel remorse. Why is that?

But when I close my eyes at night, the images often return. The massive beam pinning Sensei to the futon. A skyscraper bent over like a pipe cleaner. The sound of Miyamoto's skull striking the hard wood at the base of a doorway. The futile cries of the dying: "*Taskette!* ***TASKETTEEEE***!" Dragging Miyamoto's body out to that peaceful garden, then hurrying to load my precious boxes in the car as he bled to death on the frozen ground.

And there are other misgivings as well. Of the cash that was in the safe, I sent most of it to Mika—but not all of it. I kept a large sum to complete the tasks assigned to me by my mentor. I packaged up the items Sensei wanted Mika to have—including the majority of the cash and jewelry—and shipped them to her Tokyo address from a post office outside of Kyoto. But that didn't take all the money I'd set aside for the task. I kept the rest.

I don't know if Mika or her father ever went to Kobe to check on Sensei's house, to see the destruction with their own eyes. I never asked, and I didn't have the courage to face her anyway. I could never have found the words to tell her about her uncle's lonely, painful death. And I didn't want to see her again knowing she was about to be married. Especially not after what Sensei, in his dying moments, had said about true romance. So, after I sent her the packages, I never saw or communicated with her again.

友

Portentous rumblings, indeed. When I read Jack's words for the first time, I felt as if the ground beneath my own feet had shifted, revealing the flaws within the foundations of both of our worlds. It is difficult to express my sense of horror—in particular, the description of Jack's final meeting with Miyamoto and his role in the man's death. Death, I say—not murder.

Here we can see why the clinical signs of trauma were so neatly and mysteriously listed by our narrator, early on. How he must have suffered! But I still admit to a nauseating confusion that has made me wonder if I even knew this version of Jack. The former student with whom I had been corresponding all these many years. My very own intellectual progeny, in fact—my own precious offspring, as it were, which, to my mind, implicates me in some way. It caused me to speculate further: to what extent do parents share in the guilt of their children's crimes? Or teachers, mentors, coaches, pastors, or priests? Those of us, in other words, called to provide not mere information, but formation, character, integrity, honor, the knitting together of a human soul? Sowing in hope, indeed. I recognize that some readers will find these to be mere abstractions that have grown rather stale in our postmodern age, alas. But some of us still hold onto them.

This nausea of which I speak comes in the wake of that conjecture—to what extent am I guilty as an absent participant in the senseless death of Jack's nemesis? And knowing all this, how can I embrace the spoils of Jack's adventures overseas?

And yet, dear reader, as you will soon discover, I did, and still do, share in those delightful spoils. And like Jack, I do embrace them with some queasiness, yes, but with little or no, remorse.

Chapter 12

The only person in all of Japan that I wanted to see after the quake, and after all that happened at Sensei's house, was my old buddy Jim, the restless mystic, holed up on the top of a mountain with his Buddhist cohort, looking down on all of the human misery. His temple, *Ryoan-ji*, might provide a convenient landing spot, a temporary shelter for me, and (I hoped) a long-term storage unit for the treasures I was hauling in the back of my Nissan. For one thing, I wondered if someone else might come looking for those valuables, or for me—perhaps someone like Endo. So I headed, almost instinctively, for the hills.

I arrived at the temple, high in the crisp mountain air, late in the afternoon of January 18, a day after the tragedy. I had slept in the car along the way, and my now-wrinkled clothes smelled of smoke and sweat. I parked along the same road I had first used, a pull-off near the derelict bus-stop next to the pathway approaching the temple. Snow was not an issue, luckily. I locked the car and checked it twice—thinking again that there were bad people even in

Japan—and began winding my way up the mountainside toward the hideout.

Again it was a long journey, and again, as I passed into the complex high on top of the mountain, there sat the old, broken-down monk on the massive boulder, like a statue, frozen in time. His eyes were closed, and he was facing directly into the weak sunshine. *Ryoan-ji* glistened in the background, its dusty reds and oranges charged with the grandeur of God.

On the first evening, I told the abbreviated (or, rather, heavily edited) story about my earthquake experience. I didn't mention Sensei or what happened at his house. As far as the monks were concerned, I had just run out of my building, gotten in my car, and driven directly to *Ryoan-ji*. Initially, I neglected to mention the boxes in my back seat and trunk. Nobody asked questions, or seemed to find my story curious, though I did feel Jim's hawk-eyed scrutiny burning into my eye-sockets. I couldn't meet his gaze.

The next day, I shuttled back down the mountain, mainly to watch the news coverage of the quake on NHK, and to make some phone calls, preparing for my imminent departure (Jim still had no phones up there). I got hold of my parents, who were frantic about the earthquake and had not heard anything from me. They had called the university repeatedly, as well as the US Embassy. My mother sounded very old on the phone that day, as if her palpitating heart was audible from seven thousand miles away.

I also managed to contact Professor Aoyama, and let him know I was OK. He was at the office just days after the event. "Springs-sensei! Thank you for calling! The U.S. Embassy has been searching for you!" He shouted into the receiver, his voice full of frantic exclamation marks.

"Yes, sensei. I know. My parents have been worried. I finally spoke with them."

"And where are you?"

Pause. "I'm at a friend's house. Out here in Nagano."

"Nagano-city?"

Another hesitation. "Yes. That's right. Nagano-city." There was no need for me to be any more specific. I assured him I would be back in Kobe very soon, and asked him about what details I would need to take care of in order to leave Japan. I insisted that I wished to leave Japan as soon as possible. This seemed to surprise him a bit, since the contract did not end until March, but he said he understood my desire to fly home, and that, given the city-wide damage, the schedule for the rest of the term was up in the air anyway. I wanted to know the details of departure: where I should drop my condo keys, where I should pick up any remaining salary. He was very kind, assuring me that he would arrange whatever final matters needed to be resolved at the university.

Aoyama's helpful answers motivated me even more to get out of the country, so I called Northwest Airlines over and over, trying to move up my departure date. It turns out I wasn't the only one trying to get out of Japan, and there were no seats available at the moment. Finally, I found an open flight: Feb. 1, a Wednesday, just over a week away. Then it hit me: I was finished with Japan. I would have to head back to Kobe, pack up whatever remained in my condo that was worth taking home, and say my sayonaras.

The next morning at *Ryoan-ji*, I headed down the mountain to my car with Jim and four of the other monks. I had finally told Jim about the items in my car—although I didn't tell him the whole story, of course—and he had spoken with Watanabe-roshi about my request to store six medium-sized containers at the temple, in a side chamber along with the other treasures of the temple. The *roshi* met with us both for about ten minutes, assuring me that they could handle my request "efficiently and silently," as he put it. "We are *Ryoan-ji*—the silent dragon. Silence is a specialty here."

I had no need to describe the contents of the boxes, if I chose not to, and they did not even want to know how long it would be until I returned for them all. We agreed upon a shibboleth, a secret item by which future inmates of the temple could know that I had sent an agent to recover the boxes. The only thing we omitted was a secret handshake. It was all rather mysterious, and actually kind of cool. I guess the less they knew, the better it would be for everyone. And I could not explain why, but I trusted them—about 95 percent or so, anyway.

Still, I carried that 5 percent of lingering suspicion back to the states with me. Especially considering that the contents were worth a huge amount of money, tempting to anyone, zen monks or not. Casually I asked, "So, what's in it for you?"

Watanabe-roshi smiled serenely at what must have seemed to him to be a crude, American-style question. He leaned forward and took my hand, rather gently. He was in no rush to respond. Then he said, "Why must there be anything in anything? Such an American consideration! You are Jim's friend, and that is good enough for the rest of us, *ne*?" He laughed at this last statement, as though it were a sudden discovery. I said nothing further.

So we hiked down and loaded ourselves up with everything from my car. Everything except Hemingway's valise, which I locked in the trunk. I intended to keep that one with me. By noon, we had lugged the boxes silently up the mountain and stacked them outside the main temple. None of us spoke during the entire ascent. After removing the *tatami,* and then the floorboards underneath which the treasures were kept hidden, I asked Jim if I could hold, one last time, one of the sleek *katana* swords in my hand. He agreed, and pulled one out, removing it from its crafted box and then its fine silk bag. He ceremoniously handed it to me with both hands, and I received it with both of my own, bowing. We did not speak now. I stood with it, felt the balance of it in my hands. Its colors glistened in the pale sunlight. The steel was iridescent; the blade razor sharp. I stood and swung it here and there, trying to do what I believed a samurai might do. I imagined its mighty force being swung into an enemy's shoulder blade, down and across. Its sheer weight and sharpened edge, if brought down in a precise manner, might have once been used to cut completely through a human body, from shoulder to the opposite ribcage, diagonally. The thought was scary and intoxicating. Finally I spoke to Jim, as I held out to him with both hands the lethal weapon. "I know they say the pen is mightier than the sword, but that is one spectacularly nasty piece," I sighed.

He replaced it in the bag, then the box, slipping it back beneath the floorboards. "Words are still mightier, pal. Let's get your stuff."

Now it only took ten minutes to carry the containers the short distance into the temple. "Wait!" Jim said. He rushed away and returned with a box of black plastic trash bags. "It gets dusty in here." It took a few more minutes to wrap each box in a bag, fit everything into the cramped space, and then replace everything and to lock it up just as it had been before.

When we were alone, he brushed his hands on his robes and asked, "So when do you plan to come get all this stuff?" Jim the zen monk could be cool and calm, but Jim the American could be just as blunt as I was.

"Soon. I don't know, really. But probably within a year or so. It's ... pretty important to me. And valuable." I looked him in the eye. "I need you to take care of it. If you do, I'll make it worth your while."

"No charge, pal. Just make sure we see you again, and soon, OK?"

I stayed on a few more days, putting off my inevitable return to battered Kobe as long as humanly possible. The serenity of the place, and the fun I had with Jim and the others, was intoxicating. We lounged around, playing cards or *go* or *shogi*, talking about old times, meditating, cleaning up, doing chores, or just staying quiet most of the day. It was true, as Watanabe had said: silence was one of their specialties. I read a few of the old paperbacks that Jim kept around the place. Each day I stayed "one more night," until I knew I had to leave my remote Zen hideout. I would only have two full days to wrap everything up in Kobe, but that seemed enough. Maybe even too much. The thought of heading back down to Kobe—to the scene of the crime, so to speak—caused a knot to form in my gut, and the more I thought about it, the more that knot became like a fist with fingers reaching out to squeeze my entrails.

Finally, after a very early breakfast on Sunday the 29th, I made my way back down to the car, along with Jim. We stood quietly for a few moments, until I broke the silence. "Well, thanks for the hospitality. This is it, old buddy. I can't say how long it will be before I come back for the items. But for now, thanks for helping out an old friend."

"No problem." He looked around. "Of course you realize I may not be here forever."

"Just how long *will* you be around here, anyway?"

He had no idea, of course, but said, "Life's hard to predict, buddy. Full of twists and turns. Remember the lines from the *Odyssey*? 'Sing to me of the man, Muse, the man of twists and turns.' But you already know about that, don't you?"

We peered into each other's eyes, then looked off together into the mountains. He draped his huge arm over my shoulders. "Who knows? I doubt if I'm a lifer, but I don't plan on leaving anytime soon. It's nice up here, isn't it? Anyway, you told me before you'd be back in a year, right?"

And at that moment, I honestly felt I would manage to get back within a year or two, and repeated my hopeful estimate. He thought it all over. "Well, if I do leave, the guys will pass on the instructions, along with our shibboleth. Kind of fun, like being a spy. And I love the code. A battered copy of *The Old Man and the Sea*. I like that. Read it in high school. It always made me think of Ahab, to tell you the truth. Huntin' down that big monster. I'm sure guys in your business have thought of that connection already, right?"

I smiled. "Yeah, I think that may have come up before."

We stood beside my mud-splotched Nissan. "Well, I'm outta here." I hugged him. "Keep looking for Oz, old buddy. I'll do the same."

I started to climb into the car as Jim remained watching me, his hands behind his back. He had an authoritative look in his eye, along with amusement. He had changed so much since the old days. I rolled down the window. "Don't take no wooden nickels, Zen master."

He smirked. "And don't piss in a pothole. Some things never change, yeah?"

I thought of Sensei, wanting very much to say something profound to Jim, like what Sensei had told me about the words, but I had no words of wisdom to share. "Yeah. Thank God. Some things never change!" I raced the engine, let out the brake, and slowly began inching my way back down the steep grades of the mountainside. In my rear view mirror I could still see Jim, raising his hands and crying out, "*Sayonara! Banzai!*" Just as I had done for Mika.

Darkness was thickening on that Sunday evening as I came down the snowy foothills onto the expressway towards Kobe. I had no idea if I could sleep in the condo that night, or if it was even accessible. The quake had hit almost two weeks ago, so I assumed my building, and the city in general, were now open for business. Then it occurred to me that the highways might have limitations due to damage. So I decided to take a detour, more scenic but longer by a few hours at least—truthfully, just one more procrastination. I drove through Rokko National Park, then down the back way, the road finally dumping me directly into my neighborhood. I wondered what kinds of conditions awaited me.

Just before eight o'clock that night, I tooled the Nissan into the street where I kept it parked, a couple blocks above my building. Things were cleaned up, but the damage to the neighborhood was evident. It was quiet and there were few people out on the streets. In Japan, Sundays were always the quietest nights of the week anyway. Cars were in their normal places, though, and most buildings had lights on, with people moving within. It was almost like normal—almost; damage was all around, if you took the time to notice. I was not interested in searching out further evidence of the quake, however, so I headed into my building.

The elevator was still not working, so I had to hoof it up fifteen stories. That's a tough hike when your heart's already racing from anxiety. I still had not seen anyone else in the building, but the key worked in my door, and I could hear music down the hall, so I went on in. It was a mess—I don't know why this surprised me. But the disarray took my breath away. One of the big windows was cracked all the way across. Several cabinet doors were open and the contents had spilled out onto the floor. A plant had fallen over, much of the dirt spilling onto the *tatami*. But the electricity worked and so did the water, phone, and even the cable TV. But no gas for cooking or hot water. Turning on the TV in the midst of all that clutter was surreal.

I went to work getting my stuff ready for departure. I had already unloaded most of the big items to other *gaijin* through sayonara sales. Now I dragged out my large suitcases and started performing triage on everything else. I got out a few trash bags and decided to be ruthless. If it didn't go in the suitcase, it went in the trash. Occasional pulls on an unbroken bottle of Jack Daniels helped. I did not stop until everything had been sorted out, and the suitcases were bulging. But my recall of that packing session is blurred, hazy. I vaguely remember tossing a few things out the window, perhaps even in anger. I do know it was past 3:00 a.m., or possibly even four, on Monday morning when I was finally able to settle down and get some sleep.

Sirens began coming through the cracked window early, just at dawn, and I woke up in a start. I was sweaty and my heart was pumping hard. I panicked, and looked from one side to the other. Everything seemed stable, but I had to get out of my claustrophobic apartment. I showered quickly—in cold water—and threw on some clean clothes and headed out.

That pretty much characterized my last forty-eight hours in Kobe—a kind of mindless mania softened by a haze of forgetfulness and the fug of alcohol. After coffee, I walked over to the university. The offices were empty; I was way too early. Several campus buildings had been damaged and were off limits. The main administration offices appeared to be functional, as did the building where my department was housed. I remember sitting on the concrete, holding my legs in my arms, leaning up against a wall, and gently rocking back and forth, until finally some administrators began filing in. They seemed to stare at me suspiciously—or maybe it was just my imagination. It took a while, but I got everything figured out. I could leave the keys with them on Wednesday morning, February 1, when my last payment would be available in the same office—in cash. My flight would be late in the afternoon of the same day.

Over at the English department, I found Professor Aoyama in his office. Strangely, and as I typically saw him, he was taking care of some of the mindless duties of academic administrators, amidst all the rubble. Evidently the earthquake had only temporarily halted the deluge of Japan's bureaucratic obsessiveness. But Aoyama's amiable ways, typically inextinguishable, were subdued that day. I knocked on his door, smiling as best I could. He turned, saw me, and stood quickly. "Springs-sensei, Ah! Please come in! Sit down! Yes, we have been so worried about you!"

He continued speaking in exclamation marks. I avoided his questions, and told him only vaguely of my own experience during the temblor—the version that would become my standard account. The shaking building, being woken up abruptly, falling out of bed, running down to the car, and heading out a back road into the mountains, to a friend's place out in the country. Nagano-city, to be precise.

"Did your friends in Nagano feel the *jishin*?"

I had no idea, of course. "Not really," I ventured.

He nodded, then told me how happy he was to see that I was doing well. "And you, sensei? How are you?" I asked.

He looked down at his papers. "My family is safe. We live far out in the countryside. But this has been a terrible tragedy for the university. Many professors were injured and their homes damaged or even destroyed, as I'm sure you've heard. At least fifteen students and possibly up to twenty professors were either killed directly, or are still in critical condition, at death's door." He frowned, stroking his neck. Then he looked up at me directly. "One was Professor Goto. I am sorry to tell you of this. I know that you spent some time with him. He was truly one of the great men that I have known in my life. And Professor Miyamoto has also died. It is a terrible loss for our community here." He stared back down at the floor as waves of sudden terror washed over me. "I am so sorry to bring you this very sad news; it must be a huge blow."

A long, awkward silence stretched out between us. I am sure he was waiting for me to say something, but I was tongue tied and tearing up. The sadness, the guilt, the remorse, and the fear were all there, written plainly across my face. I couldn't choke out a single word.

"Frankly, I do not blame you for leaving early like this, sensei. Kobe will be grieving for a very long time, I think." I scanned his bookshelves, trying to avoid eye contact. What else would I need to endure to get out of his office?

He asked me a question, which brought me back to the moment.

"Excuse me?"

"What I mean is, what are your fondest memories of Kobe?"

"Well ... I guess it would have to be the students. And also ... my friendships with some of the other professors here, like you." And Sensei, I did not add.

"Yes. Well. Thank you." He stood up. I stood up also, maybe a little too fast.

"You have been a great addition to our work here at Kobe University. It has been a very sad ending, though, and I regret that this is how our time together must come to a close." He hesitated once more. "I wonder how our university, and our city, can get through this."

He walked me to the door, and we said our goodbyes. And that was it. High noon on a cold and cloudy Monday, I cleared out my office, emptied my bank account, went to my favorite Indian restaurant, and ate like a Marine, realizing as I sat down to order that I'd eaten almost nothing since Saturday. That night I walked through Sannomiya and other parts of downtown Kobe. The damage was everywhere, and I could only take so much before I began to feel I was still walking on shaky, unstable ground. So I headed back up the hill, found a seat at the bar in a dark tavern near my condo filled with chain-smoking businessmen in navy blue suits, and drank beer for a very long time.

I spent most of Tuesday walking around up in the forest on the mountainside, avoiding Kobe's forlorn streets, but still peering down at them. The waves of horror kept washing back over me, and I was in a sort of constant sweat. I could not think of anyone to call, or whom I wished to call.

My final night in Kobe, I was alone and in a foul mood. I had often imagined a big going-away party, lots of fine speeches, perhaps a few mementoes. My students getting teary-eyed, clamoring for an American-style embrace (so un-Japanese). Maybe some late night karaoke, or a final fling with one of those lovely, slender young girls.

But at nine o'clock, I was eating take-out sushi in my darkened apartment, with "Kind of Blue" by Miles Davis playing softly in the background. A cold Asahi Dry was on the table next to me, the windows were wide open, despite temperatures in the low twenties. A frigid sea-wind rushed into the room, and outside, the twinkling lights of Kobe—or at least what remained of them. Ghostly dark cavities sat like blind spots, between other, lighted buildings. These voids in the skyline signified buildings that had been destroyed in the quake, or which had been pulled down in the days following it due to structural weaknesses. And beyond all that was the inky darkness of the harbor, and then the Pacific Ocean. And then, America.

友

And that was it. The next morning, I was showered and ready to leave hours before I needed to be. I dropped the keys at the designated office, and picked up my last cash payment. I loaded up my car, still unsold, and drove it to KIX, the brand new, shiny Kansai International Airport, out on a massive man-made island in the middle of Osaka Bay. I parked in one of the garages, unloaded, and walked away from it, just like that. I wasn't parking it so much as abandoning it, and for all I know the car's still sitting there, awaiting my return, covered in fifteen years of dust. I checked two heavily packed roll-arounds and boarded the flight, carrying on one bulging backpack and one small, locked, dark leather 1920s-style valise. I managed to save a couple of sleeping pills for the flight. Those, along with a few highballs, got me back to Indiana, via Detroit. My dad picked me up at the Indy airport, smiling and ready to hear about my adventures. But I was in no mood for conversation. Mom had a big meal prepared, but I wasn't hungry. After nibbling at it just enough to satisfy her motherly instincts, I excused myself and headed straight to bed.

友

I never made it back to Japan. Honestly, I've regretted that sorry vacuum for the rest of my life. Yes, I did have the best intentions. And at times I even wanted to go back. That was a few years later, when it became possible for me to remember Kobe without suffering panic attacks, or feeling nauseous. But the bottom line is that those six boxes have been sitting underneath the flooring of *Ryoan-ji*, high up in the mountains of Japan, going on these fifteen years—or at least, I hope they have.

Jim kept in touch. He sent a postcard to my parents' house in August 1998, telling me he was off to Thailand. He only wrote a few sentences, but one of them was this: "Your secret is still safe, and the brothers await a message from Ernest." That was enough, and just like old Jim. That was over a decade ago, and by now those boxes have probably all been forgotten about, like old Christmas decorations up in some grandmother's dark, cobwebby attic. Covered in dust, like my old Nissan at the airport.

Or perhaps they've been discovered and sold off, by some enterprising monk. So you see, there is some risk involved, in taking the next step.

友

Then, in 2001, the jets hit the Twin Towers in Manhattan, and we all watched in horror as papers went flying through the air, bodies plummeted down into the streets, and finally the buildings themselves imploded, tumbling down in heaps of steel, glass, cement, and pulverized human tissue. I thankfully missed watching that horror live—it was still early in the morning out in eastern Washington, and my mornings are for reading in silence, with no electronic devices allowed till noon—but the scenes were replayed over and over and over in the subsequent hours, days, and weeks. So I did see them, eventually, many, many times, like everyone else. And those unpleasant knots arose once more in my stomach, and the shakes, and the bad dreams started up again as well. If I had been thinking about going back to Japan before 9/11, the attacks put a final and decisive end to that fantasy.

Now, nine years after that disaster, my health is also imploding. I feel seriously bad most of the time, and even worse the rest. I understand now about wanting to die, at least on those days when the headaches or the abdominal pains make it hard to read, or even to lie on the couch and watch the tube. Booze only helps for an hour, then leaves me depleted and nauseous. I rarely drink anymore. I should look into medical marijuana; if only I had the energy. Then maybe I would feel like listening to some of my old records again, which would be nice. But loud sounds jar unpleasant memories. I do miss the words of the great songwriters, but in general not enough to try listening. Plus, I'm just too tired.

In short, these last pages have been terrifically challenging to complete. I hope you've made it this far and are still with me. I do have many other things I wish I could write to you, Marty. But I'm very tired tonight. Knowing that you always would read my stuff with the greatest interest and attention, has been one of the great inspirations of my life. All the editing, the advice—all just "part of the job," as you would humbly put it—all of those favors were the seeds of hope that have grown up into my life and my career, such as it is. I won't call you my muse, but you get the point. You have been my mentor, my *sempai*—you and Sensei. I know you'll do a worthy job, presenting my story to the world.

友

And so now, Marty, it's time to open the other packages. Brace yourself, and if you do have a bottle of Uncle Jack Daniels sour mash sitting around somewhere, maybe have a finger or two. Given the fact that you'll receive all this after my own demise, make a toast to me, your old student.

Do you remember the letter I sent a few years back, with the quote from the old minister in *Gilead*? About his thousands of sermons, stored in boxes up in his own dusty attic? The Reverend John Ames admits, "I wrote almost all of it in the deepest hope and conviction." I think that's what the teaching life is all about. Now I'm near the end, and I'm able to say it soberly, I think. It struck me today that I'm just about the same age you were, in our days together back in

Bloomington—I'm a forty-something English teacher of minor professional accomplishment, whose legacy consists almost entirely of the words, words, words, all sown like seeds into the hearts and minds of students. And almost all of it sown with the deepest hope and conviction.

Emerson once wrote, "To my friend I write a letter, and from him I receive a letter. That seems to you a little. It suffices me. It is a spiritual gift worthy of him to give, and of me to receive. It profanes nobody. In these warm lines the heart will trust itself, as it will not to the tongue, and pour out the prophecy of a godlier existence than all the annals of heroism have yet made good." I don't know how much prophecy is in here, Marty, but please know that these lines have all been written so as to be warm, and that I pour out myself to you, in sending them.

At the risk of sounding corny: receive all this as a spiritual gift. Above all: cherish and remember the words!

For now, that's all. I'm tired, and I'm going to bed. Enjoy the next part of the journey, Herr Professor.

—E. Jack Springs, Sept. 2010, Spokane, WA

Part Three

My Trip to the Orient

By the time I finished reading Jack's manuscript, twelve hours after first opening the package, I was overcome by the grief and sadness captured and conveyed in Jack's words. I was at home seated in my favorite chair, an overstuffed, worn-out recliner. It had been dark for several hours and my once-roaring fire had diminished into an orange glow. I reached for a box of tissues, wiped my eyes, and blew my nose. Then, I sat back and stared at the fire.

Within the confines of my campus office, I had read well over half of Jack's luminous tale, my feet often up on my desk—I had devoured it between a few trips for refills of coffee and a few for relieving my aging bladder into the enamel urinals that are one of the staples of any scholastic setting. But the remaining sunlight slowly began to slant almost horizontally through the shades of my office window, reminding me of the brevity of midwinter days in Indiana. "There's a Certain Slant of Light—,"wrote Emily Dickinson, and so, with the early dusk approaching, and my imagination completely captured by the exotic tales of my former student, I decided to bundle myself up, withdraw from the office, and carefully wend my way homeward. My prim, highly reliable Camry was the only car in the lot as the wan sun dipped below the tree line.

Once back in my chilly manse, I brewed some strong English tea, built a fire, fried yet another egg for a sandwich, and sat down in front of my fireplace to finish Jack's story. All told, it took a total of two long sittings to complete the first reading of the manuscript. Like most experienced editors, I'm a fast reader, and moreover, I had settled down enough to read it without the constant necessity of a pen in my hand for marking errors or moments of confusion in the text. In other words, I had managed to bridle my habitual need to proof a written text. I simply wanted to read the story through to the end. That level of editorial attentiveness and nitpicking would come later. One can always go back and reread, which I have done numerous times over the past year—twice straight through, both times with pen in hand, like the lifelong editor I am.

Before I began the second half of the manuscript, I perched the small gift-wrapped box, dressed up in its red, white, and blue decorations, on the table next to my chair, where it superintended the remainder of my reading task. Yes, I held steady and true to the admonition of my departed friend: the box remained unopened until I had completed the manuscript. In fact, its smiling presence, like some close friend's special gift beneath a Christmas tree, added to the urgency, not that I needed much encouragement.

In all honesty, I've often wondered about what I immediately perceived to be Jack's palpable remorselessness, his lack of guilt. But over the years I've known other victims of trauma, including classmates who were drafted and spent time in Vietnam, and so I know firsthand that the symptoms of trauma vary from person to person, and that, in this case, it would seem foolish to draw any conclusions. As St. Paul reminds us, there is always the matter of the "mystery of iniquity," a vast, unsolvable puzzle resisting our petty attempts to solve it.

Having completed the narrative, I picked up the multi-colored box. I held it up to the light and studied it, turning it this way and that. Then, suddenly, I unwrapped it. Inside I found two objects: a small key and hand-written directions to the Chase Tower in downtown Indianapolis, with information enough to admit me to the savings deposit box area and into the private holdings of Dr. E. J. Springs.

It pains me to admit this, but almost four weeks passed before I was able to make it to Indianapolis, though I did wish to discover what might be up there. But duty calls, old habits die hard, and as a well-trained workaholic/pack-rat with classes or meetings scheduled throughout the week, I found it convenient to procrastinate, and inconvenient indeed to find a four-hour window to make the trip. In fact, and based on the few clues already given, I must admit that there may have been more than a little fearfulness in my heart, regarding what secrets I might find hidden up there in the box.

Finally, the first week of February, I was sitting in my office late on a Friday morning, with nothing else scheduled for the rest of the day, the weather decent, the sky shiny and blue, and that small box with the key, which I'd placed high on the bookshelf next to my campus desk, glowering down at me. Suddenly, I reached up and took it in my hands, inspecting it closely. Without further thought, I grabbed my car keys, my coat, scarf, and hat, my brown paper bag containing a sandwich, a banana, and some bottled water, headed briskly for my car, and soon enough was motoring down the highway confidently toward my destination. In a little over an hour, I was tooling slowly up Ohio Street in downtown Indianapolis, maneuvering my car into a parking space, and scooping up small change from the bottom of the drink holder to feed the meter.

Inside the skyscraper, I spied the various tellers and other personnel whose job it is to evaluate the various souls entering the lobby of the Chase Bank. One older lady caught my eye. She resembled an ancient librarian, sort of a latter-day version of Donna Reed in *It's a Wonderful Life*. She semi-scowled at me through a winsome smile; and as she walked up to me, I noted that the name tag on her sweater said, "Edna."

"May I help you?"

I fumbled for the key, and showed it to her. "Yes. I'm here about a box." Brilliant, I thought.

She studied the key momentarily. "A safety deposit box, you mean?"

"Precisely. Can you direct me—Edna?"

Speaking her name seemed to accomplish some otherworldly magic, and her pursed lips widened into a full smile. Without a word, she unfurled her arm and gestured me through one of those low swinging doors, then toward a stairwell that led down into the bowels of the building. My platonic relationship with Edna was now officially terminated.

Downstairs, I sought out the correct attendant and was ushered into the solemn presence of a viewing room. The walls were lined with dozens of large and small boxes, and upon my provision of certain information and another presentation of the key, I was left alone with a fairly large container, approximately three feet by two feet, and about twenty inches deep. I sat there for what seemed just the right amount of time before flipping open the cover of the box to reveal its furtive contents, silently acknowledging Jack for whatever goods I might determine to be inside.

On top was a large, faded manila envelope. Nothing was written on it, and I placed it aside. Several old volumes came next. I took them out, one by one, and slowly inspected them. *Indian Summer* was on top, followed by *A Hazard of New Fortunes* and *A Traveler to Altruria*. These were all first editions of some of the greatest novels written by William Dean Howells, the centerpiece of my own academic eccentricities for some thirty years or more. They weren't so valuable at auction, but they were all neglected novels that had been highly underrated, in my view. Books you might find stashed unknowingly in a crate at an estate sale, marked by their unwitting owner at an absurdly low price. Jack had placed these books here especially, to be retrieved by someone with a very particular interest in Howells—someone, such as myself. I smiled at his thoughtfulness.

I was so intrigued by these volumes that I did not initially notice the treasures beneath them: Pound's signed copy of *Moby-Dick*, numerous other old tomes, but most importantly, another, rather large container of some kind placed at the bottom of the box. This item was wrapped in that same white and red striped holiday paper in which the small box holding the key had originally appeared. It was underneath everything else, on the very bottom of the box, a sort of foundation, and I lifted it out.

The faded wrapping paper fell away easily. It was Hemingway's valise—or at least, Professor Goto's facsimile.

My first thought was that it was too small to hold much, but I was wrong. It contained multitudes. Opening it slowly, I found numerous file folders, all stuffed with old pages. One with "Pound" scribbled on top, another marked simply "Nook Farm," along with a few more of Jack's favorite volumes. Nestled at the very bottom of the valise, one more item was encased inside another plastic, padded envelope. The box within the box within the box, like an old Chinese puzzle.

I carefully opened the envelope and pulled out a volume with a leathery, faded green cover and gold embossed lettering. With a quickening pulse, I realized I held in my hands a genuine first edition of *Leaves of Grass*, Walt Whitman's 1855 masterpiece which the poet had prepared, printed, and then held with his own hands. It was the mother lode of rare literary relics, a collection of words as impressive and as influential as any ever penned by an American.

I set Walt Whitman aside, gently, and began pulling out the contents of the manila envelope. It included a large, bulging, blue money pouch, marked Chase Bank, the kind of pouch stores and vendors use for toting around large amounts of cash for deposits. I discovered as well a map and some hand-scribbled directions on several sheets of legal pad paper, including a couple of the pages written in what appeared to be Japanese. There were photographs and business cards, Japanese on one side and English on the reverse. And another envelope, this one with "Marty" on it. It was sealed, and I quickly opened it and removed the letter. By now I was no longer surprised to find that it contained yet one more letter from the dead. This one neatly typed on old Gonzaga letterhead.

July 4, 2010

Dear Marty,
If you are reading this, I am evidently deceased. That's a euphemism I have always liked: deceased. I have ceased to exist—at least in this dimension. I have passed away—that's a good one too, so gentle, like a train rolling out of the station and away, into the countryside, gaining speed very slowly, almost imperceptibly.

Funny how that sounds now, rattling off my keyboard. Having been given my decree of death just a few months back, thanks be to prostate cancer, I needed to put some things in order. By now you know all about that, if you've made it this far.

I date this letter as Independence Day, but my own independence—from the fear and loathing of my past—really depends on your help. Dating it the "4th" is symbolic anyway, like Thoreau saying in *Walden* that he went to live at the pond on July 4. Actually, I finished this letter and printed it off the week *after* the Fourth, but symbols are important, so let's keep the date the way it is. I still believe in the efficiency of symbols, despite all I'm going through, or went through—I need to speak here in the past tense.

Do you like my small gifts? Yes, the Howells books are trifles next to *Moby-Dick* or *Leaves of Grass*, but you are one of the few people on planet Earth nowadays who can value them properly. I include *Indian Summer*, not because it is comparable in monetary value, but in particular because I love its title, and I sincerely hope that these things can commence a rebirth of sorts in your own remaining years. Together, they're worth a fair amount of money, as you surely know. And now they are yours, to do with as you and your conscience see fit.

As you are about to learn, the best interests of humanity often clash with the sordid best interests of our outer shells—our biological appetites, as it were. Thus can a rare first edition of *Leaves of Grass* be either a blessing or a curse to you—and perhaps even a little of both, as Frodo discovered about the ring. A small gift, Sensei would tell me, as he slid a priceless book across the table toward my waiting hands.

I am a sap for romanticism and human sentiment, as you know. So are you, unless I have wildly misread you over the years. If true so far, perhaps you will go another mile. Do you remember the letter at the end of *Shawshank Redemption*? The one that Red, just out of prison, finds in the old cigar box buried under the tree in a New England field, next to a stone wall that seems plucked from a Robert Frost poem? His friend Andy writes:

Dear Red,

If you're reading this, you've gotten out. And if you've come this far, maybe you're willing to go a little farther. You remember the name of the town, don't you?

Well, Marty, maybe you're willing to go a little farther than the Chase Tower in downtown

Indianapolis? Seven thousand miles or so further, in fact. Do you remember the name of the temple, on top of a mountain in the Japan Alps? I could use a good man like you to help me find a little redemption in all this.

Directions to the temple are enclosed. Also, thanks to Sensei, so is a bundle of cash, which will more than cover any expenses. Please do me the one favor and travel first class. Sensei would insist; he always wanted the best for his assistants. And don't forget to take with you the talisman, the shibboleth, our little codebook that will admit you to the stash—Hemingway's *Old Man and the Sea*. It will be our little secret, OK? Maybe it *is* a little corny, but anyway, that's how I've arranged it. As Shakespeare wrote, "some have greatness thrust upon them."

One last thing. Hope IS a good thing—maybe the best of things. Even in the desultory twenty-first century, when it seems like multi-tasking postmodern digital natives [read: our students] are doing everything they can to AVOID the words, burying them under something else, so that they won't be bothered by their wordy implications any longer.

Nevertheless: I hope … It's why we keep on teaching. Right, Marty?

Your friend,
Jack

I opened the money pouch, finding four stacks of fifty-dollar bills, bound as a bank would bind them, each bundle appearing to have a hundred bills, meaning that perhaps I held a grand total of twenty thousand dollars in my hands, courtesy of the Goto dynasty. The directions Jack provided for finding the temple, *Ryoan-ji*, were clear and well-formulated for a novice like me, a man completely ignorant about Japan and its language and culture. The pages written in Japanese would appear to be further insurance, for any wayward strangers who might cross my path and willingly aid me.

And yet, despite these ample provisions, I was paralyzed by anxieties. I wish I could report that I immediately contacted my travel agent and made urgent plans to fly to Japan, but I didn't. Again I hesitated. I've never been much of a traveler, I don't like fish unless I catch it myself—much less raw fish—and I was always clumsy with chopsticks, so how might I survive? Crab brains? Oh my! The very concept sent my elderly body into convulsions of horror, as if a refined Henry James were being recruited to sail before the mast of Captain Ahab's whaler. So I carefully gathered my booty, replaced the security box, returned to my properly parked car (with plenty of time left on the meter for the next person), drove under the speed limit back to Bloomington, Indiana, and went back into work mode, hardly even entertaining the possibility of flying off to Tokyo to attempt all that Jack had instructed me to do.

Yes, those are two of life's most bone-chilling words—I hesitated.

There was, of course, the matter of the treasure's safety. My cynical side assumed that the cache of collectibles might well be long gone by now. The earthquake had occurred roughly fifteen years in the past, and Jack admitted that he had no evidence that the boxes remained intact.

Furthermore, he had revealed very little about what was actually contained therein. Mere innuendoes, really. And finally, there was the wrongdoing involved in attaining whatever lay hidden in that dusty old temple. Those buried words came at the cost of human lives. Blood had been spilled. Morally, it all made me a little queasy, and thus, more hesitations ensued.

友

Time passed. I mulled all this over, day in, day out. I found myself becoming even queasier. And then, it was March 11, 2011, just over a month after discovering the contents of the safe deposit box, when another jolt struck: 9.0 on the Richter scale, the fifth most powerful earthquake ever recorded on Earth, eighty miles off the northern coast of Japan. Over five minutes of intense shaking, followed by hundreds of strong aftershocks, a massive tsunami that devastated coastal cities, and punctuated by the nuclear meltdown at the Fukushima power plant, flinging radiation far and wide and commencing a massive evacuation. The footage of disaster that became available in the days and weeks after that massive quake was surreal, and the devastation that Jack had reported, culminating in the great Kobe earthquake of 1995, was actually surpassed by this temblor. It was dumbfounding to witness further calamity, just as I was contemplating a visit, and to say the least, I was horrified and thus became even less willing to fly to Japan, in light of these latest events. I now seriously wondered if I had it in me, psychologically, to undertake these "minor tasks" for Jack.

友

Eventually, however, life returns to normal and one settles down. In my heart, I knew I must go—someday in the vague future. A little over two months after my deepening anxieties provoked by the destructive earthquake and tsunami of March 2011, the skies somehow opened up, and something changed inside me. To this day, I still have no concrete explanation.

I had finished all the exams and handed in my grades in mid-May. At first I was exhausted and somewhat depressed, which is increasingly how I feel every May, needing a few weeks of unwinding from a very long year. But I was also entering a period, a lengthened reprieve, due to the fact that I had been awarded a sabbatical for the 2011-12 academic year. And thus, by the first of June of 2011, when I was beginning to see my life a little clearer again, I was greeted with the happy prospect of having the next fourteen months to do whatever I pleased. I was a free man, liberated from the intestines of the academic frenzy. Indeed, I felt open skies ahead.

Yes, I did hesitate—for a long time, it is true. But all at once, earthquake-like, in early June the novel concept shook me. I must make the trip—not just for Jack, but ultimately for me as well—as he put it, for that tired old dog, too set in his ways.

I booked the flight, in the spirit of Jack's letter, for July 4th: Independence Day. A day for riddance. A day for fireworks and ice cream, for liberty and the pursuit of happiness. A day to protest the corruptive forces that rule every other day of our lives. I drove up early to the Indianapolis Airport, and parked my old Toyota in the most expensive lot, right next to the terminal, where it would await whatever I might bring back from the Land of the Rising Sun.

By the time I filed patiently off the airplane at Narita Airport outside of Tokyo, via Detroit roughly eighteen hours later, it was the 5th of July. Bleary-eyed, my back aching, I felt as though I might throw up with every footfall. I had gained a day magically by passing over another symbol, the International dateline, and so even the dates were dissimilar. The blank hallways of the Narita Airport seemed endless, a mile long each, then a corner, where one would face another mile or two. This endless maze made one consider running away in fear and loathing, back down some other interminable corridor, like the lion in *The Wizard of Oz*.

Entering Japan was assuredly foreboding. If Kafka were ever to pen a novel about an airport, I'm certain it would be set in Narita. The unsuspecting visitor flows with a mob through a doorway to discover a line of approximately seven thousand people at passport control, then is required to endure a seven-hour wait for luggage. Predictably, my bags were among the last to arrive. One overweight and silent official poked around for five minutes in my bags, looking for who knows what. He sniffed leisurely at my shaving kit, then finally waved me forward, all without a single word, just mute gestures. I was flushed out into the main receiving concourse of Narita, with hundreds of waiting friends and family members, pointing their digital cameras, holding flowers, balloons, large signs, babies, books, magazines, or sodas.

The two-hour ride into Tokyo, on a steamy bus being pounded by torrential rain, with no windows to open and minimal air conditioning, featured a few screaming babies nearby to make it as unpleasant as possible. As we pulled up to the Keio Plaza Hotel in Shinjuku, the baby directly in front of me vomited with great force upon his mother's right shoulder. The tiniest amount of yellowish spittle flew toward me, landing on my left leg as I watched with a mixture of amusement and horror. I nearly vomited myself, actually tasted the bile in the back recesses of my throat. It was the end of a cosmically brutal trip from hell, an appendix to Sartre's *No Exit*. When I finally got into my hotel room, it was already 5:30 p.m. the next day, so to speak, with the hot sun filling my southern-facing room/sauna. The view of Tokyo seemed to go on forever. Ten-and twenty-story buildings as far as the eye could see. But I pulled the curtains and fell face down into the bed, sleeping straight through for about ten hours.

Unfortunately, I was wide awake by 4:00 a.m. Though a bit timid to venture far from the hotel in the darkness of the middle of the night, I got up, showered, dressed, and headed down the elevator to see what I would see, determined to quit whatever complaining might crop up. It was still dark at five o'clock, but a hint of the rising sun was visible to the east.

Once outside, my timidity changed slowly as I wandered away from the high-rise quarter of new Shinjuku and vaguely into the mesmerizing alleyways of old Shinjuku, a half mile away. No cars were out yet except a few lonely cabs. Trains were already beginning to rumble inside the massive Shinjuku Station, or on the rail lines passing frequently overhead. I walked under one of the trestles and entered a new kind of cityscape, with bouncing bright lights still on even at this early hour of the morning. People still walked around here and there, men in rumpled business suits, and women in disheveled and brightly colored dresses and gowns.

An hour into my hike through the canyon lands of the city, I espied a familiar sight, with workers scurrying about inside and a few paying customers already sitting at tables: a Dunkin' Donuts, here in the heart of postmodern Japan. I went in, pointed benignly at a few pastries, gestured for some hot coffee, and sat down for my first meal in Japan.

Fortified by the coffee, I hiked even further afield, first into an area called Yoyogi, where I spotted a sign, in both Japanese and English, pointing toward "Yoyogi Park." Sunshine now dominated the haze of early morning, more people bustled around, and trucks and cars began clotting some of the streets as I wandered off in pursuit of the park.

The grounds were enormous and heavily wooded with evergreens, so that the urban sprawl slowly vanished away. One path led to another, and then underneath a massive red-orange *torii* gate—shaped like the Greek letter *pi*, just as Jack had described it—I found myself in front of an extensive shrine of some sort, weathered yet elegant. One old woman sat on a bench before the building, facing away from it toward those approaching. She was patiently feeding a swarm of pigeons, as incense wafted in sheets from a massive cauldron, filling the air with a spice of purity mixed with the exotic spray of foreign gods. Behind the old lady, on one side of the building, a monk in a bluish robe, his head completely shaven, swept a long wooden deck. Another old man walked his tiny dog, which, gleeful to be outdoors, pulled him forward. Branches swayed in the light breeze, as in an ancient Japanese dance. This extended moment has become in my mind's eye one of those cosmic spots of time wherein all is suddenly well with the world. I was here, in Japan, as Jack had planned all along.

I sat on a bench opposite the old woman, her face wrinkled and weathered, but her hands gentle and caring. She glanced my way, her luminous smile a promise of sorts, as the old man disappeared down the garden path with his frenzied dog. In this somewhat altered state, I watched the woman, the monk, and the shrine long enough for the sun to rise completely, filling the air with an assurance of another steamy summer day to come.

Back at the hotel, now midmorning, it was time to pack and head off for another massive maze: Shinjuku Station, where I would pick up the express train to the big mountains of Japan, and specifically for the city of Matsumoto. I ate a late lunch a short walk from the main station, in front of the sinister Matsumoto Castle, which was mysterious for its being black, rather than the traditional white of most Japanese castles. Above the castle were dozens of large black birds circling slowly, as if it were a place of great calamity, and in the far distance to the west were the majestic peaks of central Japan. I found the bus stop to take me up into the far reaches of the backbone of Honshu Island, the Japan Alps, first to the resort town of Kamikochi, then onward to the end of the rainbow: *Ryoan-ji.*

In Kamikochi, the sky was a brilliant blue, but the air was stultifying. It was still early enough in the day to think that I could make it to the temple, but the mid-afternoon jet lag tugged at my enthusiasm. I had secured no reservation anywhere, and so I inquired through hand gestures for nearby inns, acting out a person sleeping and snoring. "Ahh, *hai*!" one attendant exclaimed, nodding proudly, "*Sanko*! *Sanko*!"

"*Sanko*?" I mimicked.

He smiled in gratitude, pointing up the hill. "*Hai*! *Sanko desu*!" Then he put his small hands on my back and pretended to push me toward a building hidden amongst old trees and large emerald ferns.

I trudged up the hill, hoping I might discover a small inn. I doubt if I have ever felt so alone, yet there was something thrilling about venturing out, unaccompanied, into uncharted waters. In retrospect, my brief stay at the *Sanko Ryokan*, up in the highlands of the Japan Alps, was one of the great days of my life. It was a tiny property, owned and operated by a single family. One older daughter, called Hideko, could speak a little English, and she happily attempted over and over to tell me about their business, their history, and the marvels of the surrounding countryside, noted for its *wasabi*, which I discovered was a kind of horseradish. The *Sanko* was a small taste of what Jack, and perhaps Sensei, might consider "Old Japan." The rooms featured *tatami* mats for floors, *shoji* screens for doors and windows, and were enhanced by the rocks, ferns, moss, and stone lanterns in a lovely manicured garden just outside the window. There were wonderfully colored pillows for sitting, cross legged, on the *tatami*. The *Sanko* also featured a real hot spring, or *onsen*, bubbling up from the molten lakes of Japan's volcanic underground. The waters were considered medicinal, therapeutic, and somehow spiritually regenerative. The place reeked of sulfur, like rotten eggs. They insisted that I disrobe immediately and take a bath, which I did.

As I inched into the steaming waters of the bath, I imagined that I was now slowly experiencing Japan as Jack had, uninhibited and unembarrassed. And though

I was not used to the Japanese way of bathing in a large, open pool to be shared with any other interested parties, I found the courage to accept their offer and even to relax, as I partook of their steamy peace offering. This lowering of the curtains of my biological reality, so to speak, had an extremely humbling effect, it seemed. Just as the Japanese believe, the twenty minutes of utter vulnerability in the *onsen* soothed my troubled soul, its magical waters rinsing off the heaviness of my travels. The bath was a baptism of fire: sempiternally heated, the waters rejuvenated me as I relaxed, naked to the world.

Afterwards, they welcomed me, if only temporarily, into the family of the inn, bearing the gifts of their wonderful food and drink including a large tray of cooked octopus with soy sauce and homegrown *wasabi* and complemented by an iced glass mug kept full of *Asahi Dry*. They took turns refilling my mug as soon as I took a drink. Another platter appeared, this one holding an entire cooked fish, blackened and aromatic. I braced myself and fumbled around with the chopsticks. Hideko patiently instructed me about how to improve my delivery, helping me eat the fish as if I were a four year old. To my surprise, it was one of the most delicious things I have ever put in my mouth—fresh, wholesome, absolutely perfect. Steamed *edamame*—soybeans—were plentiful, and Hideko demonstrated how to squeeze out the contents and pop them into my mouth. Noodles, fried with vegetables and tiny shrimp, with steam rising from them, were delivered fresh from the kitchen, and they brought out the aged *sake*, served in tiny porcelain containers. Lacquered trays, steaming mugs of thick, green tea, bitter and hearty. And all of it, seated on the floor pillow, legs dangling into the pit underneath the shiny black table, with the screens thrown back to reveal the beautiful bluish-purple mountain peaks into which I would venture the next morning. Soon enough, the combination of jet lag, the soothing bath waters, and the copious food and alcoholic refreshments did their duty. I was on the brink of collapse. I slept as I rarely do, deep and long, on a fluffy futon with a stone-hard pillow for my head, dreaming of Old Japan.

By dawn I was awakened, and soon after breakfast, I handed a 10,000 yen note to Hideko and proceeded to show her my instructions, written in both languages. She studied them meticulously, with occasional nods, then summoned a local taxi for my use. After many thanks, I departed, with her and her parents standing outside the inn, bowing and bowing over and over, as the taxi motored slowly off. Just as the Keio Plaza had in Tokyo, Hideko supplied me with a few matchboxes with their name, address, and phone number emblazoned on the side, should I ever wish to return.

The taxi slowly began to climb the mountainous winding roads with severe switchbacks and sheer cliffs falling away into the tiny rice paddies carved into the terrain below. In about ninety minutes we had arrived at a remote location near the top of a mountain. Off to one side were some of the highest peaks in Japan. And there stood before me, finally, the massive *torii* gate described by Jack, under which I had to pass to find the path leading up the mountainside to the temple. Pulling out my stack of yen, I liberated another 10,000 yen note and handed it to the stunned driver. I pointed at my watch, saying, "Tomorrow?" Yes?" He nodded eagerly, jumped out of the car and pulled my bag out of the trunk. Setting it on the road, he presented it to me.

We both turned to peer up the mountain path. He still held the handle of my large, roll-around luggage, and it immediately occurred to both of us the absurdity of the immediate situation. I must labor up the side of the mountain, pulling along behind me this overstuffed piece? The wheels were good on sidewalks or train station platforms, but here they were simply useless; and so I turned to the driver, pulled out of my pocket the matchbox from the *Sanko*, and with heavy gestures, tried to communicate my desire that he return the bag, thus making my decision that I would grace the *Sanko* with a return visit. Thankfully he seemed to understand my intentions, replacing the bag in the trunk. Settled back into the driver's seat, he repeated, "*Hai Wakarimashita—Ashita, juji—OK—koko, OK!*" Then he was off, and I stood alone, clutching my small backpack containing a few essentials and staring up an empty path into the heavily forested mountains.

I was at the *Ryoan-ji* Temple almost exactly twenty-four hours, including the time up and down the path, mosquitoes harassing me throughout. I arrived sweaty and with a severe headache, breathing heavily, even though I rested several times during my ascent. Almost magically, the inmates of the temple seemed to be expecting me, possibly due to the letter I had sent a couple weeks beforehand, though I had not specified a precise date.

As instructed by Jack, I showed them the weathered copy of Hemingway's novel, *The Old Man and the Sea*. It worked its own magic, and I was immediately brought into the presence of their leader, still Watanabe-sensei, the same *roshi* who had hosted Jack some fifteen years before, but now even more gray, more bent over, and yet more sublime in appearance and tone than I could have imagined.

We had tea in a site of true grandeur—a clean and well-lighted tea room, with gigantic vistas overlooking those awesome peaks, the windows thrown open. We sat mostly in silence, across the table from one another.

"And how was your journey, sensei?"

I told him about thc challenges so far, and about my rest stop at the *Sanko* nearby the previous evening, and Hideko's generous spirit.

He nodded and smiled a moment. "And how do you like Japan?"

"Very much," I told him and described the temple experience the first morning in Yoyogi Park.

"Ah yes, the *Meiji Jingu*. It is a shrine for the Meiji family, a kind of—what is it in English?—a place of burial, a memorial place for the dead. It is quite beautiful, I think."

"Yes. And very peaceful."

He thought about this for a moment, never rushing his words.

"And how about the food? Can you eat with chopsticks?" He grinned at these questions.

I laughed and told him about learning to eat the broiled fish the night before, and how I had managed with the kind assistance of the aging daughter.

He stroked the gray stubble on his chin. There were further brief inquiries made, then Watanabe got to the point. "I suppose you are now curious about the materials that Springs-sensei has left with us, yes?" He began to get to his feet.

I followed suit, and brushing the wrinkles off of my pants, agreed. "Of course, I have come a long way, and would be much obliged to inspect them—whenever it is most convenient."

"*So desu-ne*," he said. "Why not now?" With this he led me out of the side building where we had taken our tea and down a path toward the main temple proper. It emerged out of a lush bamboo forest and stood before me, seizing my attention utterly. In respectful awe, I gazed up at its tall, round timbers, its faded colors, red and black, and its massive bell, situated above the porch in the front of the entranceway.

Inside, he took me into a back chamber, and began disassembling some floorboards. Underneath the *tatami* mats was the vault with a cover that could be lifted off, one end precariously tilted above it. One by one we pulled out the six dusty old cardboard boxes that had been stored there, protected in their black plastic bags, for these many years. Watanabe bowed gracefully, and backed out of the room, leaving me to inspect the contents privately as a breeze fluttered through the open windows.

I was sitting on a *tatami* mat in a Buddhist temple near the top of the Japan Alps as streams of sunshine, filled with floating dust particles, moved through the muggy air. It was just after noon, and the moment for which I had traveled so far had finally arrived. The boxes arranged haphazardly before me had waited patiently for my arrival, slumbering beneath these ancient floorboards next to medieval *katana* swords, old Buddhist scrolls, and other historical and religious artifacts, for a very long time. And I was about to unveil their vast abundance of materials, out of which I might choose to focus and constitute the remaining scholarly work of my life. Still, I hesitated, soaking it all in, savoring the moment.

I began slowly, relishing each treasure as it emerged, one by one, folder by folder, stack by intriguing stack. Letters written by Longfellow, Stephen Crane, and Willa Cather. Old hand-written manuscripts by the likes of Jack

London, Herman Melville, Katherine Anne Porter, Eudora Welty, Richard Wright, and Elizabeth Stuart Phelps. Files written in Japanese, many by Mishima. Unpublished tales by Washington Irving and Nathaniel Hawthorne. Unpublished pamphlets written by a young journalist named Walter Whitman. An entire file folder of original pamphlets by Harriet Beecher Stowe, another containing newspaper articles by Mark Twain from the *Virginia City Enterprise*. Old notebooks and daybooks, penned by a variety of important figures. And there were very old photographs—Twain sitting in a carriage with an old black man; Stowe lounging around a table in the backyard of her Florida plantation; William Dean Howells with his arm around Henry James at someone's birthday party; Ernest Hemingway, shirtless, smoking a fat cigar. Mishima, days before his suicide, calm in his freshly laundered white robe. And Allen Ginsberg, naked, eating a banana.

And the books! Two of the boxes held numerous first editions, many of which had been signed by the author. Masterpieces of the American canon, the books regularly assigned by professors to their eager college wards, with a few British titles for good measure. One by one I pulled them out of the cardboard containers, astonished with each one, and astonished that they had been imprisoned here for so long, ignored by man and by history. Many of the names of these books spoke of the magic they contained, their intrinsic enchantment: *The Marble Faun*. *The Minister's Wooing*. *The Princess Cassimassima*. *The Wild Swans at Coole*. *Perelandra*. Others, however, balanced this majestic feel with a darker sense of life's varied fortunes. *The Sound and the Fury*. *The Grapes of Wrath*. *No-No Boy*. *Death Comes for the Archbishop*. *The Damnation of Theron Ware*.

I inspected each one slowly and gingerly as time stood still, on that mountaintop, and on the most dazzling day of my life.

友

Patiently, I continued my investigation throughout the afternoon, with occasional water breaks outside, inventorying all I found in a spiral notebook that I had brought along for this very purpose. It was the curator part of my character, insisting that I record for all posterity everything unearthed from this sanctuary. But soon enough, one of the interns came to say that it was nearly the dinner hour of the temple, and that I was to be the esteemed guest of honor. By then, nearly everything was back in the boxes, ready for transport back down the mountain—a task that seemed unlikely, if not impossible, given the exhausting hike up.

At dinner, Watanabe was quiet, chewing his rice and swallowing large draughts of beer. The rooms were hot and stuffy. At meal's end, he continued his inquisition from earlier in the day. "Sensei, did you find the contents of the boxes to be satisfactory?"

I considered his choice of words, and agreed. "Yes, the contents were … very satisfactory." I felt no compunction to go into details, already under the hypnotic effect of the treasures left by Jack, and greedily desiring that they remain a secret between just the two of us.

"And so what are these marvelous things that Springs-sensei felt were of such great value?"

More hesitation. I am not one who is typically coy, but I took a long drink of beer, then wiped my mouth. "They are things of value to literature teachers such as myself and Professor Springs. Only that, I'm afraid."

My answer seemed to amuse Watanabe slightly, though his poker face betrayed almost no emotion, except for a brief twinkling of an eye. He also took another long draft of beer, then responded. "I am surprised he would store such things so far up here in the mountains, then. I am sure you must be annoyed that he has forced you to come all this way for such small matters."

I debated how best to respond, then said, "Yes. Well, perhaps just slightly annoyed. It has given me a chance to travel in your wonderful country, though. And to visit *Ryoan-ji*." I faltered a moment. "But we have a saying in English. One man's trash is another man's treasure. Do you know that saying? It means … I suppose it means that although many people might find little value in the things Jack brought here, I find great treasure in them. They are … shall we say, of infinite value. Yes, for me, and for the others in my field who do what I do, I would say so." Another long pause as my comments hung there, portentously. "There are great secrets in those boxes, to be sure. And yet so many people would see only things to be burned, like fuel for a fire."

Watanabe thought over my little speech. Then he nodded, "Yes. One man's trash is another man's treasure. Much of life is like this, I think."

We sat in more silence.

"And what will you do, now that you have learned the secrets contained in those boxes?"

I pondered his meaning. "Well, first I need to get the boxes down to civilization. It will be very difficult for me to carry it all back down the trail … So if you could be of assistance to me, I would be very grateful. I have arranged for a taxi to meet me there at 10:00 a.m. tomorrow morning, so—"

He smiled broadly. "Do you imagine us trying to carry those heavy boxes down the side of the mountain? And are we really so uncivilized?"

He laughed at his own joke, and so did I. "No, of course I wasn't saying that you were uncivilized."

"Relax, sensei. I understand. It is all actually a part of a small joke that Springs-sensei has played on you, just as his old friend Jim Daymon played it on him. When he first climbed the mountain, and even on his next trip, he also assumed that there was only one way up and one way down the mountain. This turned out to be absurd, of course. How could we live such a life? How would we get our food and other things up and down?

"Finally, after the earthquake, when he came with those boxes, terrified and clearly in a traumatic state of confusion, Jim showed him the back way into the temple complex. We have an old pick-up truck that we occasionally use for shopping and other matters, and it is parked down the mountain only about a five-minute walk away. But that driveway entrance is hidden by the trees, and known only to the inmates here and a select few others.

"So you see, Professor Springs has tricked you, just as he was tricked by Jim." Here he actually stopped to laugh, then spoke some sentences in Japanese to the others, evidently explaining to them our conversation. He laughed again and the others joined him, all of them guffawing with great enthusiasm, just as it dawned on me that the short cut had been kept hidden from me by Jack. Watanabe regained his composure. "I suppose he felt that you needed to climb the mountain yourself. It is the only proper way to enter a holy site, through the *torii* gate, and then through each of the subsequent *torii*. It was fitting that you should do so. I am sure this is all that he meant by it, yes?" With this, he placed his hand gently on my shoulder, and nodded some more, yet still giggling a bit.

I thought through the implications of this final twist, and realized that it made my appearance on the scene even more special, and that it would allow for my departure to be much smoother as well. "I suppose it is fitting, then. I climbed the mountain, yes."

Then I tried to ask one last favor. "So, with your truck … could you see fit to help me tomorrow? Could we load up the truck with the boxes, and take it all down to the place I left the taxi?"

Watanabe wiped his mouth, took another swig of the beer. "Of course. I was planning on it."

And so, at 10:00 a.m. the next day, the taxi was already waiting for us as we made the final turn and spotted it. The driver leaped out, and with his earnest help, we quickly filled the trunk, then the back seat, with the six boxes.

By lunchtime, I was back at the *Sanko*. Hideko greeted me, and once I described to her what I had achieved so far, I asked her about the boxes. I needed to get them to the airport at Narita, then all the way back home to Indiana, I said. She thought this over, then smiled broadly, saying, "*Kuro Neko*! *Kuro Neko*!"

"*Kuro Neko*?"

She understood my confusion. "It means … black cat … they are very reliable, and can deliver these … packages to Narita!" Initially I was nervous about this proposition, but she assured me that they were the best option, so I agreed, recalling that the boxes had been buried safely within a mountaintop temple for over fifteen years. It seemed that my mission must have some good karma, thus I released my treasures with an almost irresponsible carelessness.

Many hours later, back in the Keio Plaza Hotel in Tokyo, it was already the evening of July 8, and my return ticket was for the 10th. I lounged around the hotel that evening and got up early the next day, hoping to visit Asakusa Temple since Jack had praised its tranquilities. I hailed a cab and took a long, meandering ride to the other side of Tokyo, through kaleidoscopic curves and windblown, chaotic urbanscapes. Once there, I sat for a very long time in the temple's grand presence, trying to discern whatever lingering spirits might be nearby. *Kannon*, goddess of mercy, superintended my visit, and I watched the clouds of incense rise up slowly into the sky. There were many casual tourists, appearing much like myself, out seeing the sights, snapping photos on their digital cameras. I smiled, feeling at home in this strange place, and somehow understood that in just a few days I had been transformed from a casual, frightened tourist into another kind of pilgrim, perhaps even a citizen of the world. I felt different, transformed by the journey, and enjoyed a strong sense of victory.

The next morning, I arrived back at Narita Airport several hours before my flight. *Kuro Neko* had my precious packages, and with their courteous help, I transferred them to an international express rate, to be shipped home. For customs purposes, I informed the agent that the boxes were filled with books and papers, which was vaguely the truth, and assumed that the professional customs agents of an international shipping company could most easily handle any potential entanglements. But I did carry onboard the most precious items—file folders of manuscripts, first editions of *Fanshawe*, *Huckleberry Finn*, and *Lyrical Ballads*, Jack's personal copy of *Glimpses of Unfamiliar Japan* by Lafcadio Hearn, and the original signed edition of *Old Man and the Sea*, among other valuables—all stored snugly in a valise purchased for this task. Just a few "old books" and as such, I did not feel the need to report them to US Customs.

友

The flight back was easy. I slept for much of it, and read from my old books for the balance. Driving back down the highway toward Bloomington and home, I tried to comprehend the implications of the commodities I would soon be receiving. Then, as if magically, I was home, after almost twenty straight hours of travel. It was still July 10, 2011, in Indiana, though by then, the calendar had already turned a day ahead in Japan. As such, it truly was the longest day of my life. Once more, I felt the ghost of Jack Springs toying with me. It was another test, or set of tests, and suddenly I realized I had no real plan for the documents, my booty. I fell asleep in my favorite reading chair, *Leaves of Grass* resting on my chest, while still contemplating what I should do with these fascinating, and troubling, new treasures. And I'm still working that out.

友

In many ways, how to conduct myself in view of this trove of literary treasures, and what to do with all of these items, have become the defining ethical dilemmas of my life. But they are pleasant dilemmas, something I surely never saw coming. A surprise ending to a rather humdrum life of teaching and research. I write these final words in summer of 2012, as I complete the endgame of sending this manuscript off to my agent, and thus releasing to the world a truly fascinating tale, including my own rather minor adventure tacked on for good measure. Our plan is to publish within the next year or so.

Always, I remember Jack's haunting words. He keeps reminding me that I was enlisted by him to carry out certain tasks that he never found the courage or wherewithal to accomplish before his own demise. "I needed to put some things in order," he wrote. So my ethical dilemma has something to do with this heady idea of order, and his tragic death has transformed all my efforts into a kind of sacred discipline in pursuit of the good, the true, and the beautiful.

It remains my earnest desire to be able to say with a clean conscience, that I have acted nobly with the materials so far. I began by going through it all, piece by piece, and cataloguing one more time the contents—but this time, in much more detail than I was able to carry out at *Ryoan-ji*. As it happens, I have an old friend who deals in rare books and collectibles, and I soon discovered that there was enough of real monetary value to create several small fortunes, at least for an old academic like me, whose needs are modest and few, and whose appetites are generally manageable. Yes, there have been significant temptations involved, though relatively small ones—I love aged mahogany, for instance, and fine wines: California Cabs, French Burgundy, and Tuscan Chianti, above all. And I love fly-fishing in the Adirondacks or Montana. And old books, I might add.

One must have a few hidden preoccupations, to make all the hard work worthwhile.

For the record, the large majority of the items I've released so far have all gone into the special collections of my home university and thus are held in the public trust of a major state institution, safe behind heavy security and surveillance. Specifically, I have made a special arrangement with the Lilly Library of Rare Books here at Indiana, one of the top collections of its kind in the world, housed in an impressive limestone building in the middle of campus, and past which hundreds of students walk daily, hardly imagining the assets held within. The Lilly represents a marvel of familial philanthropy, all made possible by the prodigious wealth produced by the pharmaceutical giant, the Lilly Corporation, headquartered up in Indianapolis. The Lilly Library already owns, for example, a Gutenberg Bible, the four Shakespeare folios, and Audubon's *Birds of America*, as well as a first edition (not mine) of *Leaves of Grass*—all thanks to the burgeoning sales of insulin products, Prozac, Cialis, and other modern wonder drugs.

Slowly but surely, my scholarly plan is to edit and present to the world most of the treasures that Jack saved from the firestorm at Sensei's house in Japan. I believe these tasks are precisely the ones Jack would have assigned to me. And so those six boxes are now the centerpieces of my daily life. The recovery, analysis, and publication of the hundreds of heretofore unknown documents I brought back with me will now become the focus of the remaining years of work that God sees fit to bequeath to me. As I publish various items, I plan to turn them over to the Lilly Library here in Bloomington, where they can be viewed and enjoyed by scholars. The Lilly has been gracious enough, as part of my exclusive arrangement with them, to provide a modest honorarium for each of the gifts I have so far bequeathed, and I expect that generous arrangement to continue. These honoraria, along with the boon of my now rather considerable retirement contributions over forty years, and managed by the sanguine accountants at TIAA-CREF, have allowed me the financial means to devote myself full-time to the recovery, and then the publication of the rest of my cache of goods.

And so, as a result, I will give Indiana University my official letter of resignation, as of Jan. 1, 2013, at which time I will retire, becoming a free man during the week of Twelfth Night. Although, in keeping with academic decorum, I will dutifully teach one semester after my sabbatical ends, and then I will announce my resignation. I maintain a few of my favorite relics in a handy place, here in the house, hidden away in case some snoopy thief decides that my enticing tale warrants further investigation. I have now purchased a trained German shepherd, by the way, so I don't worry too much about keeping precious documents and volumes with me here at home. The hound is thoroughly terrifying, if you don't know him, and I call him Strider, a small token of my boyhood esteem for J.R.R. Tolkien. He prowls around the house like a secret service agent, ready to die for me, I believe—his coat black and silver, his bark able to wake the dead, as perhaps it does, now and then. But just in case, I keep my valuables locked up in a newly purchased safe.

Sometimes, I open up that safe, and carefully handle my most cherished possessions. Probably my favorite is that tall, yet thin, volume of rambling poems, bound in a musty, green cover. It was typeset by hand before the Civil War, much of it by the author himself. I enjoy sitting in my bed, often late at night, cradling the volume lovingly, knowing that its author once cradled it in his own calloused hands. Occasionally I open the book, and speak its hypnotic contents into the evening air.

Now I pierce the darkness, new beings appear,
The earth recedes from me into the night,
I saw that it was beautiful, and I see that
what is not the earth is beautiful.

Yes, I admit I'm still hoarding that first edition of *Leaves of Grass*. Though perhaps one day I will release it, which at auction might bring me as much as a million dollars or more, due to its many inscriptions by the author throughout. For now I'm holding on to it. I don't need the money and the Lilly Library already has one of its own.

It comforts me late at night to read aloud the words of the old prophetic misfit. Old Walt's lyrics sound better somehow, when read from the actual first edition. And then, satisfied and sleepy, I gingerly place it back in the safe, protected in a bright green zippered pouch designed for a laptop. I twirl the combination dial, and go back to bed, Strider right beside me on the floor, snoring away, a protector of Hobbits.

You may well ask, what of all the ethical entanglements surrounding your claim to these treasures? Doesn't it bother you even slightly, the manner in which these precious items ended up in your possession? Perhaps I could be more bothered by these circumstances, but most days, I'm not. Personally, I sleep just fine, mostly. On good nights, the words of my old friends—Jack Springer, Walt Whitman, Ernest Hemingway, and even Professor Goto—come flooding back to me, from some primeval place, underneath shelves of granite or limestone. But other times, the nightmares of my old student come back, also seeking me out. One night, it was a bloody Miyamoto, head wrapped in a towel, shrieking like a demon into the chill night air: "Help!" Another night, it was a burning house, with disembodied voices pouring forth, unidentified but filled with terror: "Blood money. Blood!" Both times, I awoke with a start. Strider stirred on the floor beside me, fully cognizant of the corrupting powers of the one ring. Yes, I remember the terrible circumstances under which these many items arrived in my home, twenty feet from my bedside. It's a shadowy moral territory, at times overwhelming, though not nearly as traumatic for me as it must have been for Jack.

Writing these sentences, I can almost hear other words being whispered in the chill night air, siren-like. And I am haunted by the words, once again. Ultimately, I choose to overlook these skeletons—always surging forward, like the good Emersonian soul that I wish to be.

友

And so the story ends here—almost. I did receive one last letter from Jack, postmarked December 7, 2011, the one-year anniversary of Jack's death, as per his own meticulous instructions to his bereaved father, a faithful servant to the last. Receiving a letter from the dead can provoke a certain eeriness, but by then I was used to it, and a buoyant comfort possessed me, as if the bonds with the dead somehow mysteriously continued—and perhaps they do. We are surrounded by a great cloud of witnesses (Hebrews 12:1), a noble line from another old letter.

And so, after all that's been said and done, I must give Jack Springs the final word in all of this, without any of my own thoughts or commentary appended. May his farewell letter grant my readers the same degree of comfort and peace it has granted me.

友

Thanksgiving Friday, 2010

Dear Marty,
If the timing has worked out the way I've planned it, you should be getting this final letter during the holiday season of 2011, about a year from the day I'm writing it. In recent weeks, I've had a spell of very fine weather, a temporary reprieve, so to speak, like C.S. Lewis's wife Joy, in *Shadowlands*.

The pain has let up so much that I've been taking walks with my dog, Caliban, a small terrier who believes he's much bigger than he really is. For a few weeks now, it's been like my very own Indian Summer. I went by car with a friend of my sister, by the name of Emily, down to Brown County one fine, blustery Saturday in mid-October, to look at the fall colors. It was my first "date" in many years. The yellows, scarlets, and purples—all still stunning to me, jaw-dropping, in fact, even after all I've been through. I've gazed with romantic yearning at the spectacle of the trees, and inhaled deeply the damp, aromatic autumn air. I've even felt the old thrill of believing that it is great to be alive. Urge and urge and urge, always the procreant urge of the world, wrote good old Uncle Walt Whitman.

By the time you get this, a year from now when my father sends it, your life should be looking a lot differently. Maybe old Professor Martin Dean has successfully completed a pilgrimage to the Land of the Rising Sun, and discovered an array of valuable commodities, the ones I left on deposit there back in the cold winter of 1995. You did climb the mountain, yes? Because it is the correct way to approach the gods.

I could have called you on the telephone, to ask you these many favors, but I couldn't justify it. Yes, it would have been the most direct way to do all this. But we got this far through the writing of letters, and so I've always felt it was important that we finish the way we started. I feel some shame in how it has turned out, despite all the years that have passed. And I do apologize, for never finding the courage to call you. I hope you can forgive me for that—and, in fact, I think you will because ours has been a friendship built on written words.

By now perhaps you've had interesting conversations with dealers and rare books aficionados in an attempt to discover what some of those items might be worth. And I don't think it wrong that you find some benefit in all this. So why not keep a few select items for yourself? It's only fitting. Even Indiana Jones got an honorarium sometimes. But also, perhaps, the treasures have caused you some difficult moments, wrestling with the moral dilemma of how they came into your possession.

I trust you will find a solution. But I can't really see any of this changing you, to be honest.

I envision you patiently staining a freshly milled molding for a bookcase in your garage workroom in southern Indiana, or fishing in a stream in the Adirondacks up in northern New York state. I see you being pleased with your lot in life as it already is, without that Ivy League polish, or panache, or whatever it is. And I hope the goods will remain in the Great Midwest, where the likes of Twain and Howells and Hemingway were born and raised. That seems proper to my old-fashioned Hoosier sensibility.

Meanwhile, my time is running thin. It was wonderful, though, sitting at the table with my family yesterday, one of the very good days. Thanksgiving dinner: a truly American invention, established by Lincoln himself, in the midst of a great civil war.

As always, Mom wheeled out a fifteen-pound turkey, roasted brown and dripping with butter and just the right amount of garlic. My dad sat at the head of table, a prince of the earth, a man of clarity, morals, and perfect punctuation, with a proper tool in each hand for carving the bird. My sister, Sue, brought along her new boyfriend Ted, all smiles, a quietly humorous corporate attorney, wearing a suit coat and a bow tie. They held hands occasionally as they picked at their green beans, or sipped their wine, smiling shyly like teenagers. We offered up a long, solemn prayer together, for health and fellowship, giving thanks for our bounteous blessings, of which there are many. Yes, I still think so.

As always, we watched some football, and Mom brought out her traditional pumpkin pie, made from scratch, of course. She whipped up some real cream, and placed hefty dollops on the wedges of pie. Some neighbors and friends dropped by later in the afternoon, as is our custom, and we played cards and carried on. Mom sang some hymns, the good old ones, accompanying herself on the piano. "How Great Thou Art," "Blessed Assurance," things like that. "This is my story, this is my song …"

It was a perfect holiday, a truly holy day, and my last one on God's green earth, I suspect. Of course, my family and I are hoping for one more Christmas together. But last night I couldn't sleep for the pain. Finally, I did get some sleep, fitfully, until very late in the day. I think I feel the old horror rising up with renewed strength inside me, doing something evil to my internal organs. The bad stuff has spread into various areas of my body, according to the physicians, including my bones. It's harder to walk almost every single day now, and my back aches constantly, a dull and nauseating ache. But here I am, composing one last letter to an old friend, between the jagged edges of pain. Right now, as I work the keyboard, a steady rain beats against the shutters outside my window.

Tonight I'm thinking of Sensei's last moments. He had only a few seconds left on Earth, but he wanted to make sure to remind me about the words. "Without words, the people remain powerless," he told me. "Without beauty, the people become ugly, and life is unlivable."

That's why most of us become teachers of literature, don't you think, Marty? For the words, words, words. I remember one clear, October afternoon, when you thundered through a lecture on the Romantics, about how words were our chance to express the Mind of God, fit for human ears, about something pulsating in us. I always hung on to that one. Remember the words, you commanded us that fine day. The sky was a shiny, cobalt blue, pouring in through the windows. You quoted Wordsworth from memory, spoke of a power rolling through us. I recall walking out into the primordial woods that day, believing I had heard a prophet. And perhaps I had.

Here's Emerson one more time: "To my friend I write a letter, and from him I receive a letter … It is a spiritual gift worthy of him to give, and of me to receive. It profanes nobody. In these warm lines the heart will trust itself, as it will not to the tongue, and pour out the prophecy of a godlier existence than all the annals of heroism have yet made good." In sentences like that, I perceive the purr of universal things, the pulse of a cosmic astonishment that still makes getting up in the morning worthwhile.

There are different kinds of friends in life, and ours was almost entirely of the spirit these past two decades or so—consisting almost entirely of written missives, sent back and forth over many miles, delivering the words without bodily presence—

except to the extent that our letters, as Whitman used to say, *do* embody us. In that sense, we were and are present to each other—in our letters. He who touches this book, touches me, sayeth Walt.

Yes, Marty, ours has been an epistolary friendship. Finally, that's why I cannot pick up the telephone and call. It just seems out of character. Written words are superior. You taught me that, and modeled it, too, because you were a lover of words and letters, and you tried to lead a life that revealed to the world that words and letters matter. Your life has been to me like a letter dropped by God in the street. And I've tried, in return, to live up to your example.

As in all of my letters, I once again send my thanks and heartfelt best wishes to you, old friend. Try not to grieve too much. I give thanks in all things (Ephesians 5:20).

Sincerely,

E. Jackson Springs, PhD
Thanksgiving weekend 2010
Indianapolis, IN

Acknowledgments

I'm grateful to a great many people over a long period of time, for aiding in the effort to begin, work on, complete, and publish this novel. First, I acknowledge the people to whom this book is dedicated: my wife Hiroko, our son Daniel, and her parents, sister, and nephew back in Japan. I owe a lot to my side of the family as well: my late parents, my late step-parents, and especially Ron and Karla Franko and the indomitable Chelsea Emma Franko.

I've had excellent colleagues and friends who have also encouraged me; I thank them all, too many to list; but in particular, I would like to name Tom Moisan, Tom Walsh, Roger Lundin, Lt. Col. Keith Donnelly, and Georgia Johnston as chief among these beloved friends, for having passed on to whatever awaits us. I miss them all very much. I gained terrific help, and avoided terrific blunders, thanks to the impeccable readership of the likes of Devin Johnston, Aaron Belz, Saher Alem, Ray Benoit, Jim Hutchisson, Matt Nickel, Janie Chang, Kevin Mac Donnell, Kent Rasmussen, Jason Ashlock, my relentless agent Jill Marr and her colleagues at the Sandra Dijkstra Agency, and the towering team at Blank Slate Press, including Kristina Blank Makansi, Donna Essner, and Lisa Miller.

Finally, and like Jack: I thank God in all things, and I'm happy to recognize that every good gift comes down from above, from the Father of Lights (James 1:17)—including all the fine people listed above.

About The Author

H.K. Bush is a professor of English at Saint Louis University, a former Fulbright Senior Scholar in Freiburg, Germany, and formerly Senior Fellow at Waseda Institute of Advanced Study in Tokyo. Professor Bush is most noted for his work as a scholar of Mark Twain, Abraham Lincoln, and Harriet Beecher Stowe. His most recent book, *Continuing Bonds: Parental Grief and Nineteenth-Century American Authorship* (University of Alabama Press, 2016), is a cultural history of the deaths of children in the nineteenth century in America, and specifically how grief influenced the written works of major American authors. Previously, *Lincoln in His Own Time*, appeared in October of 2011 from the University of Iowa Press; and before that, Professor Bush authored a highly acclaimed cultural biography, *Mark Twain and the Spiritual Crisis of His Age* (2007), and *American Declarations* (1999). In addition, he writes regularly in popular venues such as *Books & Culture*, *Christian Century*, *The Cresset*, and the *St. Louis Post-Dispatch*, among others. He blogs at halbush.com. *The Hemingway Files* is his first novel.

CPSIA information can be obtained
at www.ICGtesting.com
Printed in the USA
LVOW03s1434180517
534796LV00002B/2/P